MOSTLY HUMAN

D.I. JOLLY

Mostly Human

Published by Tinpot Publishing

Cover illustration: Tom Kyffin

Copyright of text and characters © D. I. Jolly

Back Page Photograph by Ted Titus

www.tinpotbooks.com

Third Print edition 2020   ISBN: 9798566608631

I'd like to dedicate this book to:

My best friend Reid, with big thanks to my friend

Anne who yells at me to make my books better.

I also want to say a very special thank you to my Editor

Sean Fraser

Mostly Human is incredibly important to me

as it feels the most real, and you've helped me turn it into something I feel is a little bit special.

And of course thank you to my

Tinpotterer and Cover artist Tom Kyffin,

without whom

other people wouldn't be reading this at all.

Tinpot Publishing

Contents

Prologue

"Welcome back to K505, Syn Island's number-one radio station. I'm Barbra Barker and we're here with Alex Harris, former frontman and lead singer of the hit band Waterdogs. Alex, the question on everyone's lips is; what happened to the band? Why did you guys break up?"

"Well, we kinda reached the end of our creative rope, I think; I mean, we've been a band since we were all about sixteen, and we were inducted into the rock 'n roll hall of fame three years later – we hadn't even graduated from high school at that point. *Sigh* I guess after eight years together we all felt like it was time to take a break. It's not like there was a big fight or anything ... We just all want to be doing different things at this point in our lives; there is nothing stopping us from getting back together again later."

"Wow, that's awesome. So, you heard it here first, folks: Waterdogs not drowned, just swimming in different directions. Ha, ha, ha! So the obvious question then is, what are your plans now?"

"I'm just really looking forward to spending some time with my family and exploring some of my other interests. Thanks to my sister, I can afford to just sit back for a while and relax and think."

"Oh, that's right, your sister's an investment banker, correct, and she helped you put your earnings from the band into all the proper places and turned your already awesome rock-star pay cheques into something you should be able to live off for the next couple of lifetimes. And in return you bought her a house, is that right?"

"Well, you know, my family has always supported me in everything I've wanted to do, always had my back when I needed them, so when I got this opportunity to give something back I was more than happy to help out, you know. The basic idea was I'd supply the money and my sister would supply the know-how and together we would create a family trust. I mean, yes, I get the majority of it, but my family's never going to starve or really want for anything, ever."

"Huh, I wish my brother was as sweet as you. Now, normally rock stars of your calibre are sitting on the ceiling, talking about the interesting positions their groupies can get into, buying and writing off sports cars and dying at twenty-seven. But you seem much more level headed and down to earth than even some of your band mates. How do you manage it, because you shot to fame at a young age, from high-school band to international rock sensation seemingly over night? What's the secret?"

"Honestly? My dad has been to practically every gig I've ever done and when your dad is there watching you, you want to be on your best behaviour. He-he-he ... No, I just have a great relationship with my family and I wouldn't want to do anything that could jeopardise that. Like I said before, they've always really been there for me throughout my life and I respect that, and I love them for it. You know, when I got this idea of being a musician my father sat me down and said, 'Alex, if this is what's going to make you happy, then we're with you – just don't lose touch with the family and lose control and think you can't call us. We don't want you going the way of that Kurt Corbin fellow.'"

Everyone in the studio laughed – it was a funny story and it was true, but it actually had very little to do with why I wasn't the hardcore 'fuck-the-system' rock star everyone expected me to be. Okay, well, maybe it did, but being a werewolf still took precedence.

Chapter 1

Fifteen years earlier

It was the first sunny day after a weekend of rain. A chill cut through on the breeze but the mist was a dead giveaway that it was going to be a beautiful day. Alex had woken up early that morning with the bright sunshine streaming in through his window. It was his families' annual trip to his grandparents' farm near Edmonton in Alberta, Canada, and it had rained every day since they'd arrived, which for a ten-year-old boy seemed like a cruel and personal torture. He loved his summer holidays on the farm, but this trip was going to be especially awesome, because this year his grandparents' farm dog, Sally, had had puppies and his parents had promised they would get to take one home. Which, for Alex, was a lifelong dream come true and he had it all planned out in his head. It was going to be a boy dog, its name would be Killer and it was going to be the coolest dog in the whole world.

Waking up early hadn't made much of a difference to his day. Farms weren't exactly safe places for children to run around unsupervised, so he would have to wait until one of the adults woke up before he could really take advantage of the wide-open spaces outside. So he slipped into his usual farm morning routine, making himself toast with cheese, sweet, strong tea in the biggest mug he could find, and a soft spot in front of morning cartoons with his sister Annabel, who'd woken up about fifteen minutes before. Monday-morning cartoons weren't the best, in Alex's opinion;

they were normally an hour-long collection of classic Disney and *Loony Toons.* Annabel, on the other hand, loved them much more than the weekend's *He-Man* and *Transformers* but everyone was happy with the *Scooby-Doo* double bill that followed the classic cartoon hour, which all ended around 8 am. At some point during the first hour they were joined by their cousins Frankie and Sammie, who also brought with them toast and giant mugs of tea.

Alex had been told the night before that he wasn't going to be able to learn to ride the horses today because the ground was too muddy and slippery, although secretly the real reason – he knew – was because neither his parents nor aunt and uncle relished the idea of spending the morning out in the cold and rain to teach him. For them, a weekend holed up in the farmhouse meant a weekend running around after restless children; they were all exhausted and looked forward to a quiet day where all the kids would fill their time playing out on the farmland while they could sit back and take the much-needed break from it all. It was their holiday too, after all. Of course, there was always the chance that his grandparents would take him out, but the odds weren't great. All that taken into consideration, Alex still figured it wouldn't hurt to at least ask, if the grown-ups ever woke up that is. To his mild disappointment, a good night's rest had not changed anyone's mind about him and horse riding, but that was all right because he could still go find himself an adventure somewhere on the farm, which was his favourite game anyway. But first he'd need the right 'armour', which his mother still liked to help pick out.

"All right, sweetie, now what are the rules about going out on the farm?"

"Stay out of the barn and the animal pens, keep a look out for snakes, *aaaand* … no throwing stones?"

"And stay away from the puppies. Sally's still very protective and she'll probably bite you if you try picking any of them up."

"Oh yeah, I remember that one. It's like when Uncle Jeff's dog had puppies and she kept growling at anyone who came near."

"Exactly like that. Now please don't wander off too far, your grandma's making lunch today and I don't want to have to send a search party out looking for you to make sure you're there."

"Okay, Mom."

"Also, don't throw stones."

Alex raised his right hand with his index finger pointing up for effect and held the pose for a few seconds to make sure his mother noticed, then said with determination,

"I knew it!"

Debra looked at her son's overly serious face and couldn't help but laugh. With that, he hopped off the bed and headed straight for the front door. There was an adventure to be had and he was ready to have it.

It didn't take long for Alex's gallop to switch to a meandering walk, but his imagination was always ten steps ahead. In reality, he was making his way across a field, which was in its resting season, towards the forest-lined river bank that actually belonged to the municipality. In his mind, however, he was marching proudly over a battlefield into the enchanted woods after a gang of bandits he'd been tracking for days but was finally getting close. Occasionally, he'd sniff at the air or put his ear to the ground and pretend he could hear something. He didn't really understand what he was listening for, but he'd seen a hero do it on TV once, and it seemed to work for him. Then suddenly, while he crouched there with one ear just about in the dirt, he caught the final whimpers of what sounded like a dog. Nervously, he lifted his head and listened again to try to figure out if he could hear what direction it was coming from. Turning around a few times he quickly settled on a direction and, with some trepidation, he headed off towards the sound.

It didn't take him long either. Within just a few metres he found himself staring at a wolf, an abnormally large wolf too. It was the largest, darkest, scariest thing he'd ever seen; it was also the only wolf he'd seen in real life. As he crept nearer, he realised that its front and back paws were bound so it lay stretched out as if on a rack, and there was a strange symbol branded into its side. Fear and sadness washed over the boy and held him frozen in place for a few minutes, until finally questions began bubbling up in his mind: Why was it tied down? Was it dead? Who would have done something so mean to something like that? Curiosity, of course, got the better of his fears and he started taking cautious steps towards the animal. He had always had a soft spot for animals, particularly dogs, and to see this wolf tied up like this just seemed wrong. Tears began to slip out the corner of his eyes as he got close enough to see the burnt fur from the brand and the blood pooling on the ground around the creature. It also became apparent just how much bigger the wolf was than him. Alex stood looking at it and realised that it probably stood taller on four legs than he was on two. With his eyes still filled with tears, he knelt down next to it, trying hard to avoid putting his knee into the blood-soaked sand. His bottom lip began to quiver. Alex stared at the wolf's chest and tried to work out if it was still breathing, very gently laying his hand on the side of its face and stroking it.

"I'm sorry this happened to you, Mr Wolf. I hope ... I hope you're in a better place now."

The wolf let out a deep sigh and Alex's back stiffened with fright. For an instant, he stopped breathing, his heart suddenly the loudest thing he'd ever heard. He stared at the wolf, desperately searching for signs of life, movement, anything that would tell him whether he should run screaming or stay and help. Not that Alex had the faintest idea how he would be able to help, of course, he just knew that something should be done.

"M-m-m-Mr Wolf?"

Nervously, slowly, he started stroking the wolf again, not sure what he was hoping to achieve, not sure why he didn't just run away, or go find someone who might know more about what was going on. He moved his hand over the wolf's ear. He had always liked dogs' ears; they were always the softest part. For the first time that day Alex's thoughts were focused solely on the moment, filled with the raw feeling of standing on the edge of the great unknown and looking in. He shifted his gaze from the wolf and looked around to see if he could spot anything that could either help him untie the creature or offer some clue as to what had happened. On a tree nearby he noticed a series of deep scratches and more blood; tears welled up in his eyes once again. Alex wiped them away with his other hand and sniffed; the wolf's now open eye followed the movement of his hand to his face and he looked at the boy with compassion and gratitude before letting them close again.

Alex decided that to leave the wolf tied up any longer was a crime. Still moving slowly and nervously, he pulled from his pocket the Swiss army knife his grandfather had given him for his tenth birthday and began to cut the ropes that bound the wolf's front paws. The rope was thick and Alex had to really push and saw to even begin cutting through. It was hard work and he tired quickly, but he was determined and kept pushing. Then, all at once, the knife slipped and embedded itself into the wolf's paw. In that nanosecond, the wolf let out a ferocious snarl, swung his head to the side and sunk his fangs into Alex's forearm. Pure terror erupted out of Alex's mouth and, screaming, he leapt back. But, his arm was still clenched in the jaw of the beast, he couldn't pull himself free. His feet slipped out from under him and he hit the ground. Hard. Tears and panic blurred his vision and, desperately, he started pulling on his arm, trying to wrench it free. He shut his eyes hard, dug his heels into the ground and pulled.

"Please! NO!" he shouted.

He opened his eyes again and they locked onto the bright green eyes of the wolf. He stopped dead. A look of sorrow and pity seemed to fill the creature's face, and slowly it unclenched its jaw. The wolf then let out another deep sigh and watched as the boy running as fast as he could, screaming into the distance. The wolf's eyes then settled for a moment on the barely cut rope, and then they closed.

***

Debra and Kyle were a little hungover that morning. Housebound in Debra's parents' farmhouse by rain with the rest of the family made for a very good excuse to have a mini-reunion party. As the children made their way off onto the farm, the folks arrived with cold meats, cheese and toast. Everyone helped themselves to coffee and decided that, as it was a beautiful day, they would spend the morning on the porch doing not very much of anything. After a while the conversation graduated from various degrees of grunting related directly to the severity of their hangover to matters even more mundane.

"Look at that one, if you squint it looks like a teddy bear."

"It looks like a cloud. They all look like clouds, and if you squint it just looks like rain, if you ask me."

"Jeff, you have no imagination."

"I've a great imagination, but I'm battling with the light reflecting off my plate. There's no way I'd survive actually looking at the sky. And, while we're about it, why aren't you two as bad as the rest of us?"

"Kyle has these great multivitamins we took before going to bed."

"Well, that's cheating, and why didn't you share that great idea with the rest of us?"

Everyone nodded, but Kyle raised his hand. "Erm, because we were all quite drunk, and forgot?"

Laughing, they sat back in their chairs and listened for a moment to the sounds of the farm, the wind whistling through the trees and around the house, the horses in the paddock. And, for a moment, it was perfect, exactly how they had all pictured spending their days on the farm.

And then they heard the bloodcurdling scream of a child. All six adults leapt to their feet with no regard for table, chairs or hangovers, desperate to see where it came from. From across the field Kyle saw his son, clutching his arm and running as though chased, screaming and crying in a frenzied panic. Without thinking, he jumped the porch railing and took off at a dead sprint, his wife and brother-in-law close behind. As he got closer, he opened his arms and, in a magnificent manoeuvre, caught his son with one arm, lifting him off the ground and swinging him around to catch his legs with the other arm while coming to an abrupt halt. For an instant, Alex was compelled by fear to fight against whatever had wrapped itself around him, but his terror was short lived, and he pulled himself tight against his father, his body beginning to convulse as the adrenalin got the better of his him and the world went black.

"Oh my God, oh my God, oh my God ..."

Kyle looked his son over and realised that he was covered in blood. Debra's face turned a ghostly white and Jeff quickly caught her as her knees began to buckle. Kyle, Alex in his arms, headed back to the house at full tilt. Kath was a trauma nurse, and farms being dangerous places at the best of times meant that there was always a first-aid kit at hand. Kyle, trying hard to keep his cool, lay Alex gently on the porch table, and stepped back to let the people who knew better help. Within seconds, Kath arrived with cold water and started rinsing Alex's arm only to find numerous puncture wounds, all jagged at the edges from when he tried to pull himself free. She grabbed wadding and tape and began strapping up the boy's arm as tightly as possible.

"This is clearly some kind of animal attack. We need to get him to the medical centre, now."

Her mother-in-law, Marie, nodded obediently. "Right."

Marie moved like a woman possessed though the house, grabbing car keys along the way, and was out the front door and starting the car within seconds. Kath quickly finished her makeshift dressing, wrapped a few clean tea towels around the arm, then scooped up the boy and followed with Kyle close behind her. It was 40 kilometres to the medical centre and they were aiming to get there in record time.

Jeff sat with his sister in the field, keeping her elevated and lightly tapping her cheek to wake her. He knew he couldn't really help with the medical side of things so was going to work on the problems he could fix. By the time she came to and they had headed back to the house, the car was already speeding off into the distance. Debra's face flushed with anger for having fainted, but she pushed the embarrassment aside and turned to her father, Derrick, standing in the front doorway. The look on his face was grave.

"There's a dangerous animal loose on the farm somewhere," he said. "You two need to go find the other kids and get them indoors right now. I'm going to go secure the horses."

They nodded at their father and started calling for the other children.

Frankie, Sammy, and Annabel were all at the water tank on the other side of the house. The two boys were swimming, which they had been forbidden to do without adult supervision, and Annabel was playing lifeguard while reading, something she wasn't supposed to be doing while playing lifeguard. Catching them breaking the rules made getting them back into the house easy and required little on-the-spot explanation from a clearly panic-stricken Debra. They knew they were going to have to tell the children something, but also knew that they had to be careful of what exactly they told them. Jeff led them to the kitchen table and took the hit for being the mean parent who was about to wreck another day of holiday.

"Alex has been in a little accident, nothing major, but he's been taken to a doctor just in case."

Annabel looked alarmed. "But why? What happened?"

"Well, we don't know for sure but it looks as though he was attacked by some kind of animal. Here, on the farm."

The children became wide-eyed and silent.

"We don't want you guys to worry, but until we know exactly what happened, I'm afraid today is another inside day."

There were a few long sighs and rolling of eyes. But they boys recognised their father's 'no point in arguing' face, and Annabel simply knew better. As one the three children headed back into the TV room. Jeff waited for them to all leave the room before going off to find where his sister had disappeared to. He found her sitting on the edge of her bed, tears still rolling down her cheeks. He walked in silently and wrapped his arms around her.

"I'm his mother, I'm supposed to protect him! How could I just lose it so completely at the first sign of trouble like that?"

"Hey, with all that blood I almost fainted myself. And if that was one of mine, I can't say I'd have been any different. You're a great mom, Debs, and he's a strong kid. He'll be all right. We'll give them a few minutes, and I'll call the medical centre. I'm sure he's just fine. You'll see."

Debra put her arms around her brother and they held each other for a moment. Then she pulled away, took a deep breath and wiped her eyes.

"Right, I can't just sit here. I need to go watch Annabel and make sure nothing happens to her while I'm not looking." She forced a cheerful smile at her brother who smiled back, and they headed out to watch their kids.

***

It wasn't a large clinic, constructed out of the pocket of the local farmers for when something really bad happened. A community trust had been put together, to which the farmers all paid an equal amount each month to help pay the staff and for supplies. When it opened it had been determined that the surgery could consist of two doctors, of which at least one had to be a surgeon, plus four nurses. There were four wards and eight beds. Next door was a large, rambling old house where they all could live. Every four months the trustees met with the doctors to go over how much had been spent and on what. In return, the farmers had their medical needs met and prescriptions filled. The doctors and nurses were contracted for two years, gaining experience with animal attacks and sewing up arms and legs, inevitably as a result of a farming accident or careless farmhand, the misuse of equipment and the odd gunshot from a hunting trip gone wrong. Their two years behind them, the doctors would then move back to the city

19

and new doctors would arrive. The trust had been established twelve years earlier and in all that time there had been only one case of misuse of funds, and even that was early on, before the farmers really knew what they were looking at when reading the budget reports. The doctors currently in residence were both entering their second contract there. Jenna was the daughter of one of the farmers in the area and the other was her fiancé, Clint. Love had in its way become a theme at that clinic; Jeff had met Kath there when he had returned from his travels abroad and moved back home until he could think of what he wanted to do with his life. While pondering his prospects it very nearly came to an end when he took a tumble from one of the horses and got his arm trampled. He woke up many hours later and saw 'a vision of beauty' adjusting his IV. They began chatting and quickly began dating, and when she moved back to the city he moved with her. A year later they were married.

Dr Clint Brant sent Kath to take Kyle off to get some sweet tea to help calm his nerves. It wasn't that he was panicked, but he was taking strain. Not only had he left his wife unconscious in a field, but his son hadn't really stopped bleeding until just now and was still unconscious.

"I've managed to stop the bleeding and I'm going to be able to just stitch most of the wounds, but he's going to have some serious scars. And this is definitely an animal bite, which means rabies shots, but Lord above only knows what kind of animal could do this. I mean, the teeth are too big to be a wolf, but the jaw is the wrong shape for a bear. Also, if you look here, see these rips? It looks to me like he either tried to pull his arm free, or what ever bit him threw him about a little."

Marie rubbed her eyes and took a deep breath, trying to process the information.

"Wolves, bears … Since when did we have these animals around here anyway? This happened in the woods around *my* farm, Clint."

"Well, I don't know. But let's just be happy that whatever it was didn't take his arm off, because it looks like it certainly could have."

Clint sighed and surveyed the arm again.

"He's not going to be able to use his arm much for the next few weeks. I'll write up a letter he can take to his doctor back in the city. He's going to need to get this bandage changed in the morning, so I'd like to keep him over night for observation. That way, if something develops, we can deal with it."

"What might develop?"

"Infection, mostly. I just don't want to see him tomorrow and have to tell you he's going to lose his arm because someone was playing with the horses before coming to check on him."

"No, no, fair enough. All right, I'll tell his father but, knowing Kyle, he's probably going to want to stay with him."

"That's fine, that's why we have two beds to a room. He can have dinner with Jenna and me tonight if you guys want to go home." He patted her gently on the arm. "There is one other thing though ..."

"Yes?"

"At this point, it looks pretty serious. Of course, it's still too early to tell with any kind of authority and I can't see how much damage may have been done to the nerves in his arms but, it has to be said, he might not be able to use it properly for a long, long time. Possibly even ever again."

Marie looked at the doctor in silence for a moment. "Let's keep that between us for now. Kyle and Debra are upset enough as it is. Let's not give them any more bad news until we're sure about it."

Clint forced a smile and nodded in agreement

It was about 4 pm when everyone finally left for the farm, leaving Kyle behind with the sleeping Alex. Kyle immediately settled on the adjacent bed and began to flick through one of the old books on the nightstand and let himself disappear into the pages of a fairly predictable detective novel, hoping to distract himself from the day's dramas. After an hour or so, however, there was a gentle knocking on the door and both Clint and his wife, Jenna, walked in carrying plates of food.

"We told Marie we'd feed you, and she's not the kind of woman you'd want to disappoint," Jenna laughed.

"Believe me, I know," said Kyle as he pulled himself up in the bed.

Both men gave knowing smiles as Jenna turned the nightstands into a mini dining table and set it for three.

"Has there been much movement from our little patient over there?"

"Adjusted himself for comfort at one point, maybe an hour ago, but otherwise no. Should I worry?" Jenna could see the concern in Kyle's eyes, in the tone of his voice.

"No, I wouldn't," Clint assured him. "I gave him enough sedative to last him until the morning. We also brought ear plugs to help ward off the beeping of his heart monitor."

"The beeping is okay, actually. I kinda like the rhythm of it. Also, it helps alleviate the fear that he may, you know, be in trouble ...”

For a moment the room filled with a slightly nervous discomfort, until Clint broke the ice. “No chance of that,” he laughed. “He’s a strong one, this one. And we’re taking good care of him. Nothing to worry about.”

***

Back at the farm, the rest of the family were less assured. They all sat very quietly worrying about Alex and wondering what they were going to do about whatever did that to him.

“I think I’m just going to phone again and just check.” Debra broke the silence around the table.

“Phone who?”

“Who do you think? Kyle.”

“Debs, it’s only been, what, an hour since you spoke to him ... I’m sure if there was any news he’d call. This is a ‘no news is good news’ situation. Alex has probably been asleep the whole time.”

“I know that, I’m just worried. My son is lying in a hospital bed and I can’t make it better. It’s so *frustrating*.”

She had gotten to her feet mid-sentence and had started pacing the room. Marie’s eyes followed her daughter, up and down, up and down.

“Debra, honey, come sit down or you’ll stress yourself sick. Food is the best thing for you at this point.”

What her mom was actually saying was that the more she fretted the more she'd scare the other children, who were already glancing wide-eyed from adult to adult, bewildered. Debra frowned. She knew her mother was right and so retook her seat and went back to moving food around her plate.

"I just wish he'd wake up and tell us what happened."

"Maybe it was the G'Mork." Frankie, who was only seven, suddenly realised everyone had turned to look at him.

"The *what*?" said his grandfather, puzzled.

"You know ... from *The NeverEnding Story*. Maybe it was G'Mork that got him, mistook him for Atreyu."

The room again filled with silence. Being stuck inside for four days now meant that the children had spent a lot of time in front of the television, and had already been through the limited video selection a few times. *The NeverEnding Story* had been hauled out at least twice since they had arrived.

The adults now began to worry whether they needed to reassure Frankie and the others that there weren't monsters out there hunting children, or whether they should warn them of the possibility of a giant wolf roaming the forests. The children, in turn, worried whether all of this meant that the Nothing was coming and if Alex had gotten hurt while trying to stop it. But the evening's usual routine soon put away said concerns, and the adults decided it was best dealt with in the morning and in the sober light of day. The children were packed off to bed, baths were run, teeth brushed, pyjamas found and reassuring bedtime stories told.

Annabel, slightly older than the others, had been awarded the luxury of her own room and was allowed to stay up an hour later than the others, as long as she spent it quietly reading. This, of course, suited her perfectly. Occasionally she would be seen making herself some tea after hours, slipping back and forth between her room, the kitchen and the bathroom, but she appreciated being given her own private reading time and didn't like to be disturbed anyway.

Debra still liked to keep a watchful eye on her daughter, though, more so since her twelfth birthday, secretly dreading the day she would have to start buying sanitary pads. In fact, every time Annabel was in a bad mood she would mentally prepare herself and practise the speech about how they knew this day would come, and how it's perfectly natural and how she should start with pads and not tampons. Debra remembered her own emerging puberty as a strange and confusing time, but also worried about Annabel getting enough attention. She was so independent for her age and it was easy to pay more attention to Alex. He was witty and funny even at the age of ten, and being so active you were either catching him as he dove off something, or reprimanding him about something, either way, he enjoyed being the centre of attention. Annabel wasn't really like that at all, however. She stuck to the walls, did her own thing most of the time, and when she did engage with adults it was on a mature, adult level. Her mother, naturally, worried that she was growing up too quickly.

Now, though, Annabel had happily retreated to her room and turned off the light. For her mother, this was another day that her daughter remained her innocent little girl. But then, unexpectedly, the light in the child's room was switched on again. Puzzled, Debra turned back to the door just as Annabel appeared in the doorway, a slightly confused look on her face.

"Mom, why are you standing outside my door?"

"I just saw your light come on, and wanted to make sure everything was all right, what with today being such a strange day and all. You okay?"

"Yeah, sure. Well, what's happened to Alex is messed up all right, but can I talk to you about something? Something else, I mean."

Debra suddenly wondered if this wasn't going to be about Alex, after all. It must have been fairly dramatic for the child to have had her brother whisked off to hospital like that. They retreated to Annabel's room and, the door was closed behind them, Debra sat down on the bed.

"What's wrong, honey?"

"Nothings wrong really. It's just, well … I think I've just gotten my period and …"

A light went on in Debra's head. Her moment had arrived and she launched into the speech she had been practising for months.

"Oh. Oh, that's not a problem at all, is it, hon. Don't worry about it. I'll get you a pad and we won't have to tell anyone else, certainly not any *boys*. This is a perfectly natural thing for a girl your age."

"Actually, Mom, can't I have a tampon?"

"Well, it's not really a good idea to use a tampon your first time."

"But it's not my first time."

Debra's mouth dropped open. "What do you mean this isn't your first time?"

"Well, it kinda started a few months ago. We learnt about it all in Sex Ed. I was at school so I borrowed a pad from Vicky, bought myself some tampons after school and kinda just dealt with it."

"Why didn't you tell me?"

"Well, I didn't really want to announce it to the whole world, Mom." She rolled her eyes. "It's not exactly something I want everyone to know about."

"But, but ... How did you feel?"

Annabel looked at her mother, a little guilty that she'd not mentioned it to her sooner.

"I was relieved it had finally happened, and then kinda annoyed when I realised I was going to have to deal with this every month for the next fifty years ... Mom, are *you* all right?"

"What? Oh yes. I'm fine, sorry I just thought that ... Never mind, uummm ... There are tampons in the bathroom, you can help yourself?"

"Thanks a lot. Mom, I don't know what I would have done if I had to ask Grandma."

Annabel gave her mother a hug and made her way to her family bathroom. Debra sat on the bed for a minute, not sure whether she should cry over having missed the event she'd been playing in her head. Or instead be proud of her daughter for being mature and responsible. Realising that if she was found still sitting on Annabel's bed it might look as if she had been waiting for her to get back from the bathroom and, knowing the situation, decided that that would probably be 'uncool' or 'awkward', so she quickly got up to leave. The two women reached the door at the same time,

"All right, sorted. Thanks again, Mom. I'm going back to bed. You'll let me know if you hear anything about Alex, right?"

"Don't worry about your brother, sweetheart. Dad's there with him and I'm sure everything's fine. We'll go fetch him in the morning. Sweet dreams."

Annabel stared at her mom for a moment.

"But, yes. I'll let you know if we hear anything, don't worry."

"Thanks, Mom. Night-night."

Annabel was back in bed and asleep within minutes, and Debra returned to the dinner table where the talk was of the prospect of dangerous animals wandering around in the woods near the farm and what that meant for their horses and the neighbouring dairy farm. She pulled up her chair and only half listened, her mind drifting.

"You're right, Jeff. We need to find out from Alex what happened before we start phoning people and cause a panic. In fact, I think we've all had quite a day of it today. Perhaps an early night is what we all need."

"I think you're right about that one, Dad. Debs, the kids all fine?"

"Yeah, Annabel has turned her lights off and the boys have been asleep for hours."

"You going to be all right though, Debs? I mean, you've had the roughest day of all by far."

"What? Oh yeah, I'll be fine. I'm just exhausted, I think. I can hear my bed calling."

The chatting continued while everyone helped clear the table, then said their goodnights before going off to bed.

The farmhouse was a traditional farmhouse, built to house at least two generations of a family, so there was always more than enough room to house the kids and kids of kids on summer holidays and long weekends. Debra closed the door to their room and was suddenly stuck by the realisation that not only was her son in hospital but she was going to be alone in her bed, something that didn't happen very often. Her thoughts were broken by a tap on the door; she opened it to reveal Jeff standing in the doorway holding an old, slightly beaten teddy bear.

"Kath found this in the cupboard on Friday. Figured maybe you needed an old friend to keep you company tonight?"

The teddy bear was Debra's childhood toy that slept in her bed every night until it was replaced by a boy and even then the teddy still sometimes got more snuggle time. Debra smiled and let out a short laugh, but the tears came immediately afterwards. She took a few steps back and slumped down on her bed. Jeff closed the door behind him.

"I ... I just feel so helpless, you know. Alex is normally such tough little guy and to see him like that. I don't know. I just wish someone would call and say actually everything is fine."

It would be a lie to say that the situation with Annabel had nothing to do with her tears now, but it was still a back-seat issue compared to what Alex was going through.

"Yeah, I couldn't imagine how I'd feel if I saw one of mine like that, but everything *is* fine. And Kyle's there. You watch, by this time tomorrow Alex'll be his usual self again only with a bandage."

"Yeah, yeah, you're probably right. I think I just need to get some sleep."

Jeff gave his sister a hug and retreated to his room. Debra placed her teddy with his head on her pillow and prepared herself for bed. As she climbed into bed and cuddled Teddy, she ran over the events of the day in her head: from hangover to animal attack to missing the maturing of her daughter to her own childhood toy, it had been a day in her life she'd never forget.

Chapter 2

A cold, fresh breeze slipped through the gap of the open window and gently stroked Alex's face. He opened his eyes and it slowly dawned on him that he had no idea where he was. Trying to remain as still as possible, he scanned the room. And there, at a table in the corner playing chess with a man dressed like a doctor, was his father.

"Dad?"

The two men stopped and looked up. They both seemed surprised, shocked even, Kyle to see his son so pale and strung out and the doctor to see Alex awake at all; he had expected the boy to be unconscious for at least a few more hours so he could redress his arm without having to administer more drugs. The doctor got up from his seat and calmly walked over to the bed.

"Good morning, young man. How you feeling?"

"I dunno ... Confused. My mouth is really dry and my arm hurts real bad. Where are we?"

Alex looked from the doctor to his father and, without realising, let a few tears slip silently down his face. Kyle got up from his chair, walked over and gently took his son's hand.

"We're at the medical centre. You're going to be just fine, though.

Doc here says so."

"Your dad's right," Clint patted him on the shoulder. "You'll pull through. Just a bit of a scare, that's all."

"What actually happened out there, my boy?" Kyle squeezed his son's hand.

Alex thought about it and started to feel a lump form in his throat. He took a deep breath, swallowed and gave himself a few seconds.

"I was playing in the woods like I said I was gonna, and ... and I found this massively huge wolf. Right there in the woods. It was tied down between two trees, and ... and I just felt so bad for it, you know? It looked dead and had this giant burn on one side. I couldn't just leave it lying there, Dad, I just couldn't. So I tried to cut the ropes but the knife slipped, I think, and stabbed it in its paw. And I think it got a fright 'cos it bit me, I don't think it meant to ... It looked so, so sad, and I just wanted to help it. I didn't mean to stab it, and it didn't mean to bite me ... I don't really remember what happened after that, just that I could hear my heart beating really loudly and it seemed harder to see."

More tears welled up in Alex's eyes and he could feel his heart beat speed up slightly as he thought more about the wolf and the bite. Kyle was reminded of his son's apparently irrational love for animals, especially dogs.

"This must have been a very large wolf to leave a bite like this." Clint slowly and carefully unwrapped Alex's arm. "How big would you say it was?"

Alex thought for a few seconds,

"Well, it looked like it was taller than me."

"Yes, well, a wolf can stand up to two metres on its hind legs."

"No, I mean on all fours."

Clint chuckled. "No, my boy, that's not possible, I think you might be exaggerating a little. If a wolf was over 1.5 metres on all fours, it'd be the size of a couch. Wolves just don't get that big."

"It was that big! Dad?"

Kyle frowned.

"Well, we'll have to go look for it in the woods so we can find out what's really going on, and to make sure it doesn't hurt anyone else. Doc, can I speak to you outside quickly?"

Clint lay Alex's unbandage arm down next to him and followed Kyle out into the hallway.

"I'm sorry if I hurt the boy's feelings, Kyle, but wolves just don't get that big. You know that."

"What? Oh, no, I don't really care about that."

"You're worried about how something that could leave such a large bite in your son got tied down in the first place."

"Yeah, that's exactly what I'm worried about. I'm going to have to go call the farm to tell them what's going on here, what Alex has just told us. What more do you need to do with him before I can take him home?"

"Well, I was hoping to be able to check and redress his arm before he woke up, but he apparently wakes up early. From what I've seen already, it's healing well. I should be able to redress it without having to put him out again, but he should get some more sleep anyway. I'm sure I'll be able to get it all done in the time it takes someone to get out here to fetch you."

"All right, you go do your thing. I'm going to go make the call."

The two men nodded at each other, then Clint walked back into the ward and started washing his hands.

"Where's my dad gone?"

"He's just gone to go call your mom to come pick you up."

He turned to look at the boy, whose face brightened slightly with a faint smile.

"I just need to take another look at that arm of yours to make sure it's healing properly, and then you'll be free to go. But you must try to get some more sleep over the next day or so. I know it's not exactly what you want to be doing while on holiday, but your body fixes itself fastest while you sleep. You got me?"

Alex's face turned thoughtful, as he waited for the doctor finish his prep.

***

The farm was in northern Alberta, a few hundred kilometres

north of Edmonton. Debra had been born there, and she and Jeff had spent their holidays on the farm once they had left for boarding school in Edmonton. Kyle, in turn, was born and raised on Syn Island, the man-made prison island in the mid-Atlantic. Although originally a maximum-security prison, its inhabitants put in the work and the good nature to turn it into a functioning international city over the course of a few generations. The couple met one day when Debra was backpacking around the world and stopped on Syn Island for a week of sightseeing. Her luggage had been lost in transit from the UK and until the airline could track down which flight her bags had gotten onto there wasn't anything more they could do to help her. Kyle was at that moment saying goodbye to his best friend Peter, who was moving to Brazil to pursue some woman he had met in a bar two nights before, and overheard the airport employee giving Debra the bad news. Feeling somewhat despondent himself, having just lost his best friend to a near-perfect stranger, he decided it was his turn to roll the dice on a stranger too. He walked up to her as she stood slightly lost and confused in the middle of the arrivals lounge, wondering how she was going to get anywhere with all of her worldly belongings having taken a random flight to somewhere.

"I know I need a drink, and it sounds to me like you need one too. Now, from where we are standing I can see a bar. I'm going anyway, but I could really use some company if you'd like to join me."

Although she never actually said it, in that moment Debra thought to herself she had just met the man she was going to marry. Without hesitating, which was so unlike her usual fastidious self, she followed him to the bar where they spent the following few hours drinking and complaining and flirting. Then they took a cab back to his flat and there they stayed for the rest of the week. Eventually the luggage arrived but by that time she had found herself a bar job and Kyle had bought her some new clothes. The next time she boarded a plane it was back to Canada to introduce Kyle to the family.

The reception area of the little medical centre had an assortment of less-than-comfortable couches, a small desk and chair, and a phone. Kyle had planted himself on the chair and was running through the farm's morning schedule in his head trying to work out who was most likely to answer the phone.

"Hello?" Came a bleary voice.

"Hey, Jeff, it's Kyle. How you doing?"

"Oh good, good. How are things on that side? Everything okay?"

"Yeah, everything's fine actually. Doctor says Alex can come back to the farm, so if you or someone can come get us?"

"Uummm, sure no problem … No one's really awake yet. Well, except Dad, who's already out working, and the boys, so, uhmmm, so I guess I could wake up Annabel to watch the kids and then I'll be on my w— Oh, no, wait … She's awake anyway. Okay, give me ten minutes to shower and I'll be on my way."

"Or you wake up Deb and she can come?"

Jeff frowned at the phone. "You wake her up, I'm not that brave."

Kyle chuckled knowingly. "Point taken, see you soon."

"Any idea yet about what happened?"

"I'll tell you all about it when you get here. We might have to go hunting later, but I'll see you just now."

When Kyle turned down the hall the doctor was waiting for him outside Alex's room.

"Something wrong, Doc?"

"No, no, nothing's wrong exactly, in fact, things are good, surprisingly good. Your son's healing fast … extremely fast; to the point that I now need to remove some of the stitches I did yesterday."

The two men looked at each other in a silent confusion for a minute.

"Okay … So what does that mean exactly?"

"Well, I … I don't really know. If you'd asked me yesterday for an impromptu diagnosis, I'd have guessed he'd have many months of physiotherapy ahead of him. There seemed to be some serious damage there, Kyle. But now … now. I don't know. But come, I'll show you."

Back in the ward Clint gestured to Alex's arm. Kyle was expecting to see stitches and scabs, but what he saw were red marks, some swelling and patches of rough skin. Even those wounds that seemed really deep, possibly even debilitating, just the night before were little more than abrasions. He turned the boy's arm over a couple times, just staring at it, until Alex broke the silence that had fallen over the room.

"Dad, I … I don't feel very well. My body hurts all over and I'm really sleepy."

Kyle lay his son's arm back down on the bed and turned a worried expression up at the doctor.

"All right, I'm going to give you a little injection that'll make you feel a bit better, but it's also going to make you sleep again, so why don't you close your eyes now."

Alex nodded and let his eyes flutter close. Clint retrieved a small vial from the locked wall cabinet, filled a small syringe with its contents and injected it into Alex's arm.

"Now, I gave him a rabies shot yesterday just to be sure, but considering how fast it's healing, I'd like to take some blood and run a few tests ... See if there is an obvious reason for this."

"Sure, but would the rabies injection explain why his whole body hurts?"

"Could do. Could also be from the shock, his body flooding with adrenalin, which puts all your muscles on edge. In fact, that's actually the most normal thing about his situation at the moment. I'd be more worried if he felt perfectly fine."

Kyle stroked his son's head while Clint got together the instruments he needed to draw blood and remove the stitches. When it came time to work Kyle stepped out of the way and just watched. He wasn't normally squeamish about blood but somehow it felt different watching it happen to his son. Once it was done Clint excused himself to get the blood into proper storage.

Jeff smiled at the doctor as they passed each other in the corridor and knocked lightly on the doorframe as he walked into Alex's ward.

"Anybody home?"

Kyle looked up. "Oh, hey, the Doc will be back in a second then we can take Alex home."

"Why do you look so worried, bad news since we last spoke?"

"No, apparently he's healing really well. And I mean really well. But I just watched Clint draw some blood which I now know was a mistake."

"Could be worse. I decided to be the modern man and be in the delivery room with Kath when Sammy was born."

Kyle grimaced.

"Never making that mistake again."

"All right," said Clint as he returned, clipboard in hand, "I just need you to sign a few forms, then you can take him home. He'll probably sleep for the rest of the morning and will be a little groggy for a few hours after he wakes up. I'll let you know what I find out from the blood tests. Otherwise, when he does wake up he'll need food, and something sweet to help calm his nerves, sweet tea's better than chocolate. But chocolate will do the trick too, and lots of water."

Clint had a pleasant smile, one that showed that the young doctor remembered all too well what it was like to be a child.

Jeff scooped up his nephew and carried him to the car while Kyle followed the doctor back to reception to sign the paperwork, before heading out to the car.

"So did Alex get a chance to tell you what happened?" Jeff asked turned onto the road back to the farm, Alex already nodding off in the back seat.

"Yeah. Said he was bitten by a bloody great wolf."

"A wolf? Jesus! It's a miracle he's alive."

"That's not the half of it, apparently the 'wolf' in question was tied down and it sounded like it had been burned or branded."

"What?" Jeff shook his head in disbelief,

"Yeah that's kind of what I thought. Said he was playing in the woods, found this gigantic thing tied down, looked dead, he decided leaving it like that was cruel so tried to cut the ropes, accidentally jabbed it with the knife, and it bit him."

"Too kind for his own good sometimes that one ... So how big is big, you reckon?"

"Not sure really. He said it looked like it'd be taller than him when still on all fours."

"That's not possible ... Surely."

"That's basically what the doctor said. Personally, I wouldn't know, we don't really have wolves where I'm from."

"That's a thought. Do you have any animals on Syn Island?"

"Not really, some birds, people have imported pets, but that's about it."

"That must be weird being a kid in all that, no nature anywhere."

Kyle laughed. "You get used to it, but I do like that my kids get the balance coming here for holidays."

He turned to look at his son sleeping in the back seat, arm back in a bandage, and stared at the drops of blood on his trousers. "Or I did, anyway."

The car then fell back into silence as both men wrestled with the idea of who or what could have tied down a beast that size. And why? The drive home wasn't nearly as frantic as the drive out had been and before either of them had time to flesh out any solid theories they were back at the farm.

In the time since Kyle had called everyone else had woken, and Debra had taken to sitting on the front door step waiting for her son to arrive. As the car pulled up a part of her hoped Alex would just bound out of the car like he usually did and everything would be fine. But the sombre look on the faces of her husband and brother burst that bubble, returning her to reality and she fought back a few nervous tears. Kyle opened the back door, unclipped the seatbelt and lifted Alex into his arms, remembering suddenly having to carry him around as a baby and how small and fragile he had seemed then. He was bigger now, but was apparently still fragile.

"Is everything all right?" Debra tried but failed to hide the fear in her voice.

"Everything's fine, he's perfectly fine. The doctor just gave him something to help him sleep while he tended to his arm. Should be awake in a few hours."

"Then what's with the looks?"

"I need to talk to your dad about trying to find that thing, or whatever it was that did this to him."

"Thing? What do you mean, 'thing'?"

"Well, Alex says it was a giant wolf, but Clint says wolves just don't get that big."

Debra's face went slightly pale.

"Let's get inside so I can tell everyone at the same time and we can make a plan. And this little guy is not as light as he used to be, I'm gonna put him in our bed so the boys don't lose their room."

Concerned silence was fast becoming the theme for this family holiday. It wasn't their normal way. As far as families go, this one could be loud and talkative; someone always had a joke or two to add to every conversation, while they set about solving the world's problems. However, none of them seemed to know what to say when it came to either being thankful that Alex was still alive, or what to do about what could be a giant wolf in the woods.

Kyle put Alex on the bed and watched him for a few minutes, thinking about his children and how different they were. He had grown up an only child and had often wondered what it would have been like if he had siblings, if it would have made his childhood easier or harder. One thing he did know was that he wanted his kids to be friends when they were adults. Like their mother, he worried more about Annabel than he did Alex, but not for the same reasons. Annabel didn't like to be the centre of attention; she was smart, funny and interesting in her own way and, he felt, should not be made to feel she needed to be more like her extrovert younger brother. It was an argument Kyle and Debra had had many times in the past, but were destined to never have again. He bent down to kiss his son on the forehead, then crept out of the room to find the family all sitting around the breakfast table waiting for the update. Like his son, he enjoyed the odd flight of fantasy and for a moment envisioned himself a master spy with vital information on how to bring some unseen evil organisation down, with his father-in-law as president sitting at the head of the table and the various advisors and generals on either side. There was the temptation to start the conversation by saying, "I bet you're all wondering why I called you here today," but thought better of it. Now may not be the time to be cracking jokes, he thought. So he sat down and turned to his inner lawyer.

"Alex is fine. Doctor says he's healing extremely well, astonishingly so, in fact, and there's no need for worry. He's been given something to help him sleep, so he should be out until this afternoon."

The adults and Annabel all heaved a quiet sigh of relief, but the boys were still eager to hear about how he had been hurt in the first place and if there was an epic battle involving swords and magic.

"So what happened to him?" said Marie quickly.

"Well, that's where this story gets interesting."

He smiled and looked at the children, who all, including Annabel, suddenly looked disappointed, without even trying to argue, clambered out of their chairs and left the room. As the door closed everyone could hear Frankie.

"It's not fair, we never get told what happens. I bet Alex got into a fight with a dragon or something and they don't want us to know so we won't go try fighting it ourselves."

"Oh, yeah?" You could almost hear the smile in Annabel's voice. "So, what colour is it then? The dragon."

Kyle cleared his throat so he could continue, spelling it all out for the eager listeners.

"Wolves don't get that big."

"How on earth would you tie something like that down in the first place?"

"That's not possible."

"Oh my god."

"That poor boy."

"That poor creature."

"That dumbass. Who tries to free a giant wolf with a pen knife ...? Honestly, what was he expecting, a new best friend?" That was Derrick who, now that the alarm had settled, was simply ticked off.

"Dad!" came a chorus of voices.

"What? Don't look at me like that; you were all thinking it. Anyway, one thing's for sure, we need to arm up and go looking for that thing."

The men looked at the men and the women looked at the women and once again silence descended on the family.

"I'm in," proclaimed Jeff, to Kath's horror.

Kyle locked eyes with his father-in-law, who nodded and said, "All right, you two follow me to the garage where we'll get the guns and you three stay here and keep an eye on the kids."

"Not a damn!" announced Marie. "If you think you three are going to go hunt the big bad wolf while us little ladies stay at home and watch after the kids then, you've got another thing coming. I'm not going to sit here while you live out your Neanderthal fantasies. I'm coming with you; I'm a better shot than you anyway."

Kath and Debra applauded. Secretly the other two men wanted to join in but opted not to for fear of what Derrick might do to them if they did. With a cheeky smile, he simply replied, "Yes, dear."

Chapter 3

At some point every summer holiday the Harris family would travel from Syn Island to Canada to visit Debra's family on their farm. How long they stayed would depend on how much time Kyle could get off work. Usually around two weeks. Every time they went Alex would end up playing in the woods near the river, and he secretly looked forward to it. In his mind it was an enchanted forest full of magical creatures and adventure. A stick of the right shape became a sword and the imposing tree would become some terrible monster that was plaguing the nearby village. He'd fight his way past countless thieves and bandits to discover that it was all being masterminded by the monster, which he would then valiantly slay, sometimes twice. He still wasn't sure why the hero always needed to save the princesses, but he would anyway, because that's what always happened on TV.

Knowing that he always played in the same place made the search for whatever bit him a little easier. It didn't take long to spot the first bloody handprint, but it did stop everyone in their tracks. It wasn't the sight of blood that did it, but that it was Alex's blood. Derrick led on from that point and they followed a trail of broken sticks where the tree had obviously lost the sword fights, until they came upon a small clearing and the burnt carcass of something large. Very large. The wolf lay on the ground, still tied up, but now it looked as though it had had fuel poured over it, and set alight. You could still make out the form of a wolf, but it had almost no fur, and the smell of burnt meat and hair still stung at their noses. An ice-cold shiver made its way down the spines of all four of the search party as they considered what could have happened had Alex not escaped when he did. And yet, as they crept closer, a growing pity started to swell in their hearts. It was suddenly clear to them why he had felt so compelled to help the creature. They say hunters who shoot elephants are always reduced to tears when they get close to the corpse, something about bringing down something that big gets to people. The inert form of the wolf was having a similar effect. When they left the house to track down this creature they were a hunting party, now as they looked at it they were its mourners. Derrick was the first to find his voice.

"It's definitely a wolf. Look at the bone structure, the form of the back legs and the shape of the jaw … But who on earth would do something like this?"

"Well, he was right about the size; this thing's massive. Oh my god, look! There in the ashes … Alex's army knife."

Kyle pointed towards what had once been the animal's front paw, tears welling up in his eyes as he realised what courage it must have taken for a ten-year-old to get that close to something so big and scary, believing he could save it. As those tears started to roll down his cheeks, Jeff put a hand on his brother-in-law's shoulder.

"Well, whatever happened here, it's over now. Whoever did this is clearly gone and I don't see any trace of them. I get the feeling that if Alex hadn't have found this thing we would never have known anything about any of this … The fact that the knife is still here probably means that whoever it was didn't know Alex was ever here."

The comment was intended to reassure, and whether he knew it or not, he was right. Kyle knelt down next to the carcass and picked up what remained of the knife and slipped it into his pocket.

"I don't think there's anything more we need to do here. Let's leave this poor animal in peace and go."

Meanwhile, back at the house, Kath and Debra were sitting through *The Wizard of Oz* for the umpteenth time, giggling to each other. Occasionally one of them would say something like, "Neanderthal fantasies," and roll their eyes. And then they'd erupt into helpless hysterics all over again.

Frankie turned his attention from 'Follow the yellow brick road' to his mother and frowned. "Sshhh! You're wrecking the movie for everyone."

Both women fought hard to stop themselves from laughing as he turned his attention back to the television. Annabel bit her bottom lip and hid her face behind a book. She too had seen *The Wizard of Oz* many, many times growing up and although she still enjoyed the film she felt that once you knew all the words off by heart you didn't really need to watch it anymore. She did however sing along to most of the songs, even if it was wordlessly in her head.

Debra leaned in closer to Kath and whispered, "I'm going to go check on Alex. You want something to drink?"

"Is it too early for wine? No, no, just kidding, a cup of tea please."

Annabel looked up at her mom and, with a toothy grin, made hand gestures to indicate drinking. Debra rose from her seat and headed off to the kitchen to fill and switch on the kettle before going into her bedroom where Alex was asleep. She slowly and quietly opened the door, trying to make as little noise as possible, then crept up to the bed to look at him. He'd shifted around a little, making himself more comfortable, but was still sleeping peacefully. She gently stroked his head causing him to shuffle a little but, not wake up. She breathed a quiet sigh of relief that he really was just fine, and crept out again. She went back into the kitchen to make two cups of tea and one of coffee before returning to the lounge to finish watching *The Wizard of Oz*. Debra had never really liked the movie, but both she and Kath needed the distraction from thinking about what was happening out there, beyond the safety of the farmhouse, their husbands wandering through the woods looking for the big bad wolf. It wasn't fair. Not because the others got to go on an adventure but because they had to sit and wait to find out what was going on. If something terrible happened they would only know about it after the fact. It made them feel slightly helpless, an emotion that neither woman was really used to.

The movie had only just ended and the women had moved onto the porch when they spotted the others heading across the field back to the house. They both stood and thought about running to meet them, but stopped themselves. It wasn't long before they were all sitting around the dining table discussing what the search party had discovered in the woods. No one really wanted to go into too much detail about the state of the animal they had found, but enough was said to calm the hearts and minds of those who had stayed behind.

It was approaching lunchtime, and the children were playing outside. The two boys were back in the water tank with Annabel watching them as she read her book. Kyle was in a chair at his son's bedside; he had come in to put Alex's Swiss army knife on the bedside table and decided to watch him for a while before joining the others. The women were on the porch drinking tea and coffee. Meanwhile, Derrick and Jeff were tending to the horses, which seemed more out of sorts than usual.

Kyle joined the women on the porch just as Marie said, "And Alex has the same beautiful big brown eyes as his father."

It wasn't the compliment that drew him as much as the colour of his eyes. Kyle wasn't one who took much notice of eye colour; when he looked at someone he saw mouths and jaw lines, hardly ever the colour of their eyes.

"Sorry, what did you just say, Marie?"

"Oh come now, Kyle, no need to fish for compliments. You know I've always loved your eyes."

"No not that … What colour are Alex's eyes?"

The women at the table looked at each other.

"They're brown, honey, just like yours. Why?"

Kyle frowned. "Well, I'm not sure actually … But I remember, when we were leaving the hospital thinking how blue his eyes were. Like yours, only paler. Much paler. I'd never really noticed it before; I even remember wondering why I'd not noticed it before. Weird."

Everyone looked concerned, more for Kyle at this point than anyone else. Only Debra knew that he had been under a lot of stress at work, waiting to hear about a potential promotion to director of his department, which would put him on the board and secure his career. Kyle worked as a criminal lawyer for a big-name firm, and if the promotion came through his name would go from being on his door to also being on the wall as you walk into the building. He was an exceptional lawyer, very highly regarded, and deserved the promotion, but he was still relatively young, and many wondered whether it made financial sense to replace the current director who was retiring.

Marie thought for a moment. "Well, I've heard of people's hair going white after a shock. Do you think it's possible to happen to the colour of people's eyes?"

Everyone looked at each other and then at Kath, hoping that because she worked in the medical field she would have an answer.

"Well, I've never heard of that before, but just because I don't know doesn't mean it's not possible. Why don't we phone the doctor and ask him?"

Just then Alex stepped out onto the porch, still wrapped in a blanket and looking very sorry for himself. His face was grey, his lips dry, and his eyes were indeed ice blue.

"Mom, I'm hungry."

Everyone turned to look at the boy. There was a stunned silence as everyone at the table realised that his eyes had changed, virtually overnight, from dark brown to pale blue. Debra shot up from her chair.

"Oh, sweetie, I'm so glad you're awake. And, sure, of course we can find you some food. You must be starving. Come with me."

Alex took his mother's hand and followed her meekly to the kitchen. All the while the others sat in silence, still in mild shock at Alex's eyes. Initially Kyle had almost been tempted to disregard what he thought he'd seen, perhaps it was Clint who had blue eyes and he had just mixed it up in the turmoil of his head, but coming face to face with it like that had taken even him by surprise. He got to his feet and walked into the house, picked up the telephone and dialled the doctor. It rang a few times before Clinton answered.

"Medical Centre, good day."

"Hey, Clint, it's Kyle. Kyle Harris."

"Hi, Kyle. What's up? Nothing wrong, I hope?"

"Not exactly, no. He's a little weak still, and been sleeping a lot. But none the worse for wear, I don't think. It's just ..." Kyle struggled with the words. "Well, I was just wondering; you've heard of shock turning people's hair white?"

"It's not that simple."

"What do you mean?"

"Well, theoretically it is possible, but it's by no means sudden. Hair is dead, it's not suddenly going to change colour."

"And eyes? Is it possible for that kind of thing to happen to eye colour?"

"You mean can shock make someone's eye change colour?"

"Yes."

"Yes, in fact, that's more likely than hair changing colour. Eye colour is not as fixed as is popular belief."

"Really?"

"Absolutely. Apparently David Bowie's strange eyes are a result of him falling out of a tree. Now, I take it something like this has happened to Alex?"

"Wow. Yeah, seems his eyes have gone pale blue, from dark brown, overnight."

"Don't worry about it. You might just want to take him to get a check-up when you get back to Syn Island. But, honestly, I wouldn't worry. They may even change back."

"Oh, thank God. Funny, though, how we all know about the hair suddenly changing, which, as you say, isn't quite true, but *I've* never heard of eyes! Anyway, thanks, Clint. Will you call when you have the results form Alex's blood tests?"

"Yes, of course, but it probably won't be today."

"That's fine. If you're not worried, I'm not worried."

"Good. Have a good day, Kyle. Say hi to your boy for me, will you?"

"Will do. Thanks."

Kyle put the phone down and looked through into the kitchen. Alex was at that moment sitting at the table eating. Kyle thought about everything that had happened over the last twenty-four hours. Between the anxiety of waiting for work to call and how he'd failed in protecting his son, he couldn't help but feel a strange, angry calm wash over him. It was nothing new to him. It was often how he felt in court, and managing it helped him win cases, but in this situation he had no channel for his anger.

"Debs, can I talk to you quickly?"

The look on Kyle's face instantly told her it wasn't meant as a question and followed him out of the room.

"What's the matter, love?"

"I've just gotten off the phone with Clint who says the eye colour thing is perfectly natural, nothing to worry about."

"All right, but then why do you look so angry?"

"I'm just stressed out. I didn't sleep very well last night either."

"So why don't you go get some rest now?"

"Think I'm gonna go for a walk to chill out, but first I need to tell you something. This morning, when Clint checked on Alex's arm, he found that he's healing so fast that he actually needed to remove some of the stitches."

"What do you mean ...? Mom mentioned Clint being concerned about possible long-term damage to his nerves, is this linked to that?"

"What? No, although he did mention something about physio. But, no, apparently he's healing so fast Clint wanted to take blood to run extra tests."

"Extra blood tests? Why didn't you tell me that before?"

"I didn't want to worry you."

"Worry me? Kyle, I'm his mom, I'm supposed to worry." Debra knew Kyle was under a lot of stress, but so was she, and couldn't stop herself. "Our son is bitten by some ... some *monster* in the forest, and the doctor takes blood to run additional tests because there's something strange going on! It's a big deal, Kyle, everything that happens is a big deal. How dare you decide to keep this from me!"

Kyle was already worked up and knew he should have just gone for a walk and explained himself afterward, he knew it, but he was at that point too angry to stop himself.

"Oh, please, forgive me for trying to protect you! I'm not the one who fainted at the first sign of danger. I'm so glad *you're* here to protect our children."

It was a mean thing to say, and Kyle knew it, and even though it was said in a harsh whisper, Alex, who was still sitting at the kitchen table, could hear every word his parents were saying.

Debra, her cheeks flushed red with rage, replied through gritted teeth, "Yeah? Well, at least I have parents our children can actually fucking visit! It's still safer here, even with monsters, than under the bridge with your mother!"

The gloves were off and it all quickly spiralled out of control. They started hurling abuse at each other, screaming every horrible thing they could think of at the same time.

Kyle's parents had been in a car accident when he was a teenager. His father had been killed on impact and his mother had suffered mild brain damage that manifested itself as memory loss, and developed into an addiction to pain medication. She was in and out of mental-health and rehab clinics for years after that and would often try to break out to get her hands on more drugs. Kyle was a boarder during the school year and was fostered during summer holidays. He inherited his father's estate, which meant that there was enough money to put himself through school and college, and, with his mother declared legally incompetent, the family home was sold. Kyle was just fifteen years old.

Alex had stopped eating and now simply sat listening to his parents fight it out. As hard as he tried to ignore it, every insult, every word of blame and accusation reinforced what he was thinking:

This all started because of me. His heart began to beat faster and faster, a fury he'd never known before building deep within him. Alex closed his eyes and his breathing become very short and sharp, his heart beating ever faster. With every high-pitched slur, every blind retaliation, his mind filled with even greater fury until he couldn't stand it any longer, and burst from his chair in a blind rage.

"Now you listen to me!"

Alex roared, his voice so deep that it seemed to echo off the walls, reverberating like that of a demon across the room. Both Kyle and Debra spun around to see their ten-year-old son in the hallway. Their mouths dropped open. Alex's eyes seemed to be glowing green, his mouth open wide and what appeared to be saliva dripping from his teeth, teeth sharp and long. His breath was deep, and loud, his hair, now jet black, stood straight up.

"STOP IT, STOP IT RIGHT NOW! I'M SICK OF IT! STOP!"

Alex thrashed his head from side to side as he spoke, his voice carrying with it a ferocity that sent shivers down both their spines. With clenched fists, Alex doubled over to take another deep breath. He then quickly straightened up, threw his head back and screamed. It was so loud that it could be heard from pool to the barn. Quickly, what started as a scream seemed to change into a howl and Alex dropped to his knees. Debra shook with fear and, without thinking; Kyle stepped between her and Alex. Every muscle in Alex's body began to stretch and tense. He took another great breath in, and then let out another even louder howl. Derrick and Jeff were already running as fast as they could towards the house, the boys were out of the pool and clinging to Annabel who, having no idea what was going on, was leading them towards the porch and hopefully an adult. As Alex tensed, his clothes started to stretch taut and then rip, revealing a layer of coarse hair, turning to fur that seemed to cover his arms and chest, steadily spreading before their eyes across his entire body. Debra clung to her husband's back, her eyes wide, screaming silently. Marie, Kath and the children stood paralysed by fear at the door from the porch, looking on in terror. What was happening? *What was happening?*

Alex's heart rate had become a deep, sonorous hum in his ears, but the anger was dissipating, only to be replaced by fear, a terrible fear that clawed at him, ripped through his gut. He looked at his fists and saw black hair growing to cover his arms. He closed his eyes as his head forced itself back and, at the sound of bones cracking and muscles pulling and ripping, he howled again.

Jeff and Derrick burst through the front door and found themselves face to face with the horror of a human face contorting itself into a snout and to catch the final deafening howl as Alex transformed completely into a wolf, pitch black, dark as the night. Debra's world began to go black. Kyle felt her hold on him loosen and turned just in time to catch her and sink to the ground with her in his arms. Kath braced herself against the doorframe and slowly fell. Jeff stumbled back out the door, bent double and heaved, spewing vomit across the cobbled porch.

"G'MORK!"

The two younger boys screamed in unison and turned on their heels, running as fast as they could from the house. They were followed closely by Annabel, with Marie in pursuit of all three. Derrick remained paralysed by fear and disbelief.

The wolf was suddenly aware that his heart had begun to slow down; he could make out the familiar figure of a man on the floor, holding someone else he knew. He spun around to see more people he was sure he recognised. They were all terrified, the horror etched into the faces, the fear in their hearts. Pure terror. Everything was so different, yet the same. His breath started to quicken again as he scanned his surroundings, his mind beginning to race and panic setting in. He turned around, and around. In an instant he found himself on all fours, large black paws where there should have been hands. Panic grabbed hold of his heart and instinct took over. He raced down the hallway, past those huddled on the floor and through an open door, a bedroom. There he headed for the smallest, darkest spot, a place he'd be safest. Eyes wide, he leapt onto the couch in the corner and, ripping it apart with lethal claws, quickly clawed his way into the body of the couch, hidden except for his green eyes, which glowed in the darkness. He stared panicked out through the hole he had created, terrified at the visions in his head of someone or something reaching in to get him.

By this point, Marie had caught up with the near-hysterical children, scooped them up in her arms and held them all as tight as she could.

"It's all right, it's all right. I've got you," she whispered. "You're all going to be okay. Don't worry, don't worry. Just breathe."

Jeff managed to pull himself up and staggered inside to get to his wife and sister. He knelt and wrapped his arms around Kyle and Debra, still huddled motionless on the floor. Derrick stood for a moment, replaying what had just unfolded: the wolf disappearing down the hall, his son staggering in after it only to wrap himself around his daughter and son-in-law, and his wife disappear into the garden after the terror-stricken children. Eventually his eyes settled on Kath, who looked back blankly at him.

"Jeffrey, your wife needs you." Derrick's voice shattered the stunned silence.

Jeff turned to see his father wide-eyed and pale, a sight he'd had never encountered in the old man before. Slowly he removed his arms from the couple cowering on the hall floor and headed out to the porch. He sat down next to her and she allowed herself to topple onto his lap and close her eyes. Derrick took a few steps into the house and, back against the wall, slid down to the floor.

"Thoughts …?" Kyle turned his head to look at him.

"None."

Silence. A deathly hush.

"I've read that parents fighting can have an adverse effect on their children but this is *ridiculous*." Kyle's feeble attempt at some kind of normality, to shake the absurdity at what had just played out in front of them like some B-grade move.

A weak smile played at Derrick's lips. "And we always thought it was Annabel who was the over-achiever."

They both managed a half-hearted snigger.

"I guess his teachers were right," Kyle went on, a dry laugh bubbling up from deep inside. "He is a little monster."

They both started chuckling, a nervous sort of chuckle but it helped clear the air, shrug off the terror that had settled on all of them.

Jeff, catching their half-hearted laugh from the porch, poked his head in at the door. "And if you though potty training was bad, now you have to housetrain him."

Laughter began to fill the room, a near-hysterical laughter, but one that seemed to ease the tension nevertheless.

Debra groaned and shuffled a little before opening her eyes,

"What ... What's going ... ALEX!"

She sat up as her memory flooded back, consciousness taking hold. The laughter came to a sudden stop.

"Where is he? *Where's Alex?*"

The three men looked at each other,

"He's in there ..." Kyle nodded toward the bedroom. "In our room."

She looked up at her husband. "And the wolf? Where's the wolf?"

Kyle looked at his wife. "The wolf? The wolf in the woods ... or the wolf that's our son?"

"No..."

Debra's eyes instantly filled with tears as she came to realise that it hadn't been a dream after all. Kyle squeezed her hand, then got to his feet and headed off down the hall towards the bedroom. Debra made movements to try get up, to follow him, but her father reached out to hold her back.

"Wait. Just a minute. Let Kyle do whatever it is he needs to do."

She stopped and turned to watch as her husband slunk into the room.

Kyle looked around. His eyes finally coming to rest on the hole in the couch and the bright green eyes shining out. He wasn't exactly sure what he was going to do. His plan had been simply to find Alex; that being done, he was now drawing a blank. He wanted to try connecting with the boy- the wolf- but he worried that the wolf might try connecting its teeth to his throat. The two stared at each other for what seemed an eternity before Kyle decided to take the creature in front of him for what it was: a large dog, backed into a corner. Very slowly, he crouched down to get to eye level with it, and nervously extended his hand out.

"Alex?" he said in the calmest voice he could muster. "It's all right, son, you can come out now. Come on, boy, come to your dad."

The wolf's eyes glinted, shifting from the man to the door and back again, uncertain. Kyle continued to offer reassurance, trying to lure his son from inside the couch. Slowly, very slowly, every muscle in its body rippling with tension, the wolf started to edge its way out of hiding. In back of his mind, Alex knew that this was his father and that it was safe, but at the same time he was fighting an almost overwhelming sense of confusion and fear. His tail had tucked itself between his hind legs, an entirely new sensation for him, one that felt both strange and comforting at the same time. The world was now new and exciting and yet so much the same. He looked at his father's face, a face he'd seen almost every day since the day he was born, and yet it seemed like he was looking at it for the first time.

Meanwhile, Marie and the children, hand in hand, were slowly making their way back to the house. As scared as Annabel was, she also believed that, being older than the boys, meant that she needed to act brave, even if she didn't exactly feel that way. Marie herself had no idea what they would find back there, but she knew it was better to have the children indoors rather than running wild and scared around the farm. She was using her concern for the children to overpower her own fears. Watching her grandson turn from a ten-year-old boy into a wolf with shining green eyes was not something she could readily wrap her mind around. As they approached the porch she spotted Jeff and Kath seated just outside the door talking to someone in the hallway. Jeff turned to see his mother walking up with the children, all holding hands, still clearly terrified. He tapped Kath on the shoulder and pointed at the little group making their way back to the house. Like Jeff, Kath began to wonder how they were going to explain what had happened when they themselves weren't quite sure. In truth, they were both still numb from shock. Under any normal kind of circumstance, seeing their children so panicked would have prompted them both to leap into action, but they just sat there. It also occurred to Kath that if her young children tried to tell anyone what had happened during their holiday, people would likely think they were crazy and that they would need to work out a story to tell all the children. But they had just seconds in which to do it.

Jeff, thinking something similar, leaned his head in the door and said to the others, "Here comes mom and the kids. What are we going to tell them?"

Debra and Derrick looked at each other blankly.

"That it's about time we all go for ice cream," suggested Derrick quickly. "They, like us, are scared and confused and I still don't know of a better remedy than ice cream. Also, it'll buy us time to think ..."

Instantly Debra felt a tug at her heart at the thought that all the other kids were going to get ice cream and Alex, who had spent a night in the hospital, was trapped in a room, in another body. Her pain showed on her face.

Back in the bedroom, Kyle was still trying to coax Alex out from inside the couch.

"Alex, look, it's safe out here, I promise. It's just me and you, kiddo, and you know me. I'm your dad, you can come out now."

Alex crept very slowly, a little closer to the hole he had clawed into the upholstery and poked his nose out. Almost by reflex he sniffed the air and was suddenly abuzz with a new sensation of being able to smell, *really* smell, in detail. The shock of such a new and intense sensation caused him to panic and leap forward, out of the couch and onto his father's lap for protection. Kyle's eyes widened with fear as the beast leapt from its hole towards him, mouth open and eyes glinting in the half-light. Frankie's association of the G'Mork suddenly made much more sense. He wrapped his arms around the wolf that was his son, half to protect the boy and half to protect himself. It took a moment, but it soon became clear that the thing was not going to maul him, tear him to shreds, and gently he started stroking its head. It seemed the most natural thing to do.

But Alex was no wolf pup. As far as canines went, he was about as big as an Alsatian, an adult Alsatian, which Kyle was finding somewhat uncomfortable to have sitting on his lap. He continued to stroke its head until the wolf made a sniffing sound and licked his father's face.

Kyle frowned and said sternly, "Please don't do that again."

Alex looked back at him and whimpered in apology. They stared at each other for a minute until Kyle all but whispered, "How do you feel?"

Alex leaned his head to the side the way dogs do when asked a question, then made a series of noises that sounded as if they were meant to be words but weren't. The part of him that was still human wanted to say that this was the most different feeling he'd ever had. In all his wildest dreams, and nightmares, he couldn't have imagined that anything could ever feel like this. And yet he was fine, at the same time.

The brief silence was broken by a rhythmic thumping of Alex's tail against the floor.

"It's still you in there, isn't it?'

Alex tilted his head from side to side again, curiously.

"You, my son, are not a monster out of some horror movie. You're still the boy I know and love."

Alex thought for a moment, tried to figure out if he could find the answer to his father question, to make sure it was still him in here. The first thing he noticed was, again, smell. He was still hungry and his nose seemed to pick up on that, finding the sandwich his mother had made and which still lay on the kitchen counter. He could smell it, so intensely that he could almost see it, and he began to feel drawn to it. Then he turned to look at his father and once again tried to form words but only managed what were little more than soft growling noises. Sighing, he thought for a moment. He found it difficult not being about to express himself in words. The whole ordeal, from first being bitten and then the time in the hospital, had not yet worn off, and making the transformation had only added to his exhaustion. It was only now that he was calm that he realised how tired he still was. He locked eyes with his father and tried to lick his lips, to indicate food, hunger, but ended up licking his nose instead.

Kyle frowned. "You're hungry?"

Alex yawned, which showed off his massive teeth, sharply pointed. Kyle caught his breath but remained still, then shook his head. He had had a small epiphany.

"You're hungry and tired, right? Just like the doctor said. You're still my son, you're still my Alex."

This time he was not just trying to convince himself. He believed it. He kissed the top of the wolf's head.

"All right then … Jump up on the bed. I think sleep is the best thing for you right now. When you wake up, we can work this whole thing out together, all of us as a family. And I'll make sure we have food and water for you."

Alex appeared to nod. He then stepped off his father and, in a single bound, leapt up onto the bed. He then walked in a small circle a few times and curled himself around himself and was asleep.

Kyle got to his feet, pulled the corner of the blanket over the sleeping wolf and quietly left the room to re-join the others. His wife was still on the floor, her back against the wall, with her father next to her.

"Did I miss anything interesting?" Kyle was inappropriately cheerful, but Debra was still a little shaken.

At the door to the porch sat everyone else. They turned to look at him, but still no one said a thing. It was a strange kind of silence; it wasn't fearful or even uncomfortable. To Kyle it felt like standing in a room of sleeping people. He took a moment to think.

"Listen," he continued, "we need to talk. All of us. You too, kids. So how about we all head to the kitchen. Grandpa and I will make coffee, tea and hot chocolate for whoever wants and we can discuss what's just happened here and what we're going to do about it." Turning his attention to the children, he continued, "But there's nothing to worry about. You understand? No one's in trouble, no one's going to get hurt and there is absolutely nothing to be scared of, I promise."

He put on his best lawyer smile to show the children how sincere he was, in the hope that the same courtroom charm would work on them. And it did. Slowly everyone got to their feet and made their way into the kitchen to find seats at the table. It didn't take long before they were all seated, blowing gently on their drinks and staring anxiously at Kyle.

Looking around at their expectant faces, he found himself wishing he had more time to spend with his extended family. His job, however, dictated otherwise and, of course, Syn Island being off the coast of Brazil was so far away from Canada. So he rarely got that opportunity to spend this kind of quality time with them. On more than one occasion during the school holidays, Debra and the children had made the trip to the grandparents' farm alone, leaving Kyle at home to work. As a teacher, Debra had the same holidays as the children, and it was something he had been very envious at one point. He looked down the table at everyone and forced another smile.

"So ... It appears that Alex is now ... in fact .... A werewolf, it seems..."

As one, they all erupted, loud protests on the part of the adults, and scared whimpering disbelief from the children, with the exception of Annabel, who said nothing. Kyle tried to listen to what everyone was saying and to gather a few key points he could use to bring order to the conversation, but he quickly realised that between the profanities and tears there wasn't much logic or reasoning in any of it. He shook his head and took a deep breath.

"QUIET!"

Every man, woman and child stopped what they were saying and looked at him blankly, as one. Kyle finally had the stunned silence he was looking for.

Back in the bedroom Alex's ear twitched nervously and he pulled himself into a tighter ball, but didn't wake up.

"Thank you. Now I know this is scary and hard to believe, but let's look at the facts here: Alex was bitten by a strange wolf, yes?'

Everyone was still at a loss for words.

"Yes?"

The family nodded dumbly.

"Right, and we all saw Alex turn from a boy into a wolf?"

Somewhat sheepishly, the family nodded again.

"Then we must conclude that Alex is now, in fact, a werewolf. As hard as it is to believe, it's also the explanation that is most ..." He frowned. "... logical?"

Silence tightened its grip on the family.

"But he's not crazed. I mean, he's not out of control like in the movies. Once you spend some time with him, you'll realise that he's very much the same, only different. And, Frankie," Kyle turned his attention to the boy and smiled encouragingly, "you were right; he does look just like the G'Mork, well done and thank you."

Almost despite himself, Frankie smiled and blushed a little

Debra stared blankly at the table and said, "Nightmares. Alex had nightmares about the G'Mork, you know. And now he's become him."

Her words had a strange ring to them, and as she came out of her trance she realised that she must have said it out loud. Kyle immediately latched onto the idea and ran with it.

"That's perfect. We can tell people that he's our new pet. G'Mork, or Mork for short. That we brought him back from your parents' farm. Alex must have told everyone he knows, and a few strangers too, I bet, that we're getting a dog an—"

Debra slammed her hands on the table, cutting him off.

"Our son *cannot* be our pet dog! Kyle, I'm *sorry*, but that's a little too much to ask!"

Kyle took a deep calming breath. "I know this is an insane situation," he reasoned, "but we *have to* find a way around it and if we can do it together as a family then maybe we can help Alex have … have a normal life. He's still our son, our terrified little boy and it's our job to look after him still. Debs, we have to find a way. We *have* to. What other choice do we have?"

Kyle had learnt many tricks in his time, to help him project calm while spinning out of control on the inside, and he was putting as many of these into action as he could remember. He meant what he said, but at the same time he was desperately trying to come to terms with what he was saying; his son the werewolf, he could barely stand to believe it even though he knew it was true.

Just then Jeff found his voice.

"Frankie, Sam, now you two need to listen very carefully, this isn't something you can tell your friends about. This is a big secret, bigger than any other because if you do tell someone, anyone, they might try to take Alex away and none of us will ever be allowed to see him again. Do you understand?"

The two boys looked at each other, then they back at their father and nodded. Kyle winked at Annabel, who smiled nervously in re-ply. Derrick took hold of his daughter's hand. He could tell that she was trying hard to come to terms with it all, but it was all happening too quickly for her. She felt responsible for it all, and just couldn't fight off the overwhelming guilt and failure. She was his mom, it was her job to look after him, and something terrible happened. She turned to look at her father, but he too found himself at a loss for words.

Chapter 4

Alex slowly opened his eyes, yawned and stretched, before gently sniffing the air. The smell of bacon cooking somewhere nearby tickled his nose and breakfast came to mind. He looked at his hands, and they were hands. He peeked under the covers and discovered that, yes, he was once again a boy, a completely naked boy. Instantly, he thought it must have been a dream, but he wasn't quite sure whether he was happy or disappointed. He sat upright. He was still in his parents' room and there was a gaping hole in the couch against the wall. In that moment, he realised that there were no lights on and the heavy curtains remained drawn, bathing the room in a subdued darkness. And yet he could see fine. A shiver ran down his spine and the word *dream* slipped from his mind. It *had* been real, and he was afraid. What did all of this mean for him? Was he going to be allowed to go home with his family? Would he have to go stay with wolves in the forest? Alex's lively imagination began to race in all different directions at once, his heart started racing and he could feel his cheeks flush. Quickly he wrapped a blanket around himself and ran out towards the kitchen in the hope of finding someone to talk to, someone who could reassure him.

Kath stood at the stove cooking breakfast when he appeared alongside her, blanket draped over his ten-year-old frame and looking as if he'd seen a ghost.

Kath caught her breath. "Alex! It's you, as *you*. What's the matter?"

His breathing was heavy and laboured. Something was clearly wrong. So she knelt down next to him and her mothering instinct took over. She wrapped her arms around him.

"Sshhh, shhht. It's all right. What happened?"

In Alex's mind flashed memories of the day before like still frames coupled with a burst of raw emotions, fear, excitement, an urge to run as far and as fast as he could. He began to shake in his aunt's arms. Debra appeared at the door from the porch, ran over and scooped him up in her arms,

"Oh thank goodness. I'm so glad you're okay."

She then proceeded to kiss him all over his face. Whatever emotional roller coaster he had been on had come to an abrupt halt and he fought to get free while not losing grip of the blanket.

"Aaw, Mom! Mom! It's … Mom, I'm fine. *Mooooom!*"

Despite her best efforts, Kath giggled, loud enough to be heard by the blushing boy. Debra stopped the barrage of kisses and put him down, satisfied with a job well done. Alex frowned, wiping the girl germs off with the blanket.

"What's for breakfast?"

The women laughed. Alex was back.

"Eggies and bacon sound good?"

Eggs and bacon were by far his favourite thing to eat. The morning had suddenly taken on such a normal tone that everyone seemed to forget for a moment the events of the day before. Alex, happy with what was happening in the kitchen, made his way to the room he shared with his cousins to find clothes. Quickly he pulled on the swimming shorts and T-shirt that still lay in a heap next to his bed. As he slipped his arm through the sleeve, he realised that the puncture wounds in his arm had all but vanished, along with the stitches and any sign of scars. His arm was perfectly healed. Alex considered for a moment a long-sleeved shirt, but then thought that this would probably make it all too obvious so strolled back to the kitchen, as casually as he could muster, in the T-shirt in the hope that no one would notice.

"Gee, that was quick."

Alex shrugged his shoulders. "Well, you know, I didn't have to spend time taking clothes off ..."

"Well, there's no arguing with that logic." Kath couldn't help but laugh and shook her head. "But while I've got you here, I'd just like to check how your arm's doing."

Alex instantly looked nervous and guilty and, despite his best efforts, wasn't hiding it well, which also drew his mother's attention.

"Alex ... what's the matter?"

"It's nothing. My arm's fine. I mean ... the same. Not fine, but fine, same."

Kyle walked into the kitchen in time to catch his son's awkward comment.

"Hey, bud. You up and about?" He put his hand on the boy's shoulder. "What's up?"

Alex turned to his dad, a sad and guilty look on his face, then turned around a few times looking for a way to escape. But there was none, so slowly and nervously he held out his arm and said nothing. Kyle knelt down and looked it over.

"But there's not a mark on it."

Kyle looked up with worried eyes at his wife, who knelt down next to Alex and put her arm around him.

"Oh, honey, this isn't something you need to hide, it's great that you've healed so fast. You don't have to hide things from us. You're not in trouble."

A smile slipped across the boy's face. Then he wriggled free from his parents and galloped out onto the porch to join in whatever game his cousins were playing while they waited for breakfast. A sense that maybe everything would be actually be all right settled in the kitchen as they slipped back into the usual morning routine.

When the phone rang, Kyle kissed his wife, took a sip of his coffee and wandered down the hall to answer.

"*Hellooo.'*

"Morning, Kyle? It's Clint Brant. I have some news. We have Alex's blood tests back."

A shiver of cold fear rushed over Kyle's body, and threatened to send him into a blind panic. The blood drained from his face and he stared wide-eyed back at his wife in the kitchen.

"Kyle? Hello? You there?"

"Erm, yes? Sorry, b–bad connection. What did you say?"

"Yeah, the joys of living in the middle of nowhere. I said I'm calling about Alex's blood results."

Kyle was trying hard to sound and act normal but couldn't stop himself from feeling like he was about to throw up.

"I just thought you'd like to know that there doesn't seem to be any obvious reason why Alex seems to have recovered so fast."

"Well, actually, Debs and I were talking about that last night and apparently he's always been a bit of a quick healer."

Everything he learnt about truth avoidance during his law career seemed to have evaporated. The doctor had caught him entirely off guard and for the first time in many years Kyle found himself feeling a fool.

"Right, well, as I said before, it's not really a problem, but if you like I can investigate further, see if there is a reason on a genetic level?"

"No, no, really … Don't worry yourself about it at all. Alex seems to be much better today and we're heading back to the island in a few days anyway, so if something comes up we'll take him to his regular doctor. But thank you so much for your help, Clint. We really do appreciate it…"

The words were coming out short and fast, and Kyle found himself smiling dumbly at the phone.

"It's, uummm … only a pleasure. I'm just happy to hear the boy's feeling better. Well, in that case, enjoy the rest of your holiday and with some luck I won't see you again for some time," the doctor chuckled.

"Ha! Yes, thank you."

Kyle did his best to fake as genuine a laugh as he could and did a pretty good job of it before hanging up. He took a long, deep in breath and held it as long as he could to try calm down.

While Debra stared at him desperate to know what had caused her husband to turn into a nervous wreck on the phone.

"Well, that was close," he said to an anxious Debra hovering in the hallway. "I'd forgotten all about the doctor taking a blood sample from Alex." He could see the panic rise in Debra's eyes. "Don't worry, don't worry ... Everything's come back clean. Doc clearly didn't look that closely and I've told him to leave it."

He quickly moved across the room and wrapped his arms around his wife to comfort her and, truth be told, to garner a little comfort himself. Although he had never mentioned it, he often offered support to her as a way of reassuring himself. She nestled against his shoulder.

"So, what are we going to do now?"

He kissed her gently on the forehead.

"We're going to take every day as it comes and deal with issues as they arise. Just as we've done for Alex before this, only now we don't have to listen to him complaining that he wants a dog."

Debra let out a tired little laugh and shook her head. With Alex in their bed they had curled up for a night of broken sleep on separate couches. Kyle's fast wit and sense of humour was what she loved most about him. He was the only man she'd ever met that could keep up with her family. She looked up at him, a curious look on her face,

"I know what we can do. Amanda gave me the number of this doctor back on the island. He's apparently very alternative, while also an actual doctor. She said he's very spiritually aware and open-minded. Maybe he can help us."

"Honey, Amanda's an idiot. I know she's your friend and all, but really, the woman's a loon."

"Kyle, our son's a werewolf, we're in no position to point fingers at other people's personality quirks. Maybe some of her spiritual ramblings are just hocus pocus, but maybe not ... This guy's supposed to be very level-headed and down to earth, while also open-minded."

"Open-minded and down to earth, that makes it okay then?"

"Well, I don't know, but what else are we going to do?"

"Do we really want to involve other people in all of this, though? And if you've not even met him, how can we trust him? What's this guy's name anyway?"

"Dr Cooper. Rajan Cooper. And I've got an appointment to see him when we get back anyway. She recommended I see him to help balance out my stress levels during term time. So I can check him out and, if it goes well, I'll make an appointment for Alex."

"Yes, dear." Kyle rolled his eyes in mock ridicule.

Debra smiled a naughty grin and playfully slapped him. "Damn straight, yes dear."

Kath looked over at them, wrapped up in each other's arms, giggling, and couldn't help but admire them for how they were sticking together, supporting each other in the face of the insanity around them. She knew that they were stressed beyond belief and it gave her hope that they gravitated to each other for support in times such as these.

Alex made his way over to where his sister sat on the grass watching their cousin's sword fighting with sticks. As he flopped down next to her, she stopped reading and looked at him with wide eyes. Frankie and Sammy stopped playing too. He looked up at them anxiously and smiled. He knew they had all seen him turn the day before, and could feel their stares like fingers poking at him. Annabel looked up at the other two boys and then back at her brother, who was now obviously uncomfortable. She turned to her cousins.

"All right, you've had a look now. Yes, he's a boy again. So carry on with your game. Nothing more to see ..."

Alex smiled to himself. If anyone asked him, he'd say that he didn't need his sister to look out for him, but he knew that he did some times. And she always seemed be there for him when he needed her most.

"We were just wondering if he could turn back into the G'Mork and we could play NeverEnding Story." Sammy was scoping out the boys' options.

"I'm not the G'Mork!" Alex looked at his cousins in mock shock.

Annabel put her hand on his shoulder, mimicking her mother whenever Alex began to get defensive about something.

"We know," she laughed, "but you looked just like him and, besides, think how cool it'd be to be able to play NeverEnding Story with, like, proper characters."

The idea actually appealed to Alex in a strange kind of way. He had always like Darth Vader way more than Luke Skywalker, so why not the G'Mork, even though it scared him a lot more than Vader did.

"Doesn't matter. But I don't know how to just ... change."

His voice drifted slightly, sounding a little disappointed. He was still very confused about the whole thing. It also seemed to him that everyone else knew more about this than he did, and that worried him.

The boys shrugged their shoulders and returned to the game.

"You all right?" Annabel was looking at him with a curious expression.

"Yeah, I'm fine. Great. But, hey, check it out."

He held out his arm free from cuts and wounds. Annabel looked at the arm, turning it this way and that to try to find some kind of injury. There were no signs. None at all.

"This the right arm?"

"No, the left ..."

They both cracked up, rolling around on the lawn.

"But, yip, see?"

Alex held out his other arm for his sister to see.

"But … but?"

"Dunno. It was like this when I woke up. Oh … and I can see in the dark."

"Oh, rubbish! That's *so* not fair."

Alex smiled confidently and Annabel was clearly impressed.

"That's so cool! Like proper *see* or just, like, sometimes when you've been sitting in a dark room for a long time?"

"No, like *really* see. I didn't even realise the curtains were closed."

"And what about when you were … well, you know?"

"When I was changing? Well, it was strange. I mean, I still felt like me, or at least I think I was still me. I just felt, erm … *different.*"

He dropped his head to one side as he looked at his sister, trying to find a way to describe the feelings. It was the first time he'd tried to put it all into words, and found that there just weren't any. She could see him searching his mind for an explanation.

"Don't worry about it. You'll have more time to think about it and learn how to explain it to me."

"*What?*"

It hadn't occurred to Alex until that moment that this was something that would continue to occur. He had dealt with it with his mind still in holiday mode. Suddenly it hit him as something that would be with him for the rest of his life. Every day was going to be different. The weight of it all hit him at once and he felt something significant change inside him. For a moment the world went a little dark. The hair all over his body prickled slightly, his mind draining of all thought. Far away he could hear a voice that sounded like that of his sister, and she was screaming. He thought for a moment that he should try to pick up on what she was saying, or get closer to her, but the thoughts quickly evaporated into the void and he started to feel like he was falling right along behind them. Then all he could hear was his thump-thump of his heart, which had started to beat so fast it was more of a hum. Suddenly the void fractured and his lungs filled with air, and his whole body screamed. What came out was an ear-splitting howl.

Annabel had taken a few steps away from her brother as his body began to convulse and contort. She screamed for help as tears started to run down her face. Then, for a moment, Alex pulled himself into a tight ball on the ground and was still, but she could see that all his muscles had tensed. Then he seemed to erupt into a howl. The sound seemed to attack her and she slammed her hands against her ears while staggering backwards, desperate to get away from it.

The boys had bolted the moment Alex had started convulsing. The idea of their cousin being a wolf wasn't so cool anymore, and their boyish admiration quickly gave way to fear. By the time Debra and Kyle reached their children, Annabel was on her knees, staring in terror into the green eyes of the pitch-black wolf, slowly stepping out of what was left of boy's clothes. Annabel reached out a timid shaky hand.

"M, M, M ... Mork? Good, good boy, Mork. Good boy. P-p-plea ... please just don't hurt me."

Once again Alex's first reaction was to sniff the air and he picked up a smell he'd not noticed before, yet was so familiar that it was almost comforting. He could make out the image of a girl on her knees on the grass, holding out a shaking hand and, even though the image was almost alien, he knew it was his sister. And knew that he had to protect her. Slowly he took a few tentative steps towards her, sniffing every step of the way. It dawned on him that the smell that made him so comfortable was that of her; it rang so true with him that his heart slowed down, and calm began to settle over him. He put his nose against her hand and sniffed it a few more times just to be sure. Satisfied that it was indeed her, his tongue slipped out of his mouth and he began licking her hand. She cringed at how ticklish it was, threw her head back and laughed, then shuffled forward so she could scratch behind his ears. A tingling sensation ran all up and down his body and his back right leg started shaking uncontrollably.

Kyle and Debra looked down at their children. They couldn't decide whether what they felt was pride or abject horror. Yes, their children were bonding, but one of them was … well, a wolf. Debra let out a happy laugh as tears slipped down her face and she wrapped her arm around Kyle's waist. He, in turn, put his arm over her shoulders and they watched as the children rolled around on the grass wrestling in the way a child and a large dog do. Annabel laughed and Alex made *arff* noises.

Then Derrick appeared from behind the house, rifle in hand.

"What's going on?"

Annabel screamed in alarm and fell backwards, while Alex leaped between her and their grandfather with a violent bark. Then he locked eyes with the man with the weapon and a deep, gravelly growl rumbled out of him.

"Dad, I … I think you need to put the gun down."

Derrick looked down at the girl and the wolf on the lawn and slowly let the rifle swing down to his side, hanging on its strap.

"Sorry, I just heard the scream and the howl and, well ... I forgot, I guess."

He dropped down to one knee, his hands out in front of him.

"It's all right, boy, you know me. I'm your grandpa."

Alex looked at the older man now down on his knees and lifted his snout to sniff. Again the scent was both familiar and comforting. He sniffed a few more times to try to place the smell. Derrick had owned and encountered many large dogs in his life and knew how to introduce himself, slowly edging closer and closer to the wolf. Making sure not to move so fast as to seem threatening, but also not cowering to show weakness.

"It's all right, little Mork, it's all right. Come give me a good sniff. That's a good boy."

He was falling into the same trap as everyone else, captured by the visual aesthetic of the animal, and so treated him as a wolf rather than a boy. With everything else that was going on in Alex's mind, having the people around him speak to him in slow and simple-to-understand phrases did actually make things easier for him to wrap his mind around. In the moments before his grandfather had appeared, he'd all but let his human understanding of play go in favour of the animal's understanding of it. Likewise, when they had been interrupted, he had reacted as a wolf would, hackles raised, growl at the ready. Now that things had calmed down he found himself able to grasp the differences.

Because the changing was so new to Alex, he found himself, much like any puppy, very cautious, and so only very slowly stepped towards his grandfather. Part of him knew who it was, but that part wasn't in charge and this person wasn't as familiar as the smell of his sister or father. He looked across at his parents who were watching with bated breath to see how things were going to play out, praying that he would recognise and accept his grandfather. Realising that there were many pairs of eyes watching him, Alex's tail began to slink down between his legs.

"Don't worry, boy, no one's going to hurt you." The calming voice of his grandfather washed over him once again.

Derrick again edged himself closer to the animal, close enough so that he could put his hands right up to Alex's snout. Between the smell, the voice and being at such close range, the wolf in Alex decided that this man was indeed family and let his tongue flop out of his mouth in a pant, while his tail shot back up and started wagging. Sighs of relief seemed to echo from the onlookers.

Inside the house, however, Kath had forgotten about breakfast as she, Jeff and Marie tried desperately to calm the two panicked boys who had burst through the door. Frankie was crying, Sammy trying to explain what he understood was happening outside. Although many words came out, not a lot of explanation was being offered. Somewhere in the middle, Derrick had rushed past the window with a rifle. The calm outside the house was almost directly proportionate to the chaos inside of it. Jeff's stress levels were slowly but surely reaching breaking point. While his nephew being a wolf was a matter in itself, it seemed minimal compared to the potential issues that would inevitably arise as a result if his children witnessing their cousin transform into a wolf; he could barely understand it himself and he couldn't think how they were going to come to terms with it. To make matters worse, since Alex's incident in the woods, the horses on the farm had been getting more and more restless, and one had even managed to kick open the barn door during the night and was now missing. He knew his father was going to have to go find it; he also knew that if the horse was seriously injured Dad would have to put it down, and he knew, too, that he would have to go with him. Jeff picked Frankie up and tried to console him while Kath knelt down and wrapped her arms around Sammy.

Outside everyone was sitting in a small circle watching Alex, who in turn looked back at all of them, until Debra and Alex locked eyes and for a moment she saw what Kyle had seen the night before. She saw her son looking back at her from behind the eyes of the wolf. Tears rolled down her face, sending a strange, unexplained sense of guilt through the young boy. Alex let out a soft, sympathetic whimper and the emotion hit her like a wave. She took a deep breath and, without a word, stood up and started towards the house. Alex knew it had something to do with him but he couldn't understand what he'd done. He knew, though, that she wasn't up set with him, but still wished he could undo whatever it was. He was too young to fully understand how he was affecting the people around him, but he knew that he was. He dropped down and lay on his front paws, staring after his mother. Kyle reached out a hand and scratched his head.

"Don't take it to heart, my boy. This is just going to take some getting used to. But once we have a handle on it, everything can go back to normal again. It's just that right now everything's new; the first time these things are happening so we need to learn from them. Everything will be all right in the end, you'll see."

Alex let his vision drift past his mom to the house and twitched his ears towards the sound of crying children and thought, *no. No, it won't.*

As though he had heard the boy's thoughts, a tear suddenly slipped from Kyle's eye and ran down his cheek. He looked away quickly to try to hide it, but turned to look right at Annabel, who had been silently crying since her mom had headed back to the house.

Alex's mood suddenly shifted from mild sorrow to desperation: he no longer wanted to be a wolf. Closing his eyes as tight as he could, he focused as hard as he could on being a boy again, tensing his muscles until his entire body began to tremble. Then, all at once, it felt like he had broken through a wall in his mind, as if he were falling, weightless and free, until he landed with a bump. He looked around to see the horrified looks on the faces of those around him. Annabel had hidden her face in her father's shoulder, while Derrick and Kyle looked on in horror. Alex sat motionless for a moment. He was a boy again, a naked boy. There was a stunned silence, before Kyle summoned up his courage.

"How the hell did you do that?"

Alex quickly covered himself up with his hands.

"I ... I'm not sure. Err ... I just focused really hard and tensed my whole body."

"Oooh-kay then ..." His father's eyes grew wide. How was he supposed to react to all of this?

Inside the house, Marie had dragged Debra off into the lounge, away from the children. Her daughter had been trying to fight against it but simply couldn't any more. She wept into her mother's shoulder, desperate to try to explain her feelings, but unable to find the words.

Every fibre in her being longed to be able to go back and stop it all from ever happening, to protect him from this new life; her heart cried out for it. Disappointment and regret swum through her veins like ice, cutting its way along and turning her blood cold. No matter how hard she tried, there was nothing she could do but cry. A helpless sorrow washed over her. One moment they ran freely and the next they just seemed pointless. How would tears help?

All she wanted to do was dry her tears, and lay on the couch with her head in her mother's lap. Marie, in turn, couldn't help the silent tears from sliding down her own cheeks. The shock had worn off, and now the cold hard truth was setting into the hearts of the whole family.

Alex blinked his eyes a few times and collapsed onto the grass, unconscious. The others just stared at him, unsure of what might happen next. Was it worse to see the body of a young boy contort in pain and transform into a wolf or watch a wolf shudder its way back into a naked young boy? Kyle had had enough, but he had no idea what to do about it. Visions of his mother crawling along the floor looking for the pills she had scattered across the room in her stupor flashed through his mind; he remembered when he had to identify his father's body and how his mother, who at that point was still suffering from post-traumatic stress, scolded him, instinct told him not to cry and that everything would be all right when his father arrived. Kyle had always wanted to create a safe environment for his children, an environment where they could grow into the best versions of themselves and go on to live happy lives. He looked at his son now, sprawled naked on the grass, and watched as the dreams he had for his children shattered. He turned his gaze to Annabel, and put his hand on hers.

"I know you love your brother, and I know you protect him more often than anyone gives you credit for. But no one, no one, thinks this was your fault."

Her father's words echoed around in her head for a moment then all her anxiety burst out at once.

"But I'm his sister, his *big* sister. I'm supposed to stop him from doing stupid, stupid *shit!* Shit like this, like petting giant dead animals in the woods, while you and mom make money and pay bills and buy food and stuff."

"Sshhh … No, no, sweetheart. Your job is to be a little girl. That's all. Alex is Alex and this wasn't your fault; it's no one's fault. This is just something that … that simply *is*."

Kyle's voice was as calm as he could make it, but he could feel his courtroom cool beginning to slip. He knew that it wasn't just Alex's life that had changed; the whole family's lives were changing and no matter how much he wanted to he wouldn't be able to stop it or turn it back. He wrapped his arms around his daughter and she pulled herself onto his lap and sobbed. Derrick got to his feet, draped his jacket over Alex and hoisted him into his arms. Gingerly, he carried him into the house and back to bed. In that moment Kyle's heart broke as he too felt the full weight of the situation and knew it was going to crush Alex the child and leave only Alex the unknown.

Chapter 5

Derrick tucked Alex into bed and gently stroked his cheek in the way you would a sleeping baby. Knowing no one could see him, he allowed himself a single silent choked-up moment for the tears to flow before sitting back in the chair to hide from the rest of his family. All throughout the house the family was breaking down, fighting a desperate battle against fear and uncertainty.

As with any profound sadness, when the drama finally ended and some sort of calm descended once again, the family, pale-faced and exhausted, all drifted towards one location, the kitchen. The half-cooked breakfast now sat cold on the stove and no one seemed the have the energy to actually make anything. With the exception of Alex and Derrick, the rest of the family sat quietly around the table as if waiting for the spell to break. The situation reminded Kath of how it had felt in the hospital after a school bus had rolled back home. Many of the children had died despite the best efforts of the medical staff on duty that day. At the end of it all, the doctors and nurses ended up just sitting in the staff lounge, not making eye contact or speaking. Then suddenly the chief of medicine walked in and told a story about a separate tragedy, one that that had taken place when he was a medical student. The way they got through it, he said, was to think about the people they had saved that day, that although it had been a terrible, terrible tragedy, it would have been much worse without them. Kath couldn't see a silver lining to Alex's situation but it had distracted her from everything long enough for her to muster her energy to start cooking.

Down the hall, Derrick sat staring at his sleeping grandson and wracked his mind for everything he had every heard about werewolves. He didn't often have time to read fantasy, but he enjoyed a good movie. One image came to the fore, one key symbol that shone from every werewolf movie he'd ever seen: the full moon. Werewolves and full moons went hand in hand, didn't they? But Alex had turned in the middle of the day, and full moon wasn't for another three days. Werewolves were also all crazed monsters. Was it the full moon that brought that out in them? He couldn't help but think that things were likely to get a whole lot worse before they got better. Hands of ice seemed to reach into his chest and wrap around his heart, turning his blood cold. He wondered how long it would take everyone else to have the same thought, or if he should tell them. Alex shuffled a little in bed and sniffed the air a few times before he opened one eye.

"Bacon?"

Derrick blinked a few times at him.

"What?"

"I smell bacon."

The old man sniffed loudly a few times too.

"I can't smell anything."

Alex blinked his eyes and focused on his grandfather, a bleak smile playing on his lips.

"Oh, well ... uummm, I can."

"I know this is scary, my boy, but you must admit that that's pretty impressive. Maybe if we take this one step at a time, we can find the good in all this?"

Alex cracked half a smile and nodded to his grandfather.

"I see in the dark too."

Derrick mind suddenly flashed with childhood fantasies and let out a little laugh before leaning in closer.

"I've never told anyone this, but I've *always* wished I could do that."

"Really?" Alex laughed.

"Oh yes, if I could have had one superpower it would be to be able to see in the dark."

They smiled at each other for a moment before Derrick's expression turned grave.

"My boy, there's something we need to talk about before we go back in there." He nodded in the direction of the kitchen.

"What's that, Grandpa?"

"It's going to be full moon in about three days ..."

Alex paled visibly.

"I don't know how or when it's going to affect you, or even if it will. But I want you to know that whatever happens, we're going to get through it together, as a family, do you understand?"

What was left of Alex's smile faded.

"I'm scared, Grandpa. I was just trying to help that wolf. I didn't know this was going to happen, I didn't mean it. And now Mom and Dad are sad, and Annie's scared. Everyone looks at me differently. I promise, didn't mean for this to happen ... I'm sorry, I'm ..."

His bottom lip had begun to tremble so much that he could barely finish the sentence before tears streamed down his face. Derrick got out of his chair to sit on the bed next to him, and put his arms around the weeping boy. Alex allowed himself to cry for a few seconds, but took a long sharp breath in and gently pulled away from his grandfather.

"But I'm not going to let it, Grandpa. I know things have to change but I'm not going to let it take over my life or anybody's life. I'm going to take control of it, and own it and make it as easy for everyone else as I can. It's not fair for everyone else to suffer because of me."

Alex took a few more deep breaths. His voice seemed lower and calmer than it ever had before.

"Maybe it'd be best if I just stayed here on the farm. You could teach me how it all works and I'd be able to be a wolf without the risk of people finding out. And Mom Dad and Annabel could carry on living normal lives a—"

Derrick put up a hand and cut Alex off short.

"No."

His voice was firm and clear, and left no room to argue.

"Listen to me very carefully. As much as Grandma and I would love to have you, and you are always welcome here, living here isn't going to allow your family to have a normal life. Because it wouldn't be normal without you in it. It's going to be hard, yes, but I promise you that they won't want you to live here on the farm; they love you and *want* to help you learn how to deal with this."

A relieved smile slipped across Alex's face and he put his head on his grandfather's shoulder.

"Now get some clothes on and let's go see if we can find that bacon you were talking about."

Derrick stood up from the bed and grabbed a towel from the hook behind the door.

"Here," he said, tossing it at the boy, "you go get ready, and I'll see you back in the kitchen?"

All wrapped up, Alex made his way into his bedroom while Derrick went to join the family and find out if there really was bacon on the stove. He stood in the doorway to the kitchen and looked over his defeated family: Kath was cooking, Kyle was making coffee, Jeff still consoling his children, and Debra had Annabel curled up on her lap. Marie sat at the head of the table, staring at the fruit bowl. Never had he seen a group of people look more helpless in his entire life.

Alex announced his arrival by taking hold of his grandfather's hand. Derrick looked down at the boy and realised that someone needed to be strong for the ten-year- old who thought his family would be better off without him.

"Did you know ..." he announced, causing everyone to jump. "Did you know that our little Alex over here could not only smell food being cooked from a bedroom at the end of the hall, with the door closed, I might add, but he could also tell that it was bacon?"

Alex smiled nervously as everyone turned their attention to him.

"And ..." Derrick continued, "he can see in the dark."

Derrick gave Alex's hand a reassuring squeeze as the room fell back into silence save for the sizzle of bacon frying. Jeff took a deep breath and decided that someone needed to say something.

"That's all well and good, Dad, but can he spell 'Constantinople'?"

Immediately, the spell seemed to be broken, the tension easing. Derrick felt Alex's hand squeeze right back.

"Uummm ... Can *you*, son?" Grandpa was stepping up to the plate.

Jeff's mouth dropped open, his eyes darting around in his head as if he were searching his mind for the word. Then his mouth closed and a blush rose to his face and he broke into a laugh that quickly spread around the room. Alex realised that his grandfather was trying to normalise some of what was happening, and this is what his family did: they poked fun at each other. Although he knew he was never going to be the carefree boy he had been two days before, his spirits lifted. He suddenly felt like part of the family again and could feel the lump forming in his throat. He would have to watch himself from now on, making sure that whatever it was that was happening to him didn't become public knowledge. In the back of his mind, enveloped in fear, sat the image of the wolf that bit him, the one tied down and branded. But he locked that image away, tried to stop thinking about it.

As they all sat down to breakfast, everyone tried to keep off the topic of Alex and his new abilities, but it was perhaps inevitable that the conversation would eventually turn in that direction.

"So, Al, your eyes glow, you can grow a load of fur. What else you good at?" Sammy simply could not hold back any longer.

All eyes turn on the boy again. With the watchful eyes of his whole family on him, Alex slowly finished chewing and swallowed before, taking a quick breath to steel his resolve.

"Well, I'm fairly good at English, and Mrs Roland says if I apply myself I could get good marks in Math. Also, I can do this really strange thing ... howl at the moon."

Giggles erupted across the table.

"No, it's true. She thinks that with just a bit more focus I could really do well in Math. I don't believe her either, but what you gonna do, right?"

He turned to look at his grandfather for confirmation that he was saying the right things.

"Well," his father's voice interrupted the sniggers, "you also healed from that bite really fast, didn't you? I mean, there's not a scratch on you, anywhere. I actually think some of your older scars might have healed too."

Alex looked down at his hands. He had always had a scar on his left thumb, above his nail, but, yes, the scar was where it had always been. However, the white marks on his forearm, from when he had slipped down the jungle gym in the playground at school a month before, had vanished, and his inoculation scars were gone too. He looked up at his father, who instantly recognised the look of excitement on his son's face and felt the panic rise. But not the same despair-driven panic he'd been suffering the last couple days. This was because he'd just realised that his overactive, accident-prone son suddenly felt invincible. The threat of pain and permanent damage was gone and he knew Alex would want to test the boundaries. How far could he go before he found the new line? Kyle's mind raced. How on earth were they going to stop Alex from climbing to the top of the highest tree now that falling down and hurting himself was no longer a problem?

He locked eyes with his son and frowned sternly, then throw one hand up in the air and said in a fatherly this-is-not-a-joke voice, "Stop that thought right there, young man. Before you're even allowed to think about going outside you, me and your mother are going to sit down and discuss some new rules about what you can and cannot do, especially where other people can see you. Is that clear?"

Alex tried hard to hide his smile.

"Yes, Dad," slipped from the boy's mouth in the least sarcastic tone he could muster given the circumstances.

Kyle put on his unimpressed face and narrowed his eyes. Suddenly he felt like the boy's father again, that he was actually in charge. Alex quickly looked down at his plate and continued eating; he knew that look and knew not to argue. Also, he was hungrier than he could ever remember being. Once breakfast was finished he made his way to the fridge and scouted around for more to eat. To everyone's horror, Alex took his fork to whatever leftovers he could find and started shovelling it into his mouth. He seemed not to be able to eat fast enough, and the more he ate the hungrier he seemed to get.

Whereas the other children had left the table once they'd eaten and calmed down, the adults watched in astonishment as Alex proceeded to eat everything he could lay his hands on in the fridge. Within minutes, he found himself gnawing on a lamb bone from a few nights before. In that moment he seemed to suddenly become aware of himself and stopped dead. Slowly his eyes looked down, focused on what he was doing, then moved to the side and he saw his family staring at him. Derrick coughed nervously.

"Full yet?"

Alex removed the bone from his mouth and cleared his throat.

"Yeah. Think so ..."

"In that case, you should probably wash your face, and then come sit down. There's something we all need to talk about."

Alex returned the bone to the fridge and walked to the table, wiping his hands and face on a kitchen towel along the way. All eyes moved to Derrick. The old man took a long, deep breath, then reached out to take his wife's hand. A large part of him didn't want to have this conversation, was scared of what the outcome would be, but he knew it was important, and the sooner it was brought up the more time they'd have to prepare.

"In a few days ..." he said, hesitating, "it's going to be full moon."

The grim realisation washed over the people at the table like a wave against a shore. Everyone knew what he was saying. They all knew werewolves and full moons went hand in hand, but they hadn't put the two and two together until that instant. Why had Alex been changing if not for the full moon?

"But I have a theory about it all," Derrick went on. "So far, it's seemed like these transformations have been happening when

Alex gets upset. Now maybe the full moon side of things is just another myth, like the mindless monster, but then maybe not. My theory is that if the moon does play a part, then perhaps the fuller the moon becomes the easier it is for Alex to transform and, on full moon, well maybe ... if the stories hold any truth, then maybe he'll be forced to change."

Alex's eyes widened with fear.

"What, I'm going to be stuck as a wolf?"

The old man put his hand on his grandson's shoulder.

"If the legends are correct, you'll only be forced into being a wolf for one night, one night out of every lunar cycle, so about once a month, and then again, maybe not. Like everything else about this, err, *situation* we really don't know what's going to happen. All we can do is take what we think we know and try to plan accordingly."

Grim looks passed around the table; whatever normality had been returned during breakfast was fast slipping away again. Derrick deliberated whether to talk to Alex's parents privately before mentioning it to everyone else, but decided that it was best to bring things out into the open. It was, after all, actually only happening to Alex – the rest of the family was just on the side-lines.

"The real problem and the sad truth," said Kyle, distracted, pausing to take a sip of coffee, "is that we actually have no idea what's going to happen. Up until yesterday none of us believed werewolves even existed. So there's no telling what's going to happen."

Derrick tightened his hold on Alex's shoulder as a sign of support, but Alex slumped down onto his arms on the table anyway.

"I'm ... I'm scared."

Kyle shifted over and put his arms over his son,

"Don't worry, my boy. We're all here for you, to help you. I just wish we knew more and could *do* more. But we're going to do everything we can."

Alex turned his head on his arms so he could see his dad and smiled nervously at him. He desperately wanted to ask *how* they were going to help, but knew there was no answer.

"Dad?"

"Yes?"

"Can we go get ice cream while we talk about these new *rules*?"

At those words, the other children, who had been eavesdropping from the porch, bounced back into the room excitedly. Kyle realised that at this point it would be all but impossible to say no without wrecking their entire day. Besides, it would be a break back to normality. And there'd be no more talk of the wolf with all the kids around.

"Okay," said Kyle, "here's what's going to happen ... Alex, Debra and I will go get loads of ice cream and bring it back so we can all have ice cream for the whole holiday. How does that sound?"

Annabel caught on instantly what was going on in her father's mind and smiled.

Jeff laughed. "But we don't mean *only* ice cream for the rest of the holidays, boys."

"Aawww!" was the chorus.

"Now go outside and play, its beautiful weather out there. Go, go, go!"

With the boys back at taking on imaginary ninjas, Annabel pulled up a chair.

"Can I come with for this little family chat, Dad?"

Kyle looked over to Debra, who reached out and patted Annabel's hand.

"Not just yet, honey. I think it's best if we talk to Alex about it first, just so that we have all the information available before we start burdening you with this as well."

"Your mother's right, Annie; let us get a handle on it first. We're not trying to keep you out of the loop, we just need some time with it first."

It was clear that Annabel understood. She was old enough to know that children weren't readily drawn into situations the adults were determined to solve on their own.

It was at least a half an hour's drive to the farm that sold the home-made ice cream the children loved so much, so Kyle and Debra didn't want to waste any time before heading off. Derrick gave them a few cooler boxes and some frozen ice packs to stop the ice cream from melting, and the three of them, Kyle, Debra and Alex, set off. Normally, on any kind of long drive, Alex liked to listen to his music and daydream, staring out the window. On this occasion, however, he didn't even bother to bring it with him. He knew there was a lot of talking that needed to be done; the only problem was he didn't really know what he could say that would give his parents any more information than they already seemed to have. Once they got off the farm and onto the main road, Kyle cut right to the chase.

"Right, you want the good news or the bad news?"

"Is there good news?" Alex replied flatly.

"Of course there's good news, but let's start with the bad news, shall we? That way we might end on a high note."

Debra could tell Kyle was using his lawyer's voice on Alex, which meant that he was trying to suppress his own emotions. She knew this because she had learnt similar tricks at teacher's college.

"The bad news is that, between your mother and me, we really don't know what's going to happen and we can't help you any more than being there for you and dealing with what you tell us is wrong."

Alex took a deep breath and pushed down at his fear. He had reached the day when he needed to learn that his parents couldn't protect him from everything, the day when a note from your mom won't get you out of trouble, and he was too scared to allow himself to be scared just in case the wolf reappeared. The blood drained from his face and he fought against the urge to lapse into total despair.

"And the good news?"

His tone was dull, defeated, and that shocked both his parents. To them it seemed that their son, who had been so full of life three days before, had all but been crushed under the weight of what was happening to him.

"I'm afraid that's not all of the bad news," Debra went on. "You've probably worked this out by now, but you can't tell anyone about this. And I mean anyone. For a start, they won't believe you and, if they do, we're scared they might react badly. Also, you're going to have to stop playing sports at school."

"Huh? Why?"

"Because if you accidentally scratch someone deep enough or lose your temper from being knocked down or from losing, you might change or infect someone else. Until we know more about this, about what's happening and what really brings on these changes, it's just not a risk we can take. Just imagine if you caused this to happen to someone else, how would you feel?"

The thought hadn't crossed Alex's mind and it was the straw that broke the camel's back. He burst into floods of uncontrollable tears; it was just too much for him to handle in that moment. Kyle quickly pulled the car over and both he and Debra climbed into the back seat and wrapped themselves around their son.

"I don't want this! I don't want this to be true," Alex wailed. "I can't be this responsible. Make it not true, please make it not happen, please, please! I DON'T WANT TO BE THIS *THING*! Just, someone, please wake me up ... *Pleeeeeeease!*"

He couldn't hold back the tears. He just wanted it to not be happening. He so wished he could just be a ten-year-old boy and not have to deal with real problems. As the tears continued, his mind began to empty and after a while there were no more thoughts, just a dull empty sorrow, and with that the tears stopped. Debra and Kyle, still a little unsettled at his outburst, slowly unwrapped themselves from around their son. Seated between them, he was a grey shell, red-eyed and utterly defeated. Debra fought back her feelings of helplessness as well as her own tears, which she knew would only make the bad situation even worse. She knew, too, that Kyle was fighting his own battle. A long time seemed to pass as the three of them sat in silence in the car.

Eventually Alex cleared his throat.

"So you said something about, uummm ... good news?"

Kyle searched his mind to remember the good news he had promised, and then locked eyes with Debra.

"Well," she said, taking a tissue to the boy's face, "I know a doctor back on the island we're going to take you to, to try figure this whole thing out."

"Yes, and from what I know about werewolves and from what's happened to your arm, you'll be able to survive anything, you're like, uummm ... like a superhero with superpowers. Only thing is that, until we know the extent of your 'powers' and how best they can be used, we need you to take it easy."

Alex tried not to, but couldn't help cracking a smile when his dad called him a superhero and nodded to show that he understood what his parents were talking about.

"I know, Dad, I'm just a little ... scared. But if I'm a superhero can I have a code name like superheroes do?"

"Absolutely! In fact, we've kinda come up with one already."

Alex dropped his head to one side and raised his left eyebrow.

"Really?"

"Yeah! Well, Frankie did it really, because he thought you were the G'Mork from *The NeverEnding Story*. So we started calling the wolf Mork, because it does look like the G'Mork. What do you think?"

Alex tried, and failed, once again to hide his smile.

"Mork. Yup, I can be Mork. Alex and Mork."

Alex breathed it in for a moment, and let it find a space in his mind.

"Can we go get the ice cream now?"

He put on a brave face and a broad smile, excited and terrified at the thought of having 'superpowers'.

"Yes I think we've been parked here long enough," Debra smiled at her husband. "Let's move on. I for one could really use some ice cream right now."

Chapter 6

Kyle woke suddenly to the sound of breaking glass. He blinked a few times to help his eyes adjust to the dark room and shot a glance at his watch, which told him it was just after 2 am. He looked over at his wife and had to hold back a scream when he saw her lying dead still, eyes open, staring a hole in him. Slowly she leaned up very close.

"You hear that?" she whispered.

A cold shiver ran down Kyle's spine.

"Yes."

"Go check it out, there's a golf club under the bed."

"Why would there be a golf club under the bed?"

"In case someone tries to break in."

"What happened to you being a modern woman who takes charge and doesn't need a man to look after her?"

"Fuck you," Debra hissed, her eyes still big as saucers. "Now go find out what that noise was."

Kyle slipped quietly got out of bed, pulled on some pants and found that there was in fact a golf club under the bed. Slowly and with club in hand, he made his way into the hallway where he and found Jeff and Derrick, both holding clubs of their own and heading towards the kitchen and the source of the noise. As they turned the corner, fear hit them like a wall, stopping them dead. There, just beyond the now shattered glass of the kitchen doors, stood the large black wolf. It turned slowly, with undeniable aggression, toward them and locked eyes with Kyle. He immediately tightened his grip on the golf club. The men knew that the wolf had to be Alex because the broken glass lay outside on the porch, not inside. However, as Kyle continued to stare, he realised in a way he couldn't have before, how much humanity there had been in it the past few times Alex had changed. What stood before him now was more the monster from the horror stories than his son. It seemed larger, the hair seemed blacker, eyes brighter. It took a few slow steps towards them and for the first time in their lives, they experienced real life-threatening terror. Kyle swallowed hard.

"Alex ... Mork?"

The wolf sniffed at the words, then his back stiffened, his head bent back and he let out a deafening howl, so loud that the remaining glass in the door rattled and some loose shards fell out. The three men dropped their improvised weapons to cover their ears. The howl echoed like a shockwave through the entire house, spreading terror among everyone within earshot. Kyle fought to keep his eyes open as his body contorted against the noise and watched as his son allowed the howl to fade away. To the wolf the room flooded with the smell of fear, a familiar smell he was sure he recognised as a distant memory. A sound like thunder rolled into the house and the wolf turned to see the horses bolting out across the field. Immediately, its instinct kicked in, took full control, pushing all familiar memories aside, and he took off into the night after them.

It took many hours and many cups of sweet tea and hot chocolate before everyone had calmed down to the point at which they could start thinking logically about what their next step should be. Unfortunately, the sun had already started to rise by then and the children refused to be left alone. Annabel sat with her parents on the porch where Alex had last been seen before he disappeared into the night. Everyone knew that they had to find him; what they didn't know was whether he'd be naked and human or still covered in black fur. The idea horrified everyone; no one really knew what to do or how they were to start looking.

Derrick had taken time away from cuddles and cocoa to go set out all the horses' food for when they found their way back. He had learnt through years of experience that a hungry horse will find its way home sooner or later. It took awhile, but eventually the two younger boys drifted back to sleep in front of the television and Jeff could slip out to tell his parents that they were leaving. As much as he wanted to stay and support his sister, he and Kath had thought it best to extract the boys from the situation, get them out of there. He had to look out for his family. It wasn't that he was afraid that something might happen to them or that they were in real danger; what worried him and Kath most was how they were processing all of this, how they were dealing with it in their own minds. Being woken up by the demonic howls of a werewolf was damaging enough to him and Kath and couldn't imagine how it was going to affect their two young sons.

Derrick set out to the porch.

"We need to get started on a search for Alex. We can start by tracking the marks left by the horses' hooves."

Kyle blinked sleepily then got to his feet and headed into the house to get out of his pyjamas.

"Annabel, sweetie, would you mind going and keeping an eye on your sleeping cousins for me? I need to speak to your mother quickly."

Annabel knew that it was more an instruction than a request, but she obliged nonetheless. Derrick turned to his daughter and started explaining Jeff's position and his decision to leave. She took a deep breath and turned to look at her brother still standing in the kitchen.

"No, I can't say I blame them either. God knows I wish I could take my family away from this situation."

Jeff saw his father and sister glance over at him through the broken kitchen door and walked over to join them.

"I take it Dad's told you?"

Debra reached over and touched his cheek. "It's fine. It's fine. I understand. Honestly, I do. I'm not angry you're leaving, if anything I'm actually a little envious."

"You want to come with us or you want to be able to take your family away from it all as well."

"I'm going to go with option B on that one," she smiled wanly. "Only a bad mother would even consider option A – running away."

Derrick had listened too many of his children's conversations over the years, and always waited for what he felt was the right moment to add his opinion, and in this conversation it was now.

"You're not a bad mom, dear ... And this isn't your fault. Every single one of us let Alex out to play that day, and all the other children, for that matter, and when you were younger you two played in the same woods all the time. None of us could have foreseen this happening. Hell, until it happened none of us believed any of this stuff was real. If anything, your sense of guilt makes you a better mother than most."

Tears instantly started running down her face. All this time that she had blamed herself she had never taken the time to think about how she used to play just where Alex had, and in very much the same way. She had simply taken on the guilt of a mother when something horrible happens to one of her children.

Eventually, Derrick spoke up.

"Okay, enough with the pity party, everyone."

His tone was matter-of-fact but amused. It was the first time any of them had really smiled that day and, considering that Kyle and Derrick were about to go hunting for Alex, the chances of smiling again that day seemed fairly slim. Jeff had agreed to wait until either they or the horses returned before hitting the road with Kath and the kids.

The horses' trail was not hard to find. It was the only lead they had for which direction Alex had gone and they were going to follow it until it didn't make sense to any more. It didn't take long before they started spotting the occasional paw print in the torn-up ground. Every time one of them spotted one there was a momentary sense of achievement, and they knew there were at least on the right course. It was an hour after their search had begun when they found the first carcass. One of the older horses lay torn to shreds in the middle of their path. To Kyle's surprise, Derrick quickly looked away. Although the body had been mauled virtually beyond recognition, its head was mostly intact; Derrick looked again briefly then turned away and closed his eyes for a moment. Kyle put a hand on his father-in-law's shoulder.

"You okay?"

"That horse was twenty-four years old; I helped his mother give birth to him. I've known him his whole life."

Kyle tried to think of something supportive to say that would seem more sincere than just "I'm sorry" but before he could come up with anything, Derrick looked at him and said, "Come, we need to keep moving."

They edged their way around the dead horse and searched for more tracks to follow. At roughly the same time both men found a set of horse tracks, unfortunately, however, at this point the horses appeared to have scattered, all going off in different directions.

"Okay, so what now?"

"Look around and see if you can find anything that looks like a paw or sharp indentations where his claws might have dug into the ground."

Kyle turned his attention back to the ground in front of him as he searched the tracks for anything that looked canine or even human.

"Over here."

Kyle quickly made his way around to find Derrick pointing out a series of paw prints heading off deeper into the woods, in the opposite direction in which the horses had run. He looked back at the carcass of the horse and the carnage around it, and then looked at the tracks left by the horses. As Kyle re-examined the new set of paw prints Derrick had discovered, and he realised that they weren't as deep as the hoof prints, or even paw prints spotted earlier.

"Looks to me like, while Alex was busy here, the other horses kept running so when he was done he headed off in his own direction."

"Well, it looks like we're going this way now."

Derrick pointed ahead and set off along their new path, Kyle close behind him. They walked in silence, following the ever-lightening paw prints, desperate to find Alex before the prints vanished altogether. Eventually they found themselves in front of an old hollowed-out tree stump, and there, inside, slept a large black wolf. Kyle's heart sank. Why was his son still a wolf? It was midday and blazing sunshine. Derrick slowly pulled the tranquiliser pistol he had tucked into his belt under his shirt.

"What the hell is that?"

"Don't worry, only tranquilisers, it's not going to hurt him."

"You're not shooting my son with anything," Kyle hissed.

"Well then how do you plan to get him back to the house?"

"He's recognised us before. I think he will again."

"Do you? That's nice, and what if he doesn't? What if he treats us like he did *his* favourite old horse?"

The older man's tone was flat and hard, showing no wiggle room on his plans. Kyle stopped for a second and thought. He knew he was probably wrong, but as a father he had to try.

"Wait, wait ... Look, how about you take aim and I'll try talking to him. If he attacks, you can tranquilise him, but only if he attacks me. Agreed?"

Derrick frowned, and then nodded. Slowly and quietly, he dropped to one knee and took aim while Kyle moved over to the side so that he could see Alex and not be in Derrick's way.

"Al—"

Kyle stopped himself and thought for a minute.

"Mork ... Mork! Wake up, boy. Come on."

The wolf twitched it ears a few times, then blinked. Kyle could see his brilliant green eyes glint in the shadow of the tree. It moved its head to see where the noise was coming from. Kyle locked eyes with the creature and could instantly feel his blood turn cold. He could again see the lack of humanity in the wolf's large green eyes, but for some reason it didn't seem as severe as it had the night before. His hands began to quake ever so slightly as pictures of the tranquiliser shot missing or not working began to play in his head. Taking a deep breath, he forced himself to try again.

"Mork, come on ... Come here, boy. Come on."

Slowly the wolf got to its feet without breaking eye contact, a low growl revealing its fearsome teeth. Before every closing state-ment Kyle had ever given in court he would pause, take a few deep breaths and try to order his thoughts while waiting for the voice in his head to tell him to just go for it. As he stared into the eyes of the wolf he realised he was waiting for that same voice now. He took a one last deep breath and made a decision.

"Mork! Come here now!"

The wolf leaned back and its tail dropped. Some part of it still recognised Kyle as an authority figure. Slowly, timidly, Mork stuck his head out and sniffed the air, catching sight of the second figure. He looked back and forth between his father and grandfather. Slowly but confidently he took a few steps forward, out of the hollow. Kyle's hands were still shaking when he reached him but he gently began stroking the thick black fur. They stayed like that for a few minutes, Kyle not breaking contact with Mork, Derrick not lowering the gun and Mork gently sniffing at his father's free hand.

"Home?" Kyle broke the stalemate.

Derrick nodded in agreement and both men got to their feet. Mork took a few steps backwards, the look on its face that told the men that he was confused. Kyle cleared his throat again.

"Come, Mork. Home time."

Immediately he strode away, back in the direction from which they had come. Derrick waited a moment and saw Mork slowly but obediently follow his father. Still holding the tranquiliser pistol, he walked behind them, unsure and uneasy, but hopeful.

Chapter 7

Kath packed while Jeff tended to the returning horses. Annabel and Debra sat anxiously on the porch while Marie made regular cups of tea and coffee.

Debra drifted into the kitchen.

"You know ..."

Marie started and tipped a cup of hot coffee down the front of her apron.

"Aaahhh! God dammit! AAHHH! Fuck!"

Debra rushed over, grabbed the nearest dishcloth and started dabbing at her mother's lap. She looked up to apologise and saw that Marie had dropped her face into her hands and had begun to cry.

"Mom?"

Debra stood up and wrapped her arms around the older woman.

"I'm just so sorry for Alex and I'm scared for him and you and Kyle and your dad and everyone."

Marie had been playing different scenarios in her head of Alex being found dead, or not being found at all and being left alone in the woods, or still being a wolf and lunging for Kyle and Derrick. At no point had she hoped for the best or pictured a happy ending, in her head, it was all bad. Nothing good could come of all of this.

Debra didn't know what to say. But there was no need to. Within seconds, Kath and Jeff and the children were in the doorway, alarmed at the cry.

"We're fine, we're fine. Mom's just had a little accident, that's all," Debra indicated to the others that all was well.

"Mom," Kath stepped up, "why don't you sit down and I'll finish making the coffee? I mean, there is no use us all trying to act busy when we're just as anxious as each other waiting for Dad and Kyle to get home."

She was blunt, but right, which was one of the things Marie both loved and hated about Kath. Sometimes she wished Jeff had picked someone a little more affectionate, but at the same time knew that Kath really did love him deeply and wouldn't ever do anything to hurt him.

Reluctantly, everyone made their way to a seat around the kitchen table while Kath finished making the drinks and Debra cleaned up the spilt coffee. Within a few minutes everyone sat silently blowing on their drinks and avoiding each other's eyes in case they were expected to speak. Jeff shifted his vision from the bowl of fruit in the middle of the table to the window behind his mother and spotted Kyle emerging from the woods in the distance. His heart rate shot up and a prickling shiver danced along his cheeks. A slight gasp escaped his lips and everyone looked up at him, and then turned to the window.

Mork trotted along happily behind his father, who had spent most of the walk back trying to work out what he was going to say to the family. Then the thought, 'What am I going to do about Mork full stop' struck him and he stopped, turned to look at the wolf that had faithfully followed him out of the forest. Mork stopped and turned its face up to him. Sensing the uncertainty, the wolf began to growl slightly and to look around anxiously.

In the kitchen Debra rose from her seat and headed out towards them. Mork, catching sight of an unidentified figure, immediately stepped between her and Kyle, a warning growl deepening in its throat. Debra stopped dead in her tracks. She stared at the black wolf unblinking. As his green eyes narrowed, she could feel her nerves getting the better of her. Derrick took careful aim with the tranquiliser pistol, as Kyle took a cautious step towards Mork.

"Down, boy! That's your mom, you know her."

Mork didn't break eye contact, but softly sniffed the air. Again he recognised the smell as one that was both personal and familiar, as someone he knew well, but also the unmistakable smell of fear. Turning his head to the side, the brightness of his eyes seemed to dull slightly and Debra felt confident enough to take a few steps towards him and kneel down. Mork took a cautious step towards her and sniffed at her hand. Sensing the connection, the bond, his tail lifted and he relaxed. Slowly, Debra began to stroke the fur on Mork's back and looked up at Kyle. The look on her face as if to ask, "Now what?" He understood that look completely.

"One thing's for sure, we're going to take care reintroducing him to the family."

"Maybe tranquilising him isn't such a horrible idea at this point."

From the tone of his voice, both Kyle and Debra knew that the notion must have been going through Derrick's mind for some time.

Kyle knelt down next to Mork.

"Mork, your grandfather is going to give you something that's going to put you to sleep. Do you understand?"

"*What?* No, we can't just put him out." Debra voice was slightly panicked.

"Just until Jeff, Kath and the boys leave, dear," Derrick tried to assure her. "I don't want something happening to one of those kids if we can avoid it."

Kyle looked hard at his wife. He didn't really want to do anything of the sort, but understood the method behind Derrick's madness and had to agree. Debra sighed and turned her head away, determined not to witness it all.

Kyle then looked back at Mork.

"Do you understand? This is going to hurt, and you need to stay calm."

Mork lay down, panting. Kyle looked up at Derrick, who was taking aim.

"Wait, wait ... Can't you do that close-up?"

Derrick shook his head. "It's still a gun, if I do it close up it might do some real damage. Now, both of you, take a few steps back. Alex was bitten because he was close to a wolf who got a nasty surprise."

They backed away from Mork, and Debra turned her head just before the trigger was pulled. A dart shot through the air and struck Mork in the right rump. He winced, his initial whimper growing into a deep-throated growl. And yet he stayed calm. The pain faded quickly and with it went his consciousness.

"All right, that should have him out for a good eight to twelve hours."

"I give him four actually," Kyle interrupted. "When I was at the doctors with him he kept waking up early from his meds. I think it may have something to do with the whole werewolf thing."

Both Derrick and Debra looked at Kyle nervously as he bent down and scooped Mork up in his arms as if he were just any other dog.

Debra stepped closer and mumbled under her breath, "Why can't we drug *Jeff's* kids?"

They headed back to the house. Kyle took Mork straight to the lounge and placed him on a couch, thinking that he'd be close enough to hear when he woke up. He also draped a blanket over him, and then joined the rest of the family in the kitchen.

"So ... that's it then," Kath patted Jeff on the shoulder as he and Kyle walked in. "We'll get the car loaded while you rest up. Then we'll leave this afternoon."

"What's this now?" Kyle was taken aback.

"Jeff's going to sleep for a bit while we help Kath and the boys pack and load up the car," Marie explained. "Then they're going to head out."

Kyle offered a thin, tired smile and then yawned. Sleep sounded like the best idea he'd ever heard. Marie looked at him and smiled warmly.

"Would you also like to lie down awhile? I mean, you had to go hunting for your Alex this morning while the rest of us were here at home."

Kyle offered a goofy smile through misty eyes and nodded his head. He wanted nothing else but to go to sleep and recover some strength and sanity.

"All right then, chicken. You go take a nap and we'll wake you before the others leave."

"That sounds ... amazing, thanks."

He yawned again and staggered off towards his bedroom without a second thought. His eyes closed as he sank down onto his pillow and was asleep within minutes. Jeff too went straight to bed and was almost instantly out for the count. Derrick, meanwhile, checked on how many of his horses had returned and tended to a few minor injuries, while Marie and Annabel made a Thermos of coffee and mounds of sandwiches from the lunch leftovers for the drive, and Kath and Debra busied themselves with the packing and loading up of the vehicle.

Just an hour or so later, Annabel quietly put a cup of coffee next to Kyle's bed and gently shook him.

"Dad. Dad, it's time to get up. Uncle Jeff, Aunt Kath and the brats are leaving, DAD!"

Kyle sat up quickly, wide-eyed and, for an instant, unsure of where he was. Late for a meeting. He blinked at Annabel.

"Huh? What?"

"Jeff and Kath are leaving, come say goodbye."

"Already? Okay."

He stretched, then got to his feet and followed her out to the front of the house. The boys were already in the car and everyone else was midway through hugs and kisses and apologies.

"I guess this is what it means to be a grown-up, putting *my* family before my family."

Said Jeff with a forlorn look on his face. As much as he wanted to hide his conflict about the situation, he simply couldn't, no part of him was sure that either option was the right one, and it showed.

Debra hugged her brother for a third and final time and whispered into his ear, "Don't worry about it. We're actually fine."

Jeff forced a smile before he spotted Kyle at the front door with Annabel.

"Oh, you're awake! Good. Well, good to see you again. Debs was just saying that once things get sorted, we should make a plan and come visit you on the island."

"Yeah, of course," Kyle took a few steps towards his brother-in-law. "That'd be great, we can go see if there are any sights to see."

Jeff chuckled and the two men hugged each other, then Kyle went on to embrace Kath while Jeff gave Annabel a quick squeeze. The family stood shoulder to shoulder and waved as the car turned down the drive and disappeared into the distance. Once they were fully out of view Marie allowed herself a few parting tears, which made Debra feel worse than she already did.

"Right, we need sundowners." Derrick started back inside.

"Honey, it's four in the afternoon. The sun doesn't start going down until at least seven."

"And werewolves don't exist, what's your point?"

Marie opened her mouth to come back with a comment, but all she could manage was a little laugh, as the family moved back into the house and into the kitchen. Kyle fetched a few bottles of wine, while Annabel set glasses for everyone, including herself. Kyle poured her a small glass of sherry.

"Hey, it's not every day that your brother splits his trousers and turns into a werewolf," and he ruffled her hair. "Cheers, everybody."

Annabel took her first sip and, from the corner of his eye, Kyle noticed her pull a face as the tartness of the sherry gripped the back of her tongue. She'd be okay, he decided. This girl has a head on her shoulders.

Mork slowly emerged from his drug-induced sleep, unsure and a bit sick. He quietly sniffed the air for safe, familiar smells, then silently slipped off the couch and followed his nose out the front door, heading towards one of the outbuildings behind the house where the dogs were kept. Alex had been hoping to adopt one of the puppies before they returned home later on in the holidays. Mork arrived at the entrance to the kennel and found himself face to face with Sally, the family's Great Dane. Behind her, curled up asleep, were her six puppies. She sniffed at him while he sniffed at her. Instantly she licked the side of his face and all but grabbed him by the scruff of the neck to bring him into the kennel. Mork lay down with the other puppies and went right back to sleep, warm and safe.

Back at the house, the rest family lost track of time and before they knew it the sun had set. Annabel had excused herself from the table to check on her little brother, but then she reappeared in the kitchen with a slightly confused look on her face.

"Dad, where'd you say you put Alex?"

"On the couch, sweetie. In the lounge."

Annabel bit the inside of her bottom lip as worry spread across her face.

"Uummm, no ... He's not there."

As one, everyone leapt to their feet and made a dash to the lounge.

"Oh my God, Kyle. *Where's he gone?*" Debra could hear the panic in her own voice.

Kyle blinked a few times and wished he hadn't had so much wine.

"I don't, I don't know! But how far could he have gotten without us hearing him?"

Derrick cleared his throat: "Well, the front door's open, so possibly quite far."

Debra threw her arms in the air, as fear and fury filled her face.

"Well, who left the fuckin' front door open?"

Kyle put his hand on Debra's back to try to calm her"

"No one on in particular, dear," said Derrick calmly. "When in your life has that door ever been closed during the day? Huh?"

Debra slumped onto the couch in a fit of frustration, any pleasure she may have experienced since sitting back with a glass of wine snatched away.

"You two found him once already today, you can do it again." Tears started to stream down her face.

Gently, Marie took Annabel by the hand and led her back into the kitchen, ostensibly to make a cup of sweet tea, but really because the child didn't really need to watch her mother have another panic attack. Annabel, of course, was reluctant to leave in case she could help in some way, but was also willing to accept that her grandmother knew best.

Debra's breath started to grow shorter and sharper as the panic set in. Derrick and Kyle sat down on either side of her and put their arms around her.

"Sshhh, my dear. We've found him before, and we'll find him again. It's going to be all right," her father tried to reassure yet again. "And I'll fetch Sally to help us, no creature knows the smell of that boy better than she does."

"Oh great, that's all I need," Debra let out a tearful laugh, "to have my mothering skills put to shame by the fucking dog."

Both men laughed and Annabel, arriving with a mug of sweet tea for her mother, couldn't help but snigger too.

Debra looked at her daughter. "I'm so sorry for you too, sweetie, as if Alex didn't take enough of our time."

"Oh, don't worry about me, Mom. We'll make a plan and sort it out. I think you're both great parents, you should hear what some of my friends say their brothers are like. Compared to them Alex, even as a wolf he's a dream."

Everyone smiled at Annabel, and Kyle ruffled her hair. She had a knack for saying the right thing at the right time, which made it very hard to remember exactly how old she was.

"Alright, dear, you sip your tea." Derrick got to his feet. "Kyle, you go get some shoes and I'll go round up our Sally."

Without a word, Kyle stood up and headed back to his room, Annabel instantly took his place next to her mom and Derrick headed over to the front door where he stopped dead and looked out into the sky and thought, *the full moon is rising.* When Kyle appeared in the hallway beside him saw what the old man was looking at, he swore under his breath. The two looked at each other.

Kyle gritted his teeth, pulled on his second boot, and whispered, "Let's go get Sally. The sooner we can get this over with the better."

Derrick nodded and together they headed towards the kennels at the back of the house. Kyle looked down as they made the short walk behind the house.

"Derrick, stop."

Derrick turned to find Kyle indicating toward the ground.

"What's the matter?"

Kyle dropped to his haunches and pointed at a faint paw print on the soft dirt path leading to the kennels.

"Look, I think this might be Alex's. See how big it is and we've not seen Sally all week."

Derrick crouched down next to Kyle and looked first at the print, then along the path for more and spotted a few dusty prints leading into the kennels.

"He's in the dog house."

Derrick sounded amazed at the thought. Kyle allowed his eyes to follow the same path Derrick's had taken.

"Well, that was easier than I expected ... But what do we do about that moon? It's getting brighter."

"We could tranq him again, that's for sure."

"No, no, we can't. We need a better way of dealing with this."

"Okay, then let's try reasoning with him like we did in the woods."

Kyle swallowed hard and remembered the creature they'd encountered in the kitchen the night before. They stood up and slowly began walking towards the kennels.

The kennels consisted of three large wooden doghouses on a concrete slab behind the house. Running along the border of the concrete was a chicken-wire fence with a small gate that had been rusted open for years. Only one of the doghouses was occupied.

When they were built Derrick had had four dogs. Sally was the offspring of two of the older ones and was now the only one left.

Derrick spotted Sally sleeping outside her doghouse. He put his hand on Kyle's shoulder and touched a finger to his lips. The two men peered into the house and saw Mork curled up around the puppies, fast asleep. A sigh of relief escaped Kyle's lips.

"What the … What do we do?"

Derrick shrugged his shoulders and mouthed back, gesturing with a series of complex hand movements, "Dunno. Go fetch Marie."

Kyle quietly went back to the house. Marie was with Annabel and Debra in the lounge. He took a deep breath and tried to remind himself that he was, in fact, a very good and expensive lawyer.

"Mom? Dad's having trouble with Sally's leash, can you please just help him so we can get started?"

He didn't want everyone to rush outside and crowd the doghouses. Werewolf aside, Sally was still a very big dog who'd just had puppies.

"Her *leash*?" Marie smiled at him and followed him outside. "What on earth does the old goat want with—"

"Okay, I lied," Kyle interrupted. "Mork's asleep with the puppies in the kennels and we're really not sure what to do. Dad's waiting for you, sorry."

She looked at him in amazement.

"Lawyers," she mumbled to herself, rolled her eyes and giggled.

At the doghouse they found Derrick crouched down, softly stroking Sally's head.

"You always were like that boy's second mom, weren't you, girl? Yes, you were." He turned to look up at them. "If you can think of a better idea, please tell me."

Kyle managed to fight back the urge to laugh. Marie just shook her head. Derrick turned back to his dog and scratched her ears. Marie bent to look inside the doghouse and saw Mork curled up around the sleeping puppies.

"We should probably leave him in there," she mouthed.

"Problem is, Mom," said Kyle, "the moon's rising, and last night when the moon was up he was more animal than boy. What if he does something to the puppies or Sally?"

Marie gave Kyle a curious look, but understood what he meant.

"I still can't think of a way to get him out of there. We might just have to monitor him, see what happens and work it out as it happens."

Derrick looked up. "I think she may be right, son. I also get the impression that under a full moon the tranquilisers may not work."

Marie looked at her husband. "What makes you say that?"

"Well, Kyle said he kept waking up early in hospital despite how much sedative he'd been given, and if I'm honest I shot him with the same dose we give the larger horses and he woke up within a few hours."

"Sorry, you gave my son how much tranquiliser?"

Derrick cringed a little. "Oy, don't you go focusing on the wrong part of the story here, son, point is, it didn't work, did it?"

Kyle frowned, but knew the old man was right.

"I'm going to go tell Debra and Annabel that we've found him."

He got to his feet and headed inside while Marie moved to sit next to Derrick on the far side away from Sally.

"What we going to do?"

"I don't know, love. I just I don't know. Alex asked me yesterday if he could stay with us on the farm so his family could live a normal life."

Marie let out a groan that only a mother could as her heart cracked a little.

"It was as if in that moment I could see the child step out and the adult step in," Derrick said, as he brushed his cheek with the back of his hand. "Poor kid."

He put his arm around his wife and they rested their heads against each other, both letting their minds wander off in different directions, away from their problems, in the hope that some kind of inspiration would hit them. Marie turned her head slightly and watched as Debra, Kyle and Annabel slowly made their way towards them.

Despite their anxiety, it was quickly decided that they would all just sit there until something happened. Anything. No one wanted to be left out of the loop or alone, so they all just sat there quietly waiting. The hope was that, being still slightly drowsy from the tranquiliser and around other animals would hopefully calm him and he'd stay sleeping.

Chapter 8

Once the moon was well and truly up and Mork hadn't as much as rolled over, everyone started to think that maybe, just maybe it wasn't going to be so bad after all. Debra could see Annabel's eyelids start to flutter and took her off to bed, with Kyle and Marie not far behind. Annabel crawled into her parents' bed, citing that she didn't want to be alone, and neither Kyle nor Debra were up for argument, so they just crawled in around her.

Marie made coffee and went back out to Derrick, who sat with his back against the fence looking out at the night sky. She handed him a mug and sat down.

"What did you tell him?"

"Huh?"

"Alex, when he asked to stay here on the farm, what did you tell him?"

Derrick blew on his coffee and took a little sip.

"Oh, uhmmm ... I told him that we would love to have him, but that he not being with his family would be less normal for them than him being a wolf."

She smiled at him and kissed his cheek.

"You going to stay out here all night?"

"I don't know what else to do, Marie. Can't help the boy much, can I? Can't do anything else for him. Can't make Deb's problems go away, can't force the last of the horses to come home. But I can sit here and watch over him and make sure he's safe until morning."

She took his hand and squeezed it.

"My hero. All right, let me get you a blanket and pillow. I don't need you getting sick on top of all this."

***

Derrick woke up early as usual. He was curled up on the concrete outside the doghouses, cocooned in Marie's blanket. Blinking, he looked in to check on Mork, only to see his naked grandson staring sheepishly back at him.

"Grandpa? Can I have that blanket please?"

Chapter 9

To his surprise, Derrick found Kyle in the kitchen waiting for the coffee to brew. And Kyle, in turn, was surprised to see Alex wrapped in a blanket, traipsing behind his grandfather. The boy ran from behind his grandfather and leapt into his father's arms. The force of the impact very nearly toppled him, Alex was a lot stronger than he looked. But he closed his eyes and held onto his son anyway, allowing all other thoughts other than the relief of having his son back to dissipate. Full moon was over and that meant they had bought some time to really start finding solutions. Derrick waited until the hug was over to hand Kyle a cup of coffee and gesture towards the kitchen table.

"So, I know why I'm up this early, what about you?"

Kyle blow on his coffee and smiled.

"Never been much of a later sleeper, seven or so hours does me, doesn't matter what time I go to bed. Also, Annie rolls around a bit, which makes it a little trickier. What about you?"

"Well, putting aside the concrete floor I was sleeping on, I'm a farmer. I get up early. There are things to do."

"Early?" interrupted Alex. "You slept for ages! I was watching you all the time."

The two men turned to look at the boy.

"How long have you been up then?"

He blushed a little and tightened the blanket around him.

"I don't actually know, but it felt like forever."

"And what exactly do you remember of the last couple days?"

Alex searched his mind for ways to turn the pictures into words, and dismiss those he didn't want to remember. A cold shiver ran down his body, causing him to shudder. Kyle reached out a hand and touched him on the shoulder.

"It's okay, son. It's okay."

"I remember, or I think I remember, feeling cut loose and free and just running. Like it was the only thing that made sense, to just run and run. I don't know, Dad. I mean, I can remember things, but I don't know how to explain them. They make sense to *me*, but I don't know the words to use. I ... I don't think you'd understand."

Kyle pursed his lips. As impressed as he was that Alex could recognise that he wouldn't be able to fully understand what it felt like to be a wolf, it still stung that his son knew that they were now so different.

"I understand what you mean, kiddo. Sometimes in life there are things that you'll experience that your mother and I simply will not or cannot understand because we're not you. But trust me when I say, don't explain it like that to her. She doesn't like to think of you as a separate person. To her, you'll always just be her little chicken." Kyle ruffled his son's hair. "So, with that in mind, I need you to be brave for me for just a little longer. I know it's been a hard few days but you're handling this all like a champ. I'm so unbelievably proud of you, but the hard part is still to come."

Alex paled slightly and stared blankly at his father.

"I need you to break rule number one."

"Rule number one? Rule number one … You mean never wake up Mom unless someone's life is in danger?"

"That's the one. Can you do it?"

A naughty grin spread over Alex's face.

"I think so."

"Good. Your sister's in there, too."

Alex let out a laugh, "Wow this is going to get very interesting very fast, isn't it?"

Kyle chuckled, "Yes, yes it is. Okay, let's go."

Kyle laughed quietly as they crept into the room where the two were still fast asleep.

Alex leaned in close to his father and whispered, "Do we do this gently or can I jump on them?"

Kyle considered his son for a moment.

"Werewolf or not, if you jump on your mother while she's asleep she might kill you. Let's pull the blankets off – that way we have something to defend ourselves with."

Father and son, still sporting childish grins, each took hold of a corner of the blanket and silently mouthed a countdown. Four. Three. Two. *One!* Then all at once they pulled and ripped the blanket clear off the bed. Debra and Annabel both sat up quickly, disoriented, instantly fuming.

"Dammit, Jeff!" Half asleep, Debra yelled out.

Kyle erupted into hysterics.

Annabel's mouth was open to say something, but she fell silent when she saw her brother smiling at her.

"Alex?"

Debra spun around and spotted him nervously smiling at her. She stared at him in silent disbelief for a moment. Then all at once both she and Annabel leapt out of bed and dived onto him, Annabel hugging him and Debra kissing him all over his face as he tried desperately to wriggle free.

"Mom, sis, no! Get off! Aah, come on, hey, stop that. No, *Mooom!* Dad, help!"

Eventually Alex did manage to wrangle himself free and made a quick dash to hide behind his father. The room filled with laughter. Alex's arrival freed them of stress so quickly and so completely that in that moment there was nothing else to do but laugh, a true, honest joyous laugh.

Alex eyes flitted from one to the other. He knew what was happening, they were releasing built-up fear and anger. He wasn't sure how he knew it, but the smell in the air told him so, and he had already decided that his instincts were something he couldn't help but trust, even if he didn't really understand why.

"Oh, thank the Lord, Alex!"

Marie's voice cut through the laughter as she walked in. She flung open her arms, engulfing the boy. Her arrival also egged them all on to get the day started, one they hoped would be less tempestuous than the last few, and Alex finally slipped off to his room to find clothes.

"What happened?" Debra found words.

"Your dad brought him in this morning. Said he was like that when he woke up."

"Thank God, and now that full moon is over I feel like we've got time to come up with something more concrete."

Kyle and Debra stared thoughtfully at each other until Alex's voice rang through the room.

"Hey, where's everyone else? Where're the brats?"

Everyone turned to look at him and Debra bit the inside of her lip, turning to her mom for support. Marie smiled at the boy, who had reappeared in the doorway.

"They went home yesterday, sweetie."

"Oh, why?"

"Your aunt had some work crisis and they had to rush home."

Alex narrowed his eyes as he realised his grandmother may not be telling the whole truth. The harder he stared at her the more he could tell that she wasn't, and although she seemed normal, he could detect a faint sense of fear from her. He turned his head to the side and gritted his teeth.

"Gran, why … why are you lying to me?"

He knew she was lying, of course, but wasn't quite sure he would actually get away with confronting her like he had. Marie's mouth dropped open and everyone turned to look at him. Not because anyone was angry, but because they were astonished that he could know. His heart rate sped up and he took a scared, slow step backwards. Forcing himself too take long deep breaths, his eyes darted from his mother to grandmother and then to his sister. Then, out of nowhere, Annabel's voice broke the awkwardness.

"Aunty Kath wanted to leave because she was scared of Frankie and Sam having nightmares about Mork."

Marie blushed, and Annabel forced a look of confidence. Still confused that his grandmother would hold the truth from him, way back in Alex's memory there was the blurred recollection of Mork hearing people talk about leaving and packing. A pang of guilt ran through him as he realised how scary it must have been for the others, from the other side, and how he wished he could just leave it behind and go home too.

"Alex?' His father's voice was like a knife through his growing anxiety. "Why don't you and Annie go start making breakfast? I'm sure you're hungry and we can all sit down as a family and discuss what's going to happen next, okay?"

At the table, Alex gorged himself on bacon and toast, once again famished. It wasn't until he heard his name that he looked up from his plate and saw his grandfather looking at him.

He swallowed and said in a strained voice, "Sorry, what?"

"I said, it'll take me a while to get used to your new eyes."

The boy frowned and tilted his head.

"New eyes? What do you mean *new eyes*?"

"You not notice? Looked in a mirror lately? Your eyes are blue."

"My eyes are brown, like Dad's."

Derrick smiled nervously, "Not any more, they aren't."

Alex looked back down at his food and took another bite; the truth was that a change in eye colour was just another detail he didn't know how to deal with, one other thing he had no control over. He was, however, thoroughly enjoying how much flavour everything suddenly seemed to have. This was a change he definitely *could* handle. It seemed as though he'd eaten nothing but sand until that moment. Eggs and bacon had never been filled with such intricate flavours and the tea was stupendous – as if he could taste the different seasons the plant had faced while growing. But he kept his thoughts to himself. He didn't need even more attention than he was already getting, thank you very much. For the first time in days a genuine sense of calm came over him.

Just then a fly buzzed past and, as quick as lightning, without thinking, he spun his head and in one snap, caught the fly in his mouth. He blinked a few times and smiled nervously as all eyes turned to him. Sheepishly, he opened his mouth and let the fly escape. He breathed a sigh and cleared his through.

"So that just happened, any questions?"

No one was really sure what to say and there was a momentary awkwardness.

"So, tell us ... What can you remember since the full moon?"

It was Annabel who had eventually plucked up the courage. Some part of Alex's mind had been trying to find the words to explain it to himself. He had always had a way with words. In fact, up until that point in his relatively short life he had only ever really used this skill to make people laugh and talk himself out of trouble. This was the first time he really searched for the words to explain.

"Good question, Annabel. And I'd like to tell you, but I just don't really know how yet. I ... I don't remember it in the same way as I remember doing other things. I remember how things felt, how I felt, wild, free ... Maybe that's what being wild really means. Free. I wanted to run so I ran, but not just a run, I travelled when I moved. I remember the wind against my face, my fur moving in the wind, like water lapping along my whole body."

His face told everyone that his mind was more on what was going on in his head than on the people around that table. Kyle cleared his throat loudly and Alex blinked a few times to regain focus.

"Oh right ... Sorry. So, yeah, I can remember feelings better than pictures so it's hard to tell you."

Before the silence could take hold again Marie spoke up.

"So ... can you change at will then, hun? And what can you tell us about the difference about the first few times and full moon? You seem much more relaxed about the whole idea now than you did before."

Alex once again searched for the words to try to explain.

"As far as I can tell, before the moon I could feel something building like a strong, nervous, scared *thing*. The night I changed I was lying in bed almost forcing myself not to be scared and not to scream and trying to *not* think about anything really, 'cos my mind was, like, it was running around in circles until, I guess, I lost control. Now I don't know, it's still there, but less, and it feels like it's moving away rather than getting closer."

"I wonder if that means that you won't be able to change during new moon." Kyle had a strange and curious tone to his voice.

Derrick looked around to see if anyone was going to ask what he felt was the obvious question and, seeing no signs, he said, "So, then, do you have to concentrate to stay human? Like right now, does it take effort to stay as you are?"

Alex lightly clenched his teeth and frowned slightly.

"No, it's not like that, it's more like I kinda feel short-tempered. Not angry, just short-tempered. More along the lines of that I have to concentrate to not fall apart at the first sign of anything. Like when everyone stares at me, I can really feel their eyes on me and it makes me nervous, and that feeling starts changing and twisting, and that's how it starts ... Before the full moon that feeling was growing even without anything happening and now it feels like it's going away, so it's easier now, relatively speaking. Does that make sense?"

Without missing a beat, Kyle said, "When it comes to your relatives, don't expect anything to make sense."

Debra gave him an amused sneer, and Kyle grinned in reply. For a second the conversation ran the risk of drifting away from anything serious and back toward regular family comedy so, to save the topic, Marie quickly spoke up.

"Honey, how did you know I was lying to you earlier?"

Attention immediately reverted to Alex. His eyes widened slightly as he felt a little embarrassed and nervous for calling his grand-mother out on a lie. Also, he wasn't sure about how his answer was going to sound.

"A few little things I noticed, but mostly, uummm, ha ... I could smell it."

Mouths dropped open, and Alex stifled a giggle.

"You *smelt* it? You smelt my lie ...? What else can you smell?"

"Well, I didn't smell the lie as such. I could smell fear, or at least some kind of fear, and you weren't moving in time to your words. You seemed to be moving too quickly and I saw this thing on TV about spotting people lying and it said the people who aren't tell-ing the truth can sometimes be making the right facial movements but they do it too quickly. I've never been able to spot it before, but suddenly it seemed real obvious."

Everyone except his sister adopted a slightly worried frown. An-nabel, in fact, looked rather impressed and a little excited at the prospect of having a lie detector for a brother. Visions of all her favourite heroes in the books she read began playing through her mind, each with their own set of unique skills that she at one point or another wished she had. At some point she had decided that all the best loner heroes always ended up working with a team that included an intelligent and beautiful woman. With her brother as the mysterious hero, it left the role of beautiful and intelligent women open for her, one that she was more than happy to play.

"That's so cool! Do you think you could teach me how to do that?"

Her voice rang with genuine enthusiasm.

"Yeah, I think so. From what I remember from the TV show people have patterns that they follow so if I can see the same person lie a few times and pay proper attention, I think I can spot the pattern and then I'll be able to point it out to you."

"Oh cool! So what does Gran do?"

"Now wait just one minute!"

Kyle's voice cut straight through their excitement and they both stiffened.

"Alex, this is one of those things that we need to work the rules out for, *before* we let you just inflict it on everyone around you. Now, obviously, lies are bad and we don't want either of you thinking it's all right, but people are entitled to their privacy and it's not okay for you to be studying your family then telling your sister how to catch them out."

"But, Dad, you always said that nothing makes you angrier than entitlement." Annabel was slightly condemning in her tone, and Kyle made wide, unimpressed eyes at his daughter.

"That's not the point," he retaliated, "and you know it. Look, I'm not saying it's a bad thing but we do need to take some time and work out what else has changed and set parameters so that you can continue to go to school, see your friends, and to live a normal life. Alex, we want you to be able to do these things, we really do, but we need some time first. Also, if you're going to show your sister how to spot if people are telling lies, you've got to teach your mother and me as well, deal?"

Alex opened his mouth to argue his point but before he could say a word Annabel called out

"Deal!"

Marie stifled a laugh.

Thunder grumbled off in the distance and without warning all the lights in the house switched off. There were a few exclamations of surprise. As it was still morning, there was enough light to see by, but a storm was brewing so it wouldn't stay that way for much longer. Derrick got up and headed towards the power box to begin the journey of finding out why the power had tripped. Not having heard a sound of any kind as the lights went lowered his hopes that he would simply be able to lift the switch on the mains board and solve problem. His annoyance was realised when he saw that all switches were still up. Scratching his head he looked at the five curious faces peering at him from the breakfast table. He opened his mouth to speak but cut off by the shrill ring of the phone in the hall. He frowned, flipped the mains switch off and quickly walked over to answer.

"Hello? Oh, hello, Doc."

Kyle's blood ran cold. Had the doctor called to tell them he had kept looking and found some anomaly in Alex's blood? He sat frozen to his seat praying quietly in his mind while listening carefully to every word said, trying to work out what was being said on the other end of the line. Alex sniffed the air as subtly as he could and quickly realised that his father wasn't just nervous or afraid, he was terrified. The prospect of his father being this scared of a telephone call from the doctor unnerved him and immediately he could feel Mork starting to push against his mind. Taking a few long deep breaths and focusing on as little as possible, he fought back the transformation while Kyle bent his ear towards the phone as everyone else began clearing up the table.

"Oh. Right ... Well, thank you very much, Doc, but when was I going to be told about this? ... Oh, I see ... Ha-ha, I suppose ... Yes, I'll let everyone else know ... Have a good day ... B–bye."

Kyle took a deep breath and, in the calmest voice he could muster asked, "So, what the doc want?"

Alex tried to push the smell of fear from his nostrils and focus on his grandfather in the hope that it would help.

"Phoned to say there's going to be some kind of maintenance on the power boxes in the area, and apparently if I went to the last council meeting I would've known about it, but I didn't, so I didn't. Either way, we're not going to have power for at least two days."

Kyle gave a deep shaky sigh of relief that not only gave him away but the sudden and dramatic effect it had on Alex left both men focused on the young boy. With his father's exhale, Alex shuddered so dramatically that the entire table rattled and he let out an unexpectedly loud canine whimper. The boy looked up at his father and grandfather, who were both watching him nervously, and smiled. They saw it right away. His canines had elongated. Both men's jaws dropped and Alex snapped his mouth closed.

"W-w-what?"

His wide eyes darted from his father to his grandfather as he struggled to hold back the anxiety. Kyle quickly recognised what was going on.

"No, no, no, don't worry. Everything's fine. Take a deep breath and stay calm. Just open your mouth again quickly, we need to see your teeth."

Just as Marie and Debra returned to the table to find out what was going on, Alex closed his eyes and began taking long, deep controlled breaths. When he opened his eyes again, he nervously stretched open his jaw, revealing long, elongated teeth sharpening to points. Debra gasped so suddenly that Alex jumped backwards in his seat and it toppled back. Derrick and Marie lunged out and grabbed his arms, catching him and the chair before they hit the floor. The jolt was too much for Alex to bear, and he leapt to his feet.

"If you'll excuse me, I really need to go for a walk."

Debra opened her mouth to say something but Kyle stopped her when he saw Annabel pulling on her shoes and heading out the door after him.

"So teach me how to tell if Gran is lying."

Annabel was cheerful as she joined her brother. They hadn't taken a walk around the farm for ages, at least since they arrived.

Back in the house the adults were all still reeling. It was clear that Alex was in fact still not able to cope with what was going on, and to let him continue under his own steam would be stupid and ir-responsible.

Debra sat down next to Kyle and more at him than to him said, "So what do we do from here? We can't really just lurch from one near-crisis to the other."

"I wouldn't call it a crisis, Debs, but, yeah, I know what you mean.

We need to get some kind of help, we're in way over our heads."

"But if we go home, the kids are not only going to be disappointed but worried."

Kyle's eyes glazed over slightly as he looked over to Derrick and Marie, who had taken seats at the opposite side of the table for some support and guidance.

"These are your children, you need to do what you think is best."

"So you don't know what to do either then?"

"No."

The four of them sat in silence round the table, trying to come up with some kind of a solution or at least some idea on how to proceed.

"Did you see his teeth though? If he gets angry or nervous at school and shows those things off he'll be given away for sure."

Kyle thought he might have had more to say but didn't. Instead, glancing at his watch he said, "I think that storm's coming. And, besides, it's ten o'clock, too early to start drinking?"

Derrick shrugged then smiled. "Depends," he said, "Depends. What day is it?"

Kyle chuckled absently, "God, I don't actually know."

"Then, no, it's not."

Kyle ignored the bemused admonishment of his father went to find beer. "Anybody else like something?"

Marie asked after him, "Is tea an option?"

He turned and looked at the kettle and smiled again.

"No, actually," he said. "It's not."

"Oh right … the power. But you know, young man, drinking won't solve your problems."

"Aaahhh, but you see I don't expect it to solve my problems. It's just that half the reason I came here this holiday was to destress, forget about my job for a bit, and the last five days have probably been the most stressful days of my entire life. I just want to start enjoying myself a little." He cracked open the beer he'd taken from the fridge. "Look, it's clear that the more we freak out about it, the more it affects Alex. He can clearly sense, or rather smell our feelings, to some degree anyway, and I for one want to enjoy myself and what's left of my holiday. And I want my son to enjoy himself and what's left of his holiday, and somehow I think those two things are linked."

Kyle took a long deep drink. Debra, Derrick and Marie exchanged glances. None of them could dispute his point. If Alex's mood was so greatly affected by the mood of his guardians, then having a good time was in the best interest of everyone, including Alex. Smiles spread across the faces around the table as the idea of truly kicking back, relaxing and enjoying their holiday suddenly became the best way forward.

"Grab me one too, will you, son," Derrick said as got to his feet. "I'm gonna go fire up the generator."

Kyle took the broad smiles of his wife and mother-in-law to mean they were in on the plan and grabbed three more beers from the fridge and placed them on the table while Derrick headed into the pantry behind the kitchen and started pulling the crank on the generator.

Opening her beer, Debra looked at her mother. "I think it's about time we have ourselves a barbecue."

"Good idea, sweetie." Marie clapped her hands, and stood up from her chair. "Best idea yet!" And she headed over to the freezer and began scrummaging around, just as Derrick walked past and out the house, muttering about fuel.

Annabel and Alex had made it as far as the kennels and were sitting with Sally and her puppies.

"Funny thing is that I pretty much have no idea what Gran was actually saying when I caught her lying to me," Alex explained. "I mean, I could hear her speaking but I totally lost track of the actual words, it was all instinct and feeling. Almost as though her words didn't really matter because I knew they were a lie beforehand."

Annabel laughed, "There are a few too many words in that sentence but I get what you mean. It's really interesting, though. I don't think I could ever be as good as you, but I'm sure that if I practise it I could learn to spot a few things."

"Yeah, I couldn't do it before, but that doesn't mean anything. I never really tried; I just knew that's what spies did. I could always do it perfectly in my head, though."

A thoughtful look washed over his face and he turned to look at the house just in time to see his grandfather come around the corner. Derrick smiled as he saw the two sitting with the dogs.

"We've decided to have a barbecue if you two are interested in heading back inside and helping out. I'm just going to get some fuel from the shed to get the generator started."

"Cool!"

Both children simultaneously jumped to their feet and ran back inside. Neither had any real intention of helping, but they wanted take part. Also, Annabel loved making the fire and wanted to make sure no one else made it before she got there. Despite the pending storm, the wind was still warm.

Alex helped out in the kitchen while Annabel lit the barbecue on the porch under the watchful eye of Kyle, just to be safe. Derrick soon arrived with a can of diesel and got the generator going so that the fridges, freezer and lights would run.

It didn't take too much effort to slip into a kind of normality. Occasionally one of the adults would change topic of conversation when they came too close to the subject of wolves or anything that might link to Alex, the werewolf.

As the morning merged into afternoon and then to evening, and night fell, the children were all packed off to bed, leaving opportunity for more wine and 'grown-up talk', as Marie liked to put it. Kyle began to open up about his work and the stresses he was under, as though no one else at the table had a job that could possibly be as stressful as his. The rate of Kyle's drinking seemed to speed up as he got more and more morose about his job and, after about half an hour, in a moment of clarity, he decided that he was no longer making sense, even to himself, and took himself off to bed. Despite the failed attempts at restraining themselves, the others couldn't help but laugh, so wished him sweet dreams and opened yet another bottle of wine.

"No, no, no see, sshhh ... See, *I* think that it's fine that we dRINk because *we* know that we're not alcoholics because, because I, *I* don't *need* to drink, I ... because I enjoy it."

"Absoloootleee, see because, I know what you mean, I like it too."

"Yes, yes, 'cos, yes, but, we've had five bottles since ... five bottles and it's now nine now."

Derrick and Marie looked hard at Debra, not because they were angry but because at that point it took a lot of effort simply to focus. Suddenly Debra became aware of a tickle at the back of her throat. Putting her glass down, she got herself clumsily to her feet.

"I need to go to bed, 'cos—" she swallowed hard, "need to go. Right now."

And with that, Debra sped for her bedroom. In the doorway she was greeted by the sight of her husband lying naked across the bed, one hand on the wall and one foot on the floor, giggling to himself. She dropped down next of him.

"What you laughing about, my love?"

Kyle smiled and wriggled himself into a slightly more comfortable position.

"Our son ... our son is a werewolf."

Debra covered her mouth with her hand to stifle a guffaw.

"That's not funny!"

He extended one arm and held his index finger and thumb about an inch apart, paused for effect and said, "Yeah, it's a *little* funny."

"So what do you want to do?"

"I think I need to talk to him about going home."

She allowed her face to take on a more serious look for a few seconds then smiled again, leaned closer and kissed him on the neck.

"Okay, but what shall we do right now?"

Kyle closed one eye to better focus on her face and smiled.

Chapter 10

Alex woke early as usual and made his way into the kitchen to make himself toast and tea before turning on the TV to see whether there were any cartoons worth watching. He quickly discovered that neither the toaster nor the kettle were working, so headed into the lounge to check on the TV, which was fortunately on the same circuit as the fridges. He sat himself in front of it and his mind returned to the night before.

In the quiet darkness of his room he had found that remembering his full-moon experiences were much easier. He knew that his life would never be the same again, but couldn't help think that if he could find a way to control himself a little more during that time he wouldn't be such a burden on his family. Somehow *He-Man* had lost some of its appeal and, in Alex's opinion, these things never seemed as much fun when you had to laugh at them alone. He took himself to the table outside, thinking that maybe being a little closer to nature would make getting in touch with the wolf side easier. He stared blankly at the edge of the woods where he had found the wolf.

Derrick slowly opened one eye and, blinking, waited for it to adjust to the light in the room, hoping that this would ease the sharp, head-splitting pain in his forehead. It didn't. Nervously, he opened the other eye, the while mentally mapping out the shortest route to painkillers and cold water. Once he'd achieved those goals, he thought, everything would start being better. Slowly he sat up and swung his feet to the floor. Turning to check that his wife was in fact still breathing he realised that on her bedside table was a now slightly warm glass of water and a small bottle of painkillers. Nervously, he got to his feet and quietly tiptoed to the other side of the bed, picked up the glass and pill bottle and snuck out the room. Once in the hallway, he quickly opened the bottle, tipped two pills into his mouth and downed the glass of water before heading towards the kitchen. He plugged the generator into the kitchen sockets and made himself a cup of coffee while he waited for the painkillers to kick in. With his first short, hot sip, he quietly made his way to the patio and discovered Alex at the outside table, facing the woods with a very far-off look on his eyes,

"Penny for your thoughts?"

Alex turned quickly to see his grandfather and blinked a few times.

"Oh, I, uhmmm ... I don't really think I was thinking anything."

Derrick smiled and sat down across from him,

"Still dream while you're awake huh? Well, that's good. Nice to know you haven't completely changed."

"I also still like tea," Alex smiled, his eyes still on the woods.

"Two things that are the same, I'm sure we can add chocolate to that list and, I imagine, dogs?"

"And horses, which reminds me, can I still learn how to ride before we head back home?"

Derrick blew on his coffee and took a sip, trying not to think of the body of the horse he and Kyle had found while looking for Alex. "Unfortunately, my boy," he sighed, "that's one of the things that has changed about you."

Alex opened his mouth to protest and disappointment flooded his eyes, but Derrick put up a hand to stop him.

"No, look, it's not that I'm suddenly punishing you for something. I would love to take you and your sister for a ride, but over the past few days it's become apparent that the horses know there is something different about you, and it makes them jumpy. It just wouldn't be safe for anyone to take you near them right now."

Closing his mouth again, Alex realised that there was no room to argue. Derrick looked at the boy and couldn't bear the thought of wrecking the kid's day in the first half an hour so.

"But maybe when you guys come back either at Christmas or next summer we can see about getting the horses used to your smell and then you'll be able to ride."

Alex knew that his grandfather had no idea if that would work and was only saying it to cheer him up, but it was working – he did feel less defeated at the idea that there might be options later.

"You don't think we could start now before we have to head back?"

"I think you need to have more practice being you before we start putting you into stressful situations," said Kyle as he pulled up a seat, coffee in one hand, glass of water in the other and the bottle of painkillers in his pocket. He smiled at his son as he popped two pills in his mouth and finished his glass of water. "Which brings me to my next point ... Alex, I think it's time we head back home. I know you're on holiday and you want to spend more time up here but I think if you're going to have enough of a handle on this to go back to school we need to start putting some kind of structure in place."

Alex allowed his fathers words to wash over him and quickly

weighed up the idea of going home against the idea of being able to go back to school and see his friends. As much as he wanted to stay on the farm and have fun, the prospect of being able to continue with his life as normal carried a much greater weight with him now. He dropped his head and looked at the table.

"I think you're right, Dad."

There was no hiding his disappointment but he knew that he was making the adult decision and that it honestly was the right way forward. Kyle breathed in deep and looked over at Derrick. Who was forcing a smile. Derrick didn't really want them to head back to Syn Island but he too knew that it was for the best.

When Alex looked his sister was standing behind her father. Her feelings about this situation were made clear by her expression: it wasn't fair and she wasn't happy. Alex shut his eyes and forced down the lump forming in his throat.

"Maybe just you and I should go, Dad? No reason to wreck it for everyone else."

Kyle looked at his son over the rim of his mug and said with a smile in his voice, "I know she's standing behind me, Alex."

"Still ..." Derrick turned and smiled at his granddaughter, who raised a disgruntled eyebrow and joined them at the table.

Kyle put his now empty mug down. "I can't see it being a problem if you'd like to stay on longer, Annie. When your mother eventually wakes up we can all sit down together and work out exactly what we're going to do, so don't get disheartened just yet."

Annabel forced half a smile. She found herself conflicted, the idea of being overlooked by her family versus feeling selfish in a time of crisis. Suddenly her mind became a buzz of half thoughts as to what she should be doing against what she wanted to be doing and what was best for the family.

Alex threw his arms around his sister, hugging her tightly and whispered in her ear, "I really need you to not freak out around me right now. It makes things difficult."

Annabel giggled as she hugged him back, completely charmed and defeated at the idea of her brother asking her to not stress out because it was stressing him out more.

He rested his head on her shoulder and whispered again, "Thanks."

"But how did you know?" she whispered back.

"I don't exactly know, but I can smell it."

Derrick and Kyle sat astounded, not entirely sure what had just happened. Neither could remember a time when Alex simply hugged his sister for no reason.

With a quick glace at the two Kyle said, "You know, after everything that's happened over the last few days, that right there might be the strangest event of this holiday thus far. Would someone like to tell me what's going on?"

Remembering himself Alex quickly let go of his sister.

"Nothing, Dad, don't worry about it," Annabel laughed.

Their father raised an eyebrow and grinned.

"Kyle, my boy," Derrick piped up, "I think we need to go make breakfast and possibly get a few more cups of coffee going."

"Perhaps you're right," Kyle blinked.

Alex and Annabel decided to take themselves off for a walk, and while Kyle stumbled back to the kitchen to get breakfast started, Derrick set off to do his morning chores.

By the time they were done, Marie and Debra joined them at the table. Given the circumstances, Debra was happy with the idea of staying on the farm with Annabel for another week. So, after breakfast Kyle made a few phone calls and booked himself and Alex direct flights from Edmonton to Syn Island for the following afternoon and for a car to pick them up on the other side to take them home. They would have to leave early in the morning to get to the airport in time for the twelve-hour flight home. As the reality of the situation set in, Debra lost a few tears and wrapped her arms around Alex, but resisted the urge to tell him to stay.

"Oh, Mom, it'll be fine – please stop worrying."

"I'm not worried, but I am going to miss you."

"Yeah right, Mom, the nose knows, you know ..."

Alex smiled at his sister who burst out laughing, which quickly spread to the rest of the family. Even Debra couldn't stop herself.

"The bad news, though ..." Kyle took a deep breath, "is that you're going to have to go and pack up your stuff, my boy."

The laughter died away quickly as the facts of the matter came back into focus. No one wanted Kyle and Alex to leave, and they themselves didn't really want to go but everyone was in silent agreement that it seemed the right thing to do. Alex wriggled free of his mother and headed off to his room to start packing, and Annabel followed to help, spend a little bit more time with him before he left. Debra looked at Kyle.

"I must give you the number of that doctor so you can make an appointment for Alex."

Kyle sat down next to his wife and shook his head. "My love, what exactly do you think he can do to help?"

Debra raised her eyebrows. "I just think that he might have slightly more experience than us on spiritual and paranormal matters and might be able to offer some advice."

"We've spent the last few days coming to terms with our son being a werewolf ... How much more experience could this guy have? I mean, what kind of doctor is he?"

"He's an Ayurvedic doctor and, sure, he might not be able to give us anything specific, but maybe he can give some general advice. Look, I don't know ... but I just think it might help, so please just take him along, I've heard he's a very good caring man and ..."

Kyle smiled, nodding.

With Annabel's help, Alex managed to pack up his things fairly quickly, which almost negated the reason for Annabel being there, 'helping'. She was happy that she didn't have to go home right away because of her brother, but wasn't happy that he would be leaving. They sat down on the bed and stared at the packed bags in the middle of the now empty room that had been home to three boys a few days earlier. She turned her gaze towards her brother.

"Penny for your thoughts?"

"What? That's the second time I've heard that today, and I don't know. But in movies whenever someone has to leave for a strange reason they always stare at their luggage for a while. I figure that now that my life is more like a movie than real life, I'd try out some of the things the guys in movies do … not sure really, but maybe it'll help."

She fought back a laugh. "Is that why you were sitting outside this morning, staring into the distance?"

He pushed his lips together and nodded. "Yeah, stupid huh?"

She couldn't hold back a giggle any longer. "Has it helped at all?"

"Uhm … no!" Alex chuckled.

Alex pointed at the door and began laughing so hard that his stomach hurt, trying to force a few words. Annabel, confused, looked at him and quietly moved over to the door and pulled it open. Just outside Derrick, Debra, Kyle and Marie were bent over, ears against the door, hushing each other. Annabel's eyes widened as they all blushed crimson. Her knees buckled as she cracked up, with the adults all sheepishly joining in.

The morning slowly drifted into afternoon and the afternoon into night and finally, with a loud click, the generator ran out of power and the rooms filled with the darkness of twilight. Bread rolls and leftovers began finding their way onto the kitchen table. Because of the early start the following morning and everyone's late night the night before an early night seemed like a very good idea.

As always, Annabel was allowed to stay up to read until lights out but she soon realised that she was doing little more than stare at the pages, day dreaming about conversations with her brother, which then turned into saving her brother, and then into being saved by a hero on horseback. Finally, she could fight the sleep no longer, and turned off the lights and fell back on her pillows.

At the same time Alex lay in the dark of his room rolling around in the bed thinking about the coming flight home and how every time he opened his eyes, even a little, it felt like someone had turned the lights on because of how clearly he could see everything in the room. Eventually, after much frustration, he climbed out of bed, grabbed his shirt off the floor and wrapped around his head, covering his eyes. This made it much easier for him to fall asleep, which happened within minutes. His last thought as he drifted off was that he must remember to say goodbye to Sally and the pups before he left in the morning.

Chapter 11

Sleepily, Alex lifted the shirt off his eyes to see his father smiling down at him with a mug of sweet tea in his hand.

"Morning, son, you need to get up now, so we can head off soon."

Alex pulled the shirt back down over his eyes and rolled over. Kyle placed the tea on the bedside table and reached over to shake his son's shoulder but stopped suddenly when Alex let out a low, but distinct growl.

Sniffing the air, Alex quickly pulled the shirt off his face and grinned. "Good morning, Dad. You ready to go?"

"Think you're so funny, don't you?" Kyle laughed. "Now put some clothes on and we can start loading our stuff into the car."

"Right, be with you in a minute."

In the kitchen Derrick was making a packed breakfast for the drive to Edmonton airport. Kyle was still shaking his head when he arrived in the kitchen.

"Can you believe Alex just growled at me for waking him up?"

Derrick smirked. "Bet that's a sentence you never thought you'd say."

Kyle chuckled. "Somehow, I think I'm about to have a whole week like that."

Back in his room, Alex pulled on the clothes Annabel had reminded him not to pack away and discovered that he could pick up all his bags with one arm, no strain. He was the last to arrive in the kitchen, holding all of his luggage in one hand and his mug of tea in the other.

"Hey! Look what I can do."

Everyone turned to see him getting into position, his luggage balancing on the palm of his hand over his head while standing on one leg. Once he was stable he took his eyes off his hand and turned to the spellbound group at the table.

"What?" he said, his smile fading fast.

Debra shot a glance at Kyle. "Oh, nothing, honey – that's very, uhmmm ..."

"Impressive?" Alex frowned. He, personally, thought it was rather cool to be able to lift so much weight with just one hand while standing on one leg ... "I'm going to go put this stuff in the car." His voice showed he was disappointed, but he didn't lower his arm as he left the room. They all exchanged nervous looks for before Kyle spoke.

"Forget him losing his temper and turning into a wolf at school, if he punches another ten-year-old, he might kill 'em."

Jaws dropped and eyebrows rose.

"Tai chi classes," Marie announced out of the blue. As one, the family turned to look at her.

"What?" Debra said quizzically.

"Send Alex to Tai chi ... It's a really slow, calming martial art. Ancient. It's all about control and staying calm and not using your own strength against opponents, and using their strength instead."

Marie looked excited as she realised how clever she was to think of it.

"That's actually a fantastic idea, Mom! Kyle, you need to look into that as well."

Kyle's smile faded slightly. "As well? So you still want me to take him to that doctor?"

"Of course I do."

Her husband's smile turned to a smirk, "Okay, but tell me this, how do you spell Ayurveda?"

Debra looked very unimpressed and turned back to making coffee. "Look, just because you don't know doesn't make me wrong about everything. From what I've heard about this guy, he's really good and I think he can help!"

The words were fast and sharp and from the moment he saw the look on her face Kyle knew he'd gone too far. If one of them was going to take a joke to far, nine times from ten it would be him. He very rarely meant to do it.

"All right, all right … I was just joking. I'm sorry; I promise I'll call him up as soon as we get home. Unless it's after five, then I'll phone him first thing in the morning."

Debra took a few steps forward and kissed Kyle gently. "Apology accepted. Now go put your things in the car, with one hand, and only on one leg."

Kyle laughed as he headed for their room to fetch his things. Outside he found Alex trying in vain to get the back door of the car to close, every time he pushed it shut it would just swing back open.

"Alex? What's going on?"

Alex turned quickly with a scared look on his face, eyes that just wanted to run and hide.

"I … I … I didn't mean to. I didn't know the door was locked and kinda pulled on it harder than I should have and it opened – but now it won't stay closed and, and I think I broke it."

Kyle stared at the boy for a moment, not really sure how to react.

"You know, under normal circumstances, I think I'm supposed to suspend your licence." He sighed and put his bags down. "Come on, kiddo, let's go inside and see if we can't fix it somehow … You're not in any trouble. It's really not your fault."

He held out his hand, and they walked back into the kitchen together.

"You promise I won't get into trouble?" Alex looked up at his father.

"Well, if it comes down to it, you've got one of Syn Island's top lawyers on your side, so I think I'll be able to get you off with a warning, no jail time."

"So, is that it? You boys ready to go?" Derrick frowned slightly as the two emerged at the kitchen door.

Kyle looked down, then back up towards the family. "Well, no. Not really ... We have a small problem with the car."

Derrick's frown grew more severe. "The car? What kind of trouble?"

"Well, apparently old locks and new werewolves don't mix all that well."

Alex looked down at the floor and tightened his grip on his father's hand, causing bolts of pain to shoot up Kyle's arm.

"Oh, don't you worry about that! I can fix that fairly easily. In the meantime, why don't you two put your stuff in the Jeep instead? Alex, the keys should be next to my bed, go fetch them quickly."

Alex, Derrick and Kyle sat in silence while the car radio played Bob Dylan. Kyle reminisced on his memories of when he used to listen to Bob Dylan more often, Derrick remembered where he was when that specific song came out and Alex curled up in the back seat and allowed his mind to wander with the music and fall asleep.

Back at the farm, once the men had made their early morning departure, the rest of the family had returned to the comfort of their beds. But Marie woke suddenly when she remembered that she hadn't fed the horses. Scrambling out of bed and pulling on her work clothes, she made her way out to the barn and began working through Derrick's morning 'To do' list.

When Marie walked back into the house after the chores, she found Debra in the kitchen.

"So if Grandpa isn't here," Annabel asked, "who's going to go riding with me today?"

Debra turned away from the cups to look at her daughter. "Well, we can go out riding together if you like."

"Oh, cool! Yay, that'd be great."

Marie smiled and resisted the urge to join them, knowing how much Debra wanted to find new ways to connect to her daughter.

The morning had already drifted into afternoon before Annabel and Debra saddled up and went for a long, slow, quiet ride. The sun had just started to set by the time they were back in the barn, tired and happy after long, easy conversations about life, dreams, goals and, eventually, Alex. Debra had been cautious not to spend too much time talking about him, but he was the elephant in the room.

Alex and Kyle checked in their bags and found the quietest place to sit down for a meal before the long flight home. Neither spoke much. Instead they both allowed their minds to dwell on why they were at the airport waiting to board a plane and head home. Alex knew that he had to try to figure out how he was going to live a normal life and Kyle knew that he had no idea what he was going to do once they got home.

Alex had never really had the usual problem with girls that most other boys had, because he had always been friends with his sister.

In fact, the idea of girls being gross was a little lost on him and, as a result, he was always more than happy to have the hero swoop in and save the damsel in distress and live happily ever after, even if he didn't really understand what that meant. The chime of a pending announcement washed over them both but it wasn't until a voice called "Syn Island" that they both sat up and took notice.

"Repeat. This is a boarding call for flight SYI 479 direct to Syn Island now boarding through Gate Eleven."

They leapt to their feet and quickly made their way to the gate, both avoiding mentioning Alex's anxiety during take off. He loved the idea of flying somewhere, but was always a little anxious when the doors were locked and the plane started speeding down the runway. He always had the same thought: "Well, now, if I really wanted to get off I can't, I'm stuck here." This, in turn, exacerbated his anxiety. Then it was a matter of, "Oh, it's okay. I always have this feeling and I'm always fine." Which would then calm him back down. It had never been a problem; the only reason his family knew was because it had come up in conversation, and had subsequently became a little family joke every time they flew.

"Everything going to be all right? I mean, with … well, you know?" Kyle leaned over to the boy as they stowed their carry-ons in the overhead compartments.

Alex took a deep breath and smiled. "Yeah, don't worry, I'm always fine and I'm going to be fine this time too."

Kyle knew Alex was reassuring himself rather than answering the question.

"Course you are. I'm not really worried, don't know why I asked."

They smiled at each other and took their seats. Alex did his best to disguise the long deep breaths he was taking to try to keep himself calm as the doors closed and the plane began to taxi down the runway. As the plane started to speed up, Alex could feel his heart accelerate and the anxiety began to kick in. But just as quickly he came to his senses, as he always did, and instantly calmed down. Kyle watched all of this out the corner of his eye and decided to wait until Alex breathed a sigh of relief before lifting the armrest and tucking Alex under his arm.

They managed to watch at least some of the in-flight movie, but it wasn't long before Alex drifted off to sleep and Kyle opened a book. He spent most of the flight reading, but couldn't help notice a few things about his son that were different. Most notably was that he could pull his legs up closer to his body than usual. Secretly, Kyle was slightly envious of his son because he looked so comfortable. Also, every now and then a hand or foot would twitch like a dog's when it dreams.

Chapter 12

The flight back to Syn Island was long and dull. Alex woke twice to go to the bathroom and, on the second trip, managed to accidentally wake his father who'd only just managed to fall sleep. The coffee was bad, the food was worse, but eventually the captain announced it was time to put tray tables away and seat back in the upright position for landing. They both enjoyed the landing, not only because it meant that they'd be getting off soon but also because nothing interesting happened on a flight, and not necessarily a bad thing either. When you're in a giant metal tube some 32000 feet above the earth you don't really want anything interesting to happen. But landing was something entirely different, especially after a long, boring flight.

Neither of them was sure what they were going to do now that they were home, but after an entire flight not talking about it, they both felt that someone should start the conversation at some point soon before it became a thing they didn't talk about. Kyle didn't want his son to think that he couldn't talk to him about it or that it was something he should be ashamed of. Alex, on the other hand, simply didn't want to have to face it alone and needed his family to be there for him, even though he knew they were just as scared and confused as he was.

The Harris home on man-made Syn Island was three storeys, with five bedrooms. After moving in, Kyle had converted one of the bedrooms into his office and, as the kids got older, they refurbished one of the lounges to serve as a TV and games room. When they arrived home, they dropped their bags at the front door and headed straight for the kitchen where Kyle decided he would do the Dad thing and start the conversation they hadn't been having for the last fourteen hours. He pointed Alex to a seat and began scouring the cupboards to find something to eat.

"All right, my boy ... Let's talk about this wolf thing and how we're going to proceed from here. Your mother wants me to take you to some alternative doctor she's heard about. Now, I don't know how you feel about that ... You think it's a good idea?"

Alex took a deep breath and looked at his father. He could feel another small part of the child Alex slip away.

"Well, if Mom thinks it's a good idea, I say we take a look. I mean, we don't have to tell him the truth about what's going on with me, do we?"

Kyle stopped what he was doing for a second and the slightest shiver ran down his back.

"No, no you're absolutely right, we don't." He was quiet for a moment. "Oh God, Alex, I'm so sorry this had to happen. I'm so, so sorry."

He regretted it immediately of course. He needed to be strong for Alex, not sorry for him.

"I know, Dad, but we can't really change it now, so I guess we're just going to have to deal with it. But, on the plus side, I'm not as scared of being bullied at school any more."

Kyle laughed. "Were you before?"

"Not really, but definitely less so now ... In fact, now I could probably stand up for the other kids who are bullied."

Kyle's eyebrows furrowed slightly. "Actually, it's good that you brought that up. We need to come up with a reliable story as to why you miss school during full moon. And some rules, of course, things like showing off and getting into fights with bullies."

"Oh what, so now I'm not allowed to stand up for people?" Alex snapped, and it sounded harsher than he meant it to. But there was no mistaking the level of annoyance in his voice as his father crushed his mental pictures of saving the day and being the hero. Kyle's right eyebrow raised and Alex realised that he was very close to over stepping his bounds.

"No, that's not what I'm saying, but you must be justified in your actions. Like me, I'm a lawyer, and even when you know someone is guilty you have to follow the right channels to get them put away. So, even if you know someone is a bully you can't just pull them out of class and beat them up, because then you're no better then they are. Also, you're a lot stronger today than you were last week, so there's a real risk that you might do some real damage. Even when you don't mean to."

"Oh, come on, Dad, I'm not stupid. I'm not going to, like, throw him out a window! I know what I'm doing."

"Right, now you see that? I mean 'him' and 'I know what I'm doing', you have someone specific in mind; there's more to this story than you're letting on. I'm going to rustle up something to eat and we can talk about it. Maybe we can work out a strategy that won't get you expelled your first day back after the holidays."

Alex sighed to cover up a low growl when he realised that he had given himself away. And then, quite unexpectedly, visions began to flash through Alex's mind, of diving at the hindquarter of a bolting horse in the middle of a forest. He leapt back and yelped. Kyle spun around, his mug smashing to the floor and just for a second saw a wildness flash in Alex's eyes before he composed himself.

The sound of the smashing glass had jolted him back into reality. Kyle rushed over and took his son's shoulders.

"What happened? You all right?"

Alex taking a few deep heavy breaths and blinked quickly to make sure he was definitely back in the kitchen,

"I think I just had some kind of flashback."

"And what ...? What did you see?"

"I ... I was in a forest. Pouncing on a horse."

"From during the full moon?"

"No, no ... No, this horse was white and was being ridden by some-one wearing strange clothes, like in that movie Mom made us watch."

Kyle thought for a moment about the endless number of horrible movies he's had to suffer through since meeting Debra.

"Sense and Sensibility?"

Alex gave his father a blank look, and Kyle instantly knew that the name of the movie didn't really matter. But as he began to visual-ise new pictures in his mind, Alex's eyes glazed over again.

"Uhmmm ... He was wearing a sword on his belt, and it was rain-ing. It had been raining all day that day, which made the ground muddy and hard to run in." He looked nervously at his father. "How would I know that?"

Kyle took a deep breath and once again tried to hide his own fears. "I don't really know. My boy, but I'm going to be there with you every step of the way until we find out."

Alex felt his appetite slip away. "Dad, if it's all the same to you, I think I just want to go to bed and sleep … Maybe we can try all this again tomorrow?"

"Okay, yeah, that's all right, my boy. You just yell if you need anything and I'll come running. Sleep well and sweet dreams."

Silently Alex got up from his seat and, without hugging his father or even making eye contact, he slipped up to his room. The lights switched off and still fully clothed, he climbed into bed, shut his eyes and tried to clear his mind. Within minutes, he had drifted off. As he slept, his dreams faded from a fantasy of Batman saving the day into running low through long grass during a rainstorm. A calm sense of freedom washed over him as the grass brushed against his face and fur. No real direction, or purpose, just the joy and exhilaration of the moment. In an instant, the sea of grass ended and he came to a halt in a small clearing; he tilted his head back, then howled with all his might, not an angry howl, but one of excitement and joy, a release of energy.

Alex suddenly became aware that he was no longer the wolf in the dream, but was instead standing in front of the wolf, which was staring back at him. Everything began to grow darker as the mood changed from exhilaration to panic; the wolf stared right into his eyes and slowly tilted its head from one side to another.

"Mork?" Alex gathered his courage.

In an instant, the wolf leapt at him, mouth open, teeth bared. Alex threw his arms up to his face to try to fend it off, but then suddenly the dream faded to black, and yet he could still feel something pressing down on him. He fought and screamed as loudly as he could, his heart racing, until his scream turned to a howl and he heard his father's voice.

"Alex? Alex! Wake up, ALEX!"

Despite the yells, Alex still thrashed under his blanket, so Kyle grabbed it and pulled it back to reveal Mork, now wide-eyed and panting. Kyle sighed, and shook his head.

"Here we go …" he said to himself, and sat down on the bed, gently scratching the wolf behind its ear. "Well, sleepovers are out until further notice."

Mork whimpered and laid his head in his father's lap.

"You do understand me, don't you? I'm not just talking *at* you?"

Mork let out an 'arph' and nodded.

"Oh good … Well, at least that's something."

* * *

Debra would have liked Kyle to call the minute they touched down, but didn't really expect that he would. So when Marie knocked at her bedroom door to say Kyle was on the phone, she couldn't help but immediately start to worry. With the time difference, it would be fairly late on Syn Island too.

"What's the matter? Is something wrong?"

On the other end of the line, Kyle took a few deep breaths, and replied in the calmest voice he could muster. "Nothing, nothing's wrong. Everything's just fine. I've just called to ask for the name of that doctor guy ... somewhere between airports I seem to have *misplaced* it."

She frowned in mock annoyance, and shook her head. "His name's Dr Cooper."

"Cooper, that's right! Sorry to worry you, sweetheart. How're things that side? Your dad get back from the airport all right? And how're you and Annie?"

Debra's tone took another turn. "Annie's all right, but I think she's bored and worried about Alex. We went for a nice long ride, which she obviously loved, but I don't know ... I still think she's slipping away from me and I don't know what, if anything, I can do about it."

"What does your mother say?"

"I don't know; I haven't really had time to talk to her about it. Annabel is taking advantage of not having to go to bed at the boys' bedtime, even though I actually think she'd like to go read her books. The novelty of staying up hasn't worn off. She's just growing up too fast, dammit!"

Kyle chuckled to himself. "And you still think you two have nothing in common? I bet you were exactly the same at that age." He wished he could, at that moment, put his arm around his wife and kiss her and say the perfect thing to cheer her up. "Aaw, my love, these things happen. We always knew the kids were going to be all grown up one day. You should talk to your mom about it. I'm sure she went through the same thing with you, or at least something similar. Just because you and Annie can't do kid things together any more doesn't mean it's over, you'll just start doing more grown-up things together."

"I know what you mean, and you're right, you're better at being convincing when you've had three days to prepare. But enough about me. How's Alex? Any new developments? And the flight, how was the flight?"

"The flight was fine. I actually think he's more comfortable on a plane now than before. Otherwise things are fine. He had some kind of a nightmare and, well, wolfed again, so I told him sleepovers were a no until we had a better handle on this thing. But otherwise he's fine. Mork is now curled up at the foot of his bed, sleeping."

"What are we going to do about our children? I mean, I know and understand that at a certain point they change from being our babies and start becoming adults, but this isn't exactly what I had in mind."

"I know, I know … I mean, potty training was bad enough, now we have to house train him too."

Just then Annabel popped her head through the door and mouthed the words, "Night, Mom."

"Oh, honey, come say goodnight to your dad first."

Annabel's eyes brightened as she skipped across the room and took the phone. "Hey, Dad!"

"Hello, sweetheart, how're you doing?"

"Fine thanks. Went for a really long ride today. How's Alex?"

She always asked after Alex when they were apart.

"He's good, asleep at the moment. I'll tell him you say hi."

"Thanks. Anyway, I'm off to bed … Night, Dad. Sleep tight."

"Night-night, sweetheart. Put your mom back on, will you?"

Annabel handed her mom the phone, gave her a hug and slipped off to bed.

"I think I'm going to go off to bed now too, hon. I'll call this Cooper guy in the morning and make an appointment."

"All right, my love. I miss you when we're apart, but I'm sure I'll manage."

Kyle laughed, "Thanks! Anyway, send my love to your folks and thank them again for me."

"All right. Night."

"Love you."

And with that Kyle put the phone down. He wanted to tell her that he hated sleeping in their bed without her, but also didn't want to add to her anxiety.

Debra held onto the phone for a few seconds as she took a few deep breaths. She really did miss him when they were so far apart, and all the stress around Alex and Annabel only seemed to make things worse.

Marie's voice cut through her moment of silence. "So, shall we talk?"

Tears welled up in Debra's eyes, but she forced a smile and nodded. Without words Marie walked over and wrapped her arms as tightly as she could around her daughter. Debra always felt safe when being hugged by her mother and she couldn't help but wonder if Annabel felt the same way when she gave her a hug.

Debra and Marie settled down outside on the front steps just as Derrick made an appearance, mug of coffee in hand. He looked down at them not talking to each other, grateful that they had, for the most part, managed to bridge the gap that had developed when Debra was a teenager. He put the coffee down quietly, gently kissed them each on the top of the head and whispered, "It's all right, I still love you both." He then made his way back inside, set for bed.

The women looked at each other.

"Perhaps I'm not the best person to talk to about this, after all, but I can tell you that if you just love her and never lock the door behind her, or let the fights get to you, you'll never lose your daughter in the way you're worried about. I love you and that's never changed."

Debra smiled and tears fall down her cheek again.

"I love you too, Mom, and I'm sorry if I—"

Marie cut her off.

"Don't ... We don't have to dig up old things or past regrets. It really doesn't matter any more, does it?"

"No, I guess not, but I think it means I have to wait until Annabel has a teenaged daughter before we properly reconnect."

The two cackled.

Chapter 13

When he woke, Alex was pleased to discover he was human again, but still a little surprised to discover he was in his bed at home on Syn Island. Kyle had been up for about an hour already, working on a case, and resisting the urge to go into the office. Alex made his way into the kitchen where his father was working at the counter, made himself a cup of tea.

"Morning, kiddo. Feeling more like yourself this morning, I see."

He didn't want to make a joke out of the situation but couldn't help himself. Besides, he was determined to set a light tone, considering the events of the night before.

And Alex was not to be outdone. "Morning Dad, working as usual, I see ... You called that doctor guy yet?"

"No, not yet, as its half past seven in the morning ... Thought I'd wait until he was, well, awake?"

Although he understood that the reason they'd come home early was to start dealing with Alex's condition, Kyle didn't like being disturbed while working. Alex knew the look on his father's face all too well, so he quietly took himself off to the television room to let his father work in peace. He flipped through channels, telling himself that he just needed to be patient and find a way to distract himself. So decided to make the boring cartoons more interesting by doing a handstand and watch them upside down. He'd always been able to do it before, but would quickly fall back onto his feet. Flipping himself onto his hands he quickly found that it was much easier this time and wondered how he could have ever failed before. Shifting around a little he found, too, that he could easily walk around on his hands and, with only a little extra concentration, balance on one arm, which is how his father found him. Kyle stood in silence, watching in awe, until Alex caught sight of him out of the corner of his eye.

"Dad?" He tried to turn quickly, stumbled and fell on his back. Kyle quickly ran over to found Alex grinning up at him.

"You all right?"

"Yeah, I'm fine. You saw me on one hand?"

"I did, it was amazing actually."

"I know. I just kinda thought about it and decided to try and it all just worked out, well until the last minute anyway. But it was pretty cool while it lasted, right?"

"*Pretty* cool? It was very cool, so cool, in fact, I think we should go out for breakfast to celebrate."

Alex laughed, "Aww, Dad, you just don't want to cook."

Kyle grinned back at his son. "It's not that I don't want to cook, it's that I don't want to have to clean up afterwards. The difference is subtle, but it's there. And, besides, there's not much left in the house now that we've been away on the farm."

They laughed, knowing they'd thought of the perfect excuse. Alex quickly went back to his bedroom to change, while Kyle quickly gulped down what was left of his coffee, found his car keys and wallet and pulled shoes on. He had a favourite breakfast place he generally went to alone while his family were away. Alex loved going there with his dad because he felt like someone famous when they did. Kyle had been going there so long that he only went to the counter to say hello to the staff before sitting down, and when Alex was with him the people who worked there always made a fuss of him simply because he was Mr Harris's son. Also there was a pretty nineteen-year-old waitress, Melanie, on whom Alex had something of a crush. Every time she smiled at him he would blush crimson, and she'd try not to giggle. He was always embarrassed when it happened, but would always be more disappointed if she wasn't there. This morning, as they passed the large window at the front of the shop, he tried and failed to casually look in to see if Melanie was there, and she was. His heart rate rose and he could feel the excitement build up inside him. Kyle smiled to himself as he saw Alex seat himself with his back to the till so that Melanie wouldn't see him blush. Kyle smiled at her as she was politely fighting back her giggles.

"Morning, Mel. How are things today?"

"Very good, thank you, Mr Harris, although aren't you supposed to be away on holiday?"

"And here I was thinking you liked me?"

She blushed slightly. "Whatever gave you that idea, Mr Harris?"

A broad smile ran across his face as he burst out laughing, and Melanie blushed a little more. Alex turned to look at the two and wished he was brave enough to go up and join in the conversation but quickly turned back to the menu, knowing full well that his father was already ordering for them both. Kyle pulled his keys and wallet out of his pockets and placed them on the table before he sat down across from Alex, still smiling from his conversation.

"Still in love then?"

"Da-aad! I'm not in love," Alex hissed through clenched teeth, desperately hoping no one else heard him. Kyle hid his smile from his son and decided not to point out that Alex was blushing so much that he was practically glowing.

"So, that thing you were doing in front of the TV this morning was really cool ... What else have you tried to do?"

"Well, I think I'm a lot faster than I used to be because wolves are really fast, and I must be stronger if I can hold myself up with one hand and, I don't know, I haven't really thought of other things to try."

"Well, when we get home, I'll call that doctor, and then we can head into the back garden and see what you can do ... Sound like a plan?"

"Cool!"

Over Kyle's shoulder Alex saw Melanie clearing the dishes from another table. He smiled a little to himself. Since he had first met her she had become the princess or damsel in distress he would save. He thought to himself now that he was so much stronger he might actually be able to do it. But at that moment she looked up at him, caught his eye and smiled. Alex smiled broader, blushed a little and looked down shyly at the table.

As he was about to look back up, he heard his dad's voice whisper harshly, "Alex, eyes down!"

Alex's heart suddenly began racing. "Why?"

"Because they're bright green."

Alex closed his eyes and, in panic, began taking short breaths.

"W-w-what do I do?"

"Breathe. Control your breathing, take long deep breaths, in through your nose out through your mouth."

Alex looked up and locked eyes with his dad, panic shining through his glowing green eyes. Kyle looked his son's face over quickly and saw a slight shift in the shape of his jaw, and his mind cleared of all but one idea. In a flat, perfectly authoritative voice said, "Run!"

At his father's word, Alex took off like a bullet, out the coffee shop, around the corner and down the street towards the underground parking lot of his father's office where they had left the car and where he knew there was a bathroom in which he could hide. Alex spotted the door and could feel the change coming in fast so didn't dare slow down and ran into it, knocking it off its hinges. He quickly clambered to his feet and found himself face to face with a mirror. For the first time he saw himself halfway between wolf and boy, and for a moment the transformation stopped in its tracks and he got to really look at himself.

It took a moment before a stunned Kyle had taken off after him, and arrived out of breath at the now broken door to the bathroom to see his son turn to look at him, then every muscle tense and within a few seconds Alex was a wolf again. Taking deep gasping breaths, he looked down at the Mork.

"Shit ... I left ... wallet ... on the table ... back at coffee shop." Mork dipped his head slightly but kept eye contact. "And the car keys ...

Shit!"

Mork let out a whimper as he got to his feet and walking over to his father, who patted him gently on the head.

"Okay, you go sit by the car and I'll go back to the coffee shop, to tell them that my son is so madly in love with the waitress that he turned into a wolf?" Mork's eyes grew wide as he let out another whimper. "Oh, don't worry, I wouldn't really say that ... but what do I say?"

He slid down onto the floor next to Mork and sighed as he ran through stories in his head of what he could possibly say to explain away them having bolted out of the restaurant, when he heard a familiar voice.

"Mr Harris? Mr Harris! Hello? Anyone in here?"

Kyle quickly turned to Mork. "It's Melanie, quick, grab your clothes and hide."

Mork looked back at the pile of shredded boy's clothes on the floor of the bathroom. Without hesitation, he trotted over, scooped them all up in his mouth and slipped into one of the bathroom stalls, his paws on the door to keep it closed. Kyle got to his feet and walked off in the direction of Melanie's voice.

"Melanie?"

The girl was walking aimlessly through the parking lot. He hoped and prayed that she would start talking first and he could just agree with her and never actually have to explain what had happened.

"Oh, Mr Harris, there you are. You left your wallet and things when you, uhmmm ... Where's Alex? Is he all right?"

Damn, thought Kyle, and then realised that he needed to get out of this situation as quickly as possible and decided to simply wing it.

"Oh, yes, thanks so much, Mel. I was just on my way back for this stuff. Alex is in the car; I'm afraid he's been, uhmmm, very sick the last few days. In fact, I probably shouldn't tell you this, but that's why we're home from holidays so early. This morning he was feeling slightly better and, just between us, I thought it would be a nice treat for him to come out and say hello to you and save me having to do dishes. But apparently his stomach had other plans and he was too shy to use the coffee shop bathrooms, if you know what I mean."

Kyle pursed his lips together and raised his eye brows to show that he wasn't going to say any more and expected her to fill in the gaps with whatever horrible affliction she wanted.

"Oh? Oh! Oh ... Poor guy, well, uhmmm, sorry ..."

"Oh no, don't worry about it." Kyle reached into his wallet and pulled out $50 and held it out towards her. "Here, for the trouble of making a scene and for bringing me my wallet and keys."

Melanie blushed. "No, no, I couldn't. It's really okay, I mean, it's —"

But Kyle cut her off. "Yes you can, darling; heaven knows Alex would've made me leave a huge tip anyway."

He smiled as she reached out a reluctant hand and took the money.

"Thank you so much, Mr Harris, and please give Alex a big hug from me. I hope he gets well soon."

"Sure thing, but please don't mention it to him, he'd die if he knew I told anyone about it, *you* in particular."

Melanie blushed again, giggled and headed back to the coffee shop thinking of what she was going to say to the other staff members. Kyle watched her for a few seconds before he heaved a sigh of relief and headed back to the bathroom to fetch Mork and head home.

"Mork! Here, boy," he called from the door to the bathroom.

Then stopped and realised that he'd just called his son as if he were a dog, and he'd done it as though it was a normal, everyday thing. The door to the toilet opened and Mork wandered out, still holding his clothes in his mouth.

"Yeah, you better bring those along or someone will find them and feel a need to investigate." Mork turned his head to one side and narrowed his eyes. "What? Don't look at me like that – we can't go back in there; they'll wonder where you are. Come on, let's go home and I'll call that doctor."

Mork let out another whine and slumped down onto the floor.

"Oh, come on, don't look so sad, we can still go into the garden to see what you can do. Only, apparently we're seeing what the Mork side of you can do first."

Mork's tail lifted slightly, despite his best efforts to hide it.

"Well, at least I'll always be able to tell when you're faking it now. Now let's go before someone finds me having a conversation with my dog, wolf."

They walked briskly to the car, and without thinking, Mork jumped into the back. Kyle wound down the window for him before climbing into the driver's seat. Turning to reverse out of the parking spot, Kyle found himself face to face with Mork. Am I getting used to this too soon or should it be more of an issue? He thought to himself. He sighed, and reached an arm back to scratch the wolf behind the ear.

***

Annabel woke up stiff the next day and decided the best way forward was to stay curled up in bed and read, which was how her mother found her a few hours later.

"Everything all right, honey?"

Annabel looked up from her book. "Yeah, just a little sore after yesterday." She yawned and blinked a few times. "Do we have any plans for today?"

"Well that depends on you, sunshine. What do you want to do today?"

"I don't know ... What's the weather like?"

"It's good."

Debra thought for a moment to see if anything obvious came to mind, but before she could think of anything Annabel said, "You know, I'm happy to continue lying here for a while. I'm almost finished my book and we can take the rest of the day as it comes, if that's all right with you, Mom? I mean, you're on holiday too."

Debra fell silent in her mind, unable to think for a few seconds,

taken aback by not being able to argue with her daughter's sentiment.

"Well, if you're happy with that, it suits me to relax a bit as well.
You want anything to drink?"

Annabel smiled and her eyes seemed to sparkle.

"Ooh, yes, hot chocolate would be awesome, if that's okay?"

"That's fine, darling."

Annabel turned back to her book and Debra headed back to the
kitchen, determined to be proud of her daughter's independence,
but still a little hurt and sad. Marie found her halfway to the kitch-
en and wrapped her arms around her, unsure herself of what had
happened but knew instinctively that her daughter was upset.

Debra whispered through tears into her mother's ear, "I just don't
know how to get through to her. I feel like she doesn't need me at
all. She used to cry when I wasn't in the room."

Marie hushed her. "That was when she was a baby, she's growing
up."

"She's twelve, Mom. She's still a baby."

"Not in her mind ... And maybe it's best to simply be there when
she asks rather than beating yourself up about it."

Debra took a deep breath and pulled away from her mother, and
gently kissed her on the cheek.

"I'm apparently making hot chocolate, if you want."

***

Kyle couldn't help but watch Mork in the rear-view mirror. He kept hoping he would turn back into Alex before they arrived, but it didn't happen. He parked his car in the garage and let Mork out into the back garden. They sat at eye level on the grass and for the first time he realised just how big an animal he was, and that he was probably going to get bigger as Alex got bigger.

"Well, that howl you did at full moon was really something, but with the neighbours, that's not really an option here at home. Is there anything you can think of that you would like to try?"

Mork dropped his head to one side and thought. Eventually he gave a slight groan and lay down with his head on his front paws looking up at his father. After a few quiet minutes, Kyle got back to his feet.

"Well, then, I guess I'm going to go call that doctor, and ... make some breakfast after all."

Mork got lazily to his feet, stretched and followed Kyle inside, but headed for the TV room rather than the kitchen. With some negotiation between his nose and a paw, he managed to turn on the cartoon channel. Suitably proud of himself, he jumped up onto the couch and sprawled out. By the time Kyle popped his head in, Mork was fast asleep. Quietly, he found a blanket and some of Alex's clothes and placed them on the floor next to him just in case. He then headed into the kitchen to finally get some food and then back to work.

Hours seemed to pass like minutes as Kyle pored over his papers, looking for answers, arguments, points to bring up and a way to win, until Alex staggered bleary-eyed into the kitchen.

"How much of that was a dream, and how much was real?"

Kyle looked over at his son, who looked back nervously at him.

"You mean running out of the coffee shop and having to hide from Melanie in the bathroom? I'm afraid to say it was all real. Why what else did you dream?"

Alex shuffled his feet a little. "So, no light sabres?"

"No, sorry kiddo."

"Damn."

"Language, young man ..."

"Right, sorry, breakfast?"

Kyle smiled and looked at his watch. "It's almost noon, I left a few things in the fridge for you; I also made you that doctor's appointment. Believe it or not, we could get a time for this afternoon, apparently there was a cancellation."

"How did you know I was going to be a boy again by then?"

"Because I'm your dad and fathers know these things."

There was a moment of silence and Alex looked at his father as if to say, "No, really." "Well, actually, they called about twenty minutes ago to ask if I wanted to move the appointment forward and you were already you again."

Alex smiled as he turned his attentions back to the refrigerator. "So, when you said *things*, did you mean the pizza?"

"Yes."

"Awesome."

Alex pulled the box out of the fridge and set about warming it up, before heading back to the TV room to find something to watch. The following three hours passed quickly amid slices of pizza, a shower and an episode of *Bucky O'Hare*.

Chapter 14

Doctor Rajan Cooper had moved with his family from India to Syn Island when he was a child. His father, who had also been a doctor, was offered a job as chief of medicine for Syn General. Rajan had followed in his father's footsteps but, with some influence from his mother, had also looked into alternative medicines and the traditional practices of their home country. Now in his late forties he was a fully qualified medical doctor and Ayurvedic practitioner, finding that the balance between the two was the truest way of helping people.

He sat quietly reading waiting for Kyle and Alex to arrive, unaware of how the two were set to change his world. When the door opened, he got to his feet and with a kind smile ushered them to the chairs across from him.

"How may I be of assistance, Mr Harris? You weren't very specific over the phone."

"Yes, well, doctor, our problem isn't really the kind of thing I think you're used to. Or at least I don't think so, if I'm honest, I don't know a lot about all this stuff." Kyle gestured to the room around him, hoping it would do as a less offensive explanation than the terms bouncing around in his head: hocus pocus.

Dr Cooper smiled. "Yes, that's normal. Ayurveda is an ancient Hindu art of healing and prolonging life, based largely on diet and massage. That being said, I am also a medical doctor and try to find the balance between the two to best help my patients. Now you said it was some kind of animal allergy? Is this a recent development or has it been an ongoing ailment that's been getting worse over time?"

Kyle looked nervously over at Alex. "Well, Doc, there isn't really any other way of putting this, it's just that, well, my son was … uhmmm bitten by a wolf, a werewolf."

He smiled the smile of a schoolkid hoping that his teacher would believe that his dog really did eat his homework. Dr Cooper, on the other hand, was less amused, annoyed even.

"Very funny, Mr Harris. Now, if you please, what is the real reason you brought your son to me?"

Kyle clenched his jaw and could feel the heat rise to his cheeks. "No, that's why we're here, come full moon, my son turns into a wolf."

Dr Cooper switched his gaze back and forth between father and son, looking for some kind of explanation or legitimate reason as to why they were there, and found himself coming up short as the both stared back blankly.

"Mr Harris, you are a lawyer, is that correct?"

"Yes."

"Well, as a professional man yourself, I'm sure you can understand my annoyance at having my time wasted by silly jokes. I take my job very seriously, and if you have no time for the discipline that is Ayurveda and what it may offer as a legitimate treatment, then I'd at least expect you to show some respect. To me and to my profession. A little courtesy. Now, if there is no legitimate reason for you to be here, I'd like you to kindly leave."

Kyle turned to Alex. "You think there is anyway you will be able to show him?"

"I suppose I can try," Alex shrugged.

Dr Cooper narrowed his eyes and watched them curiously for a few moments. Alex closed his eyes tightly and started focusing on wolves and his parents fighting and the bullies at school and anything else horrible he could think of, but nothing was happening.

Eventually Dr Cooper stood up. "Young man, what are you doing?"

Alex opened one eye. "Well, every other time I've turned into a wolf, it's been when I've been scared or angry or nervous, so I'm tying to think of those things so that I can turn into a wolf and show you."

"So you really believe you're a werewolf and that's honestly why you're here?"

"Uhmmm … yes."

"Mr Harris, I know a very good child and family psychiatrist I can recommend, I think that is perhaps the avenue you should be pursuing. It's not healthy to entertain these sorts of delusions to this level."

Kyle sighed. "Please, Doctor, I know this sounds crazy, it is crazy; I can't believe I'm even here having to deal with this. A week ago I myself wouldn't entertain the idea that someone could be a werewolf, but I don't know what else do to. I'm a father who can't help his son, do you understand? I'm begging you, just give us the benefit of the doubt for ten minutes."

Dr Cooper looked into him, and for the first time saw a sense of sincerity and desperation.

"You honestly believe your son is a werewolf?"

Kyle sighed again, defeated. "Yes."

"And you believe you can prove it if you could just get him to transform into a wolf so that I can see it happen?"

"Yes."

Cooper thought for a moment. "All right, fine, for the next ten minutes I will believe that you are in fact a werewolf. If, however, you cannot prove it, I will stop and you will have to leave. Deal?"

Kyle nodded in agreement. He turned his attention to Alex.

"Right, Alex, rather than trying to focus on the times you have transformed in the past, focus instead on the wolf inside yourself and see if you can bring him out. If this beast is somewhere inside, go into yourself and find ... it. Also, sit with your back straight and put your hands palm up on your knees, close your eyes and regulate your breathing, long slow breaths, in through the nose, hold it for a moment then out through the mouth."

Alex looked at his father, but Kyle simply nodded, so he pulled himself upright, closed his eyes, put his hands palm down on his knees and began breathing as instructed. Then he heard Dr Cooper's voice again.

"First try to clear your mind of all thoughts, and then go inside your mind to find the wolf inside of you."

Dr Cooper couldn't really believe what he was saying, and worried he might come off as mocking. Alex tried to clear his mind and think about nothing, which he quickly realised was not as easy as he thought. But slowly he focused on his breathing and let all words slip away, and there he was, stand in the darkness behind his eyes, waiting for him, the wolf. Not threatening, not aggressive, just waiting for him. The discovery was so sudden that he almost opened his eyes in fright, but stopped himself. He focused on his breathing for a second then looked again at the wolf, which was now staring back at him. The bright green eyes sent a shiver down his spine and Dr Cooper's frown deepened. For the first time since they had walked in to his rooms, he began to wonder whether they had been telling the truth after all.

Alex continued to focus on his breathing and slowly moved his mind towards the wolf until he felt that he was face to face with it.

"Mork?"

For a second the wolf seemed too smiled, then all at once they rushed towards each other, moved by unseen force until their minds became one. Alex's body seized as his muscles tensed. Dr Cooper looked over at Kyle for a cue to step in and help the boy, but stopped when he saw Kyle raise his hands.

"No, no ... stay back."

Like waking from a dream, Mork opened his eyes with a jolt and looked around. He remembered that he was in an office with his father, but he could see no one else. Curiously, he sniffed the air for a scent, a scent that told him that there were two men present, one familiar, the other not. He twitched an ear, then cautiously padded around the desk to find Kyle sitting on the floor next to the doctor, who was backed against the wall, pale-faced and terrified, gasping for breath.

"It's all right, it's all right ... Just take long, slow, deep breaths, Doctor. He's not dangerous, I promise. Just stay calm and please, whatever you do, please don't scream."

Dr Cooper's eyes moved from Kyle's to lock onto Mork, and all words evaporated, leaving a white-hot terror. Slowly he started controlling his breathing until he could say without stutter, "I don't think I'm qualified for this."

"Well, I do, Doc ... That little suggestion you gave was the first time he's ever really had a controlled transformation since this thing began. I mean, if you think that was horrifying, you should see when it happens by accident."

Dr Cooper took another deep breath and let it out quickly. Then he turned back to Kyle. "You really think I'm the man to solve this problem?"

"I'm not sure this is something that can be solved, Doc, but so far you're the only one who's given any useful advice. I'm not asking you to fix anything, but we need help, all I want is a way that my son can live some kind of a normal life, and maybe the Hindu art of healing and prolonging life can help him do that."

Looking back at the wolf that now sat on the floor next to his desk, Dr Cooper felt a rush of purpose and intrigue.

"All right, I accept this as my karma. Now I need to know as much as you know so that I don't go back over what has already been established." He pulled himself to his feet and whipped out a handkerchief to mop his brow. "I guess my first question is, can the wolf understand us?"

"As far as we know, yes, every word."

"He's clearly not wild, and so full moon is just a myth then?"

"Well, no, at full moon he was stuck as a wolf for a few days and was much more animalistic than he is now."

"How so?"

"Not sure really, but if you see it, you'll understand. Also, we've kind of nicknamed the wolf Mork, after the G'Mork from *The NeverEnding Story*." Kyle smiled sheepishly at Dr Cooper who raised an eyebrow at him, before walking over to Mork.

"All right, then, uhmmm... Mork. Let's see what we can do about turning you back into a boy again shall we?" The doctor swallowed to bury his fear then knelt down so that he was eye to eye with the animal. "Let's try the same method as before: close your eyes, regulate your breathing and focus on the human boy, on being a human boy. Just like before, go into your mind and find him. I think it is important to remember that although you have different names you are the same creature."

Kyle had anticipated the need to prove their claim and had brought a spare set of clothes. Over the next hour Kyle sat and watched his son and Dr Cooper work through the process of Alex using meditation to change between boy and wolf twice more. Each time Alex would speak about how he found Mork just inside, waiting for him, and how every time he was less scared, and the merging of minds was less forced.

"When I turn back into a boy, it still feels like waking from a dream, even when I know what's going to happen and I'm in control of it ... It still feels different when I'm a wolf."

Dr Cooper, who was now seated at his desk, making notes, looked up at him.

"Different how?"

"I don't know exactly, it's like … Well, it reminds me of when it's Friday at school and the teacher decides at the last minute that she's not going to give us weekend homework."

Dr Cooper and Kyle both wracked their brains for what that could possibly mean to an adult from the point of view of a child.

"You mean liberating or free? It feels like there isn't anything holding you back?"

Alex looked at his father. "Yeah, kinda."

Dr Cooper made eye contact with Kyle for a second then looked back at Alex. "Are you saying that when you are a wolf, you feel freer than when you are a boy, more at peace with yourself, less stressed or worried about anything?"

"I don't know. I think so, yeah. I mean, it's like at full moon back on the farm, I can remember just running and it felt like nothing could stop me or would stop me, it just seemed the most perfect thing to be doing; I didn't want to or need to be doing anything else, it was just right."

There was a moment of silence that disrupted only by a knock on the door when Dr Cooper's receptionist popped her head in.

"Sorry to interrupt, Doctor, but your next appointment is here. Mrs Peppers."

"Oh right, yes, thank you. Tell her I'll be five minutes. I just need to finish up here."

With that, the receptionist ducked back into the lobby, closing the door behind her.

"So how are we going to continue from here?" The doctor turned back to Kyle.

Kyle took a deep breath and smiled, "Busy much over the full moon?"

"Four weeks might be a little away; also I'd be interested to see what it's like at new moon as well. Perhaps I could come to you rather than this happening in my office, where someone might walk in. I'm not sure why you've come to me, Mr Harris, but I believe that all things happen for a reason and that you have come to me for some higher purpose. I'll do some research between now and then. How about I come to you in a week? It'll have to be at night, of course ..."

"No problem, just let us know whether you have any food allergies so that we can make you dinner as well."

Dr Cooper smiled. "No, no food allergies. I'm a vegan, though, so maybe I'll bring my own food."

Kyle wanted to argue but thought better of it.

Over the month that followed, Dr Cooper came around once a week to work with Alex and learn about his feelings and transformations. As the moon waned, it got harder and harder for him to transform into the wolf and almost impossible at new moon. What interested Dr Cooper most was how much harder it was for Mork also to turn back. Throughout the weeks, however, a few things become clear, there was less of the animal and more of the boy in the wolf's personality. And, secondly, Alex took much greater strain during those transformations. After just one new moon transformation, he was looking gaunt and faint. He seemed desperate for food and ate everything prepared for dinner. Dr Cooper also knew a Tai chi teacher and put him into classes twice a week. He agreed that it would help teach the boy restraint and provide a viable excuse for Alex's incredible strength. They spent hours discussing how it felt to change from the boy into the wolf and back again. Alex was always full of questions, hoping Dr Cooper would have the answers and holding onto his every word as the gospel truth. As full moon approached, however, the general level of anxiety grew, not only because of how much more of an animal Mork was but also because the end of school holidays was fast approaching. Everyone had spent every spare moment researching werewolves and they were hard pressed to find any stories that didn't involve the victim turning into a human wolf hybrid and killing everyone with whom they came into contact. Debra wanted to start compiling different lores surrounding werewolfism for Alex to try out, but again could find only different ways a werewolf could be killed. The only consolation was the relief at how difficult it would be for him to die.

Debra took a sip of coffee and looked at Kyle across the kitchen table, also wading through reference material on werewolves.

"Has it occurred to you that Alex might be immortal?"

Kyle stopped for a moment and looked off into the distance. "No, that's impossible."

"So is being a werewolf."

He narrowed his eyes and but his lip. "I'm not sure if I should be terrified or relieved, but I am tempted to forget that we had this conversation … What's your vote?"

"I like that plan," Debra smiled.

With that, they both went back to reading. It was the night before the moon would be full enough to force transformation. Dr Cooper had moved into their spare room for the occasion, but had gone to bed earlier because he had a few clients the following day who couldn't be moved to later in the week. Alex lay awake on his bed, staring up at his ceiling, wondering what was going to happen over the next few days, and what he was going to say to his friends back at school when he saw them again in a few days' time. He hadn't seen or spoken to any of them all holiday. Annabel, on the other hand, had spent most of her time since she got home staying at friends' houses and hanging out at the mall trying to find reasonable excuses to not be at home. Although she understood the severity of her brother's situation and how it impacted the whole family, she couldn't help but feel like the third wheel. Sometimes she'd lie awake at night and hate herself for being envious of her brother and all the attention he was getting, but also how hard it must be for him that he was not able to see his friends and had to lie to them about being sick.

Alex rolled onto his side and stared at a picture of himself that he'd put next to his bed to help him focus on remaining human. As full moon approached, he found himself slipping into wolf form more and more while he slept. Under the supervision of Dr Cooper, he had begun to keep a diary of how the changes felt, and the differences between new moon and full moon. As much as he liked having someone he could talk to and confide in about how he was feeling, he was still reluctant to tell Dr Cooper everything, so he kept the diary entirely private. After the first week, when Dr Cooper asked him about it, he said that he wanted to keep some of his feelings to himself to try to learn how to overcome things by himself in case he should ever be separated from the family. It was also during that conversation that Dr Cooper first truly understood the way Kyle must have felt the first time he brought Alex to his office, the great swell of sadness for a child forced into a serious situation, and no matter how hard the people around him might wish they could help shoulder the burden, they could do little more than stand on the sidelines and offer support.

Alex had leafed through his diary before climbing into bed, trying to draw his own conclusions about the difference between new and full moon. He'd written that although it was harder to transform during new moon, it seemed much gentler human to wolf, as though he was being enveloped, as opposed to the approaching full moon, when it felt more like the human in him was being chipped away and the animal inside fighting its way out. He knew that this was only the beginning and things were going to be tricky once he was back at school, but he also felt confident that they were winning. He felt in control enough that he would be able to deal with going back to school, being with his friends. He sighed, focused on his picture and drifted off to sleep, quietly hoping to not dream about wolves.

Chapter 15

"If you've just joined us, we're sitting here with Alex Harris, talking about life after Waterdogs. So tell us, Alex, you've toured all over the world, what's your favourite place?"

"Well, you know, different places for different reasons."

"For example?"

"Well, Edinburgh, because you have cobbled streets and castles, but you also have all modern comforts hidden in between; Gothenburg, because in twenty minutes you can get from the middle of the city to the middle of a forest; Cape Town because it's like an adults' playground; and, of course, Syn Island because it's my home."

"Fair enough ... So what places do you like least?"

"All the same places for all the same reasons. Hahaha, no, the only real problem I've ever had with a place is when we arrive somewhere amazing for 48 hours and in that time we've got, like, two shows to do and a few press junkets and a welcoming ceremony then we leave. Makes it hard to get to know a place, you know. That all being said, I look forward to seeing more of the world, maybe finding a few places where people don't know who I am and taking it easy for awhile."

"So let's get personal for a minute here."

"Alrighty."

"It's been well publicised how much you like taking private time away from the crowds of fans and even the band to spend time with your family. And for years you would never speak about your family or your home life to the press."

"Yip, that all sounds right."

"But then on the flip side to that, a lot of the lyrics in the songs you've written are very dark and personal."

"Strange, I know ... I guess it's because I always used to keep a journal as a kid, as a way of dealing with my feelings, and song writing was just a progression from that. When singing these things it seemed to take them out of my head and helped me deal with them; the fact that millions of people around the world heard them didn't seem to matter as much, as opposed to just volunteering the information out in an interview."

"I mean, obviously you're a much more open person now. What happened to change that?"

"I think it had a lot to do with the birth of my nephew. He has a way of bringing light into my life and I didn't need to be as dark and mysterious any more. Reminded me that the fame will come and go but family is always going to be there."

"So, no longer being 'dark and mysterious' doesn't make you any less deep, which brings me to my next question: girls. How has a smoking-hot, world-famous, sensitive rock star like yourself avoided any

kind of serious relationship?"

"Practice."

"Oh, har, har, har, Mr Harris, we also all know about your strange womanising antics. What I want to know is if you have your eyes on someone special or if you're going to be a prowler forever?"

"Well, I have my eyes on you right now, Ms Barker."

"Whaa ... Hehehe!"

Chapter 16

"So, let me get this straight, because Annie gets to go do her final year in some fancy school, I *have* to go there? This is her special thing, why do I even have to be involved? Let her do something amazing for a change."

Alex looked at his parents over the kitchen table and put on the most obvious fake smile he could muster.

"We're not having this conversation again, Alex. It's a great opportunity for you."

"But, Dad, all my friends are going to Syn High, *you* went to Syn High. I don't want to go to special school."

"And you'll still be able to see them after school and other non-Mork days, just as you do now. Only you'll also be able to specialise in what you want to be when you, if you ever, *grow up*."

Alex gritted his teeth, threw his hands in the air and closed his eyes. After a long, deep breath he looked at his parents. "And what do I want to be when I grow up? Since when did my vote count towards that one? You're having me studying Agriculture so I can be shipped off to Granddad's farm as soon as I'm out of school."

Debra dropped her shoulders and shook her head. Alex pursed his lips and a very low growl slipped out, at which point Kyle pointed a finger at the kitchen door.

"That's it. Go to your room until you calm down and are ready to apologise."

Alex leapt up, knocking his chair over behind him, and stormed out of the kitchen, slamming every door along the way.

"Teenage hormones plus pending full moon definitely keeps things interesting. I'm sure he'll calm down soon enough."

Kyle looked over at his wife who had her head in the hands, trembling slightly.

"Honey?"

Debra sat back. "I hate to say it, but what *is* he going to do with his life? I mean, so far we've managed to keep his secret, but he's still in school. What happens when he's twenty and wants to move out and have a real life? What job can he get?"

"What are you saying?"

"I'm saying I'm scared that our son is going to have an unhappy, unfulfilled life."

Kyle leaned over and kissed her on the cheek. "Alex will find a way … He's just angry right now, but he'll calm down and find a way. He's a clever lad; don't give up on his happiness just yet."

Alex slumped down on his bed and pulled on his earphones. He resisted the urge to listen to angry music, knowing that this close to full moon it would cause him to change almost instantly. Instead he put on a compilation of classic chill-out songs. He huffed a few times but managed to control his breathing and let his eyes close. With the music on full blast, he never heard the gentle knock at his door, but picked up the smell of his sister drifting in from under the door. He poked the stop button on his stereo.

"Come on in, Annie."

Annabel walked in with hands behind her back, her head at an angle as she sat down on the bed. They looked at each other in silence for a moment.

"You don't have to be so nervous, I'm alright-ish now."

"Then you should go apologise to Mom for growling at her."

"I wouldn't say I was *that* calm."

"Alex ..." Annabel raised her eyebrows.

"All right, all right, I was just kidding. I know, I'm going to apologise to Mom. It's just hard sometimes to stay in control over things around full moon. Anyway, why do I have to go to the special school? You're the special one here, why can't this just be your thing?"

"That's not the point, Alex; this will actually be good for you. You don't have to study just Agriculture, you can take other classes as well."

"Really?"

"Yeah, it's like college. You just sign up for some other classes"

"I don't know, I just want to stay in the school I know, with my friends, where new people aren't going to ask questions."

"You'll be fine. A new school won't be that bad. And, besides, I'll be there to look after you."

He grimaced at his sister,

"Oh, will the fun … ever … end?"

Even though he said it a lot, the way he said it always made her giggle.

"Oh, relax! Now go say sorry to Mom."

Alex got up off his bed. "It's not like I growled at her on purpose, you know."

"Doesn't matter."

They made their way back to the kitchen. Alex sat down across from his mother and apologised.

Over the years, Annabel had taken on the role of peacekeeper of the family, always there to help Alex calm himself down and see things clearer. At seventeen, she was a pretty girl, but still kept very much to herself, with a tight circle of only close friends, never entertaining the idea of getting a high-school boyfriend or getting tied up in gossip. She told herself there would be time for that kind of thing later on in life and that studies were the most important thing at that point. Alex, at just sixteen, looked closer to twenty-one; he was tall with bright blue eyes, a pale complexion and jet-black hair. His shoulders were broad and his body well defined. And, opposed to his sister's ideas on dating, he wanted few things more than a girlfriend, but kept himself to himself for fear of being exposed. Unfortunately for him, looking like an adult didn't mean he thought like one and, in his own way, he ducked all the girls who threw themselves in his direction. It also didn't help that, like any animal, occasionally he'd pick up a certain scent in the air that would kick his libido into overdrive and he'd have to hold back from literally throwing himself onto the nearest female. Dr Cooper thought about mentioning at some point that if he picked up that smell from a girl, it meant that she probably liked him, but being as Alex had been just twelve when he first encountered this problem, the doctor had decided to keep it to himself.

After an early dinner and a quick shower Alex made his way into the basement, wearing only a towel. He preferred to change outside, but he also knew that if anyone saw him, it could mean the end of his 'normal' life. Even though he couldn't see the moon, he could feel it as it became just full enough to begin the transformation. He sat with his legs crossed and his eyes closed in the dark as the wolf came sprinting out of his mind and burst through him into the world. Mork stood panting, green eyes gleaming in the darkness. Over the years, Mork too had changed slightly; his hair was darker and coarser and he was bigger. The given story was that he was a crossbreed of Great Dane and wolf descent. Although he seemed more animal during full moon, it was now just part of the process. Mork and Alex's memories were perfectly shared but the distinction of their names had stuck and Mork was treated differently to Alex, and vice versa.

It had been Dr Cooper's idea to call the local authorities and warn them about the arrival of their new family 'pet', one that would occasionally need extra exercise. Over the years the neighbours had gotten to know Mork as a very well-trained animal that looked far scarier than he actually was, although they did often joke that if anyone decided to break into the Harris house they'd probably never be the same. After the first year, it wasn't uncommon to see him taking himself for walks. On one occasion he even helped escort one of the neighbour kids home after they wandered off and got lost.

Chapter 17

Alex emerged from his room fully dressed and human for the first time in three days. He was wearing his smart clothes, complete with tie, and drew his mother's attention as he walked into the kitchen.

"Ta-daah!"

"Oh my, love, you look fabulous."

"Do I have to wear this stuff? I thought I just got in because Annie got in."

"Yes, well, you did, but the headmaster likes to meet all the new students and talk about what they want to accomplish while at the school. Your sister had to go through the same thing, remember?"

"I remember but it wasn't as bad for me when it was happening to her."

Debra frowned and stuck her tongue out at him.

"It'll be fine. Now hurry up and eat something or we'll be late."

Kyle had already left for work and Annabel was sleeping at a friend's house, so it was just the two of them at the table. It didn't happen very often but when it did they always found themselves in a comfortable silence, only rarely broken by quiet niceties, odd complaints and food recommendations. The silence continued as they drove to the school, Alex watching the world rush by, still imagining himself as a superhero saving people, except that now rescuing the girl made a lot more sense to him. At the same time, in her mind Debra ran over the story of Alex's rare medical condition, which meant he needed to spend a few days every now and then in hospital or at home with his doctor, causing him to regularly miss school. This story was backed up by a letter from Dr Cooper that gave the long medical explanation.

When they arrived at the school they spent a few minutes sitting in the waiting room outside the headmaster's office. Debra tried to calm Alex's nerves by reminding him that it'd be fine, she'd be right there with him and he needed to just breathe and speak when spoken to otherwise she'd do the talking. He wasn't actually as nervous as she was, but her words did help.

"All right," the headmaster's secretary looked up from her desk, "Mr Reid would like to talk to Alex alone first so, Alex, you can just go straight through. Can I get you something to drink, Mrs Harris?"

The secretary was in her early twenties and if she didn't have his file in front of her that told her that Alex was just sixteen, she would have allowed herself to find him very attractive. Despite herself, she smiled at him as he got up and headed into the office. Fortunately, he was too nervous to pick up the scent of her hormones at play, but did stop and turn to her for a moment. His body tensed when he realised that what he smelt was blood. *Blood?* Despite herself, she blushed when his mouth dropped open into a smile and in, as charming a voice as he could muster, said, "That's a lovely dress."

Then quickly he turned and walked into the office.

"Aah, young Master Harris, please, take a seat and don't be nervous; I just want to have a quick chat with you before the year starts." Reid pulled his chair up to the desk. "The school has only about 400 students, so I like to have at least some idea of who they all are. I mean, don't know them all by name but I could pick any of my students out of a line-up."

Alex smiled. "Ever actually have to do that, sir?"

Reid laughed, "No, not yet!" He turned to the file open on his desk. "Now, I see you're focusing your studies on Agriculture, correct?"

"Yeah, my grandparents have a farm in Canada and I'm planning to move up there after school."

"Great, it's always nice to have some direction, but you have a few empty slots that we need to fill."

"What? I mean uhmmm ... pardon?"

"Well, the way things work here is that we offer courses that you can major in, like Agriculture, but then we want you to have some variety in your studies so we also offer minor subjects that you can take in your empty class slots. So, like with you, you have Agriculture major and then you need to go through our list of other classes and pick a few extra subjects."

Reid leaned across his desk and handed Alex a sheet of paper with two columns of different classes. Of all the different classes on offer, nine were highlighted.

'Now, obviously most of your time is taken up, so I've highlighted the classes that can fit into your schedule. Anything there look interesting?"

Alex looked down at the sheet of paper, then up at Mr Reid, then back to the paper,

"Does Annabel have to do this?"

Reid smiled, "No, she's only here for a year and on a very specific bursary. You, on the other hand, will be with us for a few years, so you're on the usual curriculum."

"How many of these do I need to take?"

"Just two ... You can take more if you want, and actually if you show great talent or a serious interest in a different set of subjects in the first six months you can even change your major."

Alex let his eyes scroll down the list of highlighted subjects, of which only one really popped out at him.

"Creative writing?"

"Oh, yes, do you do any writing?"

"I've kept a journal since I was ten?"

"Works for me, anything else?"

"Uhmmm, not really ... I mean, nothing's really jumping out at me."

Reid looked Alex up and down,

"Do you like watching movies or listening to music?"

Alex narrowed his eyes and sniffed the air.

"Uhmmm, yes ..."

"Well, why not try Popular Culture Studies? It's basically watching movies, listening to music and then writing down your thoughts on it, with the occasional explanation of its artistic merit, if there is any."

"Cool!"

"Thought you might like that, so I'll just put your name down for these classes and that's that. Do you play any sports?"

"Oh, no, I can't really, I have a medical condition. I do Tai chi, though, up to three times a week for the past five years or so."

"Yes, this medical condition, I read the doctor's report; in your own words, though, what does it entail?"

"I ... It's like, I just, uhmmm, well sometimes I just get really tired, can't really get out of bed, don't leave the house. It only ever lasts a few days, then it goes away and I'm fine again, but for those few days it's like I'm not even in control of my body."

"That must be very difficult. How long have you suffered from it?"

"Since I was ten, but you get used to it."

"Ten must have been an interesting age for you."

"W-why ... why would you say that?"

"Well Tai chi, started a journal and developed a debilitating medical condition."

"Oh right, yeah, just in reverse order."

Reid narrowed his eyes for a second then smiled.

"Anyway, everything else seems to be in order. I look forward to seeing you in the halls, Master Harris."

Reid stood up and held out his hand, prompting Alex to stand and take it. At that point, however, pain shot up the headmaster's arm and he winced. Realising a little too late, Alex quickly let his headmaster go and smiled nervously.

"Sorry, I forget my own strength."

Mr Reid rubbed his right hand with his left. "That was a little unexpected, you sure you don't play some kind of sports?"

"Just Tai chi, it's harder than it looks."

"Who knew! Anyway, have a good day, young man, and we'll see you soon."

Alex nodded nervously and quickly made his way out of the office and into the waiting room.

"All done, let's go."

"Really? Mr Reid doesn't need to talk to me?"

"He didn't say so … Can we go now?"

Alex turned, smiled at the secretary and walked off, not waiting for his mother. She found him leaning against the hood of the car in the parking lot.

"What happened?"

"I, uhmmm … Yeah, I might've broken his hand."

Debra's eyes widened. "How?"

"Well, I was nervous and he got up to shake my hand and I quickly grabbed it and shook it and, uhmmm … I might have squeezed a little hard."

"What did you say?"

"I blamed Tai chi."

She sighed. "Alex, you really must be more careful."

"I normally am," he said as they climbed into the car. "I don't know; I was just taken by surprise. He was actually much more relaxed and easy going than I thought he would be, and he caught me off guard." He pulled the seat belt across his chest and clicked the clasp in place. "And I also have to take some extra classes because apparently otherwise I'd have too much free time, so I signed on for some film and music classes and, and creative writing, which I think it'll be pretty cool."

"That sounds interesting. So … not as bad as originally suspected?"

"Time will have to tell on that one, Mom," Alex rolled his eyes.

His mother exaggerated a sigh. "Which reminds me, what happened with the secretary?"

The smile dropped from Alex's face. "I *really* don't want to talk about it, thanks."

Suddenly a little worried, Debra pushed on. "Come now, what happened? I didn't hear her say anything or do anything."

"It's just that ... No, no, actually, I really, *really* don't want to talk about it."

"Alex, tell me." He could tell that her tone had changed.

"As I walked past her I could smell blood."

"*Blood?* Like, human blood?"

"Uhm, like period blood, Mom ..."

Debra blushed. "You're right, don't tell me."

"Told you."

After that, the car fell silent.

"If you can smell that, does that mean that you ..." Debra could control her curiosity no longer.

But Alex cut her off, "Mom. I want you to think long and hard about whether or not you want the answers to these questions before you ask them. Remember, Mom, somethings can't be unheard ..."

Debra pursed her lips and said nothing more for the rest of the drive home.

As they pulled into the driveway, they saw Annabel on the front steps. She was clearly furious. Before the car doors opened, she stormed to her feet and climbed into the back seat.

"Ryan says he wants to be my boyfriend and doesn't want to be just my friend any more, and then ... and *then*, when I wouldn't kiss him he told me he didn't want me staying at his house."

Debra looked at Alex, who contorted his face as if to say, "Why you looking at *me*?" She sighed and without a word restarted the car and backed out of the driveway. They sat in silence, waiting for Annabel to gather her thoughts and continue her rant. Over the years, the family had gotten used to the way she would store up frustration until she could stand it no more, and would then vent it. Alex very quietly sniffed the air to try pick up if there were any hints to when the rant would start, but at almost the same time Annabel launched into it.

"And you know it's really unfair because I do like him, he's one of my best friends, but I don't know if I like, *like,* like him, but I could you know and he really caught me off guard when he told me he was in love with me. Oh yeah Ryan told me he was in love with me and what am I supposed to do with that, I mean we're only seventeen, well, he's eighteen now but ..."

She took a deep breath, and Alex let out a small whine like a dog locked in needing to be let out, which didn't affect his sister in the slightest.

"But because I'm changing schools, I won't be able to see him at school so that we can patch things up and I don't want to be the one that phones him and I'm afraid he won't phone me. Mom, what do I *do*?"

Debra pulled into the car park at the island's Eastside Mall, turned off the engine, then turned to look at her.

"Don't stress yourself about it, honey, if he likes you, he'll call you. Ryan's a nice boy, I'm sure he'll call you. Now let's go inside, grab some ice cream and think about what you're going to say when he does."

She smiled at Annabel, who smiled back. Alex just groaned.

Annabel scowled at the back of his seat, "Oh, come on! You get ice cream out of this deal and all you have to do is sit there."

"That's not true, I also have to hear the conversation."

"Then leave."

"I suppose Mork could run home and you could just bring my clothes?" Alex looked across at his mother.

"You're not running home, there isn't anyone there and, besides, the door's locked."

"So give me the keys? And what does it matter if I'm left alone, who's going to mug a giant black wolf?"

Debra looked at Annabel for support but was met with a shrug of the shoulders.

"But don't you want ice cream?"

"Why is this such a problem, mom? It's not fair."

"No, just no, I'd rather you stayed with us and had some ice cream. It seems like we do less and less as a family these days anyway, I'd like you to not run home please."

"Fine."

He dropped his shoulders, sighed and climbed out of the car along with the others. Debra rolled her eyes, annoyed that now she had this lump of a boy whom she had to drag along to something she thought he might actually enjoy. And Annabel once again felt over-shadowed by her brother. He caught the unmistakeable smell of anger in the air and turned to look at them both, a green flare to his eyes.

"Look, you're both annoyed with me, you don't want me here, and I don't want to be here. Let me go home, have your girl time, talk, eat ice cream, let me go home and relax. If you like, I'll walk home as Alex, it's not like I'm in any danger. I'm super strong and well trained. Please?"

His voice rang with desperation, and he knew that if he stayed everyone lost.

"But don't you want ice cream?" Debra sighed.

"The ice cream isn't about me, its Annabel's thing. I already took her special school, let her have the ice cream ... Also, if I'm not here then you two can go shopping and talk about boy-and-girl stuff and I don't have to hear any of it. You'll have more fun without me."

He put on his cheesiest smile and blinked at his mother, who rolled her eyes but couldn't help but be charmed. In that moment it also occurred to Annabel how conscious her brother was about the attention he got over her.

"Fine, you can go home, but just please do it as Alex not Mork."

"Works for me! Have a good day and laters."

Debra handed him the house keys and, with that, Alex turned on his heels and headed off. He liked walking; unknown to his parents, he'd walked to and from the mall many times before, both as Mork and as Alex. He found it calming, and it made it easy for him to order his thoughts. He felt a little bad about not having a family moment, but knew too that it wasn't supposed to be a family moment, it was an Annabel moment. He felt bad for her, knowing full well that his parents had to spend more time focused on him and hated when he cast a cloud over her moments. Now, as he walked, Alex's mind drifted to his new school, the classes there, and for the first time became a little excited about it all. He arrived home just in time to hear the phone; he quickly unlocked the door and ran inside.

"Windsor Castle, Greenwald speaking."

"Hey, Alex, it's Ryan."

"Oh, hi, Ryan. Word on the street is you messed up, how are things?"

"Wha … You heard about that?"

"I hear all, but don't stress, your secrets are safe with me."

"Cool, man, thanks. Is your sister around? I really need to talk to her."

"Nope, sorry."

"Well, will you tell her I called?"

"No, no reason to. She's out with Mom eating ice cream and shopping to get over having a fight with you. You've got Mom's phone number, call it and ask for Annie."

"Oh, dude, no! I don't know that I can speak to your mom now, and if she's doing all that stuff she must be kinda pissed with me still."

"Don't worry; here's what you say: first off, you apologise right from the start. Don't over do it, you don't need to say sorry a million times, that'll just annoy her, but you do need to say it once. Then you tell her you want to take her to the movies; she'll say something along the lines of 'We've gone to see lots of movies' ..."

"Why will she say that?"

"Because she's still confused and therefore angry with you, but that's okay because you want her to say something like that so that you can say, 'Yes, but this time it'll be different, because this time we're not just going to the movies, we're going on our first date, and you can pick the movie because I came on too strong and want to make it up to you, and we'll get buttered popcorn and you can put on the salt because you like doing that. Then afterwards we can go to that burger place that I like and you don't mind because it's about balance and it takes two people to make a relationship happen not two halves. So Annabel, I'm not asking you to marry me, or commit to me, I'm just asking you out on a date with the option of seeing how it goes.'"

The line fell silent for a moment and Alex strained to try hear what was happening on the other end. Then, after a few seconds, he heard Ryan's voice again.

"How … it … goes … That's brilliant, man, how do you come up with this stuff?"

"I study Eastern philosophy. Were you writing down what I was saying?"

"Yes. Thanks for the help, man."

"No problems. Just do me one favour; tell my mom that I've gotten home safe and sound."

"Oh, yeah, sure. Okay."

"Oh wait! One more thing … If you hurt my sister, in any way, I *will* bite out your throat."

"You know you're a funny dude, Alex … Cheers."

"Cheers."

As he put the phone down he sighed, "It's only funny because it's true."

Alex headed off to the kitchen to raid the refrigerator. He would, he decided, spend the rest of his school holiday much as he'd spent his holiday up until that point: lounging on the couch watching TV, wandering the house as a large black wolf, and going to Tai chi classes. He liked spending some time as Mork for a few reasons, one being that it helped perpetuate the story that Mork was in fact the family's pet, the other was that, unknown to his family, he still enjoyed the sense of freedom he felt as Mork. He'd had gotten very good at changing at will and, although it was always harder turning back, it wasn't really a problem.

***

Annabel looked across the table at her mom, hoping for some kind of insight into the inner workings of the mind of men. Debra took a spoonful of ice cream so as to give herself some time to reflect on how nice it was that Annabel finally had a problem that she really wanted her mother's help with.

"Don't stress yourself out, sweetheart, I'm sure that when Ryan calms down he'll call you."

"I know, but it's just that he's been, like, my best friend for years, and I just don't want to lose that over something stupid like 'I love you.'"

"On, honey, Ryan will come to his senses, you'll see. But you need to take a deep breath and think about what *you* want as well."

Annabel opened her mouth to voice her opinion but closed it again. She was finally beginning to think what *she* would like, instead of simply reacting to external forces. Before she knew it, she had expanded the picture in her mind. Her cheeks suddenly flushed red as she thought about what it would be like to kiss Ryan.

"Annie, darling, try to not think about it too much … Play it by ear. Come, grab your ice cream and let's go see if that sale's still on. I've been meaning to get myself a few things to wear at school this year and I could use your help."

"Mom, you and I both know that when it comes to shopping for clothes the only real help I can be is to tell you how to expensive the nice things are, and you ignore me."

"Right, then why stop now? Let's go get you something nice too and you can tell me it's a waste of money and I can tell you that it doesn't matter."

Annabel laughed; the distraction was making her feel a little better. Together they wandered through the mall, window-shopping until they had finished their ice creams. Then Annabel stopped suddenly to look at a bright pink tutu-inspired cocktail dress. Looking the manikin up and down a few times she said, almost to herself, "Shit, honey, it's no wonder you're single."

A shopper let out a splutter of a laugh, then blushed furiously. "Perhaps they should move her to the naval shop? I'm sure the manikins there would love her."

Annabel looked at the woman with wide-eyed amazement, and Debra clapped her hand over her mouth to stifle a laugh as the woman, cackling to herself, scuttled off.

"Well, that was unexpected!" Annabel squeezed her mother's arm.

Debra let out a soft laugh. "That's why I love this island so."

There was a familiar ring. "Mom, I think your phone's ringing."

Debra began digging in her bag, and pulled out the phone.

"Hello? Oh yes, hello how are you …? Good. Good, thank you … Oh? Well, that's a relief, thanks for passing the message on … Yes, of course, she's right here."

Debra held out the phone to Annabel. "It's for you."

Debra smiled broadly, which immediately made Annabel suspicious. Cautiously, she took the phone and answered nervously.

"Hello?"

"Hey, Annie."

"Ryan? How did you ...? Alex."

"Yeah, well, I was trying to get hold of you, so I phoned the house and he answered and told me I could get you at this number."

Annabel turned from her mother and began walking away from her.

"Look, Annie, I want to say I'm sorry about this morning. I ... I shouldn't have sprung that on you like that, but, but I've got an idea."

"Uh, okay?"

"Well, I was thinking about it and here's what I've decided, let me take you to the movies."

"We go to the movies all the time; why do you now need to ask so formally?"

Ryan had to keep his excitement at bay. Alex had been spot on!

"Yes, but ... but this time it'll be different, b-because this time we're not just going to the movies, we're going on our first date ...

And you can pick the movie because I feel bad about this morning and want to make it up to you. Uhmmm … and we'll get buttered popcorn and you can put on the salt because you like doing that and, and afterwards we can go to that burger place that I like and you, I mean, don't mind because it's about balance and because it takes two people to make a relationship happen not two half people. S-so … Annabel, I'm not asking you to marry me, or commit to me, much, I'm just asking you out on … a date with the option of seeing how it goes."

Ryan swallowed hard. He realized that he'd just asked Annabel out on a date, almost by accident. The thought that Alex might have just played the biggest and worst prank in the world also flashed into his mind and sweat beaded on his forehead. On the other end of the line, Annabel found herself lost for words. The silence between them stretched longer and longer until finally, after what felt like hours, Annabel found her voice.

"Yes. Yes, that sounds perfect actually … Perfect. So, yes, when?"

"Oh, right, uhmmm … what's today?"

"Thursday."

"Uhmmm, how about Friday? No, it's always super busy. Saturday? No, Sunday. Sunday night?"

"Okay, cool, that's great. So I'll see you Sunday?"

"Yes. I'll pick you up?"

"Cool. Okay, bye?"

"Wha.. Yeah, ok, bye."

Ryan put the phone down and sat in silence for a few minutes, trying to work out how Alex had done it, and what it was exactly that he had done ... And how he now had a date for Sunday night to go watch a movie he was going to hate with the girl of his dreams who also happened to be his best friend. He allowed himself to slide down the wall until he was on the floor ... Sunday had better come quickly, he thought.

Annabel, equally in shock, wandered back over to her mom, handed her back the cell phone and said dumbly, "I'm going on a date with Ryan on Sunday night."

Debra's face lit up. "Fantastic! What did he say? Was he charming and sweet?"

Annabel looked up at her mom and for the first time in ages Debra could see that her daughter had no idea what to do. She put her arm around her daughter's shoulder.

"Shame, my love," she laughed. "Shall we just go home so you can digest all this?"

"Yes, but we might have to come back tomorrow, 'Cos what am I going to *wear*?"

***

Over the years, Alex had begun to notice a few extra crossovers from Mork than before; it wasn't just being able to see in the dark and a heightened sense of smell. His hands and, mostly, his feet had grown slight webs, his canines had become elongated and he snapped at flies; he also scratched behind his ears with his whole hand moving his wrist in the motion of a dog scratching its ears. He growled, he whimpered, and when, as a human, he could also let out a very loud howl, in fact, his vocal range had increased

230

dramatically at around the age of thirteen. There were still times when he found it hard to contain his instincts, times when he would lose control and turn into Mork. These times were always near to the full moon and usually resulted in Mork sprinting down the street and as far away from everyone and everything as possible. On one occasion, it took him four days to find his way home. Mork, too, had developed slightly more human traits, such as a clearer memory and understanding during full-moon transformations. On the whole, they were both faster and stronger than both a wolf and a human, and although he was still very much an extrovert he would often find himself shying away from social events with his friends for fear of slipping and being exposed. As a result, he often felt cut off, even lonely sometimes. Over the years, he'd also grown very protective over his family and, as Mork, could be very aggressive towards people who seemed to be a threat of any kind. Occasionally he wondered just how different their life would be if he hadn't been bitten, but at those moments he would either have to clear his mind and find a way to distract himself or change.

Chapter 18

Annabel bounded into Alex's room, turned on the light and then screamed. Alex leapt to his feet, eyes bright green and growling, as his eyes tried to focus and he saw his sister covering her face in horror. He quickly realised what had happened and desperately grabbed at his blankets.

"Why are you *naked*?"

"Why can't you *knock*?"

"I asked first!"

"I sleep naked!"

"Why do you sleep naked? What's *wrong* with you?"

"I'm a werewolf!" His retaliation came out harsher than he had meant it to, but it calmed the conversation down quickly. He cleared his throat. "Besides, I was Mork when I went to bed."

"Oh, uhmmm ... Why?"

"Because I just was, remember, it's not always in my control. Now what's going on?"

"It's the first day of school. I was supposed to wake you up for an early family breakfast ..."

Annabel still held her hands over her eyes, determined not to look in his direction.

"I'm covered, Annie, you can look."

Nervously, she moved her hands away from her face, and very slowly opened one eye to check that her brother was indeed wrapped in blankets

"I'm telling Mom you growled at me," she laughed cheekily.

"And I'm telling mom you saw me naked."

"Eeew! Okay, you win, I'll keep quiet if you do. Still, do you always sleep naked?"

"If you think about it, I spend a lot of time naked ... Remember, when I'm covered in fur, I've not got clothes on. Nothing. Buck na-ked."

Annabel's mischievous smile quickly turned to disgust. "Oh, thanks for that ... Now that's a mental image I might not be able to shift in a hurry."

"Yeah, and if you don't want any more of those I suggest you leave so that I can put some clothes on."

"But ... I've seen you in PJs?"

"Yeah, Mom keeps buying them for me and I put them on in the morning to make her happy. I figure we don't need more things to fight about."

"Not just a furry face, huh?"

He smiled a toothy grin and pointed at the door. She smiled back and left, shutting the door behind her. Alex got up, found his new school uniform and put as much of it on as he could. After trying to tie his tie a couple of times and failing miserably, he called out to Annabel for help. He could smell her waiting beyond the shut door, curious to see her brother in the uniform, which he hadn't worn yet. She came in smiling to see her brother in a jacket and tie. Alex looked at his sister disgruntled as she reached over his shoulders and showed him how to do the tie properly.

"I already dislike where this day is going and it's only just started."

"Be quiet, it's not that bad, at least everyone's wearing the same thing."

"Yaaay ..."

"There are worse uniforms out there, you know."

"I know, but still ... it's the principle of the matter."

"Which principle would that be?"

"Give me some coffee and some time to think about it and I'm sure I'll think of one."

They both laughed and went downstairs. Debra and Kyle were already waiting at the breakfast table wearing proud smiles.

"Aaw! Look at you two in your uniforms, it's like your very first day of school all over again."

Alex smiled and was about to say something, but caught his father's eye and realised that it wouldn't be such a great idea after all. Everyone sat down to an enthusiastic breakfast, and even Alex was swept up in the excitement for a while. After, Annabel and Debra went off, ostensibly to make sure that she had all the books she needed for school, but really to talk about the date with Ryan. Alex looked across the table at his dad.

"Thank you for keeping that comment to yourself, kiddo."

"Today is going to suck."

"Probably, but tomorrow will be better. Speaking of keeping things to yourself, I heard about what Ryan said to Annie over the phone the other day ... Didn't know the boy had it in him."

"Yeah, who knew?"

"I'm still not sure if what you did is a good or a bad thing, but it sure is something."

"Don't worry, Dad, he smells good. Also, if he isn't—"

"You'll bite out his throat?"

Alex smiled broadly, showing off his sharp canines.

"Good boy."

Alex drained his cup of tea, repeating all the positive points his parents had told him about the new school; he was determined to keep his stress levels down. Kyle, on the other hand, was reading over a case brief, which was sending his own stress levels through the roof. Alex's nose twitched as he looked across the table.

"Everything alright there, Dad?"

"What? Oh yeah, don't worry about it, nothing your old man can't handle. Just slightly more difficult then the board might have had me believe."

He frowned but went back to his thoughts.

***

Mother and daughter sat on the edge of the bed while Annabel gave a blow-by-blow account of her date, from which point in the movie Ryan accidentally, but really on purpose, touched her leg, to a 1–10 scale she'd invented for recording how often she blushed. And Debra was loving every second of it, so both shot annoyed looks when Alex arrived at the door.

"All right, kids, it's time for school."

It felt strange driving a different route to school. Somehow, it didn't feel like going to school at all, which only made arriving at a school feel even more of an insult as far as Alex was concerned. He spent the first part of the day being led on a tour by Mr Reid's secretary. Annabel, however, had had the tour the year before when she had first been offered a position there, so went straight to class. Alex spent most of the tour taking long, slow deep breaths trying desperately to keep his hormones at bay and finally figured out what that strange smell coming from her was; quite apart from the winks he kept getting, he also realised that although he wasn't the only new student he was the only one getting a personal tour.

236

"… And finally here's your locker. There's only five minutes or so left of your first class so you might as well just get yourself ready for the second one and start there."

The young woman reached out, took one hand in hers and dropped a padlock in it. Looking at her, he decided she was about twenty-three and very pretty, but he still needed to take long slow breaths to try to contain himself.

"Thanks, I, uhmmm, appreciate the help."

"Oh, no problem, if you need any help at all you know where my desk is. You just come direct to me."

"Cool, thanks."

He smiled. A nervous, slightly confused smile because she was still holding his hand. She blushed, but held on. He took another deep breath, then lifted her hand to his mouth and kissed it. Goose bumps shot up her arm and her smell intensified. His heart rate was beginning to climb and he was suddenly unsure whether he was about to leap on her, turn into a wolf or both. She turned bright red, giggled then pulled her hand free and set off down the hall back to her office. As he watched her disappear down the hall, he could feel his eyes start to glow. He shut his eyes and took long, slow, deep breaths, focusing on staying human. Feeling his calm return, he exhaled and realised he could smell fear. Opening his eyes, he saw three of the older boys chasing a smaller boy. He stepped out in front of them and the little one ducked behind him for cover.

"You have to help me. Please help me."

"You really have bullies at such a smart school?"

The boy's face was grave as he whispered, "Sports scholarships."

Alex could feel the wolf sitting right behind his eyes, ready to pounce. The three bullies stopped in front of him.

"So, it looks like Brandy here has found a boyfriend ... And what's your name, little girl?"

Alex scowled.

"The silent type, huh? I like that."

The one who was clearly the leader placed his hand on Alex's shoulder.

"Now look here, Silence, we're the guys you *want* to be friends with at this school, and that little guy behind you—"

"Get your paw off me."

Alex's voice was low and firm, but the boy simply tightened his grip.

"So we've got a bit of attitude, do we? That's nice. But you're going to have to learn some manners."

Alex could feel a low growl building up at the back of his throat as he took the boy's hand in his own. He squeezed hard, then pulled down sharply, wrenching the kid's arm. He fell forward and banged his head hard on the lockers. Alex continued to squeeze. The boy quickly cried out in pain, dropped to his knees, begging to be let go.

"Now you listen to me ... I don't give a shit who you think you are.

You leave us the fuck alone or I'll break your hand, you understand me?"

"YES! Yes, just let me go, please let me go."

Alex looked up at the other two boys and let out another long, low growl before releasing their leader. The boy scrambled to his feet, swore under his breath and made a quick departure with his two friends. Alex could hear him telling them that he could have taken him, but didn't want to be late for class. Alex shook his head.

"Dude!"

Alex leaped back. He'd forgotten that there was someone cowering behind him.

"That was *amazing*!"

"Oh, right, yeah ... Well, I, uhmmm ... I do Tai chi."

"What?" The kid wasn't sure what Alex was talking about. "Oh, yeah, that was amazing too, but, no, I mean your voice, that growl, that's awesome. Dude, you've got to join our band."

Alex's head dropped quizzically to the side. "What?"

"Our band. I'm a Music major; I'm in a band, and we need a singer and your voice is perfect, right now we're a Tool tribute band called Spanner. Cool name, huh? I came up with it."

"Really? Well, I've never heard of Tool."

"*What?* Dude, where've you been? They're, like, the greatest band ever! What's your next class?"

"Uhmmm, Film and Music Appreciation?"

"Awesome, me too, and the rest of the band. I'll introduce you. It's this way, follow me."

Alex's mouth hung open, his shoulders dropped and a frown found its way to his face.

"Oh yay ..."

As they made their way to class Alex began to understand why someone might want to beat this person up; the dude hadn't stopped talking and still hadn't introduced himself or asked any questions. Alex was, however, learning a lot about the band Tool. Thankfully the classroom wasn't far. Alex followed the kid into the classroom where he was immediately approached by another boy wearing a very amused smile.

"Dude! You survived, I'm impressed."

"Pardon?"

The other boy put his hand on Alex's shoulder.

"Well, maybe 'survived' isn't the right word; let's go with, 'I see you haven't tried to kill Brandon yet, I'm impressed.'"

Alex smiled, and turned to Brandon. "Well, it was close, it's a lucky thing the classroom wasn't far."

"Lucky for him! I'm sure some of the teachers would testify that you were in class the whole time."

Alex laughed, "I wish I'd known that five minutes ago."

They both laughed.

"I'm Josh, by the way," the boy held out his hand. "And, as you've discovered, the little one with the big mouth is Brandon. He forgot to mention that, right?"

Alex extended a hand, and Josh shook it,

"That he did. I'm Alex."

Brandon turned to look at them when he heard his name. "Oh, yeah, I forgot. Yip, I'm Brandon, the drummer, and that's Josh. Josh is our guitarist, and over in the corner with his book is Danny, he's the bassist."

Danny smiled and waved then went back to the book he was reading. Brandon smiled broadly at Josh, and patted Alex on the shoulder. "Guess what! He's a singer!"

Josh narrowed his eyes. "Really?"

"No. No, I'm not."

"Well, not yet maybe," started Brandon, determined not to let this opportunity go. "But he saved me from the Olympians, and he let out this awesome growl. He's perfect! So I told him he can join the band ..."

Danny, Josh and Alex all sighed as one.

"But he's never heard of Tool, so I figure we get Ms Peel to let us do a Tool appreciation lesson today, and some Bill Hicks, and we'll teach him all about it."

Alex looked at Josh with a slightly desperate expression on his face; Josh put up his hands and gave that 'I'll handle this' sign.

"Brandon, down, boy. No more words from a while."

Brandon closed his mouth and sat down.

"Now that was impressive," Alex tipped his head to the side. "You'll have to teach me how to do that."

"Mincing words doesn't really work with this one. So take a seat, we're the only people in this class so you can relax a little and don't worry, we're not going to force you into singing in our band. But we are looking for a singer if you're keen. I'm singing at the moment and, trust me, no one really wants that to continue much longer than it has to."

Alex smiled and sat down.

"This is turning into a weirder day than I could have imagined."

"Yeah, Brandon has that affect on people," Josh sat down next to him. "So, you a Film or Music major?"

"Neither. This is just a filler class that Reid suggested. I'm actually majoring in Agriculture."

"Farm school?" Josh stifled an exaggerated yawn. "Really? If you don't mind me asking, why?"

"My grandparents have a stud farm in Canada; it's been in the family for years and no one else is really interested in taking it over, so I figured I'd learn how to become a farmer and go work there."

As Joshed mulled this over in his head, a middle-aged woman walked into the room and sat down at the main desk next to the white board.

"Morning, boys. I trust you all had a good holiday and have introduced yourselves to our new student?"

As one Brandon, Danny and Josh turned to face the front of the class. "Morning, Ms Peel."

And before anyone could stop him, Brandon continued: "Alex hasn't ever heard of Tool, nor Bill Hicks, so can we have a Tool/Hicks revision lesson?"

Danny quickly piped up after Brandon so that no one could agree with him. "No! We're supposed to be doing superheroes. I was promised Batman."

"Danny's right. I'm afraid, Brandon, we can do musical revision next week."

Ms Peel smiled sweetly at Brandon who frowned and slumped back in his chair. Alex slowly and nervously raised his hand.

"That's a nice gesture, Alex," Ms Peel smiled, "but there are only four of you, so you really can just speak."

"Uhmmm, okay … Well, I was just wondering how this class works, because I really don't know what it's about really."

She turned her smile to Josh, who explained, "Over the course of the year, we listen to a lot of music, watch a lot of movies, and occasionally write a report about the underlying theme of all the different media forms we explore, or we'll write a comparison between one band and another or actors, directors or characters, or whatever. Oh, and for us Music majors, our reports go into a portfolio that helps for our year project. Last year was a music video. For part-timers like yourself, I think as long as your attendance is up to scratch, you pass."

The room fell quiet for a moment as Alex let his mind wrap around this new information. "So, let me get this straight," he said, scratching his head. "Basically, I have to listen to the music that we as a group deem cool, watch superhero movies and occasionally write something about them, but it's not really going to count towards my end-of-year mark?"

Ms Peel nodded cheerfully. "Best kept secret in the school, right?"

Alex threw back his head and laughed, "Remind me to thank Mr Reid next time I see him."

The whole class, including Ms Peel, erupted into laughter and for the first time Alex felt he was with his kind of people. The rest of the time in class was spent watching the first half of Tim Burton's *Batman* starring Michael Keaton and Jack Nicholson. Alex had seen it often enough before but this was the first time he really watched it with an eye for writing a comparison between it and the other live-action superhero movies. After class he was excited to discover that Josh also had Creative Writing next, which was then followed by break, which he spent with Josh, Danny and Brandon. By the end of the day, Alex felt like he had three new best friends. He had the most in common with Josh; both easy going witty and good-natured, although Alex figured he probably had a much more volatile temper than Josh. Danny didn't say much but he was clearly intelligent and he always laughed along with everyone else, as opposed to Brandon, who hardly ever stopped talking.

Alex and Josh were in the parking lot waiting for their parents when Brandon bounded up to them. He had acquired a stack of CDs, Bill Hicks and Tool, for Alex to listen to, along with a guitar, and a how-to-play book. Alex looked over at Josh and groaned, while Brandon continued to beg.

"Just think about it, man, I mean, chicks dig rock stars."

"All right, all right," Alex laughed. "I'll give it a try and see what happens. But I make no promises about being able to play guitar by tomorrow."

He slung the guitar over his shoulder and tried in vain to stuff the CDs into his backpack, which was already overflowing with his Agriculture textbooks. The familiar smell of Annabel tickled his nose and he look up just in time to catch her say, "So, whose guitar did you steal?"

Alex tucked the stack of CDs under his arm and pointed to Brandon. "His!"

Annabel turned to see Josh and Brandon, who both wore similarly confused looks.

"Josh, Brandon, meet my sister Annabel. Annie, these are my new friends Josh and Brandon."

"A pleasure. You guys also study Agriculture?"

It occurred to Josh that it might be a bad idea to let Brandon tell the story about how Alex had got into a fight on his first day of school so he quickly jumped in.

"No. Oh, uhmmm, Music. We met Alex in ... uhmmm."

Josh turned to Alex with a blank look.

"Film and Music Appreciation," Alex smiled.

"Yes, that's the one, Film and Music Appreciation, and we have Writing together. Your brother's a cool dude, man, you should be, like, proud?"

Josh frowned, wondering why he'd made it sound like a question. Alex and Annabel smiled and for a moment there was no mistaking they were family. Another familiar smell drifted past and Alex looked at Annabel.

"Mom's here."

"Cool."

Alex handed some of the CDs to her, picked up his bag and slung it over his shoulder. Brandon was dead still, staring at Annabel. He had decided that he was in love. Josh looked around but saw no evidence of Alex's mom, but just before he could voice his confusion a car pulled into the driveway.

"Well, guys," Alex turned to the boys, "it was really cool meeting you and I'll check you tomorrow."

"Yeah, groovy man, see you tomorrow, have a good afternoon."

Brandon was still silent.

Debra looked at the guitar over Alex's shoulder, but decided not to say anything; she figured it would come up in his report-back on how the first day of school had gone. Annabel went first to explain her thoughts on the school, while Alex sat in the back and mentally edited the story of his day. He decided that his mom didn't need to know about getting a personal tour from the secretary or that he'd managed to get into a fight before making it to even the first class. His mind began to wander and before he knew it he was being woken by his mother.

"Wake up, sweetheart, we're home."

He yawned and blinked a few times, looking around to get his bearing before realising what had happened. He shook his head and blushed.

"Oops, I guess Annie's description of her day was so enthralling that I just …"

Debra raised an eyebrow.

"Your eyebrows say frown, but your eyes say funny, Mom," Alex chided her.

"Grab your stuff and come inside; and please explain to me why you have a guitar with you. I mean, obviously I didn't actually *study* Agriculture, but I did grow up on a farm and I don't recall ever needing a guitar."

"Oh, Mom, you're so old fashioned; you've heard about talking to plants to make them grow, well singing is just the same, only it applies on a wider scale. You can't talk to all of the crops one on one, that would take forever, so you put on a concert for all of them to hear. It's the latest thing in hippie plant-growing technology."

"Very interesting; pity your grandfather has horses not crops."

"Yeah, real pity that one" Alex climbed out the car, backpack and guitar over his shoulders. "I tried to explain that to the teacher but she just grunted and hit me with a shovel, so I ate her."

Alex patted his mother on the shoulder. She laughed and rolled her eyes.

"But, seriously, where do you get the guitar?"

"Met some cool guys in movie class, and one of them decided I need to be the singer in their band so gave me his guitar."

"Oh no, Alex, give it back, that's not good."

"Don't get me wrong, Mom, I tried, I really tried, but he was adamant that I take it. Gave me a stack of CDs as well, and some books on how to play the bloody thing."

He put his things down at the front door and turned to see a worried expression on Debra's face.

"Don't stress yourself, Mom, it's not a problem. Really. I got the impression they have a lot of instruments. Also, it might be cool to learn how to play. You know, music soothes the savage beast. Plus the guys are really cool, especially this one dude, Josh. We got along really well."

"Well, that's good, I guess. So it's not such a bad place? Happy to go back tomorrow?"

"Well, I wouldn't go that far. Let's start with once a week and see how it goes?"

"Huh, funny, you're a funny guy. Now go eat, then get on to your homework."

Alex smiled and headed toward the kitchen. She sighed cheerfully and followed him. She had put together a light lunch before everyone went their separate ways. Annabel to her room to do homework, Debra to her office to do class prep, and Alex to his room to investigate the new music Brandon had given him. From the band's name, he decided that it would probably be best if he used earphones. Brandon's instructions stated that he should begin with Bill Hicks' *Dangerous* and continue from there. Within the first few minutes Alex, laughing loudly, felt an idiot with earphones on. Through the course of the afternoon he made his way through the three Bill Hicks albums and was just starting on the first Tool album when the scent of his father drifted in under his door. Quickly, he pressed stop and opened his door to find his father standing quietly outside. Alex narrowed his eyes and could feel his muscles tighten up.

"So how was your first day of school? Your mom said you met some nice people and now have a guitar?"

"Yeah?"

Kyle smiled a thin smile. "Can I come in?"

"Uhmmm, sure."

"So, tell me about your day; who are these kids you met? Where did you get a guitar? And why on the first day did I receive a phone call from the school asking about what I planned to do about some boy's broken hand?"

Alex forced a smile. "I can explain that."

Kyle's eyebrows furrowed and Alex couldn't help but notice the disappointment wash over his face.

"Good, please continue."

It would have been clear to anyone that Kyle was trying hard to stay calm and it was twice as obvious to Alex, who, in turn, was trying hard to ignore it. So much so that he forgot that he was actually in the right and just needed to explain things clearly.

Alex took a long deep breath and stammered, "It's ... it's not as bad as it seems."

"You broke his hand, you know that?"

Kyle's voice was harsh and aggressive. Something inside Alex switched and, like a wolf chased into a corner, he turned on the offensive, barely managing to contain a growl.

"Well, it's not like I was looking for a fight or even *started* it, in fact, if you'd side with me for once, and give me a moment rather then pouncing on me, I'd be able to explain. Three big jocks against one band geek who begged me for help. What was I supposed to do, huh? Leave him to get beaten up! Why don't you take a step back, get the *fuck!* Out of my room and come back when *you* can tell me what *you* would have done in my situation!"

Alex rushed forward, grabbed his father by the shoulder and hip, spun him around and literally threw him out the room. Kyle hit the ground hard and rolled twice before he realised what was happening. Alex, eyes bright green, stood in the doorway. He had never spoken to anyone like that, let alone his father, but he was livid that he was being painted the villain when in fact he was defending someone out-classed and out-numbered.

Kyle looked up and felt the fear run cold down his spine as he saw the pure fury on his son's face. The dramatic change of scent snapped Alex back as though he had woken suddenly from a deep dream and saw his father obviously terrified.

"Dad, I ... I don't know what came over me. I'm ... I'm sorry." He dropped to the floor, his head in his hands, trying desperately to hold onto his humanity. "I was just ... I just ... sorry."

Alex clenched his jaw and tried to focus, but within seconds Mork emerged, equally confused and afraid.

"It's okay, son, it's okay ... I'm sorry for pushing you without hearing your side first. I'm going to go now and tell your mother that Mork will be eating with us. You take all the time you need. Annabel will fetch you when dinner's ready."

Kyle got to his feet and walked away, making sure not to turn his back on Mork. He headed straight for his office where he meant to lock the door, but as it closed he just dropped to his knees and, like Alex held his head in his hands, taking short quick breaths, his entire body quaking in fear. Physically, he'd had stopped being a match for his son years ago, and knew that if Mork really lost control there wasn't anything anyone could do to stop him.

Meanwhile Annabel and Debra sat wide-eyed in the kitchen at Alex's altercation with his father. Then there was the sound of doors closing, followed by silence. Annabel knew in her heart that Alex would be Mork and headed tentatively to Alex's room, while Debra went to look for Kyle in his office. Annabel found Mork standing facing the corner, ears flat, his tail between his legs, whimpering slightly at every exhale. Debra knocked gently on the door to the study.

"Sweetheart, let me in ... What's just happened?"

Secretly, the entire family held that fear in the back of their minds at all times. Debra slowly opened the door to see Kyle hunched on the floor, his clothes dishevelled and hair ruffled, and her heart sunk. Debra held a silent, unforgiving terror in her heart that, in an uncontrollable moment of rage, Mork had finally bitten Kyle. Trying desperately to prepare herself for the worst, she took a deep breath and stammered, "Di-did he ... bite you?"

Kyle looked up sharply. "What? No, no. God, no, nothing like that."

Annabel scanned the room for some sign of a struggle or of blood, then slowly lowered herself onto the floor next to Mork, put her hand on his head and gently scratched behind his ears.

"It's all right, it's all right; everything's going to be all right."

She tried to fill her voice with calm confidence, hoping it would make it seem like she herself believed it. Mork slumped down and covered his face with his paws. She continued to scratch his head.

Debra sat down in front of Kyle on the floor. "What happened?"

He shook his head. He wanted to hide his fear and be strong but as he reached out to her his hands were still shaking, and he was so pale he was almost green.

"I've never seen any ... *thing* so angry before, let alone my own son. The rage, Debs, the rage! He literally threw me out of the room, like I was nothing. I don't think I've ever been so scared in my life; he looked like, well, like he could have done anything. I think we should call Raj. "

Debra's eyes grew wide and she took a few long, controlled breaths. "All right. Okay, I'll, uhmmm … I'll go do that."

She moved silently to the phone and made the call.

By the time Dr Cooper arrived, Kyle had retreated to the bedroom, to be left alone for a while, and it was left to Debra to explain as best she knew. The doctor immediately went to Mork and spent most of the evening there going through calming exercises to get him to sleep. When they were done, Debra was the only other person still awake, sitting quietly in the kitchen waiting for him.

"I've been going over this again and again in my mind and I think I'm just going to say it. Is Alex becoming a danger to the rest of the family? Is he losing his mind? Becoming like the werewolves we've read about in all these fucking horror books?"

There was desperation in her voice that she could no longer hide. Cooper reached across the table and placed a sympathetic hand over hers and held it tightly.

"No, I think he probably lost his temper in a mist of teenage hormones mixed with animal instinct. I think, from what you told me, he probably felt like he was being treated unfairly or like he was being ignored, that his side of the story wasn't being considered, as all teenage boys feel from time to time. And, as all teenage boys do at some point, he reacted, only with Alex it's coupled with the instincts and reactions of a wolf, so he reacted as any animal pushed into a corner, as though his life were being threatened."

Tears rolled silently down Debra's face. "S-so you d-don't think we're in danger?"

"No, and I don't want to tell you how to raise your son, but I think yelling first and asking questions later isn't a method that will work with him. I've spoken to too many teenagers whose parents have brought them to me to 'sort them out', and all they want, all they need, is for their parents to listen to their side of the story before just assuming that because they did something wrong, they were in the wrong."

Debra bit her bottom lip. "We try so hard, you know … and sometime we forget he's not just a normal boy. Oh God, I know it's bad, but I just wish he was a normal child, then I wouldn't have to be so afraid *all* the time … That sounds awful, I know, but I'm not just afraid he'll attack us, or other people, I think constantly about what would happen if someone found out what he was. Raj, I don't want someone to come and take him away."

She pulled her hands free and covered her face, realising that in her distress she had opened herself up more than she'd meant to. Cooper quickly rose and walked around the table to put his arms around her. A part of him wanted to reassure her that everything would be all right but at the same time he knew that giving her the opportunity to let her emotions out in this way was healthier. She cried until she simply couldn't any more, and staggered her way to bed. Cooper called his wife to say he wasn't coming home and set himself up in the spare room.

Chapter 19

Mork slunk into the kitchen the next morning, ears down and tail between his legs. Debra looked down as he walked in.

"I've called the school and told them that you won't be in for a few days. Dr Cooper's written a note that Annie's taking in. He's gone home already but he'll be back this afternoon to do some more work with you. So you can go back to bed if you want."

She gave him a sympathetic smile and his ears and tail perked up a little. He turned to his father for a moment, trying to think of a way to apologise. Then, in a fit of frustration, slumped off to the lounge. He jumped up onto his couch, curled up and went back to sleep. Before leaving for work, Kyle quietly crept in and sat across from Mork, staring at him silently. He thought about waking him to talk about what had happened but wasn't exactly sure what he'd say. Also, he couldn't shake the fragment of fear that was still haunting him. Slowly he got to his feet, walked over to Mork and gently scratched his ear before heading out.

Annabel dropped the letter off with Mr Reid's secretary first thing in the morning and was surprised at the level of concern she showed.

"Is he going to be all right? Poor thing, at home all alone ... Does the doctor say when he should be back at school?"

Annabel tilted her head to the side as she looked the secretary over. "Oh, don't worry, Alex will be just fine. If he's not back tomorrow, it'll be the next day for sure."

"Well, that's good to know," The secretary breathed a sigh of relief.

It occurred to Annabel that the woman was rather young, quite pretty and probably not very bright. So she smiled uncomfortably and beat a hasty retreat.

Mork woke to the sound of the phone ringing, which annoyed him because he was unable to answer it. After a few rings and a click, a woman's voice played into the answering machine.

"Hi, Alex, it's Judith, the secretary from school. I'm just calling to find out how you are, but I guess you're probably sleeping, poor thing. Sweet dreams, angel. Hopefully see you tomorrow."

Mork wandered over to the answering machine and wondered if he'd be able to delete the message without making it look like he'd messed with the machine. After some deliberation he decided that he'd have to either be Alex to do it properly or he'd draw Dr Cooper's attention to it. With that in mind he returned to his room, bounded up onto the bed and stared at the picture of himself, running through his routine for transforming. The conscious mind was willing but when the wolf and boy came face to face, the mental projection of Alex was still raging furiously and very quickly turned back to Mork. He came to as if waking from a nightmare, tail down and hair standing on end, wishing he could find some away to communicate this to Dr Cooper when he arrived. He lay back quietly, confused, wondering why he still came across so angry when all he really felt was regret. It wasn't long before he had drifted back to sleep, and didn't stir until woken sharply by a loud knock on the bedroom door. Mork leapt up and looked around to find Dr Cooper stood smiling at him from the doorway.

"Good afternoon. Glad to see you've got more spring in your step today. As it's almost two o'clock, I was thinking we should work in your room again, in case your mom gets home in the middle of a meditation."

Mork hopped off his bed and padded past Dr Cooper into the hallway, then turned around, grabbed onto the doctor's trousers with his teeth and gently pulled on them as he took a few steps backwards. Cooper knew what this meant and followed him through the house to the answering machine and saw the flashing light. He pressed the button and Judith's voice repeated the message.

"Oh, I see," said Dr Cooper flatly. Mork dropped his ears and looked pleadingly up at the man. "I'm guessing you want me to delete this?" Mork nodded. "All right then, but you're going to have to explain this to me later, you realise that don't you?"

Mork's mouth opened, his tongue lolled out and he nodded again. Dr Cooper laughed before deleting the message and the two of them returned to Alex's room to meditate. Cooper put on some classical music, filled the room with the smell of lightly heated lavender oil, wrapped Mork in a blanket and started a guided calming meditation, which ended with Mork coming face to face once again with his human self. This time, however, Alex was much more relaxed and, as usual, they crossed over, with Mork transforming into Alex again. He blinked open his eyes and, with controlled breathing, allowed himself to settle back into being human. When he was ready, he exhaled and stretched his arms and back.

"So ..." asked a curious Dr Cooper, "why is the school secretary calling you at home?"

"I think it's because she has a crush on me."

"And why would you think she has a crush on you?"

"Well," Alex continued cautiously, "she gave me a private tour of the school and then she phones me at home to check if I'm okay and, well, I think I've finally worked out what the funny girl smell is."

Dr Cooper couldn't help but laugh. Alex blinked a few times, then rubbed his eyes before looking up at the doctor.

"We really need to talk, Doc."

"Look, I understand it's hard being a teenager, and I can only imagine what it must be like to be a teenage werewolf. If you apologise to your father, he'll forgive you, in fact, he's probably already forgiven you."

"No, no, it's not that really. I can deal with that. What I'm worried about is that when I tried to change back on my own I found that the inner me was still so furious, screaming inside myself ... violent even. That's never happened before. I always kinda thought that Mork represented the emotional side and Alex the rational ... but now I don't know."

Dr Cooper put his hand to his mouth and stared at Alex for a moment and then, parting his fingers, said, "I think this is a conversation we should to have with your family."

Alex fell silent and rubbed his eyes again, trying to buy some time to think before having to answer.

"All right, let me put some clothes on and I'll meet you there."

Dr Cooper nodded, stood and left the room. Alex sat in silence for a few more minutes, staring at the pile of CDs and the guitar he'd got at school. It dawned on him in those moments that, in a way, he was looking at the life he had always wanted. Before he had been bitten, people had always said he would grow up to be an actor or a rock star. He then realised that it hadn't been hormones that had made him lash out but rather a spike in frustration at the life he was being forced into, and he could feel another small part of the child inside himself fall away. He knew that he was going to have to lie to his family in order to protect them, it wasn't their fault and they shouldn't have to suffer the guilt. He would tell them it must have been the hormones and he'll work harder at keeping himself in check. Alex closed his eyes and focused again by taking a series of long, deep breaths before going to face his family and tell them everything they expected to hear. Getting to his feet and pulling on some clothes he made his way into the kitchen where everyone was waiting for him. He took his seat and for a moment there was an awkward silence.

"Uhmmm, sorry."

Everyone looked at each other, except for Alex who looked at the table.

"I'm gonna try harder to keep hold of myself and stay focused. I think Dr Cooper's right, you know, hormones and things. I don't know, just new school stress and I did kinda spend the afternoon listening to angrier music than usual, so, yeah, sorry. I'll … I'll do better."

Debra and Kyle looked at each other.

"It's all right, my boy," Kyle ventured. "We understand that this must be a difficult time for any teenager and we can only imagine how much more complicated it is for you. And I'm sorry, too, for not hearing your side. I won't do that again; my stress at work mustn't come home with me, so I'm going to try harder too. We love you, son, don't forget that, no matter what, we're always going to be family."

Alex looked up at his father for the first time since sitting down and smiled then moved his gaze over to his mother, who, as he expected, had tears in her eyes.

"Aaw, Mom, no need for that."

"I'm allowed," mumbled Debra, with a childish smile.

Then Alex, in a moment of insight and wisdom, turned to his sister. "And thanks, sis, you're always there for me, I really appreciate that and I don't think I say that often enough."

Annabel looked down and made a tutt sound as tears began to well up in her eyes.

"Oh, that's not fair," she said, her voice upbeat but cracking.

Kyle reached across and put his hand on Debra's and gave it a comforting squeeze while Dr Cooper put his hand on Annabel's shoulder. The girls dried their tears and the boys all smiled, and yet in the back of Alex's mind he couldn't shake the lingering sadness of having to lie to the people he loved about how he was really feeling.

"So what's for dinner? 'Cos I'm famished!"

It took a little longer than usual but by the time the food was on the table, it was a normal family night. They ate, cracked jokes and laughed. By the time Dr Cooper went home, everyone was ready for bed to ensure a good start in the morning. Annabel spent an extra half an hour or so on the phone to Ryan, making plans for the weekend and filling each other in on their day, whereas Alex lay awake trying to read his favourite author to cheer himself up, but very quickly tossed the novel and wrote a sad, dark poem entitled "Gaps in clouds, like scars in the sky". For him, it meant that sometimes things that can look so beautiful can carry with it so much pain and leave deep vicious scars that no one can see. In reality, it was about finally being offered an opportunity to pursue the life he really wanted, but knew he was going to turn it down ...

The next morning Alex woke with a start to Annabel banging on his bedroom door.

"Get up! We're going to be late!"

He'd slept through his alarm. He felt a general sense of sadness wash over him at the thought of having to face a day at school where he'd have to lie to everyone about being sick, turn down the offer of singing in his new friends' band and pretend to take a serious interest in agriculture, which, since facing his true desire, now felt excruciating. After a few deep breaths, he made the conscious decision to not let it show, and just get on and do it. Jumping out of bed and quickly pulling on his uniform, he managed to reach the door before Annabel could assault it again.

"Why didn't you wake up when Mom knocked before?"

"I didn't hear her. Transformation can really take it out of you sometimes, you know."

"Eat it in the car, we need to go." Debra was already waiting at the front door.

Arriving at school, Alex was thrilled to discover that his day started with double Media. He was looking forward to the class itself, but didn't much like the idea of lying to his new friends. As he slowly made his way to class, he thought up the exact wording he would use when explaining to his friends where he'd been and, more importantly, why he couldn't join the band. By the time he reached the classroom the door was closed and everyone was already inside.

"Oh, you're back, I'm so glad you're feeling better!"

He turned to see the secretary bounding down the hallway towards him, preceded by that same smell that he'd been getting off her from the moment they had met. He dropped his bag and held his arms out, waiting for a hug. Judith jumped at the last moment and he caught and held her with ease, spinning around twice before putting her down. Without a word he smiled and pulling into the secretary, who after a moment of hesitation kissed him back. A moment later he unwrapped his arms and took a step back, his heart beating hard in his chest.

"So, I erased that answering machine message you left me and I'm guessing we can't really do this sort of thing in public, can we?"

Judith blushed and went a little weak at the knees. "No, but, uhmmm, I need to get to, and you need uhmmm ..."

"Well, I finish at two-thirty and I'm free the rest of the day, and I have trusting parents that won't ask where I am. What time do you finish up here?"

"Three?"

"Meet you outside of school?"

Judith blushed even harder. "Alright," she giggled. Well, uhmmm, bye."

And with that she quickly made her way back down the corridor. Alex smiled a broad confident smile and walked into class.

"Good morning, everybody!"

The class turned to face him as he stood mysteriously triumphant in the doorway.

"Mr Harris," said Ms Peel, "Welcome back. Glad to see you're feeling so much better."

"Sorry I'm late,' he said as he took his seat alongside Josh. "I'm still not exactly sure where everything is and I got a little lost."

"That's okay. You're actually just in time, we're about to start watching *Batman Returns*. I'm afraid you missed the end of *Batman*."

"That's all right, I've seen it before."

"Marvellous, but I do need you to stay behind after class. There are some notes you'll need and I just want to have a chat."

"Sure, okay."

With that Ms Peel nodded, switched off the lights and started the film. And yet, try as he may to stay focused, Alex's mind continued to drift toward the possible outcome of his planned after-school activity, and finally ended up with his head on his arms on his desk, only half paying attention to the film, which he'd also seen half a dozen times. And then, somewhere in the distance, he heard the Penguin cry out, "I'm not a man, I am an animal!"

And before he could stop himself he whispered to himself, "I know how that feels, bud."

His eyes turned from the screen to meet those of Ms Peel. For one terrible moment he thought she might pause the film and draw attention to his off-the-cuff comment, but she simply made a curious face and turned back to the movie. But the moment was sobering and it brought him back to earth with a thud, out of his head and back into the room. It wasn't the shock of almost being forced to explain something unexplainable, but the words, 'I'm an animal' had struck a chord, repeating itself over and over in his head. And then, all at once, he could feel his heart rate shoot up, and control begin to slip away.

"Alex? Dude, you all right?"

He turned to Josh who was staring at him, but no words came out.

"Dude, you're sweating, a lot."

Alex wiped his forehead and managed to gasp, "No."

By that point, any hope of holding onto himself was lost. In what looked like a single motion, Alex leapt from his seat to the door, and was out the classroom. His mind immediately turned to the new school buildings Judith had pointed out during his initial tour, all the classrooms were still empty. Ms Peel and the boys tore after him, but by the time they reached the door he was nowhere to be seen.

"Right, boys, follow me!" she announced and they all headed off at a run to Mr Reid's office. Judith had little time to protest as they marched past her desk and through the door.

"Alex Harris has just had some kind of fit and practically ran through my classroom door and now we don't know where he is."

The blood quickly drained from the faces of both Mr Reid and his secretary. The headmaster looked at Josh.

"Are you his friend?"

"Yes, sir."

"You know his sister?"

"Yes, sir?"

"Good, she's in Finance. Find her and tell her what's happened; maybe she has an idea of what to do. Judith, you phone his parents and get them here ASAP. Ms Peel, you and the other boys start looking for him. I'm going to call his doctor, and then come help with the search."

For a moment everyone stood motionless until Josh broke the silence.

"Right."

He hotfooted it out of the office in search of Annabel. Judith began frantically searching her files for the Harris' numbers. Ms Peel turned to Brandon and Danny and started issuing orders, and Mr Reid began searching his desk for that business card he prayed he hadn't tossed out.

Josh arrived first at the Accounting class, and thanked God he could spot Annabel as he burst through the door.

"Alex," he panted, "Alex has had some kind of a stroke, a fit *thing* and ran like a crazy person out of class and we can't find him."

"*What?*"

Josh stopped and thought for a moment. "Okay, maybe not an actual *stroke*, I didn't mean that ... But he started sweating and breathing funny, and then just ran out of room and disappeared."

Annabel gritted her teeth, scanned his face in the vain hope he was joking, but then quickly rose from her chair and headed for the door.

"Where are the boys' bathrooms?"

"Follow me."

Judith tried to keep herself calm as she dialled Kyle's number, not because she didn't want to worry him but because she was so upset herself. She could also hear Mr Reid on the line with Dr Cooper.

"No, I didn't see it myself, but I know he was off sick yesterday ... You're on your way, really? That's amazing, thank you, Doctor."

This instantly upset Judith even further. Why was Alex's doctor dropping everything and rushing to his school to find him? Could it really be that bad?

"Harris ... Hello?"

"Wha... Oh, sorry, uhmmm, this is Judith from Mr Reid's office."

"Sorry, who?"

"Mr Reid. The headmaster of TSF?"

"I'm on my way."

Kyle could hear the fear in her voice and knew instantly what must have happened. Debra, however, was in class teaching and her phone was off. Judith tried calling a number of times before giving up and heading out to help with the search.

Kyle recognised Raj Cooper's car in the parking lot as he pulled in. Heart racing, he, like Dr Cooper and Annabel, knew that they needed to find him before anyone else stumbled across him and then try get him out before someone found a massive wolf hiding near a pile of shredded school uniform.

Mork was breathing in short gasps. Whereas after fighting with his father he found his inner self violent, now the boy inside sat weeping, whispering.

"Why couldn't I keep control; why couldn't I get through one day?"

Mork snapped back as a familiar smell drifted in from under the door. His sister and someone else were getting close. He wracked his brain for a way to let her know where he was without alerting the other person, whose smell he recognised but couldn't place. He knew he'd left scratch marks on the door and hoped and trusted her to know what to do.

Annabel and Josh raced through the corridors looking for any sign that might lead them to Alex. Annabel stopped for a moment to order her thoughts.

"What's that building over there?" she asked.

"It's going to be the new science building or something like that. Why? Do you think he's in there?"

"I don't know, but I'm going to find out, you continue to look here."

"Okay, meet back here in five?"

"Let's make it fifteen, sweetheart," she winked at him and ran off.

Josh blushed and stammered before remembering that he was on a mission and ducked into the next room.

Annabel knew that Alex would look for somewhere secluded in which to hide. It didn't take long before she found herself standing in front of a claw-marked bathroom door in the unused science building.

"Mork? Mork, are you in there?"

Her voice released him from the terror that had gripped him, and a series of whimpers escaped him. She quickly ducked into the room, struggled for a moment to find the light switch then spotted her brother. He looked more defeated then ever before.

"Oh, Mork, don't worry, Dad's on his way."

Mork sniffed the air and she turned just in time to see the door open behind her and her dad and Dr Cooper walk in. Kyle spun around to lock the door behind them, but the door locks had not yet been installed.

"Dammit! I'll stand outside, and tell everyone we've found you and that it's being handled by the doctor."

Dr Cooper made his way over to children and knelt down.

"Is there anything I can do to help?" Annabel looked at him.

"You can sit with us if you like, join in the meditation."

She nodded nervously, then sat down next to them.

Kyle stood resolute in front of the bathroom door, scrolling through his phone for the school's number, hoping he could call off the search, when a boy of about Alex's age hurtled towards him. It occurred to him that there was no plan to replace Alex's school uniform, which had probably been destroyed.

"Whoa, son, where's the fire?"

"Oh, uhmmm … Sorry, sir, I'm just looking for my friend who's gone missing."

"You mean Alex?"

Josh narrowed his eyes in confusion. "Yes?"

Kyle smiled and held out his hand. "Hi there, I'm Alex's father, Kyle Harris."

Josh took his hand and shook it. "Josh. A pleasure to meet you, sir."

"Nice to meet you. We've found Alex and his doctor's tending to him now. You can relax, son, he's going to be fine."

"Oh good. So what actually happened?"

Kyle thought for a moment on the best way to approach the matter.

"Well, you know how when there's an earthquake, you have the initial major quake, then for a few days afterwards there's the risk of smaller aftershocks?"

Josh thought for a moment. "No, but I understand the concept."

Kyle laughed and shook his head. "Well, that's what's happened here. This was just an unexpected aftershock following the main quake two days ago. It doesn't happen too often and he'll be fine by this afternoon."

Josh looked down at the floor, still a little confused. "Oh, well, good that he's going to be all right."

"Yes, yes. Perhaps we should've kept him home today but he didn't want to miss too much school in the first week, but I assure you he'll be back to normal in a few hours."

"Back to normal?"

Kyle tightened his jaw for a moment. "Well, normal for Alex. It's a longstanding illness that he'll have to live with for the rest of his life." Kyle let his gaze slip past the boy. "If I'm honest, as a father it's not always easy to face up to the fact that your kid's sick, is always going to be sick and there isn't anything that he can do about it. You know what I mean?"

Josh smiled nervously and looked around for a reprieve, someone who could help alleviate the awkwardness of the situation.

"Well, no, I'm afraid I don't, sir. I mean, Mr Harris."

"No, of course not, and I hope you never do. Right, well, you can go back to class. Tell your teacher that Alex won't be coming back to class today and probably not tomorrow either. Also, if you see the headmaster or the secretary, that's a good lad, and thank you for helping look for him."

Josh continued to smile like a fool but was grateful to be able to leave, which he did at speed.

Inside the bathroom, Annabel witnessed for the first time in her life her brother struggle, and fail, to turn back into human form. Above all, it stuck her hard how painful it looked. Mork slumped onto the ground defeated.

"Don't give up," she pleaded.

Dr Cooper sighed in frustration, wishing he could just ask what was going on inside.

"We're going to get through this," he tried to reassure the boy. "Okay, Mork, look into your sister's eyes, find your humanity there. Don't think about Alex, focus on Annabel. Annabel, I need you to sit as still as you can, try to keep your breathing and blinking regular. You up for it?"

"Uhmmm … I'll try."

They locked eyes and Dr Cooper started guiding them through the meditation again, adapting it to include Annabel. Mork focused on his sister's eyes, trying to fight the waves of anxiety and fear until at last he felt the link break and the transformation finally begin. Within moments the bright green eyes turned blue and Alex sat where Mork had been. Washed in sweat and tears.

"I ... I ... feel ..."

Alex reached out a hand to touch Annabel's face, but collapsed onto Dr Cooper and started whimpering from sheer exhaustion.

"Go fetch your father."

Annabel jumped up and quickly went to the door; cautiously, she opened it to see her dad talking to Mr Reid and the secretary. For a moment, they all stopped and stared at her as she poked her head out from behind the door.

"Uhmmm, Dad, we need your help, and possibly some blankets."

The secretary who was losing her grip on herself quickly snapped, "I'll go get some from the nurse's office."

As she scuttled off, Mr Reid turned to Annabel and headed for the door. Then a flash of inspiration hit Annabel.

"We're also going to need a plastic bag for his clothes, he threw up a little on his uniform. And when I say a little, I mean a whole lot."

The headmaster made a slightly sickened face. "Right, of course. I'll be right back with that."

"Quick thinking," Kyle smirked.

"What can I say, not a werewolf's sister for nothing."

The two then ducked back into the bathroom. Dr Cooper looked up at them as they approached, Alex now unconscious in his arms.

"Any idea how we're going to get him out of here?"

"Annabel told the headmaster Alex vomited on himself so we need blankets and a plastic bag for his clothes."

Dr Cooper looked at her and smiled, impressed.

"Someone should wait outside for them then. Even if they think they understand the situation, they don't, and it looks far worse when you don't know."

Annabel sighed and left. She tried to make it look like a chore but, after watching her brother's struggle so, she was relieved to be able to take a moment from it all to collect her thoughts. Mr Reid returned first, followed quickly by the secretary. Annabel thanked them both then asked to be left alone while they wrap Alex up and carry him to one of the cars. Mr Reid smiled graciously and turned to leave. Judith, however, searched her mind for a reason to stay but had to follow so as to not look conspicuous. Annabel took the things inside and scooped up the torn cloths and tried to avoid looking at her naked brother.

"Alex's trousers are still mostly intact, someone want to put them on him?"

Kyle took them from her. "You're doing great, sweetheart," he said. "I'm very proud of you."

He then gently pulled them onto his sleeping son and wrapped the rest of him in the blanket. He cradled Alex in his arms and, with the help of Dr Cooper, got to his feet. Naturally, he struggled a little, Alex was no longer the little boy he had been when this had all started. Dr Cooper held the door open and they made their way to the parking lot and Kyle laid Alex on the back seat of Dr Cooper's car. Kyle wanted to take the boy home, but he had a court date that he couldn't miss, whereas the doctor had already had his appointments pushed back. They shook hands, Kyle kissed Annabel and they all went their separate ways. It had been a long, long day.

Chapter 20

Alex opened his eyes. He felt drained, exhausted, his pallor grey. He pulled himself up from the pillow, reached for the water next to his bed and gulped it down. There was a brief note on the bedside table:

You're off school until further notice – Dr Cooper

He swung his legs off the bed, pulled on his clothes and headed cautiously to the kitchen.

"Well, good morning, sleepy head. How you feeling?" Debra and Dr Cooper were chatting over a cup of coffee.

"Tired, confused … and what's the meaning of this?" Alex held up the note to Dr Cooper. The room went quiet for a moment,

"It's obvious that something's out of balance, and I feel it's best that we get you back in control before you return to school."

Alex sighed, clenched his jaw and rolled his eyes. Parts of him wanted to growl and vent his anger, but he was almost overwhelmed by the sense that it just didn't matter, that nothing mattered.

"Whatever! I don't want to talk about this now … Have I missed dinner?"

Debra cast a concerned look at Dr Cooper. "Uhmmm, no, honey, it's going to be ready in about fifteen minutes, but Dad's stuck in court and your sister's at Ryan's tonight so it's just us for dinner."

"Okay, well I'm gonna go shower."

He turned abruptly and walked out. Debra turned back to Dr Cooper. "What do you think's going on?"

Cooper sighed. "It's hard enough being a teenage boy in a new school, I mean, I bet every boy in that place feels like they're turning into a hairy beast just dealing with normal puberty. But with him ... it's just more extreme."

"With Alex everything has always been more extreme, even before he was a werewolf," Debra let out a defeated sigh. "I just don't know what I'm going to do with him."

"I wouldn't worry too much, Debra. He's a smart boy; he'll sort himself out. He's just ... teething. I'll sit with him this evening and see if I can't get to the root of the problem. It might be as simple as that and he can go back to school tomorrow."

"I hope so."

Alex sat in the shower, allowing the water wash over him and drown out all other noise. He closed his eyes and tried to piece together what had happened to him that day. It was easy for him; he knew precisely why there was conflict. He felt as though Mork was holding him back, keeping him from fulfilling his dreams and it made him frustrated and angry. What he didn't know was what he would say to Dr Cooper and his parents. His mind was consumed by the internal debate: his unwavering loyalty to his family and his desire to protect their normal lives from his abnormal one. He moved from the bathroom to his bedroom and collapsed on the bed, still wet and wrapped only in a towel, his mind still slowly spinning downwards. A gentle knock at the door woke him from his morbid daydreams.

"Can I come in?" Dr. Cooper's voice.

"Yeah, just one second," Alex coughed. He quickly ran the towel over himself and pulled on some clothes, then opened the door.

"So, what's going on with you?" Dr Cooper walked over and sat on the bed.

Alex was still debating the answer himself. "You see, the problem is, I …" He hesitated. "I'm starting to feel like it's me and everyone else. I can't really talk to you, because you're so apart of my family that I might as well be telling everyone and it's everyone including you I'm trying to protect."

Cooper cocked his head and thought very carefully about what to say and how to say it. "Well, yes … I suppose that since you're no longer a child, we need to change the rules. What if I make a promise that from now on what you tell me we keep between us, just us, doctor/patient confidentiality? I am your doctor after all."

Silence settled on the room for a moment as Alex willed up the courage to open up about his feelings. Then he slumped to the floor with his back against the wall.

"For the first time in my life, Mork is stopping me from really having the life I would choose. I want to join that band, I want to be a famous rock star, and I want to … I want to be able to tell my new friends the truth. I believe Mork is fighting me because I'm blaming him for it all, and, yes, I suppose hormones are playing their part, so you aren't totally wrong, but the real reason is that I'm not happy with this planned *normal* life ... It's not what I want; it's not working for me any more, but I can't think of a way that works for me and my family, so I picked them and ... well, I'm miserable for it, which makes me feel like a bad person and ... and I blame Mork for all of it."

Alex took a deep breath and felt a cold shiver run down his spine. He was starting to feel very exposed, vulnerable even.

"So ... can I go back to school now?"

Dr Cooper was slightly dumbstruck. He hadn't realised how hard it would be to hear Alex confess to being so unhappy.

"Yes."

"I'm sorry, Doc, I didn't mean drop all of that on you. It's just that ... that's what's wrong. But I need to learn how to control myself better."

"Well, I can help with that, or at least I can try."

Alex held out his hand. "Deal?"

Dr Cooper smiled and took it. "Deal!"

Alex traced his eyes along the lunar map to see when the next full moon was. Dr Cooper sat with him in silence for a few minutes, wondering if he should say something or whether Alex had more to say.

"It's full moon again soon. It's always full moon soon."

"You sure you're going to be all right, Alex?"

"Yeah, I think I just need to get hold of myself a little, you know. I'm the only one who can really do this right. I mean, at the end of the day it's really up to me to do it or not do it."

It was the doctor's turn to take a long slow breath. "I'm sorry it has to be that way."

"Thanks, Doc. Don't worry, I'll be all right. Really. In other news, how long until dinner is ready?"

"Now that you mention it, I think it's probably done by now."

Debra tried to hide her concern behind cheerful banter, but Alex could smell the fear all through the house.

"Don't worry, Mom, I'm not totally crazy. I've just got a lunar tick." He pulled a silly face and frantically blinked one eye.

Both Debra and Dr Cooper laughed instinctively, which cut through the tension.

***

The next morning Alex woke up a good hour before his alarm clock was set to go off. He crept out of bed and quietly made his was through the house to see if there were any leftovers he could polish off before everyone else woke. His dreams still dancing about in his mind, he couldn't shake the visions of a wolf running through the desert to some unknown, unreachable destination. Dreams like that had become common for him; usually, he enjoyed the sense of freedom that came with them but this time it just felt like a harsh reminder of how trapped he felt. The subtle creaking of floorboards that only he could hear prompted him to start making coffee for everyone else.

"Morning, family," he quipped as they finally made their way into the kitchen

"Morning, son. Why are you awake this early? Wolves are supposed to be nocturnal."

"Yes, well, this wolf went to bed at eight last night so getting up at six just seemed natural."

Annabel was the last to arrive and Alex instantly noticed a difference in the way she smelt. It wasn't anything obvious, just a very subtle change in an otherwise familiar smell, definitely still Annabel, but different somehow. It reminded him of Judith and then remembered that Annabel had gone over to Ryan's house the night before, and he realised what it meant. He managed to contain himself but was determined to find an opportunity to drop the hint that he knew precisely what had happened there.

"Alex, did you eat *all* the leftovers from last night?" Debra stared into the fridge.

"Oh, yeah, sorry, I woke up really hungry."

"Fantastic. Well, I guess it's cereal for breakfast then."

He smiled a toothy smile in way of a fake apology. Kyle laughed and began to help get breakfast ready, which gave Alex the opportunity he was waiting for. He locked eyes with Annabel, smiled, tapped his nose and said as quietly as possible, "Have a good night then?"

The blood rushed to his sister's cheeks and her mouth dropped open. He quickly put his finger to his lips and winked at her. She felt an urge to cry and blurt out the whole story. Secretly she'd been dying to tell someone about her night from the moment it was over but didn't really have anyone she felt like she could trust. Alex having worked it out for himself took that worry away and it seemed natural to confess everything to him. Him not blurting it out but in fact letting her know that he was going to keep her secret made her feel safe, offering a deeper kinship with her brother, something she didn't think possible up until then.

All through breakfast and the drive to school Annabel thought about how she was going to tell Alex about her night with Ryan, and Alex about how he was going to explain himself to his classmates and Judith.

Attached to the door of Alex's locker was a pink handwritten note.

Please come straight to my office once you get this. Mr R Reid.

Alex rolled his eyes and slowly made his way to the headmaster's office. He'd been hoping to put off seeing Judith for as long as possible. At the office he said with a nervous smile, "Morning, darlin', how are you today? I found this on my locker door."

He held out the pink slip and tried not to look like too much of a twit.

"You're here, I mean back, I'm so glad," Judith's eyes lit up when she saw him. "How you feeling?"

"Me? Oh, I'm fine. Don't worry about me, strong as an ox. I believe Mr Reid wants to see me?"

Judith giggled, which made Alex slightly more nervous, and he tried to sniff as subtly as possible.

"Of course, go right on in."

Alex narrowed his eyes as he headed into the office. It was empty, no sign of the headmaster. The door closed behind him and he turned to find Judith smiling at him.

"See, the truth is that Mr Reid is out all day today at board meetings, and when your mom called to say you'd be back at school today, I just thought that, as we couldn't have our little date yesterday, we could pick up where we left off?"

Alex's heart leapt about in his chest up and he felt a stirring in his groin. He took long, deep breaths in the hope that it would add some clarity to the moment but before he could really order his thoughts she stepped in close and whispered, "I'm not wearing any panties."

Alex didn't even try to fight it. Passion took over and before he realised what was going on, his tongue was in her mouth and she was guiding his hand up her dress. In a remarkable moment she pulled away from him, smiled, then dropped to her knees and gave him his first ever blowjob. Alex looked at her through wide, anxious eyes for the first few moments then closed his eyes and focused on his breathing, on staying human. After a few minutes he opened them again and looked down at her and, despite his attempts not to, began to laugh. Judith pulled back and looked up at him.

"Are you laughing at me?"

"No, no, I'm laughing because this ... is awesome."

"Oh, you're so cute."

She winked at him and went back to what she was doing. It didn't take too much longer before he crinkled his face, and started to groan uncontrollably. She quickly pulled her mouth away.

"Oh no, I'm not done with you yet."

He decided not to say anything in case what he said was just stupid and it all came to an abrupt end. She unzipped her dress and let it fall to the floor and suddenly he was standing, penis out, in front of a naked woman. He quickly pulled his shirt off. She bit her bottom lip as her eyes traced him up and down. Then she took his hand and led him over to the desk.

"Have you ever done anything like this before?"

He thought for a very moment about what the correct answer would be.

"No?"

She giggled again. "Well, don't worry. You just relax, I'm going to help you."

Judith turned around and bent over the desk, then reached around and guided Alex into her. After a few seconds of fumbling, he relaxed into what was happening and found him self surprisingly calm. He had always been afraid that sex would get his heart rate up too high and he'd not be able to keep himself from transforming. He was still a little worried about what would happen at the end but he tried to push that thought out of his mind and enjoy the moment. It was not very hard to do. Judith began to moan and push back against him more vigorously as he found his mind torn between wanting to get to climax and hoping he could hold off long enough to satisfy her. He quickly gave up on the idea of prolonging the experience when he let out groan that sounded more animal than man. Gambling with himself, he focused entirely on what he was doing and how good it felt, then quickly pulled out just as he finished.

"What's wrong?"

"Huh, uhmmm, well ... sorry?"

"What? Oooh!"

She giggled, then turned around and propped herself up on the desk facing him. He wondered what he should do but nothing came to mind so he just stood in front of her, his arms at his side, trying not to stare at her naked breasts. A sudden urge to leave washed over him, but before he could voice the urge she pulled him closer again and kissed him.

"You should probably get to class. And don't worry, you'll last longer with practice, and I think we should get plenty of practice."

Alex took a deep breath, forgetting for a moment his urge to run, and cleared his throat. "Agreed," he said.

Alex pulled his trousers up from around his ankles, then searched around for his shirt while Judith slipped her dress on. As he buttoned his shirt something occurred to him.

"Can I quickly try something?"

She looked at him and smiled, "Okay ..."

He walked over to her, slipped his hand into her dress, flipped out her breast and kissed her nipple.

"Thank you," he said.

The scene quickly flashed through his mind and Alex blushed at Judith, who bit her bottom lip.

"It was my pleasure."

She turned around and Alex quickly zipped her dress up and they headed for the door, which opened just as they reached it. They froze as they stared at a surprised headmaster.

"Why are you two in my office?"

There was a brief silence before Alex said, "I just wanted to come and apologise for what happened yesterday, sir. I really didn't mean to cause such a fuss at school."

A part of Mr Reid really wanted to believe the boy, because the reality of the situation was more than he wanted to deal with.

"That a very nice sentiment, Mr Harris, but sadly it makes me wonder which class you left to come offer your apologies. Or why would you wait half an hour in my office when I wasn't supposed to be here today? As I'm sure my secretary informed you. And the question I really, deeply don't want to ask but feel I have to is, what is that on the floor?"

They turned to look at the mess Alex had left on floor in front of Mr Reid's desk, then looked back at him.

Mr Reid's face was scarlet, the veins in his neck fit to burst. "Judith! He's sixteen and a student. You are faculty ... This is *illegal.*"

Alex's heart stepped up a few notches and panic started to creep up on him.

"I lied to her, sir."

Rushed out of his mouth before anyone else could say anything, Judith and Mr Reid both turned and said to look at him.

"I ... I told her I was 18 and that, uhmmm, because I'm a legal adult, it's not illegal."

Mr Reid frowned.

"She has access to your school records, son."

"Yeah, I know, I told her we listed my age as a few years younger on my school sheet so that I could get in because I had to miss school because of my illness. *I* made this happen, sir, I manipulated the situation. Don't punish her, sir, it's my fault. I've lived with an illness for a long time and I can't live a full, normal life, so I thought I'd try speed up the better parts in case ... in case my life runs out."

Listening to himself, Alex realised that woven into his little lie was a strong thread of truth and it worked towards calming him. He knew exactly how manipulative he was being, but it was necessary. He felt a little bad for Mr Reid, who really had been backed into a corner, but he couldn't let Judith take full blame. The headmaster glared at them both for a few seconds before speaking.

"All right, both of you sit down. Actually, Alex, would you please clean up your mess, then sit down. I'm afraid I'm still going to have to call your parents."

Judith moved very quickly and quietly to the chair in front of the desk and sat down, eyes cast down at the floor, panicked at the idea that she'd broken the law. Alex looked around the room, spotted a box of tissues on the desk and quickly pulled a few free and cleaned up before slipping into the chair next to Judith. Mr Reid moved slowly to behind his desk.

"The reasons behind this aside, I cannot just let you get away with it, either of you. We're going to tell your parents that I caught you two kissing in my office and we're going to see what they have to say. Judith, if they insist you be removed, I'm afraid my hands are tied, but you can't be punished by the law. Alex, I'm going to have to suspend you for two weeks. I'll have your teachers put together a list of what work you must have done before you come back. If it's not done, we'll have another meeting and you may be expelled. Do you both understand?"

"Yes, sir."

"Good."

His tone was firm, authoritative, leaving no more room for excuses, lies or negotiation.

"Sir, you'll have to call the school where my mother works; her phone will be off by now, and I think it's best if we deal with her and not my lawyer dad."

"I think you shouldn't say anything further, Mr Harris. But thank you for the advice."

Mr Reid flipped through his contact list and made the call he dreaded making.

"All right," he said as he replaced the receiver, "your mom will be here in about ten minutes.

The ten or so minutes it took for Debra to arrive felt like a lifetime. Alex could tell by the look on his mother's face that he was probably in trouble. Big trouble. Mr Reid stood up from his desk as she entered.

"Mrs Harris, thank you for coming down. I'm sorry, however, that it has to be under these unfortunate circumstances."

"Of course ... But tell me, what exactly are the circumstances? You were rather vague on the phone."

"Perhaps you should have a seat."

Debra stared daggers at her son, who shamefully got up from his seat and pulled up another.

"Right, well, here it is ... I came back to my office much earlier than expected and found these two in here in an ... intimate circumstance. Nothing too bad, but still, Judith is staff and I'm sure, as a teacher, you're well aware of the consequences. Alex has currently been suspended for ten school days and, unless certain school requirements are met, he may not be allowed to return. Normally, expulsion would be on the cards, but he is a new student and potentially a very good one, so I'm going to give him a chance. Now, Judith is twenty-four and, as you may or may not remember, she's my secretary. By all accounts, I should fire her on the spot, but as your son pointed out to me, he is a mature-looking lad, and she is a very good secretary, so I thought I'd confer with you as to how she should be dealt with. If you'd like her removed from the school, you just need to say. How would you like to proceed?"

Debra looked Judith up and down, then over at Alex, who smiled sheepishly and waved at his mother. Debra dug in her bag, pulled out her car keys and held them out towards him.

"Go fetch your things and go wait in the car. We'll discuss this with your father when he gets home. You don't need to be here for the rest of the meeting, your fate will be decided later."

"No, but Mom, it's not her ..."

"Do not even *try* to argue with me."

There was no mistaking the severity in Debra's tone, and Alex knew better than to answer back. He took the keys and skulked from the room, straight to the car, his school bag flung over his shoulder. It had become common practice to keep at least one CD of calming classical music in each car. He slipped it into the player and sat with his eyes closed. The mix of carnal excitement and the concern for Judith made for an uncomfortable cocktail of emotions. Also, that he might have tarnished the family name in some way filled him with a sense of failure.

Debra returned to the car within minutes, which made him even more nervous. He knew better than to ask questions so silently he handed her the car keys. Lips pursed, she turned the ignition and they drove off without a word. It was only once they'd pulled off school property that she turned to him.

"So, you and the school secretary, huh?"

To his surprise, he could hear a slight lift in her voice.

"Yeah."

"So, did Reid walk in just before or just after?"

It occurred to him that these were not the questions of an angry mother.

"Tell you what Mom, ask again and I'll tell you who's the real *headmaster* of that school."

Debra lurched slightly as she tried to contain herself, but lost control very quickly and erupted in helpless hysterical laughter, which instantly set Alex off too.

"I ... I can't believe you hooked up with the secretary."

"I can't believe you're fine with this."

She wiped tears of laughter from her eyes. "Well, I'm not! Well, okay, maybe I am ... I don't know. But you have to admit, it's funny, she's, like, ten years older than you and, of course, she's gorgeous. Hahaha! But, Alex, in the *headmaster's* office, you little shit!"

He shook his head in disbelief.

"Your father's going to be so pissed!" she went on before stopping for a minute. "Actually," she said, "maybe not ... He won't show it, of course, but he may even be a little proud. After all, you're not the first Harris to seduce a member of school staff, you know."

Alex covered his eyes with his hands. "Oh my God! Stop!"

He cracked back up into helpless fits of laughter. For a moment he felt entirely at ease, like he was part of the family and not the family burden. As he blinked away the tears, a flash of light caught his attention and he turned just in time to see the grille of an eighteen-wheeler careening through a red light and heading straight for them.

They never felt the impact, never heard the squeal of tyres or the shattering of glass.

Chapter 21

Kyle had been sitting outside Alex's hospital room for three and a half hours before Dr Cooper eventually emerged.

"How is he?"

"Stable, alive, but it's a miracle. He's still unconscious; apparently, he's been given a fairly strong sedative as well as morphine to help him sleep. Between the two they should also work to keep his mood low and calm, if you know what I mean."

"Thank God. Can I go in and see him?"

"His left arm and leg are in casts and there's some damage to his face. Quite a lot actually. No broken bones, but it looks like the car window must have burst inwards when the truck hit them. It's actually amazing he doesn't have more severe injuries; normally in these situations the side that's hit is more like a beanbag than a body."

Kyle shut his eyes and turned away. Nothing in him was ready or able to deal with that kind of mental imagery.

"We both know what's kept him alive, Doc ... How long should it be until he wakes up?"

"Given that it's him, I don't know, maybe ... five hours tops, but maybe as little as two."

"Rajan, I need to ask you the biggest favour." Tears began to well in Kyle's eyes and he had to swallow before he could speak. "I ... I just can't, I need you to ..." His voice was broken, desperate.

Dr Cooper put on a brave face and nodded. Kyle turned away in a weak attempt to hide his pain.

"Thank you, I have to go be with Debra. I know he's my son, but I just—"

Dr Cooper allowed himself to cut Kyle short.

"You don't have to make excuses. Go do what you have to do, and I'll do what I have to. I don't want to be anywhere else either. Together, we'll get through this."

Kyle wished in that moment that he had the capacity or personal strength to wrap himself around Dr Cooper and just let go, but he couldn't bring himself to do it, so he simply walked away.

Dr Cooper took a deep breath and then returned to Alex's room to sit by his bedside and wait for him to wake. It was more than two hours before Alex stirred and opened his eyes. Instantly, he knew he was somewhere strange, and couldn't move easily, but there was a very familiar smell.

"Doc? Doc, is that you?"

Dr Cooper quickly got to his feet, rushed to the side of the bed so that Alex would be able to see him without having to move.

"Alex. Yes, it's me, I'm here."

"What's going on?"

"Don't try to move. You've been in a car accident. Your left arm and leg have been badly broken. How much can you remember?"

Alex searched his memory for something useful but nothing came.

"I ... I don't know."

"How do you feel?"

"Strange, tired. But there's no pain?"

"You're still feeling the effects of the morphine and Benzo."

Alex let himself swim through his mind again.

"I've not felt this far from Mork in a very long time."

"What?"

"It's almost like ... like he's not there; but he is there, he's always there, lurking in the back of my mind. I know I put on a sad face about it sometimes, but I feel safe knowing he's always there watching over me, looking after me. Like you, Doc, always there when I need you, helping me, making sure I'm going to be all right.'

He managed a wan smile. The doctor tried to smile back but couldn't hide the pain in his own eyes.

'What's up, Doc? I smell sadness. You sad?"

"Alex, you need to take a deep breath and focus, there's more ..."

Alex tilted his head to the side, in curious. An ice-cold shiver ran down his spine as his memory began creeping back.

"Mom. Mom was in the car ... She was driving. How is she? She all right?"

Dr Cooper put his hands on Alex's hands. "I'm afraid your mom suffered far more serious injuries than you. The doctors did everything they could to try to save her, but ... but it was just too much."

"No. No ... no. Please don't say it, Doc. Please don't tell me what I think you're about to tell me."

"I'm so sorry, my boy. I'm so, so sorry. It's a miracle that you survived. Your mother, I'm afraid, wasn't so fortunate."

Alex turned his head sharply away. "No, no, no – no! Please, no. Please ... Fuck you, no! NO! NOOOO!" He started thrashing from around on the bed.

"Alex! Alex, stop!" Dr Cooper squeezed his hand as tight as he could. "Alex! Look at me!"

Alex stiffened himself flat against the bed and screamed so loudly that the doctor had to cover his ears. Anxious, he watched Alex carefully, trying to determine whether the heightened emotions would have any effect on the boy. But to his surprise, Alex's teeth hadn't begun to elongate and his eyes weren't turning green. What he saw was the animal inside reacting to the news but struggling to emerge in bodily form; the boy's body was too damaged; too many chemicals to work through.

Tears streamed down Alex's face as he tried to haul himself off the bed. Dr Cooper wrapped his arms around the boy and held him as tightly as he could. Within seconds, a team of nurses was at his side to help subdue the boy and injected another dose of Benzodiazepine into his IV. Immediately, Alex's thrashing began to subside and he finally crumpled, weeping, into Dr Cooper's shoulder. It only took a few seconds for the drug to take its full effect and Alex once again slipped into the dark chemical blackness. Dr Cooper stood up and composed himself.

"Thanks everyone, very well timed."

The nurses all looked on in astonishment. How could one patient have made that much noise?

"Some set of lungs he's got, hey? Never have I ever heard anything like that outside of an opera house."

The nurses smiled politely but none of them were convinced. The doctor heard their whispers as they returned to their station. It was all such a damn mess, he thought to himself. Rajan Cooper put his head in his hands and for the first time since the accident allowed himself to cry.

Chapter 22

Alex remained hospitalised for a further three days for observation. Meanwhile, Kyle had put together the paper work to get Debra's body flown to Canada to be buried on the family farm. Annabel had taken on the task of calling family members to inform them of the tragedy, so spent most of the time crying into the phone. Ryan kept trying to find ways to comfort her and eventually, when Annabel had exhausted herself so from crying that she fell asleep, took over the job from her. The rest of the family had all headed to the farm the moment they heard the news. They wanted to deal with it together, as a family.

On his discharge, Alex didn't say anything on the drive home. He was quietly relieved to be leaving the hospital, but still anxious about getting into a car. Kyle had to help him into the house, as the hospital had insisted he use a wheelchair.

"Right, I'm gonna go upstairs and pack some things for you. If you're tired, let me know. Annie's made up the downstairs room for you."

"Thanks, Dad. When exactly is the flight again?"

"Tomorrow afternoon."

"And today is ...?"

"Saturday."

Kyle had managed to set his feelings aside in order to focus organising as much as he could. Despite getting a final sedative just before leaving the hospital, he was already more alert, and wondered if he wasn't building up immunity to the drug.

"Dad, when do we land in Canada?"

"Leave Sunday afternoon, and arrive very, very early Monday morning."

Alex's head dropped. "It's full moon Monday. You know that, right?"

The blood drained from Kyle's face as he turned to face his son, leaving him with an overwhelming sense of failure.

"Which of course means that, as there isn't an earlier flight, I have to stay here. Which means ... I can't go to my mother's funeral."

Kyle put both his hands over his mouth, paralysed at the realisation that he'd overlooked one of the most important details his family had to take into account when travelling.

"What's going on?" Annabel walked in on the conversation. Annabel's eyes instantly teared up when she saw the grey face of her father. "What's happened?"

"I, uhmmm ... I can't go." Alex used his one good arm and leg to steer the wheelchair towards his new room.

"Wait! What? No, Da-aad?"

"I forgot to check," Kyle dropped his hands and took a deep breath. "I forgot to check the lunar calendar."

"What? No, but time difference, surely that'll do it? No, he *has* to come."

"Time difference is four hours, flights about twelve, gives him about an hour's grey area when he could turn on the plane." Kyle's voice was flat. He'd given up. It was the final straw and broke his spirit completely. All he wanted to do now was go to bed and hope for a better tomorrow, and that's exactly what he did.

Annabel turned to follow her brother, who had managed to hoist himself onto the bed. He was lying on his back trying to find the most comfortable position for his good arm so he could sleep. She stood at the door, unsure of what to say or how to say it. After a minute of them staring at each other, she eventually walked over and climbed onto the bed with him. Alex put his arm around her and she began to cry. He swallowed hard and managed to hold back his own tears.

"Congrats on losing your virginity."

Annabel laughed a little through her tears, but said nothing. They just lay there until they fell asleep.

Kyle couldn't bear sleeping in his own bed so had unofficially moved into Alex's room. He lay on the bed and let his thoughts tumble into the dark realisations he'd been so actively trying to avoid. Despite almost dozing he was relieved to hear his phone ring, and reached for it quickly, desperate for whatever distraction it would offer.

"Harris speaking."

"Kyle, it's Raj. How are things?"

"That a trick question, Raj?"

"Sorry, man. But I have news. Good news, good news, and not-so-good news."

"Okay, give it to me in that order."

"Good news is I managed to swap all Alex's blood samples with yours."

"Good."

"The other good news is that the tests I did on his blood show no abnormalities for him, so he's fine."

"Wonderful, thank you. That is good news. So what's the bad news?"

"Well, your blood work came back from the labs and your cholesterol levels are getting dangerously high. It's very early stages, but I think we need to talk about changing your diet and lifestyle, otherwise you're on the road to have a heart attack."

"Hell, man. Really?"

"Yes, but don't worry, I specialise in this sort of thing so I'll help you out here."

"But I eat fairly well anyway. I mean, thanks to you and Alex, we don't have a bad diet in this house."

"True, but it'll be offset by a high stress job, so you need to eat slightly better than most people to counter that, eat things that actively bring cholesterol levels down."

"Well, that sucks."

"Well, you could just quit your job."

"Raj, my wife's just died and I'm now the single parent of two, somehow I think being unemployed isn't going to bring my stress levels down."

"Point taken, but at least you seem to be getting your sense of humour back. Do you want me to come over to do a final check on Alex before the flight?"

"Funny you should bring that up ... I have a massive favour to ask, another one. You know when the next full moon is?"

"Yes, Mon— Oh, God."

"I see you've already worked out where I'm going with this."

"How did he take it?"

"He worked it out first and just took himself off to bed. Annie had a little freak-out but went after him. I don't know what to do any more so I'm in bed too. Failing to not think about my massive shortcomings as a parent and how I'm only ever going to fail my children from this day forth."

His tone was such that Dr Cooper couldn't tell how much of it was in jest and how much he believed.

"He didn't transform?"

"Well, no, he was given more drugs just before we left the hospital. Which raises an interesting point: if we sedated him before the flight, do you think it could counter full moon?"

"Is that a risk you really want to take? On a *plane*?"

"How about trying to get Mork into Canada and not Alex?"

"You're the lawyer. Can that be done in a morning?"

"No."

"My friend, you're in deep mourning, and bargaining. I will come by tomorrow morning before you all leave and we'll make a plan."

"I have never felt more useless and helpless in my whole life, Raj. I feel like I couldn't have more completely failed him."

"You are a fantastic father, Kyle, and the horrible deed has already been done. What's happening now is you needing to say goodbye. Alex just has to say goodbye a little sooner than you, but I'll be with him and we'll get through this."

Kyle could feel the lump forming in his throat. "Rajan, you're a true friend. I'm not sure what we would have done without you all these years. My family wouldn't be the same if you weren't a part of it. Think I'm gonna try get some sleep now. I'll see you in the morning?"

"All right, you rest, and I'll see you tomorrow."

Kyle put the phone down next to his pillow, rolled over and was asleep within minutes.

The next morning, Alex's first back at home without his mother, Annabel prepared breakfast and no one really spoke. As usual, Rajan Cooper let himself in and, as he appeared in the kitchen doorway and saw the numbed faces, Debra's absence struck him like a blow to the chest and he turned away for a moment to compose himself.

"Tea, Dr Cooper?" Annabel called from the kettle.

"Yes, that'd be lovely, thank you, Annie. Alex, how are you feeling?"

"The casts itch, but fleas are worse so nothing I can't handle. Otherwise, I'm peachy. How's you, Doc?"

Dr Cooper sat down across from him and looked him up and down. Alex didn't even try masking the pain. He also didn't think he should try. It took a while before Dr Cooper noticed what had changed.

"Alex, what colour are your eyes?"

"Blue? Green? Depends on the time of the month, something I never thought I'd say. Originally brown, but that was before we met."

"Well, they're grey now."

"Really?" Kyle butted in, and moved around the table to see. "Wow, that's creepy."

Annabel, cups of tea in hand, also trotted across the kitchen to take a look. "I don't think they looked like that yesterday," she said.

"Maybe it's from all the medication?" Alex reasoned. "Or the pain? I'm still very tired all the time, actually."

Dr Cooper sipped his tea and thought for a moment, but Alex came up with his own answer first.

"Well, Mork turned my hair black and my eyes blue, maybe this is more about him than me? Which reminds me, what happens with the broken arm and leg during full moon?"

Cooper shrugged his shoulders. "Well, we can't risk taking the casts off beforehand, if that's what you're asking. So I'm afraid we're just going to have to wait and see, but I know the name of a very good vet that I can call to reset your legs when you turn."

Alex rubbed his face in frustration. "So you'll be staying with me while everyone else is away?"

Kyle and Annabel quietly cleaned up, trying not to intrude on the conversation, Kyle out of regret and embarrassment, Annabel for fear of weeping again.

"So, about cleaning myself ..." Alex smiled another defeated smile.

"A nurse will be around this afternoon to administer a sponge bath like in the hospital."

"Oh, goodie! I'll be sure to wear my good underpants."

Dr Cooper rubbed his eyes, wishing he had a way he could fix everything.

"Sorry, Doc, I'm just, you know, fucked up."

"Alex!"

"You know a better way to put it, Dad?"

Kyle lifted a finger as if about to make a point. "No, you're right; right now I think we're all a bit fucked up. But I also think that, between the four of us, and that includes you, Rajan, we're going to survive this as a family and still be a family at the end of it. Alex, I'm sorry about the funeral, I really am, but Annie and I have to start packing and getting things ready."

"Yeah, I know, Dad. It's not your fault. I'll be all right, and I still love you. That being said, could someone get me upstairs? I wanna talk to my sister a bit and get some things from my room."

It took all three of them to get Alex and the wheelchair up the stairs, but once up there Annabel could push him around. She wheeled him into the corner of her room before she started her final check to make sure she had everything.

"So what did you want to talk about?"

"Actually, I figured you'd be the one who wanted to talk. How are *you* doing? Has anyone stopped to ask you yet?"

She stopped mid-fold and looked at him. "I'm trying to maintain a sense of numbness, the less I think and feel about it the more I can get done."

"I hear you there. How's Ryan after the other night?"

"It was strange, awkward being naked in front of someone. I liked it, though, and it felt right to be doing it with him. I was so bursting to tell you about it the other day but then, well, you know ..."

"Yeah, I know, I could smell it."

"That reminds me, what exactly did you smell?"

She looked worried and slightly grossed at the thought, but still wanted to know.

"Oh, don't make that face, it wasn't that bad; you smelt like you do only with a very, very subtle difference, like suddenly it was you only with a drop of lemon, for a strange example. I guess it was you with a drop of adulthood."

She smiled warmly, the first real smile in days.

"You know the whole school knows you got busted with the secretary."

"What?"

"Apparently, you were busted making out with the school secretary."

"We're not going to talk about that. Don't bring it up again."

Alex closed his eyes and thrashed his head about as if trying to turn from a distant thought or memory. Annabel rushed over to him and put her hands on his hand.

"Alex? Alex, what's the matter?"

"Nope, no, we can't talk about that. Change the subject."

"Okay, okay. Would you like to borrow some books? Most are in my room and you'll be stuck in a wheelchair for awhile, even after full moon."

He opened his eyes. They were now touched with green.

"Yes, that would be very nice, thank you. What do you recommend?"

Annabel stepped cautiously back. "I'll grab a few things I think you'll like, and you can just go through them and read whichever you think looks interesting?"

"Groovy, sounds like a plan, only you can leave out those teeny-girly books about falling in love and high-school drama. I have enough troubles in my own life to read about someone else's experiences along the same lines."

"Fair enough. How about classical literature? Know who Oscar Wilde is?"

"Wrote plays and poems, yes, one novel. Haven't read it. Didn't know you had it, lay it on me."

"Really? How do you know about Oscar Wilde?"

"I like writing poetry and a girl in my school last year did a presentation on him for English class, 'Who in literature inspires you?'"

"Who did you pick?"

"I was Mork the week it was assigned; arrived back in time to see everyone else's."

"Pity. Who would you have picked?"

"I don't know, maybe Guy Endore?"

"Guy Endore, Guy Endore?"

"Come on, you know this ... Wrote *A Werewolf in Paris*?"

"Ha-ha, very funny. Also, you hate that rampaging werewolf stuff."

"Yes, but it's easier to name him than it is to work out who wrote *Melion*."

"*Melion*?"

"Really? Do you just not read any werewolf literature?"

"I've read up on werewolves, just not that one, I don't think."

"*Melion* is the poem thing about one of King Arthur's knights who gets turned into a wolf ..."

"Oh, I have read that one! His wife turns him into a wolf so she can run off with someone else. Of course I know that one, I've always wondered if that one was actually true."

"What do you mean?"

"Well, you've had dreams about being a knight who turns into a wolf, so I've just always wondered if it's not transferred memory from whoever wrote that story and if he was basing the story on his life. Fits the bill, doesn't it? I mean, loses his temper and turns into a wolf but stays very tame."

"Yeah, yeah, I have actually thought about that myself. Only problem is I can't control the dreams and no one knows who actually wrote the story so there's no lead to follow, no way to confirm it. Would be interesting, though, if it were a true story based on one guy's experiences. Stuff like that makes me really wish I know what happened to the wolf that bit me."

"What did happen to that wolf?"

"Dunno. Dad said it wasn't there when they went back."

"Pity."

"Yeah … Annie, could you do me a favour and wheel me over to my room for a bit, help me get some things?"

"Sure. Of course."

Alex knew his father had been sleeping in his room but didn't expect it to smell some completely of fear. After collecting his laptop, CD player, earphones and CD bag, Annabel left him near the top of the stairs so that she could quickly finish packing.

Stranded at the top of the stairs, Alex allowed himself to think about his mother and their final moments together, trying to hold onto that laughter. But all at once his mind flashed to Judith and the guilt he'd been hiding from hit him like a wave. If I had just accepted the plan, my mother would be alive, he thought to himself. It's my fault she's dead. It's my fault, it's all my fault. He pressed his eyes closed and thrashed his head from side to side, trying to suppress the urge to scream or howl.

"DAD!"

The intention was to get someone's attention so he could get help with the stairs. His voice carried through the house like a gun-shot, and everyone came running. His cheeks flushed as he saw the panic on their faces.

"Sorry, I didn't mean to scare you guys; I just wanted to get your attention so I could get downstairs. Full moon around the corner, you know, I get a little ... grumpy. Sorry."

"No, no it's fine, don't worry. Let's get you downstairs."

As they carried him Annabel said, "Sorry, man, I didn't mean to just leave you like that."

Alex put on a smile and waved his hand. "Don't worry, I'm cool. It was just a moment, I'm fine now."

Kyle couldn't help but worry. Full moon always brought dramatic mood fluctuations. And now, coupled with an actual tragedy, who knew how it would turn out.

It wasn't easy for Alex to get around on his own, but he could manage by pulling himself along with one leg. So once back on the ground floor, he got himself to the TV room and hoped he could distract himself enough with cartoons to not think about every-thing else. Dr Cooper slipped into the room and sat down next to him,

"So, how are you *really*? How you holding up?"

"Honestly?"

"I'm not sure, but let's try,"

"I feel like I'm stuck the middle of a war between my body and my mind. I don't want to think of anything, but I can't do anything, so I have to think about things and all I really want is for it all not to be true but even just saying that is making me feel like I could lose control. Plus the fact that in a couple of weeks I won't even have a scratch to show for the crash that killed my mother. I'm clinging to a twig here, so if it's all the same to you, I'd like to just go back to watching cartoons for a bit and not have to think about anything."

Alex turned back towards the screen and Dr Cooper slowly got back to his feet and walked out, unsure of what, if anything, he could do that might give comfort. His concentration was broken by a knock at the door. Both Ryan and Dr Cooper were surprised to see each other.

"Uhmmm, is Annabel here?"

"Aah, you must be the infamous Ryan. We've actually met before, I'm Rajan Cooper, Alex's doctor." He extended his hand to the shy young man. "Annabel's just upstairs packing if you want to go up."

"Cool, thanks.' Ryan moved to take a step but stopped. "How's Alex doing, Doctor? I mean, I don't know a lot about his disease, Annie doesn't like to talk about it, but I hear he got pretty banged up in the accident."

"We're still waiting on the final results but so far it looks like he's going to make a full recovery, just a few scars. He's in the TV room if you want to say hello."

"Thanks, I'll pop my head once I've seen Annabel. Thank you, Doctor."

Ryan dashed up the stairs, and knocked sharply on the door to Annabel's room.

"Hiya, Annie. Thought I'd come by to see how you were doing before you guys all ship off to Canadia."

"Aaw, you're so sweet," she said as she put down the clothes she was holding, and walked over to him. "I'm as good as I can be, I think."

"Good. That's good." He kissed her on the cheek then sat down on the bed. "Sooo ... you're not freaked out about last week, are you?"

She regarded him with some apprehension. "Which part of last week?"

"You know, the *us* part of last week?"

"No. Should I be? Is something wrong? Are you breaking up with me?"

Annabel's voice got steadily more shrill as her eyes filled with tears. Ryan sprang back up, took her in his arms and held on tight. "No, no, no, not at all. I'm just ... I just ... I was so happy about it, and it was so amazing, then ... well that awful thing happened the next day and I was worried that it was going to make it strange between us? I don't know, forget I said anything. I'm sorry."

She wiped away tears as she pulled away slightly from the hug. "No, I'm sorry. I'm kinda a wreck. I'm sorry you're freaking out about it. You can take some comfort knowing that I'm not freaking out about it."

"I think it's also this Canada thing. I mean, I'm just going to miss you. Last week was awesome. I just … Okay, I'm going to stop talking about this now. How's Alex?"

She leaned forward again and kissed him gently, resting her head on his shoulder. "It's sweet that you're worried about him. I'm worried too. I don't know how he's doing and I'm terrified he's blaming himself because he survived."

"Heavy."

"I haven't actually worked up the courage to ask him about it. Not that he'd definitely tell me if I did, of course."

"Well, you've got the whole flight to talk about it."

"I what? Oh yeah …"

"Or maybe after the funeral he'll be a bit more able to deal. Also, isn't he on like serious painkillers? It's amazing that he's alive at all, isn't it?"

"It's a miracle, but I'm starting to think he wishes it was the other way around."

"Fuuuuuck! That'd be so much worse."

"What?"

"Could you imagine your mom if she survived and Alex had died? I think you would've lost your mom either way."

"You know, sometimes," tears welled up in her eyes, "sometimes you're very smart."

"Oh yeah, you landed the whole package with me, you lucky girl you." And he leaned in for a kiss.

There was a discreet cough from Kyle in the doorway, and Ryan leapt back.

"Sorry, sir. I wasn't, I mean I didn't, I mean ... Hello, Mr Harris."

"Relax, Ryan," Kyle laughed. "I'm not going to lynch you for kissing my daughter. That being said, Annabel, you almost done?"

"Yeah, just got to get my things from the bathroom and close the bag."

"Good, because we need to start making a move soon, which means ... I'm sorry but, Ryan, I need you to give us a little space to get the last few things in order before we leave."

"Oh, right. Yes, sir, absolutely."

"Thanks, I'll give you a few minutes. Annie, I'll be in the kitchen."

"All right, Dad. We'll be right down."

Kyle met Dr Cooper at the foot of the stairs.

"What's the matter, Doc?"

"I'm just a little tired is all, nothing a nice cup of coffee can't fix. Would you like some?"

"When did you start drinking coffee?"

Dr Cooper put on a pained smile. "Five days ago, about ten in the morning."

Kyle laughed despite himself. "We'll have you throwing back a beer or two by the end of the week, Raj."

"Week and a half alone with Alex and anything's possible, I guess."

They made their way to the kitchen and put on a pot of coffee. In the background they heard the front door open and then close and Annabel walked in pushing Alex's wheelchair. They were sitting around the kitchen table, quietly drinking their coffee, when there was a knock at the door. Kyle checked his watch.

"That'll be our cab. Annie, get your stuff."

"My suitcase is already at the front door."

"All right, good. Well then, let's grab it and go."

It took only a couple of minutes before the car was loaded and everyone was saying their goodbyes. Annabel kissed her bother's cheek and fought back her tears.

"I'm sorry you can't come with us."

"It's just one of those things I guess." Alex shrugged his shoulders.

Then Annabel stepped back, her eyes wide and covered her mouth with her hand.

"What is it?" Kyle and Dr Cooper quickly turned to her. "What's wrong?"

Then they saw what she saw: Alex's irises had gone from a dull grey to almost entirely black. Alex looked up, confused.

"What now?"

Dr Cooper leaned a little closer and said in a low voice, "Your eyes have gone black. But don't worry, we'll look into it the minute we're done here."

Alex sighed and shook his head. "Right, you guys have to go or you'll miss your flight. Have fun, and say hi to everyone for me. And don't forget to say goodbye to Mom for me ..." He dug his hand into his pocked and pulled out a small folded square of paper. "I, uhmmm ... I wrote this. If one of you wants to read it that's cool or you can just put in with her."

Kyle took the paper and slipped it into his pocket. He desperately wanted to say something, but there were no words. And Alex was right, they did have to go. A final hug and a shaking of Dr Cooper's hand.

"Thanks again, Rajan, for all your help."

And they were in the cab and away.

Dr Cooper wheeled Alex back into the house.

"You want I should take a look at your eyes now?"

"No."

"Alex, it's not your fault what—"

"No, no, please, just give me some time to *not* think about it. I just need to not think about it for a bit longer, please. Let me just get through full moon, then we can do this, but right now I ... just, no."

"Okay, okay, I'll take you back to the TV room. What would you like for dinner?"

"I don't know. Pizza? Whatever you want is fine. We can even do the super-healthy stuff if you want, I don't care."

"I'll have to remove your casts a little later to prepare for transformation tonight. I'm not really sure what'll happen, but I'll be here the whole time. You know that, right?"

"Thanks, Doc."

Dr Cooper stood for a moment longer and then left him watching TV, unsure of what more could be done or said. Against his better judgement, he ordered pizza, he didn't want to leave it too late in case the change came before the food. After they had finished, he sat with Alex for a few more hours watching whatever was on, just so that Alex could see he wasn't alone. Eventually, though, he had to break the silence.

"All right, it's time to remove your casts, but remember that once they're off you can't move at all."

Alex turned away from the screen to look at Dr Cooper. "Okay, but how's that going to work when I start transforming?"

"I have no idea," Dr Cooper smiled nervously. "We're going to have to wait and see."

Alex took a deep breath and a shiver ran down his back. "Will the fun ... ever ... end?"

Together they got Alex to lie down on the couch and, slowly and carefully, Dr Cooper cut and folded away the plaster of Paris casts on his leg and arm. After a quick inspection he was amazed to discover how much it had already healed and how little scarring there was.

"You need me to bring you anything?"

"No, I'm all right, thanks. But if I were you I wouldn't stand so close, I really don't want something bad to happen."

"We've gone through the transformation so many times together. I can't imagine why you'd think something would happen now."

"Well, I'm just worried that, with what's happened, I'm gonna have less control of Mork than usual."

"You must remember, Alex, that you and Mork are one and the same. You are the wolf and Mork is the human. I do understand that in wolf form you are more inclined to act on emotion and in-stinct, but do you really think it'll lead you to attack me?"

"I don't know ... I don't know what's going to happen. I don't know what this is going to feel like or how I'm going to react. In fact, the only thing I do know is that I'm terrified that I'm going to lose con-trol and do something terrible. So, Doc, I think I want to be alone for this one."

"You don't have to face this alone, I care about you and I want to help you."

"You can't help, no one can. No matter who's around, it's always me who has to actually transform, so let me just get through this, then help me. Mork with a broken leg and arm is going to be a strange thing. And a trapped, hurt animal does things that it maybe doesn't mean to. That much I can guarantee."

Alex's mind flashed back to when he was bitten and his face went pale, his eyes green.

"Doc, it's happening now. Ple-please just go, just leave."

Dr Cooper nodded his head, got to his feet and left the room, careful to hide how deep Alex's words had cut.

Alex closed his eyes and tried to control his breathing. With the full moon imminent, he knew that there was no way of stopping the transformation once it started so he didn't even try. He simply held on and hoped the ride would be over soon. Then, all at once, pain shot down his arm and leg like an electric current and it felt as though his limbs were on fire. He gritted his teeth and tried to hold himself together for as long as he could, but it didn't take long before the pain got the better of him. His back arched and he wailed. Twisting and contorted in pain, he threw himself off the couch and onto the floor where he continued to scream.

Dr Cooper burst into the room but was struck still by what he found. Alex lie on his back, half man half wolf, twisting and screaming as sweat poured off him. He watched as the broken arm and leg shifted back and forth between human and wolf, each time causing Alex to recoil in pain. The torture went on for a full ten minutes, then just as suddenly as it had started the pain faded. Alex rolled from his back onto his stomach and a calm washed over him as he rode the transformation to its final stages. Then came the tsunami of rage and, in an instant, every fibre of his being wanted to lash out in all directions, to destroy all it touched. His muscles screamed to move and he obeyed, diving through the sheet-glass window and disappearing into the fading light. By the time Cooper reached the front door in pursuit, Mork was long gone.

Chapter 23

Pain and anger drove him forward like a whip against his back, forcing him to keep going, forcing him to go faster. Mork ran like he'd never run before, screaming in his head as loud as he could, entirely beyond control, eyes wide in fear and panic and sorrow. In wolf form, his emotions could not be contained; all his feelings came rushing to the fore and overwhelmed him. If he could have cried, he'd have been weeping, screaming, but he couldn't, all he could do was run. Life as he knew it seemed to fade away, the world around him a blur; all physical pain disappeared and eventually the only thought in his head was one paw in front of the other. It seemed as though days had passed when he eventually reached the end of the island and dove head first into the waters off Syn Island.

He gasped as the cold hit him, and he struggled to find his feet on the soft sand amid moving tides. Much of the island was rimmed by docks, but beaches had been built for entertainment and leisure. He stood on the edges of his height, the cold water lapping at his chin, hoping it would wash away his pain. Then he threw back his head and erupted with a deafening howl to the night sky. Slowly, he made his way up the shore. Exhausted and freezing, he lay down on the beach and for the first time since the accident allowed himself too think back to the moments after the truck hit. At once he could see his mother hitting the steering wheel, contorting and falling limp in her seatbelt. In wolf form, the full memory of the car accident was as clear as day, from every drop of his mother's blood against the windscreen to the joy in her laughter just a moment before. He felt weak and helpless. Every part of him wanted to find a way to change the memory, to change what had happened, to end the nightmare. But there was nothing he could do and it crippled him. Mork howled and howled at the moon as if it was the cause of his misery, as if it had killed his mother. The pain in his heart overwhelmed that of his glass-shredded paws, run even more ragged by sharp stones and brambles as he fled, leaving a trail of bloody paw prints.

It had been eight hours since Dr Cooper had begun his search for the only wolf on Syn Island and although he wanted to keep looking he simply couldn't go on, especially at the wheel of a car. He had been awake for some twenty hours and the fatigue and angst were beginning to take their toll. As he turned the car around to head back to the house, he was struck by an uncontrollable urge to cry. Quickly, he pulled over and the tears flowed without stop. Alex had been his responsibility for only a few hours and he had lost him to the streets and wilderness of Syn Island. Debra had felt like family to him, too, but he had needed to stay strong for everyone else, and the idea of Alex missing the funeral because of Mork, coupled with knowing why, had simply become too much for him. He cried and beat his fists against the steering wheel and cried some more. He no longer wanted to be the one always in control, the one always reaching for the positive, the one hiding his own frustration and inadequacies, he just wanted it to all be different. It was some minutes before he came back to his senses, at least enough to realise that sitting at the side of the road feeling sorry for himself would help no one and decided that if he couldn't find Mork he needed to be where Mork would find him. So he headed back to the house.

Rajan Cooper woke up on the couch in the TV room. He had had a restless, troubled sleep, and a deep anxiety still hung over him as he yawned and stretched. There was no indication that Mork had returned, so the doctor looked at his situation and weighed up his options: either continue with the search or wait and have faith. He turned on the kettle, then started clearing up the broken glass.

***

Mork limped down the street, exhausted but determined to make it home before he collapsed. The pads of his paws were now just a bleeding mess that shot pain up his legs with every step. A cool breeze swept down the street and he had stopped to try to find some hint as to where he was when a very familiar scent tickled his nose. With newfound strength, he forced himself to press on down the street and quickly made his way to a nearby doorway. Grudgingly, Mork started scratching the door to attract the attention of the people inside, leaving a fresh bloody paw stain every time. When the door finally opened, it was Ryan who stood in front of him, his expression even more confused than usual. Mork looked up, blinked and then collapsed at Ryan's feet. As in a distant dream, he heard Ryan's whisper.

"Mork?"

Then, like water rushing over him, the darkness took him and Mork lost consciousness. Ryan, in near panic, looked down at the animal at his feet. His first thought was how he would have to tell his girlfriend that her family dog had died.

"What the hell is that?" His mother, peering cautiously from behind the door, pointed.

Ryan leapt, startled. "It's Annabel's dog, and I think he's dead."

"No, look, it's breathing. But what is it doing here?"

"It is? It is! Oh, thank God. Uhmmm, I think Alex's doctor is looking after their house. I'm gonna call and see what's going on."

"Okay, sweetie, but I'd call the vet first, just look at his paws and the blood on the path."

"Holy shit!"

"Language, young man."

"Right, yeah, sorry. What could have happened? He's, like, the most well-trained dog in the world."

"Well, maybe he didn't take too well to being left at home? But pick him up and bring him inside. I'll get some towels you can put him on. Then go make those calls; we can work the rest out later."

Ryan looked down at the massive creature and hummed again. It wasn't until his mom reappeared a moment later and saw him crouched down next to it that she realised how big Mork actually was and would take both of them to carry him inside. Ryan then called the vet, who arrived twenty minutes later, just after a frantic Dr Cooper, who thanked everyone profusely, but explained that the family had left very specific instruction on which vet to call in an emergency.

"Thank you for all your concern, but I can handle it from here. I feel bad enough as it is that Mork got out under my watch so, Ryan, if you could just help me get him to the car, I'll see to it that he gets the best care."

***

Mork woke up a day and a half later to the sound of Hindu chanting and the smell of incense. Slowly he looked around and saw that the source of the chanting was a small CD player in the corner and that he was in fact on his own bed at home. His attention then went to his bandaged paws and steadily his memory started to return. He lay back down and remembered picking up a familiar scent that lead him to someone safe, then darkness. As he lay his head down and closed his eyes, flashes of his mother's laughing face merged with images of the truck impacting the car. Mork's eyes shot open. Dr Cooper was standing at the door, watching over him.

"Awake, I see. I need to take another look at your paws to see how much they've healed over the last twenty-four hours."

Mork raised a paw to the doctor and snorted. The expression on Dr Cooper's face was one of concern but Mork couldn't work out if he smelt anger or fear, perhaps both. Cooper unwrapped one of the bandages and inspected the wounds on the paw.

"As expected, it's healing well, and fast. In fact, you can probably walk on them quite comfortably, but they might feel a little tender. At the rate it's going, though, if you just wanted to sleep a few more hours you'll probably be just fine by tonight."

Nervously, Mork closed his eyes once more determined to fight off the memory of the car accident and, without realising, drifted right back to sleep. Dr Cooper gently scratched behind Mork's ear before returning to the lounge where a team of handymen was replacing the broken window.

"Why not just have the mutt put down?" the one in overalls sniffed.

"Wha—? Oh no, extremely rare breed, almost impossible to replace. Also, he's normally very well behaved. Just had a moment, I suppose."

The man turned to look at the broken window, then back to Dr Cooper. "That's one hell-of-a-moment, if you don't mind me saying. I mean, I understand, but I think I'd consider having my children put down after a moment like that."

The other two laughed as they began packing away their tools. Job done.

When Mork woke again, it was dark and all the comings and goings of the day had ended, leaving the house eerily still. Quietly, he hopped off the bed but fumbled slightly when his bandages slid across the polished floor, causing him to upturn the bedside table smash the lamp as it came crashing to the floor. Of course, it wasn't long before Dr Cooper swept in to investigate the noise.

"Breaking things again, I see?"

Mork whimpered and held up a bandaged paw. Dr Cooper then realised what had happened and began to unwind the bandages.

"There. Much better already. See? And there'll be no skidding around on polished floors either," the doctor said, turning each of the paws over in turn. "Now I need you to come with me. There's something I think you should see."

Mork got to his feet and followed the doctor down the stairs, out through the kitchen and into the back garden.

"Right, now look up."

It didn't take him long to realise what he was looking for. As he peered into the night sky, a waning moon shone down onto him, clearly indicating that the full-moon period was over and that, under normal circumstances, he should already be human again, or at least be able to try to transform again.

"You've been asleep for just over two days. I think the stress you've put on your body, coupled with all the emotional stress, is what's keeping you from turning back. That being said, I'm sure that if we sit down we can do this, get you to transform, so don't panic. How-ever, it's just past two in the morning and I was asleep when you broke that lamp, so if it's all right with you I'm going to go back to bed, we can both get some much-needed rest, and we can deal with this in the morning?"

But when Dr Cooper discovered Mork asleep on the couch much later that morning, he let him be, and it wasn't until the afternoon that they were both ready to start the process, one that could take hours. Candles and incense were lit, lights were dimmed and soft chanting music was put on in the background. While the two sat with their eyes closed, Mork would try to follow every word of the meditation. It was always harder to turn Mork back into Alex than the other way around and in this case it took an inordinately long time, less violent than when Alex had argued with his father, but nonetheless exhausting for both of them. By the time they had succeeded and Alex had transformed into his human form, the candles and incense were long burnt out and the music had looped three times.

Dr Cooper looked at Alex struggling to wrap himself in a blanket. "I took the liberty of ordering you three full roast chickens, they're in the fridge, waiting."

"H-ha-have I ... ever told you I l-love you, Doc?"

Cooper smiled and left the room to give him some time to dress and compose himself. Within minutes he was in the kitchen, stuff-ing his face with as much food as he could get his hands on and following every third or fourth mouthful with large gulps of water. Everyone knew better than to watch him eat after a long trans-formation. In the time it took him to devour everything placed in front of him, Dr Cooper filled him in on what had happened, par-ticularly those incidents that Mork's memory had clouded over. Alex sat alert, with renewed strength and not a single scratch or mark on him.

"So … what am I going to do now?"

"Well, what do you want to do? Your dad and Annie won't be back for another week."

"I think I want to go back to school. My suspension must be over and, even if it isn't, I'll go have a meeting with Reid. I'm sure he'll understand."

"Are you sure that's a good idea? I mean, how are you feeling, inside?"

"Yeah, well, what else can I do? Sit around here, alone? Do you really think that's going to help? On the inside I feel, I don't know … grey. Maybe if I get back into routine, do something *normal*, it'll take my mind off of everything for at least part of the time."

Dr Cooper considered Alex's argument for a moment. "All right," he said. "Tomorrow morning I'm taking you to school and we'll talk to the headmaster. Now I know there's been a lot of this today, but perhaps you should go take a hot shower and get yourself to bed. Get as much sleep as you can so that you'll be ready for school in the morning."

"All right, Doc, and thanks again. Not just for the chicken … for everything. I really don't think I would've made it this far without you."

Cooper smiled. "It's been an interesting journey, I have to say, and it's not over yet, but I'm happy to be part of it. Now get yourself upstairs, young man. I'll see you in the morning."

Alex saluted with his index finger and headed to his room.

"*Oh My God!* What are you do— I heard you were so hurt, but you're fi— I ... I ... I don't understand."

Judith's voice was shrill, as she looked him up and down in the doorway. Realising that there wasn't a scratch anywhere on him, the blood seemed to drain from her face.

"The severity of my injuries have been greatly exaggerated, I'm fine. Mr Reid in? Can I see him?"

Alex had prepared a story about sitting in the back seat against the opposite window, and the truck striking the front half of the car, so missing him by an immeasurable amount, but he also didn't want to say anything he didn't have to, so kept it vague when he could. The door to Mr Reid's office opened quickly as the headmaster peered out to see what all the commotion was about. He was equally astonished at the sight of Alex in reception.

"Mr Harris? I ... don't understand."

"Can I step into your office so that we can talk about it?"

"Yes, please do." And the headmaster ushered him in, shutting the door on the flabbergasted Judith.

It occurred to Judith that she was hurt by Alex's nonchalance, that she had been used by this teen with the rampant hormones. And she was not amused. She had spent so much time worrying about him and looking forward to seeing him again, and to come face to face with him apparently entirely unharmed and not even so much as a hello cut her deeply. Tears began to roll down her face and she was suddenly glad to be sitting alone.

In the office, it hadn't occurred to Alex until that moment how the room brought back memories of the day his mother died.

"Take a seat, Mr Harris. I've been rather worried about you. We all have; we heard reports that you were all but dead, half your body crushed in the, uhmmm ... the accident. It's more than a little alarming to see you now in perfect health."

"I wouldn't go as far as to say perfect health, sir. Physically, I'm all right, but there's a lot more to it than that. Anyway, sir, the reason I'm here is because I can't remember if my suspension is over yet, and even if it isn't, I was wondering if you'd let me come back to school ... please?"

"You being here now raises the question, where's your sister? I thought you'd all gone to Canada to attend your mother's funeral?"

Alex closed his eyes and took a long, controlled breath. "Yes, well, sadly, due to the sensitive nature of my illness coupled with the emotional stress of ... well, everything, I suppose, I'm currently medically unfit for air travel. Which is what brings me to you now. Rather than sit idly at home, I thought I could come back here, get my mind off of things for at least a few hours a day."

Reid nodded. "Of course, of course. I know a few boys who are going to be very surprised to see you. Like I said, to the best of our knowledge you were at death's door."

"I was. I think I even knocked a few times, but luckily for me no one answered."

Mr Reid let slip a burst of laughter before quickly regaining composure. "Right, well, before I let you head off to class, I do need to ask, how are you?"

"Honestly, sir, the reason I'm here is so that I don't have to think about that. Can't we just go with your door is always open if I need to chat, and let me distract myself for a bit?"

It became clear to the headmaster that whatever chance Alex's illness had left him to have a childhood had died right along with his mother. The person who sat across from him now was an inexperienced but none the less hardened adult. To now treat him like a child would be wrong. He also felt a great swell of pity for the young man and it took a moment before he could speak without his voice cracking.

"Very well then, my door *is* open if you'd like to chat. Let's leave it at that, shall we?"

"Of course. You wouldn't happen to know where on the schedule I am right now, sir? Also I need to be put onto the school lunch program as my guardian and I don't really agree on the correct diet for a teenage boy."

"As luck would have it, Judith can help you on both counts."

Alex smiled and tried not to roll his eyes.

"Thank you ... sir."

With that, he got up from his seat and quickly left the office. Judith was still at her desk feeling sorry for herself.

"Hello."

"Oh, so you're actually going to greet me now?"

Alex tightened his jaw to prevent himself from not reacting and give him a moment to think before speaking again. "I'm sorry I was a bit abrupt just now."

"Apology accepted, I guess," she sniffed, head down as she continued to tap at her keyboard.

Her tone was disinterested and it was enough to push Alex to near breaking point. All the pain and anger rushed to the fore and all he wanted to do was spit it out. But he restrained himself once again.

"What day is the schedule on today, and would you please sign me on for school lunch?"

Judith shook her head, determined to hold back her tears. Every cold word out of Alex's mouth felt like a knife in her back.

"Will that be all then, Mr Harris?" she spat at him.

"Well, no actually ... I'd also like to remind you that my mother has in fact just died, in a car accident in which I was also involved, and that because of my injuries I was unable to even attend her funeral. Remember, too, that the last memories I have of her involve ... The only reason she was here was because we ..." He stopped himself from venting further, knowing he'd already gone too far. He turned for the door and stormed out. "And, you know what, fuck the schedule, I'll work it out myself."

Behind him he could hear her erupt into tears, but chose to ignore it. There was only so much he could be expected to cope with on a day like today. And Judith was not something he cared to deal with.

Alex arrived at his locker a couple minutes later to discover that it was covered with cards, all wishing him well and apologising for his loss. He quickly scooped them up and stuffed them into the locker. According to his existing schedule, he decided that there were two options of possible classes, both taught by the same teacher. He grabbed his books and headed off, all the while mentally preparing himself to tell the same short lie to everyone individually, all with the aim to show that he was in fact 'fine'. And that is almost exactly what he did in every class for the rest of the morning.

As the bell rang at the end of his third class, he sat quietly while everyone reached for their bags and headed out for recess. Recess worried Alex more than classes did. In class, there was at least some control over how much time could be spent talking about him, but recess meant that there would be more questions, more curious looks, more speculation. The Maths teacher stared at him for a moment or two and waited for everyone else to leave before approaching him.

"I know you're fine, Alex, but are you all right?"

He looked up at the teacher. "I'm okay, sir. Thanks. Just taking a break from telling the same old story a million times before I head out to lunch and get asked it twice as many times in half the actual time again."

"As a Maths teacher, I frown on your exaggeration but as a human being I totally understand. I'll leave you to it then ... And don't worry about tonight's homework, if you forget to do it, well ... I'm sure I'll understand."

Alex laughed quietly to himself. He ran through a quick breathing exercise before gathering his things and heading out to check whether he had been signed on for lunch. As expected, as he made his way through the halls, everyone turned to look at him, their conversations dropping to whispers when he came into sight. It didn't help, of course, because he could still hear but still he made an effort to ignore it.

In the cafeteria, he hoped he would find Josh, Danny or Brandon, whom he'd not seen since before the accident. When he walked in the whole room fell into a hush; even the serving staff turned to look at him. His heart rate began to steadily climb and, after a quick scan, he realised that his three friends were nowhere to be seen. An unwelcome but familiar voice broke the silence.

"You're looking good for a dead guy."

Alex turned to see Brandon's bully sitting on a table surrounded by his crew.

"I beg your pardon?" Alex pretended to have missed what he had said.

The bully got up from the table and ambled over.

"Didn't you hear? Rumour had it you're dead."

Something about the way the bully spoke made Alex's muscle's tighten and his blood simmer. "Well, you shouldn't believe everything you hear," was all Alex could muster.

The bully held out his hand. "Look, we got off on the wrong foot … I'm Rick and I'm really sorry about what happened with your mom."

Alex tried to ignore whatever it was about Rick that got under his skin, and took his hand. "Alex. And thanks."

Alex loosened his grip on Rick's hand only to realise that Rick had started squeezing as hard as he could.

"Yeah, man, and the funeral was amazing! You *really* shoulda been there."

Rick looked back at his friends and laughed in a way that prompted them to laugh with him. For a brief moment before he lost control, Alex knew that what Rick was doing was showing off, putting on a performance for his friends, trying to rebuild the reputation that had been tarnished on Alex's first day. But that moment soon passed, and Alex hooked him as hard as he could, dislocating his jaw and smashing several of his teeth. He then grabbed Rick by the throat, hoisted him clear off the ground and slammed him right through the nearest table. Two of Rick's friends leapt to the boy's defence, but without a moment's hesitation Alex kicked one in the stomach so that he doubled over, vomiting blood, then grabbed the second and slammed him against a wall.

The terror that rose in the boy's eyes immediately brought Alex to his senses. He took a sharp breath and jumped back. Rick lay unconscious among the debris of the table, blood pouring from his mouth, while the second boy lay doubled over, still vomiting. Looking up wild-eyed, Alex realised that the other students stood backs against the wall, and an almost overwhelming smell of fear filled the room. He turned around and walked out. His intention was to clear out his locker, head home and wait for the call to tell him he was officially expelled.

The moment Alex's back was turned, the cafeteria erupted into screams of panic as some of the students tried to flee and others rushed over to help the injured boys. Immediately, the head cook dialled the headmaster to report the incident.

Mr Reid leapt over his desk, stumbled, hit the ground, rolled and came up running. As expected, he found Alex packing his bag. The boy's outward calm stuck Reid as slightly frightening. Alex turned to look at him as he slowed from a run to a march.

"I know, I'm expelled. I understand. I'm just gonna pack up my things and leave. But if you wouldn't mind waiting a few days before you called my father? I don't think he needs more stress in his life right now."

"No, you need to stop packing and come with me."

"But, sir ..."

"But nothing! Come with me right now. You don't understand what you've done."

Alex stopped what he was doing, dropped his head and followed Mr Reid back to the office without a word. He retook his seat in the headmaster's office and waited.

"Sir, I was just going to leave and wait for you to call to say I was expelled."

Reid's voice was firm, angry, but very controlled.

"It's not that simple, Harris. Rick is an athlete, that's what qualifies him to be here. At fifteen, he's one of the fastest sprinters in the country, possibly the world, and what you have done today might very well have jeopardised his future livelihood. That aside, putting two people in the hospital isn't just expulsion, it's assault."

Alex's shoulders sank as he looked down at the floor.

"I mean, what were you *thinking*?"

"I wasn't thinking. For a moment, I felt totally free, totally out of control, driven only by instinct."

"What could possibly have happened to prompt your 'instinct' to throw a punch that sent the kid through a bloody table?"

"First, he offered his sympathy about my mom, then he followed up with, 'It was a beautiful funeral, you shoulda been there' while trying to intimidate me and laughing with his friends ... I lost it. I just lost it."

Mr Reid sighed and shook his head. "Alex, you asked me to let you back so that you could come here and calm down, and all you seem to have done is inflict your pain onto other people."

"I wanted to see my friends from film class. I wasn't even really that hungry, plus I figured Judith hadn't signed me up for lunch. The only reason I went to the cafeteria was to find them. I was gonna leave when I saw they weren't there; if Rick had left me alone, none of this would have happened."

Alex could feel his heart rate begin to rise; he stood up and started pacing around the room. "I didn't even want to come to this bloody school, you know. I just wanted a normal life. And I hate farming. Judith liked me first and when I tried to do what a normal person would do, my mother died. And now some other kid doesn't have a future, well, you know what, fuck him! My future died when I was ten, and if he wasn't such an arsehole he wouldn't be in this situation. *All* I want is to be a normal kid with normal kid problems, is that really too much to ask? Am I really such a monster that I can't even have that?"

He had stopped pacing and was facing Reid, pleading, as though the headmaster might be able to solve his problems. Tears had welled up in the boy's eyes. Mr Reid looked Alex up and down. Never had he been more convinced of sincerity in his life. The boy honestly wanted Reid to provide the answers to his questions, to know what he was supposed to do next.

"Goddammit, you're not expelled, yet." Reid took a deep breath. "You are, however, suspended until further notice. When your father gets back, we'll make an appointment and together we'll figure out a way to justify not expelling you. In the meantime, I'd like you to think about what kind of subjects you'd like to transfer into. Agriculture clearly isn't working for you, so I'd like you to change to something more suited, perhaps Writing or maybe Music. Writing is a good way to get your stress and frustration out of your head. So that it can be dealt with in a way that doesn't involve damaging school property. Now, if you wouldn't mind calling your guardian from Judith's desk and ask him to come pick you up."

Alex listened with disbelief. How could someone who had no real reason be so totally calm and understanding of his needs and frustrations?

"Can I hug you, sir?"

"No, but I appreciate the gesture. Take my card and ask your father to call me when he gets back so we can sort this whole thing out. I warn you now, though, there will be repercussions as a result of your actions today, and they won't simply go away with time. Rick's parents are very much within their rights to file assault charges. Students and staff are going to be interviewed for witness accounts. There is a very real possibility that there isn't a way to not expel you. I want to help you ... so if I can, I will. But I'm also never going to admit to having said that, so keep it too yourself."

He pointed at a small card holder on the corner of his desk; Alex walked over and took a card

"I understand, sir. And thank you, sir."

"Yes, well, don't forget to close the door behind you."

Alex turned and walked out. He called Dr Cooper and asked to be picked up, promising to explain everything when he got there. Back at his locker, he saw paramedics hurrying in the direction of the cafeteria and it occurred to him that he could so easily have killed that boy. He was still so unsure of his own strength but knew that parts of Rick's face had broken under the impact of his fist. Either way, he decided it would be best if he left sooner rather than later and headed quickly towards the school entrance.

Waiting for him on the steps were Josh, Brandon and Danny. Alex knew he would run into them at some point, but after throwing Rick through a table he had begun to hope he could simply leave and try to forget that this day had ever happened. For a moment it was like a Mexican stand-off, three to one, neither side saying anything, all four boys just staring at each other. To nobody's surprise, it was Brandon who broke the silence.

"Dude, the accident. I heard you were smashed up and broken, almost dead? We were really worried about you. What happened?"

"Well," Alex kicked a pebble around with his foot, "as you can see, I'm fine."

"And back there, in the cafeteria, what happened there?"

"I'm just not dealing with things as well as I thought I was, I guess."

The group fell silent again before Josh spoke up. "So is that it, you're being expelled?"

"Suspended until further notice."

"What does that mean?"

"That I can't come back until the issues of today have been properly resolved, and even then maybe not. But, uhmmm, if you guys are still looking for a singer for your band, and you're still willing to hang out with me, I'd really like to give it a try."

Josh, Danny and Brandon looked back and forth at each other, and Alex felt his heart begin to sink. Were they ready to abandon him, this loose cannon? Just when everything seemed bleakest, Dr Cooper pulled up and honked the horn. A strange mixture of relief and disappointment washed over Alex; as happy as he was to have a way out of the situation, he also wished he'd gotten an answer from the boys, instead of having it left open. He smiled at the three, adjusted his bag on his shoulder and headed for the car.

"Alex, wait!"

He turned to see Danny walking towards him. "Alex, man, look, we don't actually know what happened today. The story around the school is that Rick said something really harsh and you went berserk. We don't care, and we're all really sorry about your mom. So ... practice is Thursday; learn the song 'Hooker With a Penis'."

"Groovy."

They smiled at each other as Alex ducked into the car.

"Berserk?" Dr Cooper looked at him.

"Just drive. Please. I'll tell you in a minute."

Dr Cooper frowned, worried that he'd made a mistake by allowing the boy to go back to school, but drove off without a word. Alex waited until they were off school property before he launched into the full story, starting with his arrival at Mr Reid's office right up until he climbed into the car. He spoke in a low voice, ashamed, without looking up. By the time the story was over they were both at the kitchen counter drinking coffee. Dr Cooper waited until Alex had finished before he said anything.

"So, let me get this straight, you upset the headmaster's secretary, possibly crippled a fellow student, incapacitated another and you're *not* expelled?'

Alex thought for a moment, it seemed a lot stranger when Dr Cooper said it.

"I can't say I'm thrilled about what's happened, and I'm glad you haven't been expelled, but I can't imagine what your father's going to say."

Alex winced.

"For a moment I knew, I knew he was just being a show-off and a bully. He had no idea what his words meant, or how they would affect me. And I lost it, I felt completely out of control. God only knows why I didn't transform. I felt so wild, so … so free."

"I shouldn't have let you go back so soon. So close to full moon and your emotional wounds too fresh."

"You alright, Doc?"

"NO!" Dr Cooper stood up quickly and walked a few steps. "I'm supposed to be looking after you and in all the time I've had you almost nothing good has happened. What am I supposed to tell you father when he gets home? Broke the house, lost you for a few days, then when I did find you I sent you back to school where you almost killed someone and could be expelled, again. I know you're having a hard time, but I'm trying to meet you halfway here. You asked me to let you go back to school and ... and I trusted you to be honest with me about your emotional state. I wish I could carry this for you, Alex, but I can't! I need to be able to trust that you're telling me the truth so that I can help guide you."

In the five years Alex had known Dr Cooper, this was the first time he'd heard the doctor yell or speak like this. It also occurred to him that in all those years this was the first time perhaps that Dr Cooper had felt like this: an unfortunate cocktail of anger, toward Alex and himself, with a generous helping of guilt for good measure.

"Doc, it's not ... I mean, I didn't do it on purpose. I'm ... I'm sorry, I just wanted to ..."

Alex was resisting the urge to shift the blame onto being a werewolf. He had never liked using it as an excuse for anything; he felt it was too easy a way of getting out of trouble. In his mind, he believed that if he began using being a werewolf as an excuse it would take over his life and he would lose another part of himself to the wolf, which at this point added to his growing resentment. The fact was, however, that everything that had gone wrong in his day was indeed because he was a werewolf and he knew it. Deep in the back of his mind a small black ball of sorrow began to grow. Dr Cooper took his seat again, and regretted immediately that he had resorted to raising his voice. But he didn't know what else to do. He loved Alex and felt like he was failing him at every turn. He understood now how Kyle and Debra must have felt every day and it broke his heart.

Neither of them said another word, just sat in an uncomfortable silence until the doctor left to return to work. Through the course of his day, Cooper ran over various ways to apologise for what he'd said and how they were going to move forward. But by the time he pulled up in the drive of the Harris home, he was no closer to any answers. Exasperation remained etched on his face, the muscles in his shoulders and back taut. And matters were to get worse, much worse. When he opened the door, the blood drained from his face, panic gripped his heart with an icy hand and he could feel his entire body tense up with fear.

Chapter 24

The entrance hall was littered with broken furniture and splattered with blood. Trembling, Dr Cooper cautiously followed the trail of destruction out the hall, down the passage and back into the kitchen where, based on the pool of blood, it must have started. Turning quickly, he followed the spatters of blood upstairs into the bathroom on the landing, where he found Alex lying on the floor in a pool of his own blood. Dr Cooper rushed to his side but as he touched his arm Alex's eyes shot open.

"Don't touch me!"

The boy scurried away across the floor; his eyes had again turned black, gleaming against the contrast of his pale white complexion. Tears welled up in Dr Cooper's eyes.

"What ... what's happened here? What did you do?"

Alex's voice drifted in and out of coherence, as if what he was saying were little more than random thoughts verbalised without intention.

"It doesn't work, nothing works, I've been bleeding for hours, I have no control over my life, Mork is me, I'm nobody, and I can't even, can't even ... I'm going to outlive everyone, Doc ... silver knife didn't even make a difference." Alex slid the silver carving knife along the floor towards Dr Cooper. "I don't want to be this any more. Everything good in my life is falling apart because of Mork. My mother's died, my school career is fucked, my friends are terrified of me, my family don't know what to do with me; I almost killed some stupid kid. I don't want to be a werewolf any more; I just want to be a normal kid ... I don't want to know the horrors of the world. I ... I just wish acne was my biggest problem, but it's not, is it? Why can't I just be a normal boy? Huh? Please? Isn't there anything I can do? Please? Please! I'll do anything. I'll eat lentils if that will help, please."

Alex broke down into helpless tears and Dr Cooper's heart broke. He looked down at the blood-covered boy, the one begging him for some kind of salvation or mercy, and understood for the first time why this was a curse. Guilt welled up in the doctor and he took a few cautious steps forward, then sat down and wrapped his arms around the boy. Alex turned his face towards Dr Cooper and wept into his shoulder until exhaustion took hold and he fell asleep. Gently Dr Cooper scooped the boy up and carried him to bed.

Back downstairs, he turned the kettle on and settled at the counter. How did this all happen? Why? And why did the boy not transform into his wolf form? History had showed them that this was what happened in times of stress. Was it the sorrow, the loss of blood or the silver that had prevented the transformation? His questions prompted him to list other high-stress times when Alex *hadn't* changed. How were the circumstances different? Up until then no one had thought about it from the point of view fighting against the wolf. The doctor was determined that, by the time Alex eventually awoke, he would get to the bottom of this.

***

It was already late in the afternoon of the following day when Alex slowly opened his eyes and quickly discovered that having them open hurt much more than having them closed. He had a splitting headache and a growing sense of nausea. He turned in bed and carefully put his feet on the floor as though any sudden movement might just tip him over the edge. Resting his head in his hands, he tried to sift through the blur of his memory and remember why he felt so crap. All at once the images started rushing back, the despair the desperation and how it only got worse with every failed attempt. He clamped his hands over his mouth as he lunged forward, bouncing off walls as he staggered to the bathroom and threw up into the basin. He sank to the floor and looked around. He could still smell blood, but it was now largely disguised by the smell of disinfectant.

A deep sense of gratitude, indebtedness, to Dr Cooper began to set in. Then the guilt. But most of all, clarity. This was it. The moment had come, he decided. He'd had his mourning period, he'd done every stupid thing he could think of, and it was time to take back control. Alex got to his feet, splashed his face with water and made his way to the phone at the bottom of the stairs. A few seconds later Judith's voice answered.

"Hello?"

"You know, I think this must have been the strangest, and most stressful month of my entire life, and that's really saying something."

"I beg your pardon? Uhmmm, who am I speaking to?"

"It's Alex. I figured that if I just announced who it was at the start you'd put the phone down."

"Good guess. But what's stopping me from doing it now?"

"How about 'cos I called to apologise."

"And you think that's enough?"

"No, 'cos it's the right thing to do, Judith. The bad things in my life aren't your fault and it was wrong of me to take them out on you. It's just I couldn't handle what was going on and so I projected all the anger and confusion on anyone and everyone around me. This really has been the worst time in my life, and in the middle of all of it is this shining star of pure joy that is the moment we shared, which I think is why I dumped so much of my stuff onto you. It was, like, such a precious thing, but I felt so vulnerable, so I cut loose all my own demons and that was really, unbelievably unfair of me, and I'm sorry. Genuinely, really, very sorry."

For a few moments neither said anything. Alex, still feeling like shit, had run out of things to say and was now lying on the bottom step, the phone resting against his face. Judith was dumbstruck, fighting the urge to cry.

"Are you sure you're only sixteen?"

"Pretty sure, but some days it's harder to tell than others,"

She offered a weak laugh as though allowing herself to laugh was an alternative to tears. "So what happens now then?"

"Nothing. I'm going to stay at home and you're going to go back to work. We'll see each other again eventually and we'll smile and chat like old friends, and one day we might actually be old friends, but friends is all we'll ever be. Because, once again, if we look at it honestly, I'm for the moment still a student and, well, you're not ... it's not legal, or logical or practical."

Tears slipped slowly down her face but she knew in her heart that he was right; it had been no more than a moment of insanity that had allowed them to be together but in the real world it should never have happened.

"Old friends sounds perfect to me. And, yes, I'll see you at school. I may even wave." Judith was trying hard to keep to logic and common sense. "And I'll let you know if I hear anything more about this 'Suspended until further notice' whatever that means."

"Really? Thanks."

"Shit, right … I've got to go. Speak to you later."

She spoke much quicker now and he could hear tapping away on her keyboard.

"Uhmmm, okay. Bye then."

Alex tried to put the phone back on the hook without having to look up or move his head, and eventually fell back into a lying position on the bottom step. That is where Dr Cooper found him.

"What are you doing down here?"

"Resting. My head's killing me …"

"You look awful. I really think we should get you to the hospital, you've lost a lot of blood."

"Really? Back to hospital? I was thinking more food and coffee, lots of coffee, and something cold and sweet to drink, some kind of soda. Any kind, I really don't care."

The doctor was astonished, and couldn't help but show it.

"It's truly amazing, you know."

"What? Which bit exactly?"

"Well, you spill two thirds of your blood out onto the bathroom floor and all you have to show for it is a hangover."

"If this is what a hangover feels like, I'm not even going to start drinking."

He opened one eye to look at Dr Cooper and smiled. The doctor noticed that his eyes were still jet black, but said nothing.

"Well, we both know that's a lie. Come on, let's get some food in you. Maybe it'll make you feel better and we can discuss what we're going to do now."

"Okay. Oh, and thanks for cleaning up the blood, that couldn't have been fun. I really appreciate that."

"I did my trauma training in Johannesburg in South Africa; I've seen a lot of blood in my day." Dr Cooper extended a hand and helped him up,

"Man, I feel terrible."

"Truly remarkable body you've got. I mean, I know that you're going through a rough patch at the moment with everything that's happened, but I'm glad that somewhere inside of you *that* wolf managed to keep you alive last night."

"You know, Doc, I never thought about it like that, but it still can't bring Mom back and I couldn't stop it almost killing that kid at school. I'd still trade all of this for them."

"Well, that's what I wanted to talk to you about." Alex sat down at the kitchen table while Dr Cooper set about getting him something to eat. "After last night's little episode, I started preparing a list of things we could try to maybe suppress the wolf. Not a cure, but maybe an aid, something that'll at least help you to control it more in these emotionally stressful times, without having to pour a bucketful of your blood on the floor."

"Yeah, let's not do that one again. The results were ... well, unpleasant for everyone."

Dr Cooper frowned, surprised yet again at the Harris' ability to make fun of everything. "Well, for reasons best known to themselves, you didn't transform last night despite being under severe emotional distress. I sat up last night thinking about it and, unless you also tried taking a load of pills, I believe the reason why you managed to maintain your human form was blood loss. You didn't take a load of pills, did you?"

"Nope, didn't think of it."

"Good, but if I help you find a way to suppress the wolf, you're not going to try to use it as a search for a more successful way to commit suicide, are you?"

The doctor had adopted a frank, matter-of-fact tone to his voice, one that Alex knew better than to dismiss.

"No."

"Good ... Because you know I've become rather fond of you over the years and seeing you in that state last night was very hard for me. And if that's the road you're going to take, then I won't help you and won't continue to be a part of all of this."

"What? No, Doc, you can't leave me."

"I'm not the one who's tried to leave." Cooper put a mug of coffee down in front of Alex and sat down across from him. "But if you're willing to promise me you'll never try anything like that again, I'll stay and try to help you."

Alex half smiled. "Dad's going to be really disappointed too, huh?" he said without looking up.

"I'm not going to tell him."

For the first time in a week Alex felt like he might actually be able to go back to living what would be some semblance of a normal life. "I promise, suicide is no longer an option worth considering."

"That's my boy. Now, I took the liberty of preparing you some food that you're not going to like, but it *is* good for anaemia."

"Anaemia?"

"Normally, it's a lack of iron in your blood, but in your case it's a lack of blood, full stop."

"How much am I not going to like this food?"

"Let's just say we're even for the cleaning job in the bathroom last night."

"Oh God, that means there's going to be lentils in it, doesn't it?"

"And broccoli and spinach and all kinds of other healthy things that you seem to hate."

"So what, I promise not to try killing myself just so you can poison me?"

Dr Cooper closed his eyes and shook his head. "You people, I'll never understand. I was sitting with your father and Annabel at the hospital, the doctor comes into the waiting room and tells us about your mother and you know what your father said to that poor man?"

"No?"

"Thank you, doctor, I'll tell my girlfriend she can move in." Alex's eye widened and a chuckle bubble up from inside him. "See," the doctor continued, rolling his eyes, "this is what I mean."

"Aw, come on, we're not totally heartless; we just never miss the opportunity to crack a joke. I mean, when will Dad ever have the chance to make that joke again?"

Dr Cooper shook his head, and pushed a plate of food toward the boy. Alex promptly lunged from his seat and threw up in the sink. He stared at the mess for a moment. "And that reminds me. I wouldn't use the upstairs bathroom if I were you."

"It's all right; I've called cleaners to come in this afternoon. But you do still have to eat this food."

"What if I really don't want to?" Alex stared unblinking at the doctor, challenging him. It was clear, however, that Cooper was not going to back down. "Okay, okay, just kidding."

He returned to the table and slowly began picking at his plate. It wasn't long, however, before he realised that he was starving and that if he swallowed as quickly as possible he wouldn't even taste the food. Two full servings later, Alex was asleep in front of the TV and Dr Cooper was explaining to a cleaning company what they needed to do.

It was dark when Alex woke. On the coffee table in front of him were a note and another plate of food.

Been called away by work. I'll only be back late tonight so try not wreck the place again as your father and sister are coming home tomorrow

Doc.

P.S

Eat just one more plate of food, drink two big glasses of water, then you can go back to bed.

Alex grimaced. More food? He curled his lip and shivered in disgust at the plate, then got up and headed to his room to fetch the CDs Brandon had lent him. Back downstairs, he sifted through the pack and pulled out the album featuring the song 'Hooker With a Penis', slipped the disk into the stereo, and pressed play. He turned the speakers up so he could listen from the kitchen, and then set about putting burgers together. Every now and then, he'd go back and play the song again. He listened to it a few times, attempting to sing along. By the time he had finally listened to the rest of the album, he realised that his own poems would work rather well as lyrics for this type of music. He'd take some of his stuff with him to band practice, he thought, and see what the other guys thought about it.

Once he had devoured a couple of cheeseburgers and some fries, and thrown back at least two glasses of water, Alex took himself off to bed. Sleep, however, was the last thing on his mind. He couldn't get out of his head the idea of converting some of his poems into lyrics. He told himself, though, that he'd wait until he actually spoke to the other guys before doing anything about it, but after twenty sleepless minutes he finally gave up, jumped up, found his journal and began searching for the poems he had in mind. And so he sat up in his room converting certain sections of his poems to choruses, and figuring out how they could be sung, until well after two in the morning. Every time he reached the point where he wanted to try to put music to it he would simply put it aside and start on a different poem. Eventually Dr Cooper returned and found him still awake, surrounded by sheets of paper and coffee mugs.

"Alex? What's going on here?"

Alex looked up with a start. "Hey. I'm converting poems into song lyrics. In fact, I've also written a few new ones. One about Mom, another about suicide."

Dr Cooper cocked his head and turned his wrist to Alex. "See the time? It's almost three in the morning ... Why you doing this *now*?"

"Oh, wow, I hadn't realised it was so late! Well, I, uhmmm ... listened to the song my friends want me to sing and it reminded me of some of my poems, so I thought maybe I could convert some into lyrics and then I guess I kinda got carried away."

"I don't mean to burst your creative bubble here. I mean, I love that you're doing this, I believe it can be very good for you, but you still have to talk to your dad about that whole band thing. He's not going to be happy with what's happened since he's been gone and he might not want you to pursue this."

"I know." Alex frowned. "I ... I just really want to try going after normal dreams, like a normal person, like being a rock star," he grinned sheepishly. "When I woke up this morning and remembered everything that had happened I realised that, for me to make that happen, I have to take control. And part of that means not just doing what's expected but also what makes sense to me. It's my life, and I need to have some input."

Dr Cooper let Alex's words sink in for a few seconds. "I couldn't agree more, Alex, but this is a conversation you need to have with your father. I'm sure everything will be all right; you just need to take the time to sit and talk about it."

"How *is* my father? And Annabel? In the wake of everything, I've been so wrapped up in myself I haven't really thought much about them."

Cooper thought for a minute.

"As can be expected, you've been asleep every time he's called. Annabel I haven't spoke to, but your dad never fails to say that she sends you her love. And I've always returned the sentiment on your behalf."

"Did he say much about the funeral at all?"

"No, not really. And I didn't want to push the topic over the phone."

"How much does he know? About our week, I mean."

"Not much, not yet. I don't even think I've had the time to tell him about your recovery. I don't know, he hasn't called very often, he has more than enough on his plate at the moment, I imagine. Must be something of a juggling act for him. And whenever he has called, I've always been recovering from one of the crises here on our end."

Alex nodded, then began shuffling his papers into two piles on the floor. "All right, Doc, I'm gonna go to bed now. What time do they arrive tomorrow?"

"Not sure. Your dad said they'd catch a cab home. But you just make sure you get some shut-eye. Tomorrow's another day." The doctor laughed. "Good night, Alex. Sweet dreams."

Chapter 25

Alex woke the next day to the sound of his father's voice downstairs. He leapt out of bed and ran down to find them.

"DAD!"

Kyle turned just in time to face Alex as he wrapped his arms around his father and lifted him off the ground.

"Oh, thank God you guys are home."

Kyle opened and closed his mouth a few times, trying to find words but all he could manage was, "No wheelchair?"

Alex put his father down and grinned. "Nope. When I changed back after full moon ... I was back to normal. Well, normal-ish."

Annabel appeared out of nowhere and threw her arms around Alex and whispered in his ear, "Oh, I missed you. And that poem ... it was beautiful."

"I missed you guys too. How was it? How are Gran and Grandpa?"

Kyle smiled nervously. "Let's go into the kitchen and grab some coffee," he said. "And we'll tell you all about it."

"Something's wrong."

"Your grandfather's taken this all very hard, but grab a seat and I'll turn the kettle on."

The four made their way into the kitchen, and settled around the table.

"Before we go on," Dr Cooper intruded, "Alex has something to tell you about school.'

Alex turned to Dr Cooper with wide eyes, mouth open, as if to say, "Why would you say that?"

"What?" the doctor frowned. "Someone had to say something, Alex. I could see it wasn't going to be you ..."

"What happened at school, Alex? I thought you were still suspended."

"Well, I am, sort of," Alex half smiled.

Kyle looked annoyed. "So what happened?"

"Well, I went in once I had changed back after full moon and asked Mr Reid if I could come back to school. Explained that I was unfit for air travel and didn't want to sit at home. He was fine with that. Then lunchtime came and that bully I got into a fight with on the first day? Anyway, he made a comment about Mom and I, uhmmm ... lost it a little." Alex's eyes were firmly locked on a little imperfection on the coffee mug in front of him

"How little?"

"I, uhmmm ... I might have broken his jaw and thrown him through a table. Also possibly did some damage to another kid."

"Jesus Christ, Alex!"

Alex began talking quickly, but still wouldn't look up. "I didn't want to do it. I was trying to not talk to anyone and I'd done well all day, but he stopped me as I walked into the cafeteria and challenged me."

"So you threw him through a table?"

"*No!* Well, yes, but ... he said, 'I'm sorry to hear about your mom, but the funeral was beautiful, you shoulda been there.'" The room fell silent again; Alex sighed and finally looked up at his father. "I lost control and not just a little, but totally. I admit it. It was a wonder I didn't transform right there. It only lasted a few seconds, but that's all it took. One minute I was shaking his hand, the next I was standing over some other kid growling. It's a wonder I didn't just rip his arm off and beat him to death with it."

"So ..." Kyle took a few deep, controlled breaths. "You've been expelled, is that what you're trying to tell me?"

"Actually, no ..." Kyle frowned and Alex realised he should get to the point sooner rather than later. "Well, suspended until further notice."

"What does that mean?"

"No idea, but Mr Reid says he wants to have a meeting with all of us when you get back to discuss what we're going to do. He also wanted me to think about possibly majoring in Creative Arts rather than Agriculture."

"Why's that?"

"I might have had a small nervous breakdown in his office. Might have said something like, 'I hate farming.'"

Kyle sighed. "Oh ... Anything else?"

"There're these guys. Good guys. Friends. And they kinda want me to join their band, and in the light of everything that's happened, I figured I'd ask you before I went."

"A band? That's a bit of a turnaround from agriculture, isn't it? Well, we can talk about that later."

"Also," Alex ventured, braver now that he was on something of a roll, "the bully kid, Rick ... He's on a sports scholarship and it's possible I could've ended his sporting career, which I imagine his parents aren't going to be thrilled about."

Kyle's frown deepened. "Jesus, Alex ... For Christ sake, man! I'm trying to be very level-headed about all of this, but you're making it very hard, kiddo ... I'm not happy, but I guess there isn't anything I can do about it now. I'll set up an appointment with Mr. Reid and we'll just have to see if we can save you."

"Sorry. And thanks, Dad," Alex sighed. "Now what's wrong with Grandpa?" Kyle looked down and Annabel began to tear up. Alex was suddenly a lot more worried. "What's happened?"

"Your grandfather's had a heart attack. He's okay, well, not *okay-okay*, he'll pull through. But he's very weak. He'd apparently been sick for a while but, stubborn as he is, he just soldiered through it, then the news of Mom tipped him over the edge."

"So what does it mean?"

"It means that Uncle Jeff has moved to the farm to take over for a bit."

"Okay ..."

"And he'd like you to go up to the farm for a month or two to help out."

Alex's heart lurched. He was instantly agitated; it was clear he wanted to say something but struggled to find the right words. "But what about school?"

"Well, you've taken care of that, haven't you?"

Alex searched his mind for reasons to protest but came up short.

"Look," his father leaned in toward him, "I know it's not ideal, but maybe it's for the best."

"But, Dad!"

"Stop! I'll make you a deal, okay, but hear me out ..." Alex dropped his shoulders and nodded. "I don't really want to lose you for two months, not right now. In fact, originally I said it probably couldn't happen because we weren't sure how fast or slow you were going to recover, but looking at you now, and considering what happened at school, maybe it's not a bad thing for you to get away for a bit. Somewhere where you can run and do some hard work to shed all this extra energy. Spend some time getting back in touch with yourself, some balance."

"But ... but, Dad, I don't want to go into exile. I don't want to go away, be away from you guys, from school."

"I know it's not perfect, but if you do this, for me, for us, then you can join this band with your friends."

"Or?"

"Come now. Things aren't perfect right now, I know; it's hard for everyone and we all have to do things we don't want to be doing. But we'll talk to your headmaster and try to sort things out there. We'll explain that you need to go help your grandfather and get you the books you need. We can talk to him about changing your subjects and I'll get you some books on music to take with you."

Alex sat back in his chair, like he'd just been cut off at the knees and, without thinking, said, "I don't want to be a werewolf any more."

"I know and I'm sorry. I'm sorry that I don't know how to make it better, Alex. Really, I'm failing as a parent, I know that. And I'm sorry. Sorry that all I can do at this point is ask more of you. But it's only for two months, and then when you get back we can work on trying to make things easier. Also I do mean it when I say that getting away might be exactly what you need. It's not exile; it's ... a tactical retreat."

"You're not failing as a parent, Dad. And I get it. I understand that I'm a burden. But I don't mean to be ..."

"You're not a burden, Alex, but sometimes we need to do what has to be done. And if you can go and help your uncle and grandfather, that would be a really good thing. They *need* you, Alex."

"Okay, I'll go," Alex finally admitted defeat and conceded. He understood the rationale, and it did make sense, no matter how much he tried to deny it. "One thing, though ..." he quickly added a proviso. "Can I go after Friday only? I'd like to go to band practice on Thursday."

"Deal! I'll call the travel agent and book the tickets."

Silence once again swept over the table. Alex let his mind wander for a bit.

"What day is it today?"

"Wednesday."

"Right, uhmmm, just so everyone knows, when I was Mork I freaked out a little and bolted and ended up at Ryan's house ... He may have also called a vet, so when you see him again, Annie, and if he asks, you know what happened ..."

"Oh, lovely," Annabel groaned.

Alex tilted his head and sniffed as discreetly as he could, noting that her scent changed slightly at the mention of Ryan, but thought it best to ask in private rather than in front of the whole family.

***

When Alex found himself alone with his thoughts, he couldn't shake the sense of defeat. In a way, he loved the farm, and wanted to see his grandparents, but at the same time he didn't want to do it now. All he wanted now was to hang out with his new friends and see what developed with the band. He couldn't help but feel disgruntled, angry even, which to him seemed a very dangerous place to be, so he headed back up to his room and forced himself to get back to work on his poetry. Converting his poetry to song lyric was at least a way to stop his mind from spinning round in ever-decreasing circles. He fell quickly back into what he had been doing the night before and in what seemed like no time at all his father was knocking on his door. He had called Mr Reid and the two had chatted briefly, and had settled on appointment for that very afternoon.

Alex was glad that his father would be with him. Something about his dad being there made everything that had happened in the past week seem more real, more severe. He kept checking and re-checking where the scars would have been to make extra sure that they weren't there any more. An attempted suicide was the last thing his father needed to find out about right now. The whole idea of trying to kill himself seemed so stupid to Alex that when he thought about it he had to cringe.

The drive to school seemed inordinately long and very quiet. Kyle was still a little angry, but he knew that if he was going to be able to give his son any kind of defence he would have to keep his mind clear, open, and calm. He'd treat it as he would any other legal case, he thought. And that meant logic and common sense.

Alex was pleased to see Judith, and gave her a conspiratorial wink. She, in turn, smiled politely back.

"Mr Reid is expecting you," she said. "So you can just go right in."

Mr Reid rose from his desk as the door opened.

"Mr Harris, good to see you." The headmaster took Kyle's hand. "Firstly, my deepest sympathy for your loss. Something like that can't be easy."

"It's not. But thank you."

"And, young Master Harris, how are you feeling?"

"Better, thank you sir."

"Good, good. Now, please take a seat and we can see about sorting this all out." Alex and Kyle sat down while Mr Reid returned to his side of the desk. "Right, lets get the good news out of the way first. The young boy Alex got into the brawl with doesn't have any permanent injuries that will impede his running career."

Kyle looked at Alex and frowned, then looked back to Mr Reid, "So what *are* the extent of his injuries?"

"Well, the most severe is the jaw, plus a few missing teeth. His shoulder was dislocated and he cracked a few ribs."

"What about the other guy?" Alex interrupted.

"Yes, I was just coming to him. He was kept in hospital for a few days for observation; they took an X-ray of his stomach to check whether anything had ruptured, but it appears it was just some bruising and swelling, nothing too bad. Doctors say he will make a full recovery."

Kyle sighed. "So, what's the bad news?"

"Well, obviously the parents of these boys don't just want Alex expelled, they want to lay assault charges."

"And what do you think, Mr Reid?"

"I think Alex has a lot of potential and it would be a waste to remove him for the school system at this point, so I'd like to find a way to get him out of this and keep him at school. At the same time, though, I also see great potential in the other boys and Alex's little outburst of violence goes completely against school policy. He could have crippled or even killed either of those boys and it's a miracle that he didn't. As it stands, Rick's face will never look the same again."

Once again Kyle looked over at Alex and shook his head; Alex in turn dropped his head and resisted the urge to respond. The room fell silent while Kyle ordered his thoughts. He liked Mr Reid and felt a little bad for what he was about to do.

"Firstly, from what I've heard from my son, he was minding his own business, looking for his friends, and was about to leave when that boy, Rick? Stopped him and not only physically challenged him, but made a comment about his mother, my late wife that was not only offensive to me and my family but also potentially emotionally damaging, considering Alex's ... uhmmm ... health issues. Secondly, Alex should not have been back at school in the first place. Not only was he still suspended but emotionally unfit, which is something you should have picked up on when you had your meeting with him that same morning. Of course, I don't condone his behaviour, but had anyone have said something like that to me I might have thrown him through a table as well." Kyle could feel his blood pressure begin rise. "Thirdly, once Alex stood up to the first bully, two more stepped in to take his place as if they knew a fight was going to start, which indicates premeditated action. It seems to me the only reason they've brought this to your attention is because they lost. It's also not the first time my son has had a run-in with these same bullies. The first time being when he had to come to the defence of another of your students, who in turn claims to have had multiple run-ins with these boys in the past. Which brings me to my final point, Mr Reid, what is the school's policy in relation to gangs?"

Kyle let the question sink in for a seconds but didn't wait for an answer before he continued his onslaught. "Personally, as a parent of two children at this school, I'm not impressed. You approached me with promises of specialised education and attention for my children's individual needs and I feel like none of those promises have been met. And I'm not afraid to take this to a public forum. In fact, for me to even consider allowing either of my children to continue at this school I'm going to need your word that something will be done about this schoolyard gang that seems to have been so firmly established, and I'd like Rick and his friends to face a full disciplinary hearing. Do you have video surveillance around the public sections of the school?"

Mr Reid stared open-mouthed at Kyle. "Uhmmm, yes, b—"

"Fantastic, if I could get the video from the cafeteria and the adjacent hallway where the original incident occurred, we can see just who did in fact start these fights and determined the correct person to be punished. When is good for you?"

Reid sat in silence, contemplating the best way to respond, but when he did speak his words were controlled and calm, at a lower volume to what Alex was used to.

"I'm sure it won't have to come to that, Mr Harris. But if you insist, obviously I'll be happy to investigate the matter further for you. In the meantime, I'm happy to reinstate Alex as a student and wipe his record clean."

"Well, that's a good start, thank you, but we have a second problem, don't we?"

The headmaster heaved a sigh of relief. "Yes, yes we do. Alex does not want to be a farmer. Now, I don't know how much of this he has discussed with you, but he seems to have a much stronger preference towards his creative writing class and has bonded with some of the other media students. It seems to me that he would be far better suited there. He could focus more on his creative writing than perhaps music, as to my knowledge he can't actually play an instrument. But obviously those kind of decisions are up to you and him."

For the first time since arriving at the school Kyle smiled at Alex. "Son, would you mind waiting outside?"

"No."

Once Alex had pulled the door closed behind him, Kyle then turned back to Mr Reid.

"Sorry about that. I don't like talking about people as if they're not in the room, unless they're actually not in the room."

"No, no, that's fine, please continue,"

"Well, Alex and I have discussed it, and he would like to transfer to be closer to his friends and spend more time writing, which I support wholeheartedly. I want my children to be happy, and in the face of what's happened I think this is the best move for him. That being said, he is not going to be able to attend school for the next two months." Kyle dropped his eyes and for just a moment Mr Reid noticed a gap in his resolve. In that brief instant, he could see a man near breaking point with no light at the end of the tunnel. "Alex's grandfather didn't take the news too well and has subsequently had a heart attack."

"Oh my, Mr Harris, I'm sorry to hear that."

"Thank you. The doctor says he should be fine but he needs to have as much bed rest as possible and under no circumstances is he allowed to work. Alex's uncle is going to take the run of the family farm, but would like Alex there as support as he does have lots of work experience there. This of course means he won't be able to attend school for a good few weeks."

"That should pose no problem. Do they have internet access on the farm?"

"Yes."

"Well, we can easily arrange for major projects to be e-mailed to Alex and he can work on them there and e-mail them in. When does he leave?"

"Friday, it looks like. I'm going to call my travel agent this afternoon."

"Right, well, I can have a staff meeting with his new teachers tomorrow morning and arrange for them to compile lists of things he'll need for the next two months and he can just do things from there. It will put him at a bit of a disadvantage during examinations, of course, but he's a smart boy, and I'm sure he'll be able to catch up on any class discussions he might miss out on."

Kyle got to his feet and extended his hand.

"Thank you, I do appreciate your consideration and understanding in these difficult times, Mr Reid. I think in two months he will also have come to terms with things a bit more. He's not a violent person; I truly believe this to be a combination of stress and someone saying the worst thing at the worst time."

The headmaster nodded. "I really do understand, and I wish him all the best. Although Rick isn't a small boy, I mean, he could easily be as big as you or I, Alex must be extremely strong to lift him in the first place, let alone put him through a wooden table."

Kyle made an effort to put on a concerned face. "You know, he is a strong boy for his age; he has to stay very fit and as healthy as possible. But I was talking to him about the incident and it sounds to me like he had a mild blackout. He says he felt totally out of control of his body, which I've heard is common during massive adrenaline surges. Did you ever read about the woman who lifted a truck out of the way of her child?"

"Oh, yes, I remember something about that, crushed her hips under the weight but still managed to lift this truck and save her child. You think Alex had that much adrenaline in his system?"

"I think if you put someone under enough emotional stress, anything's possible."

"Mmm, interesting. Anyway, Mr Harris, I'm glad we could sort this out. I understand now why they say you're one of the best lawyers on the island. If I ever get into any kind of trouble I'm glad I have your number."

"Just *one* of the best?" Kyle laughed. "But, yes, thank you again, Mr Reid, we'll leave you now. And hopefully we won't have to meet under such circumstances again. Should the other parents decide to continue to push this matter, though, I will follow through with my investigation. I trust you'll be able to dissuade them. The consequences could be disastrous, for us all, I mean."

The headmaster realised that this was no idle threat, or in fact a threat at all but a warning.

"Yes, thank you, let's hope it doesn't come to that. Goodbye, Mr Harris."

Kyle turned towards for the door but stopped and turned back.

"May I ask you a personal question?"

Mr Reid looked at the man for a few seconds and sighed. "You want to know why I didn't just expel him?"

"Basically, yes. I mean, he has broken most of the rules and a few laws."

The room fell silent for a few seconds while Mr Reid considered how to respond.

"When I ... When I was ten years old I was diagnosed with cancer. I spent the next eighteen months in and out of hospitals, chemo-therapy, radiation, the works. I lost all my hair, missed two years of school and died twice, clinically, anyway. When I was finally giv-en the all-clear to go back to school I looked different. I was older than everyone else and the few friends I had meant the world to me. Then a year later I suffered a relapse and went through the whole process again. I remember coming back to school, almost three years behind everyone, and feeling frustrated and angry with myself, the cancer and the world, and I wished more than anything that someone would ... well, that someone would stand by me, be on my side. I understood then that it's difficult being the one who's different. When I look at Alex, I can't help but remem-ber how I felt and ... and I ... I know how it feels to be a sick child, to be the odd one out."

Kyle swallowed hard to clear the knot in his throat. "My parents were in a car accident when I was a teenager. I boarded and fos-tered throughout my high-school career. I can't tell you how much I appreciated knowing that someone here understands how hard it is for him. Thank you, truly, thank you for ... understanding."

***

Alex noticed that his father was taking a different route home than usual, which took a few minutes longer but missed the intersection where the accident had taken place.

"So, Dad, how was the funeral?"

Kyle bit his lip. "It was okay. A lot of folk showed up. Even Gaillard, the headmaster of her school, came. Your uncle couldn't think of anything to say so he played 'The Night They Drove Old Dixie Down'. Annie wanted to say something but didn't manage to get much out, poor thing. She was saved by Frankie who said a few sweet things. It was nice, as far as funerals go, I suppose. I read out your poem, I hope that's okay, and Annabel slipped it into the coffin with Mom."

Alex narrowed his eyes. "Frankie? But how old's he?"

Kyle let out a hollow laugh. "You know, that's exactly what I asked. He was twelve in January."

"Wow."

"I know, right? Smart kid, though. Must get that from his aunt's side of the family."

Then silence settled once again.

Chapter 26

Alex awoke excited the next day. It was Thursday and that meant band practice, his very first. Between his early morning and everyone else's jetlag the whole family was up and about much earlier than normal, which prompted Kyle to take them out for breakfast. Even though he had breakfast virtually out every day, he almost never got a chance to take the kids. He was always working and they had school. Then on weekends someone inevitably had plans or was asleep or a wolf. After the accident, Kyle had been instructed to return to work only when he felt he was ready. It was no secret how he and Debra had felt about each other. Even after all those years of marriage and two kids, they could still act like a high-school couple, going on dates, surprising each other with gifts. On some level, both Annabel and Alex felt worse for their dad than they did for themselves.

Kyle took them to his favourite coffee shop, although Alex was less keen now that Melanie had moved on to a better-paying job. Kyle still parked in his company parking spot around the corner, and they walked over to the coffee shop. As they made their way to the table, the place fell quiet. Alex, Annabel and Kyle stood for a few moments while everyone stared, not sure what to do or say. And then, in a sudden moment of inspiration, Alex leapt into the middle of the room, threw his head back, arms out and yelled.

"Ta-daah!"

The entire café, including Kyle and Annabel, burst into hysterics.

"Well done, and thank you," Kyle leaned over and whispered as they pulled out their chairs and sat down.

"Had to do something," Alex smiled. "It was either that or make a rude comment but I'm not sure everyone here would've seen the humour ..."

"Hey, Alex," Annabel patted him on the shoulder, "You're going to be really glad you chose *ta-daah!* When you see whose back for a visit."

Instinct made Alex sniff the air before actually turning around, but he already knew what she meant. He blushed as soon as he locked eyes with Melanie. It had been just under a year since they last bumped into each other in the mall. He quickly turned back to the centre of the table.

"Oh no."

He shot a glance up at his father who had his eyes closed and was biting both his lips to stop himself from laughing. Melanie bounced over to the table and kissed Alex on the cheek.

"That was some entrance!"

Alex's old crush leapt back to life like a flash, and he blushed. Kyle had now turned his head away and was holding his breath, his face red.

"Lovely to see you again, Mel." Annabel was trying equally hard not to roll her eyes. "It's been so long. How are you? Would you like to join us?"

"Sure, if that's okay with your dad."

"Yeah, that's fine," Kyle just managed to compose himself. "Please do. That'd be lovely. Right, Alex?"

Melanie took the last empty seat, across from Alex, while Kyle rapidly pulled himself together. Alex focused on the table, his eyes fixed on an imaginary centrepiece. Eventually Annabel kicked him under the table and he realised he'd missed a question aimed at him.

"Wh— Sorry, I was off in my own world ... What did I say? What did you say?"

"I said, and how are you Alex?" Melanie giggled. "How's your new school? Making nice friends?"

"Err, I joined a band."

"Wow! That's so cool. I always knew you'd grow up to be famous. What are you guys called?"

He opened his mouth to say but then his courage began to falter. "Uhmmm ... Sp— Spanner. We're, uhmmm ... a Tool cover band."

"Awesome, I love Tool."

Alex dropped his head to the side. "Really?"

"What? Am I too old to know about all the cool bands?" Melanie smiled devilishly. "Or are you just too cool for me now?"

In a moment of uncharacteristic brave, he managed to say, "I could never be too cool for you."

It was Melanie's turn to blush, and she had to remind herself that he was, in fact, much younger than he looked. "Well, aren't you just mister charming, I bet you have all the girls at school lining up outside your house."

A shiver ran down the spine of everyone else at the table, as Melanie hit tender nerve. Alex's relationship with Judith and the resulting events was still a sore point. Annabel saved her, though.

"Apparently, it's quite a *short* queue."

A look of horror rushed over Alex's face and he stared open-mouthed at his sister.

Kyle closed his eyes and shook his head, but let himself to chuckle softly, "This is all getting a bit much to handle before coffee."

Gripped by reflex, Melanie hopped to her feet. "Oh sorry, I'll go grab you a m— Oh, wait, I don't work here any more."

She blushed again and sat down, but her actions did prompt a waiter to deliver menus and take drinks orders. Melanie chatted for a few minutes longer until her takeaway arrived, but then explained that she had to run. Alex watched as she headed out, the wind just catching her fringe as she stepped onto the pavement and turned the corner ...

"Oy! You hear me? I asked what time band practice was?"

"Uhmmm ..." Alex scanned his memory to his conversation with Danny. "I don't actually know."

"Fantastic, how do we find out?"

"I could call the school?"

"You do that then."

"So, I think I'm going to break up with Ryan." Annabel dropped the bombshell.

"What?" Both men spun around to face her.

She was staring down at her food, shifting it around with her fork. "Yeah, I'm just not too sure about it now. I mean, I really like him and everything, but it's hard to concentrate on school work and him at the same time and right now I think school's more important."

It had never occurred to Alex when he had warned Ryan about treating his sister right that it might be her who would hurt *him*.

"Sweetheart," Kyle tried to reassure her, "I know that feeling very well. It's hard to have a successful professional life and a successful relationship. But your mother and I are proof that it's possible ... were proof. Either way, you don't have to give up on Ryan in favour of school if you don't want to. Just be sensible about it, and take it easy."

Annabel continued to shift things around on her plate. "No, I think I'm going to break up with Ryan. It's the right thing to do, I know it."

The monotone to her voice told her father that there was no point in arguing. She had made up her mind and was going to stick to it. He recognised it as a tone Debra would use when her mind was totally made up.

"Okay, then. That's very mature of you."

Alex knew enough to keep his mouth shut during these kinds of conversations, so it was only once they were back home that he was brave enough to offer an opinion. He had headed back to his room to sort out all his songs so he could take them along to band practice, and found Annabel lying on his bed. He knew what was coming so without saying anything he climbed in next to her and waited.

"I don't want to break up with Ryan, but I can't think of another way to calm my life down. Between school and him and Mom and you and Grandpa, Ryan's the only thing I feel in control of, it's the only part of my life I feel has anything to do with me or I have any influence over. Dammit, Alex, I don't know what to do. What do you think?"

"I think it's stupid to get rid of the only part of your life you feel makes sense right now. Because once you do that you're only left with the crazy, the stuff you can't control, and that's got to be worse, right?"

She rolled onto her back and let the tears roll down her face. "How is it that you always know how to solve my problems in easy-to-understand language?"

"Balance. You got numbers, I got words."

"That was supposed to be a rhetorical question, but that, see, that makes sense too." She sighed heavily. "I just don't know any more."

"Here's one for you ... Why do I have to go to the farm for two months if Uncle Jeff's going to be there?"

"Because, with Grandpa sick and his sister having just died, he's under a lot of stress and could use the help on the farm."

"Bullshit! Until you got back you thought I was half broken and in a wheelchair. What's the real reason?"

"That is the real reason, but also because we think it'll be good for you to get some time away from everything to really think about what's happened. Dad's worried you're blaming yourself and is scared you're going to do something stupid."

"Stupid how?"

"Stupid like hurt yourself."

Alex felt himself get warm and prickly. "Well, you can rest assured that that's not ever going to happen. I can't, I won't abandon my family. I just don't think it's fair that I have to go away for two months. I mean, how sick is Grandpa really?"

Annabel rolled over, turning her back to Alex.

"Annie, how sick is he?"

Without turning to face him, she answered, "Really, really sick."

"Is he going to be all right?"

She turned to face him, wrapped her arms around him and cried into his shoulder. It became clear to Alex that he was being sent to the farm for two months because they might be the last two months he ever spends with his grandfather.

"Why didn't anyone tell me?"

"We didn't want to upset you. You know … Mork and everything. And you're about to get on a flight and everything …"

Tears filled Alex's eyes as he held his weeping sister. Then, out of the blue, she asked, "Does it hurt?"

"Does what hurt?"

"When you transform?"

He allowed himself a moment before answering. "It's not really something you can explain; it ticks the same boxes as pain, but isn't pain. Also, the feeling hasn't changed since the first time; it's exactly the same every time. I can feel it all happening, the hair growing, the bones changing, Mork taking over."

She felt a well of pity for her brother, but the moment was interrupted by the phone ringing downstairs. Alex quickly pulled himself free.

"That'll be Judith. I called her to ask if she could find out what time band practice is today."

He bolted to grab the phone, but it didn't take long before he was back.

"So, what time's practice?"

"Four. In the school music room."

"And what's all this stuff on your floor?"

"I started turning my poems into song lyrics."

"Really? That sounds cool."

"You think? I was gonna take them to practice and see what the guys think."

"What do you mean by 'was'?"

"Well, now that it's like in a few hours, I'm starting to get nervous that it'll suck and they'll think I'm a dick for bringing them in."

"Really?"

"Little bit; more worried that they'll like them, though."

"Why?"

"Because if they like them, then they'll turn them into songs and my poems will be played to people. Which means my inner thoughts are going to be displayed to the world, open to criticism?"

"To the world? *Please*, let's not get ahead of ourselves here, Elvis. I think it's cool though that you wanna turn your poems into songs."

"Yeah?"

"Yeah."

"Cool, so can you help me organise them?"

"How?"

"No idea, that's the help I need."

She laughed. "Fine, you make coffee, and I'll see if I can neaten this all up for you."

"You're an angel. Be right back."

The two spent the next hour trying to organise Alex's writing into two folders, before they finally moved from his room to the lounge and planted themselves in front of the television with a large bowl of popcorn. Annabel took the remote because she'd been away from any kind of TV since she'd left for the farm, but that gave Alex the opportunity to work at a few more poems. He hadn't realised how many there were until he'd started this project. He'd been writing about one a week for almost five years.

By the time Kyle eventually joined them, Alex had already started to gather all his things for practice. So as not to be left alone, Annabel came along for the drive.

"What time does this end?"

"Not sure, but I'll call you? Or maybe I'll just walk home."

"I'd rather you called, but suit yourself."

"Did you get hold of the travel agent?"

"Yes, you're booked on the flight tomorrow. We have to be there at 11 am, so be sure to pack tonight and ask your friend which books you'd need if you really want to learn guitar and we can take a look first thing tomorrow."

"Oh, okay. Cool! Thanks, Dad."

They pulled up outside the school and Alex hopped out with his files and Brandon's guitar, and headed off in the direction of the music department. The others were waiting outside.

"You made it!" Brandon leapt up first. "We weren't sure if you were actually coming, but you made it. Awesome!"

Alex couldn't help but detect a slight hesitation in Brandon's voice, which made him feel uncomfortable.

"Everything all right, guys? I mean, is it still cool that I'm here?"

Josh and Danny looked at each other.

"Yeah, man, don't stress. We've just been chatting and ... well, thing is we've not actually heard you sing." Danny glanced over at Brandon. "All we've got to go on is old Talent Scout here going on about your growling technique. So, you know, we're just a little nervous that Brandy here got your hopes up and it turns out you sing like a cat with its balls in a meat grinder."

Alex burst out laughing. "It's cool, man! Let's give this a go and you can tell me, because honestly I don't know anything about this stuff compared to you guys."

"Awesome!" Brandon, Josh and Danny beamed. "Then let's do this thing."

Alex followed the others into the music room. Josh handed him a lyric sheet and Brandon put the song they were going to play on while they set themselves up. Alex put his file and guitar down and took his place at the microphone, his back to the band, mouthing the words of the song as it played. He was more nervous than he thought he'd be since their little chat. When the song ended, he took a few deep breaths to calm himself and told himself he was going to give this song everything he had, from growl to howl. If this was the only time he played with these guys then he was gonna rock it.

"Right, Alex, we know this song backwards, so if you can keep up we're just gonna keep going, 'kay?"

Alex turned to look at them. "Yeah, no problem. I've been listening to this song on a loop since the other day. I think I can handle."

Josh gave him the thumbs up, and then counted the other guys in. Alex turned back to face the imaginary audience. Behind him the band started and he waited for his cue, trying not to think about how pitch perfect the others sounded. And then he took a deep breath and gave it his all. He put his heart in it, like it was just him and the mic. He thought nerves would hold him back, prevent him from going all out. But there was nothing. Just the lyrics and his voice. He knew he'd nailed it. As the final note was struck, Josh, Brandon and Danny yelled in excitement. Alex turned to look at them red-faced and pumped up.

"How was that?"

"Fuckin' awesome, man! You rocked! That was AMAZING! I've never heard anyone actually sing like that. You're so in the band, dude. Soooooo in the band."

Alex tried to act cool for a moment, but failed to stop himself smiling.

"For the first time really, I feel like we're a real band."

Brandon and Josh high-fived each other.

"The way I feel now," Brandon piped up, "I just want to have practice every day. I told you he was the man for the job, man. *I told you!*"

Alex quickly lost his smile. "Yeah, about that, guys."

Josh turned to look at him, a frown on his face. "What? Don't tell us after that you can't join the band? That you've changed your mind."

"No, no, I'm *so* in the band, but there's a snag ... I have to go work on my grandfather's farm for the next two months."

"Where's the farm?"

"Canada."

"What?" The three other boys groaned.

"But my dad said I should ask you guys what books I should get so I can start to learn guitar. And Reid says I can transfer to Music major instead of Agriculture."

"What? Really? That's awesome, man. So, like, that's it, we're a real band?"

Alex smiled nervously again. "Well, there's one other thing ... And I don't mean to jump the gun here, but I've been writing poems for the last five or so years and over the last few days I've been listening to only Tool and converting some of my poems into lyrics, or to the best of my knowledge, song lyrics. And I was just thinking, if you guys wanted to take a look at them and maybe we could use something there and produce our own songs."

They looked at him in amazement.

"That's awesome, man. Is that what's in the folder?"

Josh quickly put his guitar down and ran over to Alex's folder and started paging through it.

"This stuff's awesome, dude. You really wrote this?"

"Well, I've been writing things like that for years, I just added bits and made choruses and things, but I know nothing about the actual music side of it. So what I was thinking was maybe you guys could find a way to put music to it. But I really don't want to feel like I'm taking over here, this is your guys' thing."

Josh looked up at him. "It's *our* band now, and we've needed someone like you for ages. This file is just the push we need to really get this thing started. For our year-end project we were thinking about doing, like, a music video. Up until this point we were going to do another Tool song but now we can actually do an original." A spark of excitement shot around the room. "We can really do this now."

"I've got another folder easily three times bigger than that one of more poems. I can work on converting them as best I can while I'm away and learn guitar while you guys put music to some of those?"

"Sounds like a plan. Sounds like an amazing, awesome plan."

The boys spent the next two hours reading through one of Alex's pieces, showing him how he could better convert the poems, and explaining the structure of lyrics as opposed to poems. Josh also compiled a list of good self-help books to help Alex learn how to play. By the time the two hours were up, Alex had a lot to think about. Once they all said their goodbyes, Alex decided that he would in fact walk home. He left his folder of songs with Josh so that the band could work on turning them into proper songs while he was away.

It was just after seven by the time he arrived home, still excited about the prospect of being part of a real-life band and finally doing something he was genuinely passionate about. Alex found his father and sister in the TV room.

"Aah, there you are! So, how was it?"

"Awesome, absolutely awesome. Such a rush. Josh gave me a list of books I should get. Apparently I don't need all of them; there's one that's a must and any one of the others, as it's basically the same information."

"Great, I'm glad you enjoyed it. Now go get cleaned up, we're going out for dinner. And be quick. Dr Cooper will be waiting for us."

Alex shot upstairs, dived in and out of a shower, pulled on some clean clothes and was downstairs and in the car ten minutes later. Given the drastic difference in diet between Alex and Dr Cooper, dinner would inevitably be sushi, the one thing they all agreed on. By the time they arrived, Dr Cooper was already seated, waiting for them.

"So, your father tells me you're going to Canada for two months. Excited?"

"I guess, but I had band practice today and that went really well."

"Oh yes, I'd forgotten about that. I'm glad you liked it; it'll be good for you." And then, turning to Kyle, he asked, "And what happened with the school? You managed to get all that sorted?"

"They're going to let him back in, but it took more than a few threats and I doubt I'm going to be invited to school social events anytime soon."

"Not making any friends that side, huh?"

"Well, I couldn't just let him sit around the house; he deserves to be unhappy like the rest of us."

"Which reminds me, Alex, I've been looking into possible options for suppressing the wolf, and I think I may even have found a few to try."

Kyle's face went blank for a moment. "Sorry, what?"

Dr Cooper turned to Alex. "Haven't had that conversation yet, have you?"

Alex shrugged nervously.

"What am I missing here, folks?" Kyle's face turned sour.

Alex stayed quiet for a moment in the hope that Dr Cooper would explain but quickly realised that that wasn't going to happen.

"See, the thing is, I've tried embracing this whole thing and it's not working. I feel more and more out of control of Mork and out of control of my life. So I asked Dr Cooper if we could start looking into ways of suppressing him."

"I thought that's what all the meditation and Tai chi was for?"

"That was all to learn control and find a balance between Mork and me."

"Isn't that a good thing?"

"No, I'm tired of walking a tight rope the whole time. I don't want *balance*, I want off."

"You mean, like a *cure*?"

Dr Cooper could see both men beginning to get frustrated and a little angry.

"Gentlemen, this is neither the time nor the place to be having this conversation. Kyle, the long and short of it is that Alex has asked me to look more into suppressing the wolf as opposed to finding a way to—"

But before he could finish, Annabel said the thing no one wanted to say: "This is because of Mom, isn't it? You're blaming Mork for her death, or at least her being dead and you being fine."

The table went quiet and Alex could feel his chest heating up, a tingle creeping across his face as emotions welled up. Taking a long, deep breath in, he exhaled the word, "Yes." He waited a moment before he continued. "Yes, that is why, and it might sound childish, but I feel justified. So I want to find a way to try to put Mork to bed. It might not work, but I want to try."

The waiter returned to the quiet table to serve the drinks. They sat in awkward silence until he had poured and left.

"Alex, it's not your fault,"

"Yeah, how not? She should have been at work. I should've been in class, but I get the scent of a girl and suddenly rational thoughts fly out the window. And two hours later my mother's dead. Tell me how that's not my fault."

"Alex, son, you can't live your life thinking that. It's not your fault someone decided to jump the red light and there is no way you could have known that your actions would have led to that outcome."

Alex looked down and wiped the tears from his eyes.

"Alex, I love you, you know that. And I will always love you. What happened to your mother is a tragedy like no other, but you cannot burden yourself with that. I don't mind that you want to look into other options, but don't exclude us, your family. Annabel and I are still here, and so is Rajan. If you decide to carry your mother's death solely on your shoulders and push us away, you'll fall. We don't want that. So take a deep breath and calm down. We're all still here for each other, we're still a family. All right?"

Alex looked up at his sister, who was crying again, then turned to his father whose eyes had gone slightly red and puffy.

"Okay."

"That's my boy. Now, what you gonna have for dinner?"

Alex smiled at his father, then turned to the menu. "Same thing I always have." He put the menu down on the table and turned his attention to Annabel. "How are you *really*?"

"What?"

"How are you?"

Annabel looked anxiously at Dr Cooper and her father, then back at Alex.

"I imagine much the same as you guys, desperately sad, with no idea when there will again be light at the end of this tunnel, but I'm going to keep soldiering on in the dark until I find it."

Kyle cracked a half smile and shook his head. "That's actually a really good way to word that," he said. "Maybe you should be writing Alex's songs."

Alex frowned.

"Oh come on," laughed Annabel. "That's more of a compliment to you than anything else." Then she turned to her father. "Actually, Dad, I stole most of that from one of his poems. I was reading through them this morning. It just seemed to make sense to me for what was happening now and how I was feeling."

"Really? Well maybe there's something in this band thing after all."

Chapter 27

Despite an early night Alex still only woke when his sister tiptoed in with a cup of coffee in the morning. Annabel put the cup down and stood arm's length away.

"Alex? Aaaalex, it's time to get up now."

He opened one eye grumpily. "What's the magic word?"

She laughed to herself. "Coffee?"

"Works for me."

He sat up in bed and Annabel quickly covered her eyes and turned away. "Whoa! Not so fast, I'm still in here."

"Oh please! I'm decent …"

"But what's the attraction to sleeping naked anyway?"

He blinked at his sister. "Really? We're going to have this conversation right now?"

"Well, I'm just curious, is all …"

"Why do I sleep naked? Well, I guess it's the same reason I don't wear underwear …"

"You don't wear underpants? *Why?*"

He rubbed his eyes and muttered under his breath, "This is so much more than I want to deal with before coffee." He lay back down and said in a tired voice, "I have an erection, now go away."

Annabel recoiled in horror and scuttled out of the room. Alex smiled to himself and made a mental note. He got himself out of bed and dressed before picking up his coffee and heading down-stairs. In the kitchen he was met by an equally tired-looking father and still slightly disgusted sister.

"Oh, relax, I just said that to get you to leave so I could get dressed. You're a smart girl, but no sense of timing."

Kyle looked up at his children. "What did I miss?"

"Nothing," Annabel frowned. "Nothing you actually want to hear about."

"Never mind then, I don't want to know. Now … what are you mak-ing me for breakfast, kids?"

Bowls of porridge, cups of coffee and a shower later, everyone was ready to face the day. Annabel and Kyle helped Alex pack up the last of his stuff.

"Alex, how exactly do you plan on getting this guitar to Canada?"

"Uhmmm, I thought about that in the night actually."

"And?"

"Nothing, no idea. What are you thinking?"

"Well, I suppose I could get you a case."

"For a guitar I don't actually own?"

"Well, I guess you could just leave that one here and we could get you a guitar of your own then."

Alex smiled for a moment then had a minor epiphany. "Why hasn't Annie complained about all the things you're planning on buying me?"

Kyle looked over at Annabel. "You tell him."

"Tell me what?"

"Dad's ordered me a new laptop and cell phone and a few other things ..."

"Well, that would explain it then."

***

Alex spent what seemed like hours talking to the mall's music store salesman about guitars, before eventually picking one out. His original thoughts about getting his own guitar were humble, cheap but good. But since learning about his sister's good fortune, he decided to simply go with the best one his father would be willing to pay for. He selected three guitars and arranged them in order of the one he wanted most to the one he'd be most willing to settle for, which was inevitably also descending order of price.

Kyle stared at them for a while.

"So, that's the one you want, huh?"

"Yes."

"Is that the most expensive guitar in the shop?"

Alex looked over at the salesman who shook his head.

"No."

"If this is what's going to make you happy ..."

"Dad, just that one song we did and the way the guys reacted to my lyrics made me happier than I've been in a long, long time, maybe ever. I mean, I know right now I don't know too much about the music but they *really* do, and I've got this voice and it's something I've always wanted to do, or at least always thought would be something I could be good at."

Kyle smiled, a large part of him relieved that Alex had decided to fight against the original plan and skip the easy way out, going instead for the much harder but more rewarding option, an option that five years ago seemed entirely impossible.

"Then we're with you. Just don't lose touch with the family and lose control and think you can't call us, we don't want you going the way of that Kurt Corbin fellow."

"Cobain, Dad. Kurt Cobain."

"I know, but the cliché is that I get the name wrong and sound all uncool and old-timery."

Alex shook his head and laughed, "You're insane, you know that?"

"I know. And it's funny what's genetic ... Now, grab the one you want and let's get a case for it, some books and head off to the airport."

"Really? I can have the one I want?"

"Yip, just don't tell your mo—"

They both stopped dead in their tracks. Kyle closed his eyes and shook his head.

"Sister ... Don't tell your sister how much it cost."

His tone was suddenly flat and distant. Alex simply nodded his head but couldn't bring himself to make eye contact. He picked up the guitar.

"So you're taking that one?" The salesman leapt back to life.

"Yeah, yeah. Also, I'm getting on a flight to Canada in a few hours so I need a nice hard case for it and a few books. I've got the titles written down here."

Alex dug in his pocket and handed the salesman a crumpled sheet of paper.

"Groovy, I'll go grab all those, and if you could just hand me the guitar I'll get all the cables and a case." The salesman smiled at Kyle. "Don't worry, the display price includes a case, a small amp and a good set of headphones so he can play it to himself and not disturb the rest of the neighbourhood."

"Thanks, Dad. That's so awesome, I can't even find words to thank you."

And suddenly all anxiety was gone.

"My pleasure, kiddo. Now you do us all proud, okay?" He could feel a lump growing in his throat. "Right! Let's take this stuff to the till and pay before you make me buy more."

When they had loaded it all into the car, they headed back into the mall to find warm clothes. It was mid-February, which on Syn Island meant mild temperatures and rain, but in Canada frozen, snow-covered wasteland. Clothes shopping, even when for himself, always made Alex miserable but he forced himself. By the time everything was done they had to head straight for airport. With the addition of the new guitar and amplifier, Alex's luggage was hopelessly overweight. He grinned at the woman at the check-in counter in the hope that a smile alone could get him out of trouble.

"I'm terribly sorry, Mr Harris, but you're either going to have to remove some luggage or pay for the excess weight."

Alex looked nervously at his father, who was waiting with Annabel at a coffee shop.

"How much am I over?"

"Well, you're allowed twenty-five kilograms and you're at about thirty-four ..."

"How much is it per kilo?"

"$35 per kilo, times nine is ..." She tapped away at a calculator. "That'd be 315 Syn dollars, sorry."

"Naa, it's not your fault, don't worry about it. I'm just not sure what to do now; I mean, my father's just spent a lot of money buying me this stuff. I'm gonna be in Canada on a farm for two months and there really isn't that much to do there. Is there really no way around it?'

He looked the woman up and down as subtly as he could; she wasn't bad looking, nothing amazing, but he knew she had his ID information in front of her and, despite what he looked like, she knew he was just sixteen. He smiled at her again anyway, figured there wasn't a reason not to try.

"I mean, could my luggage go on, like, standby and if the flight doesn't fill up it can slide through under the radar, so to speak?"

The woman narrowed her eyes curiously at him, and finally broke into a slight giggle.

"That a good sign?"

"You're not as subtle as you might like to think, *young* man."

His attempt at a charming smile now slipped into an obviously nervous one. "Sorry?"

The girl laughed again. "Oh, don't worry, as it turns out the flight is actually fairly empty. I'm sure a little extra weight won't prevent the plane from taking off. You board through Gate Three at one o'clock. Have a safe flight, Mr Harris."

Alex silently sniffed the air and got a whiff of the scent with which he was becoming all too familiar.

"Uhmmm, thank you. Thank you very much. Have a nice day."

"Oh, I will, thank you. I'm actually heading to Canada this afternoon for a bit of a vacation myself, maybe I'll see you there?"

Alex lost control of the smile for a moment and his cheeks flushed red. "Really? Awesome. If there's time, I'll treat you to a coffee on the other side to say thanks. That's if we're on the same flight? I mean, are we on the same flight? I mean ... I don't know what I mean, so I'm just going to go away now. Thank you again."

The young woman laughed, then waved goodbye. Alex turned to walk away but glanced back to check her name tag. As he looked, she caught his eye and winked.

"Alex! What's taking you so long?" Annabel called from over in the coffee shop next door.

"Nothing," he laughed as he hurried over and pulled out a chair with his back to the check-in desk. "Nothing. I mean, I think I might have flirted a little with the check-in girl to get $315 worth of extra luggage on board, but otherwise nothing."

Kyle put one hand over half is face. "Jesus, you didn't, did you?" He looked up at the counter and saw a pink-cheeked young woman behind one of the check-in counters. "Christ, you did! Well, I guess it beats paying ... What exactly did you say to her?"

"Nothing. I think I just got busted checking her out."

Annabel shook her head. "Maybe you should've asked for a First Class upgrade as well."

"You think?" He took on a serious look and pulled out his boarding pass.

"Oh, oh no."

Alex laid the ticket on the table, and both Annabel and Kyle leaned over to take a look. And there, on the stub that would generally be handed back to the traveller, was a name and phone number.

"She knows how old you are?" Annabel was mildly disgusted.

"She must do, I had to show her my passport."

Kyle frowned. "I'm not so sure I approve of this."

"Does it help if I say I'm not so sure I approve either?" Alex laughed.

"Oddly enough, yes." Kyle looked at his son sideways. "Right, now finish your coffee so we can make sure you get through the gate unmolested."

Alex downed what was left of his coffee and they all stood. Kyle wasn't one for long goodbyes and Annabel was too pissed off with him over the check-in girl to linger. So after a few quick hugs and goodbyes, Alex made his way through the security gate and off into the waiting lounge and Annabel and Kyle headed back to the car.

Alex wasn't sure what he was more nervous about, that Check-In Girl would approach him or that she wouldn't and he'd just wind himself up for nothing. Relief came when they announced boarding and he headed for the plane. He took his seat, plugged in his headphones and switched to the classical channel. He always preferred classical music to any of the other channels. He felt safer on the plane than in the airport, and figured that once on the plane everyone would take their seats and that would be that until they reached Canada. This thought worked for him right up until the moment that Check-In Girl sat down next to him.

"So, you come here often?"

His heart rate shot up immediately. "It's not my first time, but I wouldn't say I'm a regular." Alex wracked his brain to try to find something to say but failed.

"Oh, don't look so nervous, Mr Harris; flying really is the safest form of travel."

He sniffed the air in the hope that he could get a handle on himself and the situation. All he got was the near overpowering smell of woman.

"Please, call me Alex, and if I'm not mistaken you're Jenny?"

"You know my name. Are you stalking me?" She pretended to act all bashful.

But he was now ready with a retort of his own. "So, give out your phone number to lots of boys then?" He couldn't help but feel victorious.

Jenny blushed. "Uhmmm, no ... I've never actually done anything like this in my life. But I saw you checking me out and, well, I figured I'd just go for it, be spontaneous for once. I hope you don't mind."

Alex was, on the contrary, rather impressed; this girl had decided to leave her comfort bubble and had made the first move. But "Groovy" was all he could manage. He tried to say it with as much charm and conviction as he could, but it still sounded more frightened puppy than Man About Town. He smiled and put his hand on Jenny's knee.

Alex and Jenny waited for the stewardess to finish her pre-flight emergency demonstration and for the plane to take off. Because there were so few passengers on board, once the plane had levelled out the captain invited everyone to make their way to First Class. Jenny, of course, knew the air crew working their section so made arrangements for her and Alex to linger a little longer. Alone, of course. By this point, Alex was well aware of what was going on, of Jenny's ulterior motives, her whispered conversation with the stewardess at the hostess station further down the gangway. The whole thing seemed like some bizarre wet dream: teen boy, flirtatious young woman, a near-empty plane, and raging hormones. A scene straight from a Mile-High Club fantasy.

As the cabin emptied, Jenny returned with bottles of wine and a heap of blankets.

"Before this goes any further ..." Alex leaned in as she settled into the seat alongside. "I've got to ask, are you sure you want to do this?"

Her answer was difficult to misinterpret. She responded with conviction. With such conviction, in fact, that she all but pounced on him.

An hour and a half later he was seated comfortably in First Class, had finished two glasses of wine and was watching a movie of which he didn't know the title and wasn't paying much attention to. He was so confused that he felt as though his brain had shut down to prevent the intake of any more crazy. Curled up asleep on the seat next to him was Jenny. She had apparently been working since 4 am and was put to sleep by the wine and sex. Alex tried to reassure himself that although this probably didn't happen to many people, it must surely happen to some, that he couldn't be the only man in the world to be picked up this way. Stranger things happen ... He clung to these thoughts as he turned his seat into a flat bed and drifted off.

He woke later to Jenny gently shaking his arm.

"Wake up, wake up! We've got to put the seats up and get ready for landing."

"Already?"

"Yeah, apparently wine and fooling around at thirty-two-thousand feet makes you more tired than you'd think. I only woke ten minutes ago."

"Holy shit."

"I know, I was still hoping for round two before we landed."

Alex blinked and tried to recapture his happy thoughts, that this was all perfectly normal. He knew it was probably not, but it still made him feel better. On some level, he couldn't quite fathom why it bothered him so much.

"So where do you go from here?" He was almost afraid to ask.

Jenny laughed. "I have friends here. I'm gonna stay with them. What about you?"

"I'm heading north, to the farm."

"Oh yeah, you mentioned that. What kind of farm?"

"Stud. Family horse farm. My grandfather had a heart attack when he heard about my mom—" He stopped, just as surprised as she was when he realised how much personal information he'd just let slip. "Sorry, I shouldn't have said all that."

"No, no … Wow, I'm sorry, really sorry to hear that. We … we can talk about it if you like?"

She took on a softer look, no longer the carefree girl letting her hair down and cutting loose for a change, but a concerned, responsible adult. With everything that had transpired in the last few hours, it was this new look, that most endeared her to Alex.

"No, no, I'm sorry, you're here to have a good time and cut loose, while I'm kinda here to do the total opposite. I don't want to be the downer and burden you with my sad stories."

"You don't have to worry about me," she frowned. "But I understand if you don't want to go into detail. But, if I may, your mom died?"

Alex scratched his cheek and thought for a moment.

"Yeah."

"When?"

"Bout two weeks ago? In a car accident. We were hit by a truck."

"Oh no! That one on … I think I read about that. Truck jumped a red light and hit a car with two—" She clapped her hands over her mouth and nose.

Alex forced a smile. "Yeah, the details of my injuries have been greatly exaggerated in the media."

A few tears slipped down her face as her emotions got the better of her. To Alex it smelt almost like fear, but less threatening. He put his arms around her and kissed the top of her head, something he'd seen his father do to his mom when she was upset.

"Hey, now, come on ... There's no need for that."

"I'm just ... I just feel so horrible."

"Why?"

"Well, I feel like I've taken advantage of you."

"How so?"

"You must be an emotional wreck. And then I swing in and just mount you. I mean, what am I even doing here? I don't even ... I never do stuff like this and now it turns out—"

"Hey, don't do that to yourself; you didn't take advantage of me. If anything, this has been one of the nicest things that's happened to me in the last couple weeks. Gives me hope that there's still a fun, albeit crazy, world out there to look forward to."

He wasn't sure if he was lying or not, but it sounded good and it kinda made sense out of the situation right now.

"You're so sweet."

"Thanks. I'm told bitterness will come with age."

Jenny laughed. "How old are you anyway? I mean I know you're younger than me, but, as you may have noticed, I was a little distracted when I checked your passport."

The blood drained from Alex's face and he could feel his chest get hot and itchy.

"Yeah, I'm eighteen," he laughed nervously.

She blushed and looked away. "Oh, wow. I didn't realise you were that much younger."

He felt himself getting warmer still. "I get that a lot. Not to say I do this a lot, I just mean people think I'm older a lot ... How old did you think I was?"

"At least twenty-four. Wow. Just the way you carried yourself at the airport and the way you handled yourself, well, back in Coach."

"Sorry," he smiled. "Maybe I should have said something sooner, but I thought as you'd seen my passport ..."

She leaned in and kissed him. "Don't be sorry, 'cos I'm not."

"Ladies and gentlemen, this is your captain speaking. We're now coming in to land. The fasten seatbelt signs are being switched on. If you could make sure your seats are in the upright position and your tray tables are properly locked away. Thank you."

Jenny shifted back and did up her seatbelt. He did the same, and then waited for the plane to land. Having both Canadian and Syn passports meant Alex didn't have to wait in as long a queue or answer as many questions. After they retrieved their luggage, they held hands as they made their way through customs and to the main gate where they kissed one last time. Finally, Alex spotted his uncle and when he turned to look for Jenny, she was hugging her friends. He saw the opportunity to make a quick dash and took it, not even stopping long enough to greet Jeff properly.

"Good to see you! Been a long flight and still got a long drive, shall we go?"

"Yeah, sure. Car's this way."

Alex told himself not to turn around and look but couldn't help himself; he scanned the crowd for her face and found it smiling in his direction. He winked back at her and waved, then turned and quickly followed his uncle out into the darkness of the early morning. It was only when loading things into the car that Jeff noticed the guitar case.

"What's all this?"

"Oh, I've joined a band and I'm taking music at school."

"But what about your, uhmmm, condition?"

"Well, we're going to be trying a few new ways to manage it. Could we talk about this in the car? I'm a bit cold."

"Oh right."

They loaded the rest of the things into the back of the Land Rover, then got in themselves, Alex immediately leaning over to turn on the heating. Alex sighed with pleasure.

"So, two-hour drive," Jeff said as he turned the ignition. "Haven't seen you in ages. How was the flight?"

Alex thought for a moment about telling the truth, about Jenny, but decided against it.

"It was good. There were so few people on the plane that we all ended up in First Class, but I slept most of the way."

"What? That's amazing. I've only ever heard of things like that via a friend of a friend's cousin. I didn't know that ever actually happened. Why do you sleep, though? It's a day flight. It's 2 am now and it'll be four by the time we get to the farm. Your body clock is going to be all out of sync."

"I'm fairly good at just sleeping whenever. If you like you can get some sleep when we get home and I'll just stay up and do the morning chores."

"Actually, that'd be great, if you wouldn't mind."

"Not at all. I mean, you've had to drive all the way out and back in again, so it's the least I can do."

"Great, thanks. Your grandmother will probably be up, so she can help you as well just to make sure everything gets done."

"Cool."

The car fell silent and stayed that way for a while. Alex took up his usual long-distance-drive pose and stared blankly out the window at passing cars.

"I've got a question."

Alex didn't break position.

"Yes?"

"Well, it's something I've never really understood. Syn Island not having any natural resources, how does it maintain such a strong economy? It doesn't really have anything to export, does it?"

"Syn Tax."

"Alcohol and cigarettes?"

"What?" Alex was confused.

"Sin tax? That's the name for taxes on cigarettes and alcohol, meaning the taxing of 'sins'."

"Oh no, Syn with a *y*. Apparently back in the day when Synners were much sought after because of our high level of education and whatever, the Syn Island government set up a deal with the rest of the world that a portion of the taxes their citizens pay in whatever country they chose to live gets given back to Syn Island."

"So all the people from Syn Island all over the world still pay their taxes to Syn Island?"

"Yeah, if you were born on the Island you pay taxes there for the rest of your life. But it doesn't extend to family. So if Annie and I were born in Canada, we wouldn't have to, even though Dad's from there, unless we actually worked on the island."

"So everyone on the island pays taxes there and everyone ever born on the Island pays taxes there?"

"Yup, pretty much it."

"Do they teach you that kind of thing in school?"

Alex laughed. "Me? No. Annie told me about it when I asked the same question."

"Thought that didn't sound like you," Jeff chuckled. "That's insane, bloody good idea, though. Pretty much ensures Syn Island's economy forever."

"Yeah, Annie says it's a good system while we still have an advanced education system and Synners in place in high-end international business. But if their kids take over and aren't born on the island, then that money all goes to the country the business is actually in."

"All right, so how much of their taxes go back to Syn Island?"

"I don't know, some percentage, I think. All depends on what you do, where you do it, how much you earn, and I think there might be a few more factors."

"Okay."

Alex sat quietly for a little longer to see whether Jeff would strike up another conversation, then finally returned to his position staring out the window. Jeff accepted that he couldn't think of too much more to say so turned up the volume on the car radio. Being early morning, it didn't take the radio long to launch into a gentle, melancholy playlist, and the thoughts of both men turned to Debra. They shifted uncomfortably in their seats, trying to think of something else, to initiate conversation, anything that would distract them from what was really on their minds.

"It can't be very responsible for late-night radio to play sad songs like this, it's just putting people to sleep as they're driving."

"Never thought about it that way," Jeff sighed. "But you have a point … Speaking of music, what's with all the equipment? You said something about joining a band?"

"Yeah, I don't know if you know but Annie and I are being sent to this special new school that's supposed to be for people who know what they want to study at college so you start taking higher-level subjects at a younger age. Anyway, while I was there I met these cool guys who are Music majors and one of them heard me growl and decided I had to be in his band. Long story short, I tried out and got in."

"Cool! And the guitar? I didn't know you could play."

"Yeah, I can't, yet. But I've got some books to teach me."

"Oh? Oh dear … Alex, noise isn't really going to fly with your grandfather in his current condition, or any condition for that matter."

"It's all right; I've got earphones that plug into the amp, so the only noise will be in my own head."

"Okay then. That's cool. What kind of music does your band play?"

"Ever heard of a band called Tool?"

"Nope, can't say I have."

"Oh, well, I think it's metal."

"Metal?"

"Yeah, metal. The other guys in the band are amazing. They've been playing instruments for, like their whole lives and are masters. I'm just kinda the voice and the lyric writer."

"Lyric writer? I didn't know you wrote songs."

"I didn't really, until a few days ago; I started converting some of my poems into lyrics, sort of."

"How?"

"Mostly structure and picking a catchier part to turn into the chorus, adding a few bits, taking a few bits away. Not sure how good they are, but the other guys seemed to like them."

"Wow, that's great. I'm glad you've found something you're really interested in. It does pose the question, though, what about the farm? Weren't you originally going to move up here and work on the farm with your grandfather after school?"

"Yeah, that was the original plan. I don't know. I just really want to at least try living a normal-ish life, with normal-ish dreams, and try to make them come true, just once."

Alex wanted to say something about his mother, but stopped himself. He wasn't sure if it was all right to talk about her with his uncle, or whether, in fact, he should bring it up around his grandparents at all. So he decided to wait and see how they treated the subject or if one of them brought it up first.

"I understand. I mean, I got a lot of pressure growing up to take on the farm after school. I would have loved the opportunity to be in a band, or something else equally romantic."

Alex smiled with relief; he had been a little nervous about how the other side of the family would take his decision to not work the farm. Once again the car fell silent, only this time it stayed that way until they pulled up in the yard of his grandparents' farm.

Alex was greeted with a bear hug and a cup of coffee from his grandmother. Jeff helped him bring in his things, and then took himself off to bed. In the meantime, Alex and Marie busied themselves with the morning chores, which in winter mostly involved feeding the animals and checking that they were warm enough. When Alex arrived with the dog food, Sally seemed more excited to see him than his grandmother had been.

Once everything was done, he was left to himself to arrange food while Marie went to check in on Derrick, who spent most of his time in bed, shying away from company, in part because he was too weak to deal with it, but also because he was embarrassed about being so feeble. Alex made himself a sandwich, then went to his room and set up his guitar and amp before settling under the covers to reading the guitar books Josh had recommended. He stayed there until Jeff knocked gently on the door.

"Aah, there you are. Was wondering if you wanted to take a walk with me?"

"Uncle Jeff, it's freezing out there. That's why I'm all tucked up here."

"The cold still affect you then?"

"Less and less as I get older, but still."

"There's something I think you should see, though."

"Okay."

Alex rubbed his eyes and scratched his head. Being at the farm-house and seeing his grandparents and Sally had been harder than he'd expected, but he pulled on the padded jacket his father had just bought him. Jeff handed him an insulated travel mug full of coffee and the two ventured out into the cold. It was no more than a five-minute walk to the farm graveyard. Alex had been there many times before but this was the first time that he knew one of the occupants personally. Just the sight of it caused tears to well up in his eyes, and a whisper escaped him.

"Mom buried out in the snow, her worst fear comes true."

Jeff looked at him curiously. "How do you know about that?"

"Because it's one of my worst fears too, and I told her about it one day. I think she told me to try to make me feel better. One of those 'See? You're still human like the rest of us' conversations."

"Oh, well, I'm probably not going to be too good at those."

Alex smiled at his uncle. He knew he was trying but the stillness of winter crept over them and the conversation fell silent. He stared at the small tombstone sticking out of the snow and all his sadness and guilt swelled up inside of him like a rising tide. Each time it hit it made the water deeper and deeper until he felt like his feet could no longer touch the ground. He turned away from the grave and fought the urge to run.

"I need to get away from this place, these ... are the only winter clothes I have."

He shivered, but from sorrow rather than to fight off a transfor-mation. Jeff slipped his arm around Alex and almost dragged him away. When they got back to the kitchen, Alex sat down on the floor, his head in his hands.

"It's all right, Alex, I know how you feel."

He looked up.

"Grandpa!"

He leapt to his feet, wrapped his arms around his grandfather and burst into tears.

***

Over the next two months Alex spent most of his time running through farm chores, completing homework assignments or practising guitar. It helped that Marie knew how to play, and rather well too, and taught him as many Buffy Sainte-Marie and Joan Baez songs as she could remember. Jeff stayed only a couple more weeks before heading back to his family, leaving Alex alone with his grandparents.

It took Alex another week to work up the courage to actually sit with his grandfather and have the conversation about not coming to work on the farm after school. Derrick already knew, of course, but Alex still found it hard to initiate a conversation he knew it would disappoint his grandfather.

In turn, it took Derrick and Marie just as long to ask their grandson about the wolf situation. He thought about lying to them, telling them everything was on track and fine, but he hated lying, even if it was to protect them from the worst, and finally admitted that he and Dr Cooper were looking into ways of suppressing the beast. Derrick thought about it for a long time.

"What do you mean by *suppress*?"

"Well, help me control the it … maybe not change as often or be able to stop the transformations before they happen."

"So not a *cure*?"

"If there is a cure, then sure, but we're not really looking for that, just a better way of controlling things, I suppose."

"Okay, but I'm still not sure I understand, what sort of *ways*?"

"Well, we noticed that when I was in the hospital and on the sedatives, I didn't change."

"Whoa, stop right there, young man! Are you telling us that you and your doctor are looking for medications you can take to prevent you from changing?"

"No, not medical stuff, but if there are herbal remedies that can help me stay calmer, well … But more like other alternatives. Like, there are still a lot of myths around werewolves and we've not fully investigated any of those. Things like silver and wolf's bane. And Dr Cooper has already said that he's not going to write prescriptions for drugs just to stop me changing. He's not that kinda doctor."

Derrick took it all in for a moment and Marie took over.

"So what about meditation and all the breathing exercises you've been doing?"

Alex took a long breath and reminded himself that they weren't attacking him, just out of the loop.

"Up until now that's all been a way of harmonising with Mork, bringing us together, but … I don't want to be half man, half wolf. I want to have control over it, be able to manage it, be able to live a normal life and not have to share that life with him any more."

"But, sweetheart, you'll always have to,"

"I know! But … Sorry, I know I will, but I also want to take control of my life a bit and not let it *all* be governed by him, by Mork."

The room fell silent for as Marie looked back at Derrick.

"So what have you tried so far?"

Alex swallowed and thought for a moment. "Well, Dr Cooper has e-mailed a list of new breathing techniques to try, to help prevent changes, and some new meditations to focus on being human to hold back the transforming. He also has a list of things he wants to try when I get back, like allergy tests, to see how I react to certain things."

"Things like silver and wolf's bane and other mythological aspects of it?"

"Yup."

Derrick nodded in approval and Marie smiled. They understood that, out here on the farm, they were out of the loop when it came to most things around Alex's condition but they still cared and only wanted the best for him.

Once they'd cleared the air the remaining time seemed to fly by. Alex quickly came to terms with his chores and could get them done quickly and quietly without much effort. He experienced two full moons while he was there, which he spent mostly in the kennels with old Sally. As Mork, he was far more resilient to the cold than Alex, and so took long runs every day. By the end he was quite sad to be leaving the farm. He'd enjoyed the peace a lot more than he'd thought and his father had been right to allow him the space. Now, though, with his grandfather getting stronger and stronger every day, and more determined to get back to his work on the farm, Alex's new life awaited him back on Syn Island.

Chapter 28

"We're here of course with the one-and-only Alex Harris of Water-dogs on Syn Island's number-one radio station, K505. Now, as you mentioned earlier, Alex, you guys shot to fame at a very young age, how did all of that actually come about?"

"Well we all went to TFS, which is where I met Danny, Brandon and Josh. They were already a band and had done a music video as a year-end project the year before I started there. When I joined and we started writing original music, we decided to do a second video. The song we did was 'Scars in the sky', and it not only got us all top marks, but also got passed on to Syn Records, the label that took our music from the classroom and got it played on the radio. They helped us produce our first album, and that basically launched our careers. It seemed like sudden success from the outside, but because it was so structured and part of our school careers, I remember feeling like things were going very slowly."

"'Scars in the sky' – obviously a classic song now, but written about your mom, correct?"

"Yip."

"So if you're up for it, let's talk for just a minute about your relationship with your family, specifically your sister."

"Personally, I don't believe in having relations with family members, it's kinda gross, but thanks for asking – I do feel it's important to make sure everyone is aware of that."

Chapter 29

Alex sat on Annabel's bed, watching her try to pack two large piles of clothes into a suitcase that seemed far too small.

"So, where are you going again?"

"Cape Town, I've told you this."

"I was Mork at the time, it's not perfectly clear, and who are you going with?"

"Right, I'm going to Cape Town; it's a working holiday thing."

"Working holiday? You only worked there a couple weeks."

"I've been there five months, plus I'm a partner – I get to go along to all the cool things."

"Cool, can I come?"

"No!"

"Why not? I got you that job."

Annabel stopped packing and glared at him. "No. My brain got me this job, my amazing skill with maths and money got me this job, with a little help from your band."

He smiled. "Come on, I'll be your famous rock-star brother coming on holiday with you – you'll be a hit with the other staff."

"That's just it, Alex. I don't want them to like me because of you, I want them to like me because of me. I mean, you're already going to be able to hold this job over my head for the rest of my working career, how I wouldn't have gotten there without you and all that shit. I just want to have at least some friends of my own, who are my friends and not your friends or *our* friends."

"All right, all right I get it, I get it. I'm just envious."

"Haven't you been there? Cape Town, I mean."

"Twice, but for, like, three days total. ThaSpinest's why I'm envious. Seemed like a cool place."

"Any hints?"

"Yeah, the ocean's fucking freezing."

"So don't take a bikini?"

"No, you've got to take a bikini! People lie out on the beach all the time; it's *the* place to be seen. In fact, chances are there's a day planned for you to just hang out on the beach and look cool, and they'll definitely want you there for that. Not sure how a bunch of bankers could look cool on a beach without your awesomeness there."

Annabel rolled her eyes and stuck out her tongue.

"Don't you have band practice all week anyway?"

"Yeah, we've got a show booked somewhere next week Thursday. Which reminds me, when are you back?"

"Tuesday. You planning on staying here while you're in town?"

"I was thinking of going to stay with dad, but I'll pop in if that's cool."

Annabel frowned disapprovingly. "Don't you bring girls back to my place, please Alex."

"What's the point of looking after it then?"

"Why don't you just get an apartment or something?"

He lay back down on the bed and stared up at the ceiling. "We live on an island, Annie. Why do we need *three* properties? Dad's got his place, you've got this one. I paid for both of them – I don't see the need to have us all live in different places."

"Whatever ... Just make sure you clean the place up this time. Last time you 'popped in' I had to hire professional cleaners to come in and give the place an once-over." Alex sat up quickly. "In fact, let me leave you their number."

"Thanks, and don't worry, you're going to have a great time. Drink some wine, swim with some sharks, and meet someone who isn't named Ryan."

"Thanks. Right, I think that's everything packed. Let's get going.

Can we go in your car? Mine doesn't have too much gas and I don't want to be late."

"Will that bag fit in my car?"

"Oh, ha-ha! Just because you travel out of a black plastic bag doesn't mean it's the right way to do things."

"It's a stuff sack not a plastic bag, and you just don't want me driving your car."

"Oh good, so we're on the same page."

She gave him a naughty smile. He hopped off the bed, grabbed her bags and carried them to the car. In the wake of his success, Alex and the rest of the band – with Annabel's help – had invested all their money. To say thank you, they used their influence to help jumpstart her career in the financial world, and Alex had also bought her a house. He turned the key and the car started blaring George Thorogood, which made Annabel jump. Alex chuckled before turning the music down.

"Passport?"

"Check."

"Flight booking information ticket thingy?"

She smiled. "Check."

"Condoms?"

"Gross! But, yeah, check."

"Really? Cool, let's rock 'n roll."

He put the car into gear and headed off in the direction of the airport at great speed.

"Sure you haven't forgotten anything?"

She scanned her memory. "If I have, I can probably do without or buy it that side."

They pulled into the drop-and-go parking at Syn Island International, and suddenly Alex's eyes widened.

"Shit! Credit card?"

"What about it?"

"Do you have yours?"

"Of course. I keep it in my wallet; where do you keep yours?"

He smiled nervously. "Normally? Josh's wallet, if he can remember to collect it from the barman."

They burst into laughter, which drew attention to the fact that Alex Harris had arrived unannounced at the airport and suddenly a crowd of autograph seekers started to form. He quickly helped Annabel get the bag out of the car and kissed her on the cheek, only to hear someone in the crowd call out.

"Alex, that your new girlfriend? What happened to ... what's-her-name?"

Alex sighed and Annabel whispered an apology as they turned to face everyone.

"No, no, this is my sister. Now, if you'll excuse us, she has a plane to catch, and if you'd like to step to the side I'll happily sign autographs."

Annabel pushed through the crowd, then turned back to wave at her brother before heading into the terminal to find her co-workers. She knew that Alex didn't really like drawing the crowd's attention and knew, too, that he was doing it now so that she could get through without much hassle.

"Hey, Annabel!" It was Sarah. "Over here! You know what's going on outside? Apparently some rock star is here with his new girlfriend."

Despite herself, she breathed, "Oh, that's going to piss him off ... *sooo* much."

Sarah looked shocked. "What? Oh my goodness, don't tell me *you're* the girlfriend! Who's the guy?"

"It's Alex Harris from Waterdogs and, no, I'm not his girlfriend, I'm his sister."

"Oh, shut *up*! You serious? Shit, don't they invest with us?" Sarah had clearly not yet been privy to the office gossip, thought Annabel. "Oh, I get it now, you're the link! Is that how you got this job?"

Annabel sighed, "Honestly? Yeah, a little bit – but don't ever tell him that; he gives me a hard enough time as it is."

"Aaaahhh," Sarah nodded knowingly. "Must be a younger brother then. I have two of them and every time they do something that doesn't get them in trouble they act like it's an event and everyone else should celebrate the fact that they haven't messed up."

"Exactly, it's like I make breakfast every day and it's normal; he does it once and we have to talk about it all day, like he's God's gift to egg and chips."

"God, I'm so glad you're on this trip as well. Let's go find a bar and have some wine with our whine."

"Love! That idea."

They checked in their luggage ahead of everyone else and smiled sweetly at the guy behind the check-in counter to make up some story as to why they had to sit away from the other employees, and then headed through security and onto the airport bar. Two glasses of dry white wine were raised.

"To little brothers, we love them really."

"Most of the time."

The girls giggled. A few glasses of wine and high altitude made sleeping on the plane much easier than they had expected. To kill time in the final hour before touchdown, Sarah decided to interrogate her new best friend about her rock-star brother. Annabel had, of course, been expecting it since she arrived at the airport.

"So, is your brother single?"

Annabel tried not to make the face she always made when people asked her that and, as always, failed. Sarah smiled nervously.

"At the moment, yeah, I think so. He's not really the relationship kind of guy."

"Too much of a rock star?"

"Not just that; he's also not very good at it. I'm not sure if he's got insanely high standards or what, but he's better at being single."

Of course, she had a few other ideas about her brother's string of short-term relationships, but she wasn't about to begin talking about it to just anyone.

"How so?"

"Well, his last girl – sweet thing, a little dim, but very pretty and actually quite good for him in a way, down to earth and not too star struck, he broke up with her for singing 'The Night They Drove Old Dixie Down' to him at a karaoke party."

"Fuck, that's a bit high strung! What does he have against the song?"

"Nothing. It's one of his favourites, but it reminds him of our mom. So he said it was too early in the relationship to have that conversation and get that emotionally involved, and he dumped her."

"How long had it been?"

"Two months."

"Why's being reminded of your mom so bad?" Once again, Annabel tried to stop herself from making a face at the question. "I mean, if you don't mind me asking?"

"No it's fine," said Annabel. "My mom and Alex were in a car accident when he was sixteen, and he survived and she, well, didn't."

"Oh my God! I'm so sorry. I'll stop talking now. Shit!"

"No, no, it's all right. I mean, it sucks, but it's okay. It's not like it's something I don't talk about; I just don't bring it up very often, you know."

"Yeah, yeah, I do. Actually, my mom died when I was a kid; in fact, she died giving birth to my youngest brother, so I kinda know what you mean."

Due to time zones and travel time, the crew found they were all checked in with nothing to do by seven in the morning. Their itinerary meant that they would be at office functions from the second day until day four, then three more days to themselves to enjoy the city before they headed back to Syn.

Sarah and Annabel decided it was in their best interest to throw caution to the wind and embrace their 'vacation' as best they could. So they rallied and made their way to Camps Bay, to drink cocktails in the sunshine at a beachfront restaurant.

"Aawww, we shoulda brought towels and things so we could swim."

"Apparently not. My brother says the water's icy and that people come to the beach more to be seen than to swim. I mean, just look at all these people, I bet Alex spent all his free time out here perving."

"Does a rock star perv, or does he window-shop?"

"Eww, I don't know and I try not to think about it."

"Fair enough … So let's drink!"

They burst out in the kind of free-spirited laughter that comes with ordering alcohol at 10 o'clock in the morning, and it didn't take long before they drew the attention of a table of men not too far away. Annabel had grown into a beautiful woman who, because the spotlight was always on her brother, made sure she maintained a good self-image. Sarah was equally attractive, a bit older than Annabel, but that didn't stop her from having a good time. Within half an hour every guy in the restaurant could see that those two girls meant trouble in the best kind of way. Sarah seemed to draw the fun side out of Annabel; she felt safe with her and could allow herself to take more risks than usual. A few cocktails in, Sarah popped the question.

"So how come you're single? Girl like you is usually married to her high-school sweetheart by now, no offence."

"Oh, none taken. I was almost that girl."

"Then what happened?"

"I don't know. Everything was headed in that direction and one day I just woke up and decided that he wasn't for me."

"Found out he was sleeping with someone else?"

"And she was fucking ugly too! Like, I don't mean to stroke my own ego here, but she was a cow on on two legs, I swear …"

"It's always the way: grass-is-greener syndrome."

"Well, he could at least have traded up is all I'm saying."

Just then a young man in his mid twenties – tanned, surfer's body and sun-bleached hair, turned around in his chair at the adjacent table.

"Give the guy a break! How could he possible have traded *up* from you ...? I mean, I'm not saying what he did was right, personally, I think he's an idiot, but I don't see how he could have possible done better." He winked at Annabel, a cheeky glint in his eyes. "But, hey, that's just my opinion. I didn't mean to interrupt, well, yes, I did, but I'm done now so ..."

Annabel wanted to say something witty, possibly even flirtatious, to keep his attention but couldn't find a single word, so she quickly made wide eyes at Sarah in the hope that she would have something useful to say in the moment.

"Nice line, buddy," Sarah happily obliged. "But I believe tradition says you're supposed to buy a girl a drink as well. We'll wait right here."

Annabel felt a swell admiration for Sarah. But the young man, sitting with two other equally toned guys, was up to the challenge and their tables were quickly pushed together.

"It's not often in this town you're able to find two girls as hot as you two who are up to start drinking in the morning."

"Well," Annabel finally found her voice, "we're not from around here. Just here for a few days on a work thing."

"If this is what you do for a living, I want your jobs."

"So you guys from Cape Town?"

The three men looked at each other.

"No, actually, we were volunteers in a township for a few months and now we're gonna do a tour around southern Africa. But we've been off for about a week and we've been coming into the city on most weekends to party it up. Sad to say, we're leaving tomorrow."

Sarah instantly threw her voice in. "Good, that means you have to come party with us tonight because we might never see each other again, and you wouldn't want our only impression of you be that you can't hold your booze against a couple of girls, do you?"

Both tables erupted into laughter, a hand went up and another round ordered. As time ticked by Annabel started to worry that she wasn't going to be able to keep up, and considering that they were drinking in the sun, she'd not only have to stop but also go lie down. All reservations were banished, however, when the hand of the blond dude came to rest gently on her knee. She wasn't wrong about being the first to go to bed, but she knew then that she was not going alone.

Sarah, good friend that she was, noticed that Annabel wasn't just waning from the sun and booze, but also interested in going somewhere more private, and so instigated a party move to their hotel bar. She led the other two boys to the bar while Annabel led her boy up to her room. And that's where the two stayed until Annabel and Sarah met for dinner that night.

Sarah was already at a table when she arrived.

"Well?"

"Well, what? You know what happened."

"Yes, but how was it? Have you two been at it this whole time?"

Annabel laughed. "No, it was great – I mean *really* great – but we stopped for a nap, then he went back to his hostel and I carried on sleeping. What about you, what happened with your boys?"

"Sadly, nothing as interesting as your day. We had a few more drinks, then I made some work excuse so that I could take a nap. But I did kiss one of them. Tommy. You manage to catch Surfer Dude's name?"

"Yes, of course," Annabel blushed. "Jasper. But I had to ask him afterwards because I couldn't remember. I've never done that before – like, ever! Even through college, I was always the good girl who never went out before exams or important lectures, and always got good grades. Always. God, I feel like a whore."

"Bullshit!" Sarah waved her hands in the air. "Did he leave a wad of cash on the nightstand?"

"No!"

"Then you're not a whore – you're just a lucky slut. Because he was *soooo* hot."

Both girls laughed. Sarah seemed to bring out an entirely different side to Annabel. And, she had to admit, it was a side she enjoyed. It was something of a relief to be with someone who didn't cast her in her brother's shadow.

"I have a confession to make ..." Annabel looked down at her plate, avoiding Sarah's upturned eyebrow.

"Spill it, sister ... Spill it."

"So Jasper was my second."

"Second what?"

"Second lover."

"*What?* Like, ever? How old are you?"

"Twenty two ... last month."

"But what about college?" Surely, at college ..."

"I had a boyfriend."

"Since you were *fifteen*?"

"No, seventeen."

"Jesus, that the douche you were telling me about? When did that end?"

"Three weeks ago?"

"Well, then everything's on track; you've still got plenty of time for this kind of thing." Annabel smiled shyly, and Sarah feigned surprise. "But you have more to tell me, don't you? Don't you?"

"No, no ... I'm just a little sad Jasper won't be around for the next couple of days, that's all."

"Yeah, would make it easier. You get his contact details?"

"No, we left in such a hurry that I forgot."

"You want to go to the backpackers and ask for them?"

"No, I thought about that and it seems too much like stalking. I'm just going to accept it for what it was – really, really great sex."

**

The flight home seemed longer than the flight out, but Annabel was happy to see her brother and father waiting for her at the airport, and they promptly whisked her off to dinner – to which Sarah duly invited herself. Annabel was happy to introduce her new friend but she did discreetly forbid her sleeping with her rockstar brother. Sarah reluctantly agreed, but made it clear that she was not happy about making that kind of promise. Alex smiled to himself – their whispered conversation had not escaped his keen hearing. He was even tempted to make a quip, but decided against it. No point in getting up Annabel's nose just as she steps off the plane ...

Over dinner Annabel and Sarah chattered on about their trip, how beautiful the country was and how much they'd love to go back. Alex and Kyle simply smiled and nodded along.

"So, Alex, what you up to at the moment?"

The family smiled. Both Annabel and Kyle knew what was coming.

"Me or Waterdogs?"

Sarah blushed, pretending she was offended at the suggestion.

"Oh, okay! Waterdogs."

"Don't be embarrassed. I really don't mind talking about it – it's not like it's a secret. Hell, truth be told, I've always preferred answering questions about the band than talking about myself. We're off to LA in two days to do a series of TV interviews and also putting the finish to our latest album *Sitting On the Edge of Anxiety*, which will be released end of next month ... hopefully."

"Cool! So how often do you get to see your family?"

"It's not that bad actually. I make a point of trying to get back home at least once a month-ish. You know, we're all from here so we like coming home. In fact, I'll be back here in three weeks, for a week and a half, and then back to LA for about a month. From there, you'd have to check with our manager, or the publicist, or the agent or—"

"Oh, wow!"

Alex was happy that Annabel had made a new friend and had moved on – at least a little – from Ryan, who in his opinion was still running the risk of a mysterious animal attack. He couldn't put his finger on it but Annabel seemed different, something about the way she smelt.

"So, sweetheart," Kyle tried to steer the conversation back to his daughter, "how things at work? Since you started there I hardly ever see you."

"I know, I'm sorry. It's just been a little crazy – and this sudden conference on the other side of the world hasn't actually helped. It's thrown me a little. So much going on all at once. A lot of new systems to learn and they've got me doing high-end audits, which is basically reading through entire customer portfolios, looking for anything interesting or out of the ordinary."

"Why?" Alex frowned.

Annabel, Sarah and Kyle all rolled their eyes at the rock star who had no clue as to how a corporate system worked.

"To find any anomalies, dunce."

"What, like organised crime?" Alex made no attempt to hide the sarcasm in his tone.

"Well, wouldn't you like to know?" Annabel stuck out her tongue.

"Excuse them," Kyle made eye contact with Sarah. "If you close your eyes you'd swear they were still ten and twelve years old."

Chapter 30

Alex's eyes flew open, and reached for the phone next to his bed.

"It's very early in LA." He made no attempt to hide a growl.

But his annoyance rapidly turned to panic when he realised it was Annabel at the other end of the line – and she was in tears. He sat bolt upright, whipping the sheets off the brunette curled up alongside.

"Annie? Annabel, what's the matter?"

"Whe ... when are you coming home?" Annabel choked out the words.

He shot a glance at the lunar calendar he put up in every hotel room he stayed in for longer than a day.

"Leave Monday, arrive Tuesday. Four days' time. What's happened, hon?"

She took a long, deep gasping breath, and then burst out, "I'm pregnant!"

The world seemed to stop for a moment.

"Right, I'm getting out of bed now," Alex tried to clam her. "I can probably make the next flight out, which should be in about three hours. I'll be there ... at the latest, this time tomorrow."

Annabel wanted to say something but couldn't. He pulled on a pair of jeans and kissed the somewhat bewildered girl now unfolding from a deep sleep.

"Have you told Dad?" Alex tried to keep the conversation going as he whipped around the room, picking stuff off the floor and tossing them in a bag. "Are you *going* to tell him?" He put on a pair of shades to shield his glowing eyes and pulled the door closed behind him. "You know who the father is?"

Annabel erupted into floods of tears which all but defeated Alex.

"Okay, look ... You need to calm down. I'm going to check out of this place, and I'll call you back in a couple of minutes, okay? That all right?" There was no answer beyond Annabel's stifled snuffles, so at the front desk, he stopped and scrolled through his contacts for Sarah's number and dialled from the concierge's phone, all the while holding the mic of his phone from his mouth.

"Hello?"

"Oh, thank God! Sarah, you've got to get over to Annabel's."

"What? Who *is* this?"

"It's Alex, Annabel's brother? Look, I've got her on the other line and she's hysterical I'm gonna get on the next plane back to the island, but I need you to go over there *right now*."

"Jesus, what's happened?"

"I'm sure she'll explain. I've got to go, I need to get a cab and get to the airport."

"Where are you?"

"LA, but I'm gonna try catch the next flight back."

"Fuck! Okay, right. I'm on my way, don't worry."

Alex leapt into one of the cabs waiting in the forecourt "LA-X!" and sped off. He stayed on the line with Annabel, mostly just listening to her cry until he could hear Sarah arrive and he felt secure enough to put the phone down. To his relief, there was a flight to Syn Island within the hour, making just one stop in New York to refuel and take on more passengers. He checked in his bag and began the gruelling wait. Nothing rattled him more than Annabel being in trouble; at no point did anything matter more than getting to her – although he did need to at least bring Josh up to speed rather than do a runner.

A tired, grumpy voice answered.

"Josh, man, bad news."

"Fuck, dude! You need me to come bail you out ...?"

"No, I'm at the airport. About to hop on a plane back to Syn."

Josh shot up in surprise.

"What! When? Why?"

"Look, we're boarding now; I've just walked away from the queue to call."

"Alex, what's up man? You running? It's that brunette, isn't? I knew it, man, I just fucking knew it! I told Bran—"

"No, no, it's Annabel. She called me in flood of tears. Keep a secret? She's just found out she's pregnant."

"Preggers? Didn't think she had a ... *ooooh*. Right, no worries, man. Anything I can do?"

"Yeah, I don't know ... Apologise to the guys for me and make up some excuse to the press. Don't, whatever you do, tell them about Annie. She's not told dad and I'm not sure what she's going to do about it – all I know is she's fucking upset. Tell them I'm sick and had to go back to Syn to see my doctor; I'd rather they write shit about *me*, you know."

"Cool, man, yeah. Fuck! Well, happy flying, I guess, and if there is anything else let me know. I'll make sure this doesn't get out."

"Thanks. Well, have to go. I'll speak to you as soon as I land."

***

Thirteen long hours later Alex grabbed his bag, jumped into the first cab he could find and raced off towards his sister's house. As they pulled up alongside what must have been Sarah's car, he handed the driver too much money and headed straight into the house. He found both Annabel and Sarah in the kitchen, dropped his bag on the counter and wrapped his arms around his sister. The look on Sarah's face was a mix of relief and frustration. She had only just managed to stem the flow of Annabel's tears, and now, wrapped in her brother's arms, the dam broke.

"Thank you, Sarah, so much. I mean it, I really appreciate it."

With that, he picked his sister up and carried her upstairs. He lay her down on her bed, tucked her in, and then slipped under the covers next to her and dried her tears.

"So, sis, what we gonna do about it?"

Annabel fought off the urge to cry again. "I can't have this baby – look at me; I'm a wreck just at the thought. I can't do this now, and I'm too young and, oh my God, work! It's getting so insane at the moment, Alex ..."

"It's okay, it's okay ... If that's how you feel, I'll call and make an appointment, then we'll head down together and get this sorted out. No one has to know. We'll get Sarah to call you in sick for the next few days and see if the doctors write fake sick notes in this kind of situation. Now, when last did you get any sleep?"

"Off and on, but not much since I found out."

"Okay, well, don't worry – I'm here and I'll sort this all out. Sleep now, okay?"

He lay there holding her until she drifted off, then kissed her on the forehead and slipped out the room. Sarah stood at the bottom of the stairs waiting.

"You're amazing, you know that? I've been trying to get her to do that since I arrived."

"We're family, it's just … different. But I can't tell you how much I appreciate what you've done. I would've been lost if you hadn't answered your phone."

"I'm glad you called. Poor thing. What's she going to do?"

"Well, you know a doctor I can call?"

"What kind of doctor?"

"The kind that makes people, uhmmm, un-pregnant?"

"Yeah, thought as much. I'll make a call and book her an appointment. I know a guy who's very good, discreet about this kind of thing."

"Speaking from experience?"

"Can you keep a secret?"

"No, but I know where she keeps the good wine."

Sarah smiled gratefully. It was the first time she'd seen a side of Alex Harris that wasn't the rock star. "You really can't keep secrets, can you?"

They made their way into the kitchen. Alex found the wine while Sarah made the calls, then they sat down – only to stare at the table without a word. Alex finally broke the silence.

"So, you wanna talk about it?"

"Same old story really, I suppose …" she laughed half-heartedly. "I was nineteen, he was ... well, not much older. Just the wrong thing, the wrong people, at the wrong time."

"Regret it?"

"Yes and no ..." Sarah poured another glass of wine. "Sometimes, when I see other people with kids, I think about what I could have had, but then I realise I could handle being a single mom *now*, but if I'd had a kid *then* ... Well, I wouldn't have this job, this life. So it is what it is, and can't be different."

"And there's plenty of time to still have kids, right."

She bit her bottom lip, then locked eyes with him. "Well, I have some time right now to practise?"

Alex couldn't help but laugh. He was exhausted from the flight and worried to death about his sister, but ... "I thought Annie made you promise not to," he dared to remind her.

Sarah blushed crimson. "She *told* you?"

"No, she didn't have to – I've just got very good hearing. But, hey, I'm flattered," he winked at her. "Now, in a totally unrelated matter, I think I'm going to go lie down for a bit." He pulled the chair out from the kitchen counter and stood up. "My bedroom is the one at the end of the passage should you feel like you needed to lie down as well."

He picked up the bottle of wine and both glasses before he headed off. Sarah was not far behind him.

***

Alex woke up alone with a slight hangover. Slowly he made his way into the TV room and flopped down next to his sister, who sat wrapped in a fleece blanket watching the morning news.

"Apparently you're sick and missed your album launch."

"Yeah, well, I'd rather the press think that than start making up a reason I would've disappeared in the middle of the night."

"Thank you. Sarah left a note on the fridge; she says my appointment is at four this afternoon."

"What's the time now?"

"Twelve-ish."

"Okay … Are you allowed to eat before this thing or do we starve you?"

"Don't know, but I'm not hungry."

To Alex, she seemed numb, distant and sad.

"It's going to be alright, sis, I promise. This time tomorrow it'll all be behind us and life will be back to normal."

"When's full moon?"

"Starts Thursday night."

"Funny how we describe 'normal', isn't it?"

He put his arm around her and kissed the side of her head. "Don't worry. I'll still be here to protect you either way."

Tears slipped down her face but she was determined to ignore them, and quickly changed the subject.

"So, did you sleep with Sarah?"

"Me? No, she's your friend ..."

"You can't lie to me, Alex. I can see it in your eyes ..."

"Well, then, why did you ask?"

"I don't know. I'm ... I'm just trying to think about something else. You use protection?"

"Oh, yeah! Chances are if I get a girl pregnant she'll have a litter ..."

"Alex!" Annabel shot her hand to her mouth to stifle the guffaw.

"But didn't you, uhmmm, get ... neutered?"

He frowned at her choice of words but let it go. "Yeah, but it didn't take."

"What do you mean *it didn't take?*"

"I mean, I went back in for the check-up and everything, and it had all healed over. Freaked me out at the time, but, hey, it's not like this kind of thing is anything new to me, this 'Wave a magic wand thing ...' He shrugged. "Which reminds me, when did *this* happen?" He pointed at her belly.

"Cape Town. Must have been ..."

"But you told me you had condoms."

"I did. One must have broken or just not worked, I don't know."

"So who's the dad?"

"Just a guy ... Look, can we talk about something else? He's not going to be a dad, I'm not having this baby. And that's all I have to say. I don't want to talk about it."

"Okay, let's go for a drive. Getting out the house a bit will help get your mind off it."

The idea of having a baby versus having an abortion was so all consuming that Annabel doubted anything would be able to distract her from turning it all over and over in her mind. Over and over and over again, like a really bad country song on loop. It wasn't until they pulled up at the drive-thru ice-cream place that something occurred to her

"Oh shit! Just thought of something ... Dad's going to see on the news that you're sick."

"He'll probably just think its Mork related. It's more likely I'll get a call from Doc than him."

"How is Dr Cooper?"

"Good. Spoke to him a few days ago."

"So you haven't told him about me then?"

"No, you should, though. I mean, he is our family doctor; if anything, he'll write you a sick note that doesn't have the word 'abortion' on it."

"Oh fuck, Alex!" Annabel felt like she was going to throw up. "Please don't say *that* word!"

In his entire life, Alex had never seen his sister so detached, so defeated. Even when their mother had died or when she found Ryan cheating on her, she had at least reacted – screamed, fumed, complained – but now, now that the initial flood of tears had subsided, she was just grey, a blankness in her eyes.

"Are you so sure about this?"

"Sure about not being a single mother to a child whose father I cannot contact and only knew for twelve hours? Yes, I'm sure, thanks."

"Yeah, it's just one of those things that have to be asked, so don't bite my head off. Doc still thinks you might be able to get the curse that way."

"Still calling this whole Mork thing a curse, huh?"

"Yeah, I don't know another word. It's a love-hate relationship. I appreciate that my life wouldn't necessarily be what it is now without it, but there are still things I feel I can't do or bad things that might not have happened. 'Curse' might not be the right word, but it's better than 'disease'."

"How so?"

It was Alex's turn to take on a grey pallor. "Disease suggests it can be cured."

"Didn't you and Dr Cooper look into that stuff, though?"

"Yes, but none of it made any difference. Silver makes me itch and wolf's bane makes me vomit, that's about it."

"Isn't wolf's bane poisonous?"

"Yes."

"And Dr Cooper just let you take it?"

"Well, no, not exactly ..." Annabel started hitting Alex's arm. "What are you doing, woman, I'm driving!"

"You're not allowed to do things like that!"

She punched one last time, folded her arms and went back to looking out the window. He thought about his other experience with silver and decided not to tell her about it.

"It was a long time ago and a very small amount – not enough to really do anything permanent. But, yeah, sorry."

"Just because you may be immortal doesn't mean you get to test the theory."

They both knew that they were simply killing time, filling the void, but it was better than sitting in silence waiting for four o'clock.

And by the time late afternoon did finally creep up on them, they were exhausted, drained, sucked dry by their mutual attempts to keep their spirits up, to be distracted by the everyday, knowing how the following hours would change their lives irrevocably. Eventually, when Alex finally pulled up in the parking lot of the doctor's rooms, tempers were frayed, emotions heightened, angst written all over their faces. Sarah was already pacing the length of the waiting room, and Alex noted that the awkwardness he usually felt when he ran into someone he'd slept with simply wasn't there. Sarah had filled in the anonymous patient sheet on Annabel's behalf, so all she had to do was sign and wait for her number to be called. Finally, a friendly-looking nurse walked over to them.

"Patient 112? If you could follow me?"

"Do ... do I have to go alone?"

The nurse smiled. "No, your friends can come too if you want; this is just a consultation with the doctor."

The nurse turned to Alex, the look on her face telling them that suspected she knew him, but couldn't quite place him. Alex smiled, but tried to avoid eye contact. Her recognising him was the last thing they needed. In the doctor's room Sarah and Alex – his back to the nurse, just to be sure – took the chairs and Annabel seated herself on the bed.

Sarah turned to the nurse. "Surely it doesn't happen in here?"

"Oh no, just a consultation. There'll be an ultrasound to confirm the pregnancy and the doctor will explain how the procedure will work, then a second appointment is made." The nurse smiled, not at Sarah, but at Alex, confusion still getting the better of her. "Sorry, but where do I know you from? I know your face, I'm sure I do."

Alex smiled nervously. "If I told you, that would make the 'anonymous patient' bit redundant, wouldn't it? In fact, I should probably ask you to promise to never tell anyone about this should you ever work it out."

The nurse squinted her eyes, even more confused.

"Jesus, Alex, can I go nowhere with you?" Annabel struggled to maintain her composure.

"Oh! My! God! You're Alex Harris. You are, aren't you? Aren't you? Oh my—"

"For fuck's sake, Alex!"

The nurse looked at Annabel, then at Alex, then back at Annabel. "Oh m—" It was clear that Annabel was near to tears. "Oh, oh … don't worry, dear, you're not the first celebrity case we've had come through here. If I tell anyone, I not only lose my job but any chance of ever working in medicine again and that goes for everyone who works here."

"Thank you," Annabel offered a gracious half-smile. "But, for the record, he's my brother not the father."

The nurse smiled, nodded, and quickly made her departure as the doctor appeared at the door. She introduced herself as Dr Schmidt and, having immediately recognised the young man with Patient 112, again assured them all that there were very strict non-disclosure rules in place, before she began to explain the procedure in detail.

"But first things first," she said, when she saw Alex wince. "You're going to have an ultrasound to make sure you are indeed pregnant, and then we can continue from there."

She ushered Annabel over to the examination table, invited her to lie down and lifted her shirt. She then wheeled over a small screen and began rubbing gel on the patient's stomach. Within moments the screen crackled to life and a tiny dot of blue emerged on the screen.

"That, my dear, is your baby."

It was at that point all sanity left Annabel. "Alex! Alex, I can't do this."

"Do what?"

"This. This! Becoming un-pregnant. That. I can't do it."

He took her hand and held it tightly. "Okay. It's okay. You don't have to. You get to decide here. Shhh, shhh ..."

Tears ran down her face, which prompted Sarah to shed a few herself. But this was nothing new to the doctor. The minute that blue dot appears on the screen, the doctor usually knew which path the patient would follow.

"Well, in that case," Dr Schmidt smiled, "I recommend you get in touch with your own gynaecologist or, if you'd prefer, we can reschedule for a couple weeks' time for you to come in for your next check-up."

Alex looked at the doctor, then back to Annabel, who started blankly at him.

"I think we'll stick with you, doctor. Set up the appointment; we'll fill out the cards next time round. Right now, we have some things to take care of."

Annabel was confused but strangely happy that she didn't have to make any other decisions right after making what seemed like the most important of her life. Dr Schmidt grabbed a sheet of paper from her desk and handed it to Alex.

"Here is a list of things the expectant mother should start eating and doing, and also what she needs to avoid. If you could just leave your contact details with nurse at the front desk, I'll be in touch."

"Thanks." Annabel was calmer, strangely at peace as she took the paper towel from the foot of the bed and wiped her stomach clear of the remaining gel before pulling her shirt down.

Alex handed the doctor his card, then he led Annabel back to the car. Although she knew what was going to happen next, she didn't say anything or ask. They got in and drove directly to their father's place, Sarah following right behind.

Alex pulled into the driveway, switched off his car and waited for Annabel to say something. Neither had said a word since leaving the doctor's room. Sarah parked on the road outside the house and waited to see what they were going to do.

"What are we doing here?"

"Well, I figure, if you're not going to do *that* then you're going to do *this*. Then I thought the best thing to do would be to get some sound advice from someone who has slightly more experience than us, so I thought Dad … well, actually, I thought Grandma, but Dad's closer."

Annabel leant over and hugged her brother. "I love you, you know that? I'm so glad you're not normal and have all kinds of strange animal protective instincts."

He smiled. "I like to think I would've been like this anyway, but thanks, I think."

"You'll make a great uncle."

"Hey! I'm not letting it ride me, if that's what you're thinking."

"And that," she laughed and patted him on the head, "we both know is a lie."

Kyle was watching from the front door. What were those two conjuring up now? They were up to something, he knew. Alex looked up at his dad, waved and then climbed out of the car, stopping at the passenger side to open Annabel's door for her. No, Kyle thought to himself, something's up *for sure* ... Annabel followed her brother up the drive, and Kyle noticed Sarah exit her car just a little further away and make her way up behind them. Wonder if I'm gonna need a whisky after all of this ...

"Hey, Dad, you remember Annie's friend Sarah?"

"Yes, of course. But ... Alex, I thought you were sick – and in LA. What's going on, you two? What's up? 'Cos I know something's up ..."

Annabel frowned nervously. "We've got some news." She glanced at Alex.

"You're pregnant, aren't you?"

Alex burst out laughing.

"Alex!"

"*What?* I didn't say anything, I swear!"

"Oh God, you really *are* pregnant?"

Annabel smiled nervously. "Can … can we come in?"

Kyle scrunched up his face, and waved his hand to usher them in. "Yes, please do."

Alex continued to fight back laughter, both Annabel and Kyle decidedly less amused. Silently they all made their way into the kitchen and took seats at the table. Kyle looked at his daughter and waited for her to say something.

"Are you angry?"

"No."

"Disappointed?"

"No, confused."

"Confused?"

"I take it that all of you being here to tell me means you're going to keep it, keep the baby?"

Annabel looked down at the table and nodded.

"And the father?"

"A guy I met in Cape Town."

"Any way of contacting him?"

"No."

"Okay ..." Kyle reached a hand across the table and gently guided Annabel's head back up so that he could look into her eyes. "And you're absolutely positive about this?"

Her eyes welled up with tears. "I'm not really sure about much right now, but I know I can't get rid of it, Dad. That was just too much. I can't do it."

Kyle nodded. "Okay, good – I'm glad to hear you haven't totally lost your mind. But I do think you should move back in here. Just because the baby doesn't have a father doesn't mean you don't, and there are some things a pregnant woman has to do that are just easier if you have someone to yell at it about."

Annabel's face lit up. "You mean it?"

"Well, if your mother's pregnancies were anything to go by, yes, you're going to go crazy, but that's okay. God knows we do enough crazy in this household ..."

"No, I mean you're not throwing me out? Disowning me or something?"

"You really think I'd do that?"

Annabel couldn't hold back any longer, and burst into tears. "I don't know! I don't know anything any more."

Kyle got up to move around the table and wrap his arms around her. "Hey, no reason for silliness." He turned to Alex. "Go order some pizzas, I think. You all stay here tonight, and tomorrow I'll make a doctor's appointment. Then we can see how far along you are and find out everything you have to do. Okay?"

Chapter 31

"Welcome back to K505, Syn Island's number-one radio station. I'm Barbra Barker and we're here chatting to Alex Harris. So, you've always been more on the metal side of things, but what kind of music do you listen to at home? I mean, what was playing in your car on the drive over here?"

"Honestly? Rachmaninov."

"What?"

"I love classical music. I love all music actually, but classical music has always been a favourite – long before I even knew about metal. It's also good to listen to while driving, less chance of road rage."

"Wow! Well, another first brought to the world by K505. So what do you think of the music on the charts at the moment?"

"There is no music on the charts at the moment."

"Ouch! Bitter much? Are you saying there isn't one song on last week's top twenty you liked?"

"It's all just fungus music: not good, not bad, but if you leave it long enough it grows on you, like fungus. All formulated carbon-copy music being stamped out by the giant machine that is contemporary pop. Written by someone sitting in an office, performed by a

generic pop singer then digitally remastered to sound like no sound a human can make. I mean, there are reality shows – little more than game shows, really – that you can win to become a pop singer ... How much respect can you possibly have for these people?"

"Well, what about the current number one? She writes most of her own stuff and there is a very hot YouTube clip of her where she does some acoustic stuff – really amazing."

"That's even worse. Being able to do it doesn't make you an artist if what you actually produce is the same old rubbish that everyone else pumps out, so manipulated by computers that you can barely tell when it's voice and when it's keyboard. I mean, how do you do a live show of this shit when no part of it is actually performed by a live person?"

"Okay, can't say the s word on air, and we've clearly hit a nerve on this one."

"Well, what do you expect? We – the guys and I, and other half-decent *musicians – spend months practising to get it right for the recording of the album, and even longer for the live shows. These guys sing three notes into a computer and some techie produces an album of pop songs that sound exactly the same as every other song on the radio. Occasionally, some real music breaks through but for that to happen it either has to be a masterpiece or be attached to some film or scandal. I think the last time we were on the top twenty it was with a song now listed as one of the greatest metal songs in history and we were number one for two weeks. I can't tell you the name of the song that took its place or who it was by, but I remember that it was there for over a month and was remixed into like a million different dance versions. Tell me, where the artistic appreciation is in that?"*

"I remember that, I used to love going out and bustin' a move to that song."

"Oh, you've got to be fucking kidding me."

With that, Alex pulled off his headphones and stormed out. The rest of the dumbstruck crew could see the panic rise in Barbra's eyes as her Special Guest abandoned her mid-set, on live radio.

Her first thought was, Oh shit, I'm gonna lose my job for this …

But by the time she managed to switch to a commercial break, Alex was long gone. He was fuming as he made his way out of the building to his car, but hadn't even turned the ignition when his phone rang. He pulled it out of his pocket and smiled when he saw Josh's name flash on the screen.

"Dude, that was fucking *amazing*! I think you might be the first person to say fuck on public radio and in the middle of the day, during school rush-hour traffic. Your sister is going to be *soooo* pissed, but I think you're a legend, man. That chick is still uum-mming and aahing about you walking out. Where can we meet? Time for a celebration drink!"

Alex threw back his head and laughed. "Uhmmm, I don't know, I'm still a bit pissed off. You name the place and I'll head right over."

"Cool, man! Why don't you come here first and we'll work some-thing out from there."

"Groovy, on my way."

"Cool man."

"Oh shit, I can't."

"What? Why not?"

"I'm supposed to be babysitting Bastian tonight."

"Shit! Well, okay if I come there then? It'll be cool to see the little dude again. Haven't seen him in a while."

"Liar! You just want to see Annabel."

"Well, yeah, that too ... So, is that a yes?"

"Yeah, come on by. I could use the back up to make sure he grows up listening to good music."

"Awesome. Give me about an hour?"

"Laters."

"Bye."

Alex started the car and made the slow drive over to his sister's place. He couldn't help but laugh when he turned his radio to K505 and was met with the stutters and awkward silences of Barbra Barker as she tried to pull herself together and salvage what was left of her show.

He found Annabel in the kitchen. "Have you lost your goddamn mind?"

"What? I thought it was appropriate. Asking me about my thoughts on pop music, what did she expect me to say? I'm a metal singer. Oh yes, if only I had it my way I'd be making shitty pop songs too?"

Annabel rolled her eyes. "What are you doing here anyway?"

"To babysit, don't you have a work thing tonight?"

"Yes, but that's what the nanny is for."

Alex suddenly picked up an unusual scent from Annabel. "I know, but I thought maybe you could give her the night off and I could do it. I mean, I don't get to spend too much time with him as it is, and I'd like to."

"You spent all weekend with him." Annabel's words were sharp, her tone annoyed.

"Well, no, that was Mork, whom, I might add, Bastian is notably happier to see. And that's a problem for me."

"Fine, do whatever you want. I'll give Charmaine the night off and you can watch Bastian."

Alex blinked hard at her. "What's wrong?"

Instantly he felt a shiver run down his spine and sensed that he'd just made a mistake. Annabel looked up at him, furious; she opened her mouth to rant but stopped herself.

"It's a work thing and it's totally fucked up, but I can't really talk about it."

"That's new. Can't talk about it, why?"

"Because if I do I might go to jail," she smiled at him sarcastically.

"Okay ... so I guess I'll stop asking."

"Would you, thanks!" She was back to short, sharp words.

"Jesus, Annie! Put me down, why don't you? I'm just worried about you, that's all."

She took a deep breath. "Sorry, I'm just really stressed out about all this. I'm actually glad to see you and I'm glad you want to spend time with Bastian – I think it's good for him to have a male role model in his life that isn't a big, bad wolf."

"It's alright, I know you work hard. It's part of the reason I've taken a break from the band; I want to be here to help you out a bit more. Take some of the stress off so you can have some free time."

She smiled up at him. She so wanted to just vent.

"Does that mean I'm going to lose my job?" Suddenly a third voice joined the conversation. Charmaine, Annabel's nanny, locked eyes with Alex.

"I wouldn't worry, Char," he laughed. "Chances are I'll need more looking after then Bastian does."

"Ain't that the truth?" Annabel laughed.

Alex tried to look offended but failed, but before he had a chance to even attempt a witty comeback he was saved by the sound of his phone ringing. He quickly pulled it out of his pocket, and glanced at the screen.

"Oh cool, it's Marina." He looked at Charmaine and Annabel and smirked. "This isn't over, you two." He answered his phone as he left the room. "Morning ..."

Charmaine looked at Annabel. "Does he mean Marina Allen? The movie star?"

Annabel raised her eyebrows. "Yip!"

"I thought he said he was single?"

"Char, he could be married with ten kids and he'd still tell the press he's single. It's his pet hate – having the public know about his personal life."

"So he just lies in interviews?"

"Yip, *all* the time."

Charmaine chuckled, but the two stifled their laughter when Alex raised his voice.

"What do you mean I'm an *arsehole*?"

He moved away when he saw Annabel and Charmaine watching, mouths open, from the kitchen door.

"Exactly what I say," replied Marina. "You didn't need to swear at that poor woman."

"Oh, come on! That was funny."

"Oh, of course, everything is one giant joke with you! Well, what about *my* feelings?"

"What about them? I didn't talk about you ... Oh, wait, *that's* what this is about, isn't it? You're pissed that I said I was single."

"Well, we've been going out for almost three months ... Don't you think it's about time we admitted to it?"

"No! It's *our* business, Marina. Ours. Why the fuck does the rest of the world need to know about it?"

"Well, what about what I want? Don't I get a say?"

"Sure you do. What's your say?"

Alex's voice deepened to a low growl, but Marina could still detect the sharp sting of sarcasm.

"Well, I say we tell the world about us. I'm sick and tired of pretending I'm single when I'm not. *I say* we admit our relationship and go public with it." Alex took a deep breath. "In fact, my publicist has already made arrangements for *People* magazine t—"

"You've done *what?*" There was no mistaking his deep growl now as it reverberated through the house, sending a cold chill down Charmaine's spine. "*How dare you? Fuck this! Relationship over!*"

In a fit of rage, Alex bit a chunk out of his phone and sent the rest of it hurtling across the room. On the other end of the line Marina was dead silent, her fear almost tangible. To her it sounded as though Alex was about to launch himself through the phone at her and was relieved when the line went dead. All her life she'd never heard anyone so completely enraged.

Alex spat out the chunk before dropping to his knees, and groaned loudly, focusing hard on retaining his human form. Annabel rose quickly and closed the door, then turned back to Charmaine.

"Wonder what that was about."

Charmaine smiled nervously and forced conversation.

"So, all those things he said in the interview, does he come up with it on the spot?"

"He scripts some of it. I think his little outburst about modern pop was the most honest he's been in an interview for years."

"Is he going to be all right? He sounds … almost in pain."

"He'll be fine. Just give him a minute. He has a medical condition that flares when his heart rate accelerates quickly like that," Annabel sighed. "Pity though. I was going to give you the night off but if Alex doesn't calm down, he'll end up having to go home, which would mean that I'm going to need you to stay with Bastian."

"That's okay. I mean, I was fully expecting to work and even if I had the night off I'd probably stay home anyway." Charmaine hesitated. "Uhmmm, but if it's a medical thing, shouldn't we help him?"

"The best way to help him is to leave him. He just needs to sit quietly and calm down; he knows how to handle it. If we were running around him trying to help we'd just stress him out even more. Don't worry, I know the signs of when to help and when to leave him be."

Annabel smiled and switched on the kettle. A few minutes later Alex reappeared in the doorway, much calmer.

"Sorry about that. Guess I lost my temper a bit there."

Annabel looked up.

"Yeah, no shit."

"And I'm sorry about swearing like that around Bastian."

"Oh, don't worry about that. He's playing at Dad's place this afternoon."

"Oh, good."

"Dad's going to bring him back later when he picks me up. He's my date for the work dinner."

"Dad? That'll be nice. How *is* Dad? I've not actually sat down with him in a bit."

"Seems to be doing well, thinking about retiring."

"Really? What will he do otherwise?"

"Not sure. I expect I'll be having that conversation a lot. But are *you* okay?"

"Me?"

"I mean, you just broke up with your girlfriend."

"Yeah, I'll add her name to the list." His tone was sarcastic and evasive.

Annabel shook her head then turned to Charmaine. "Could you give us a minute please, Char?"

Alex rolled his eyes. "Really?"

"Yes."

Charmaine nodded nervously and scurried off to her room.

Alex sat quietly and waited for the lecture to start.

"Are you really that insensitive that you'll just drop a girl and get over it in five minutes? I thought wolves mated for life?"

"I'm not a wolf."

"Well, you sure sounded like one on the phone to Marina. You were so angry. I mean, she must have been terrified."

"Well, what do you expect? You know what she did? She got her publicist to 'leak' a story to *People* magazine that we were official-ly a couple."

"Swearing at her and destroying your phone like that is still an overreaction. I know you like to be private and all, but at some point one of your relationships is going to have to last longer than a week and eventually go public."

Alex tightened his jaw. "Not right now – please, Annie,"

"You can't keep chasing away every girl you get close to."

Alex took a sharp breath. "Just give me a little more time to get my head sorted. I promise we can talk about it later. My heart is still clanging like a fucking cymbal, and Josh is coming over."

"What? Since when?"

"He called when I left the radio station. Said he'd be an hour."

"When was that?"

"About forty-five minutes ago?"

"Oh, for fuck sake, Alex! Okay, well then you go sit somewhere and calm yourself down. I've got things to do, but we *are* going to talking about this later."

"Promise."

Alex smiled and held up his pinkie finger; Annabel tried to look unimpressed but couldn't hide her smile. She gripped his little finger with hers and then left the room. Alex sat for a moment considering the lingering smell of fear before he pulled his MP3 player out of his pocket and settled on the sofa in the lounge.

It wasn't long before he heard a car pull up and Josh's voice at the front door. Usually, Alex would play his music at maximum volume to block out as much noise as possible, but he couldn't risk Josh sneaking up on him and shooting his heart rate right back up. He took out his earphones and headed for the front door, determined to prevent Josh from trying to ask Annabel out on a date yet again. It wasn't that he had anything against the idea of Josh and Annabel dating; it was simply that he didn't want to have to stand by and watch his buddy get rejected yet again.

"Josh, my man! How's tricks?"

"Alexis! What's up?"

"You want some coffee?"

"Sure."

"Groovy, come on in."

"So where's the little dude? And why's your phone off? I tried calling you."

"My phone ... Yeah, slight technical problem there."

"You had a fight with Marina again, didn't you?"

"Wha— How?"

"All right – don't be angry, but I heard about the *People* thing."

Alex put down the kettle and turned to Josh.

"You what?"

"Yeah, well I thought I'd be good for you to have a real relationship for a change, instead of another one-month stand."

"Dude, not cool."

"And Marina is cool and smoking hot, dude."

"Still not cool, you know how much I hate my private life being front-page news."

"Yes, but we're famous so it's always going to be that way, unless you move to the middle of the desert or something, someone in the crowd is going to know who you are. It's not healthy what you do."

Alex took a deep breath and went back to making coffee while Josh took a seat at the table.

"A lecture? Really? Come on, man. Is it honestly better to do it the other way, and end up like Brandon?"

"Brandon is just as bad; just the flip side of that coin. Oh shit, that reminds me ..."

"What? What's happened now?"

"He found out Stacy's pregnant."

"Why does your face say that's bad news?"

"Because Brandon ... well, Brandon probably shoots blanks."

"What?" Alex took the seat across from Josh and handed him his mug. "How could you possibly know that?"

"Turns out that when he was a kid he got measles or malaria or something like that and it kinda killed his swimmers, there's like a one per cent chance it's his kid."

"Holy shit! He must be a wreck. When did you find out about this and why aren't we all together, I don't know, drinking our faces off?"

"Well, no one else is supposed to know, and Brandon being Brandon ..."

"Is he deluding himself, believing it's that one per cent chance that it's his kid?"

"Yip! Expect to get a strange call in the next few days inviting you to a strange gathering with no clear explanation."

"Oh God! It's going to be his engagement party all over again."

"Yip."

"Why does he do this to himself anyway? He's not a bad-looking guy, talented and, oh yeah, a fucking world-famous rock star, he could get some groupie who's twice as hot, and infinitely more loyal than Stay-bitch."

"Who's a bitch?"

Alex and Josh both turned to see Annabel, dressed in a dark blue cocktail dress, standing at the door to the kitchen. Alex gave a low whistle while Josh's face seemed too slide off his head and onto the floor.

"Brandon's shit wife."

"Oh God, Stacy! Why doesn't he just leave her?"

"Welcome to the conversation, kettle's just boiled."

Annabel quickly made herself a cup of tea and sat down next to Josh, who pulled himself together just enough to muster, "Why you dressed like that?"

"Going to a work dinner."

And before Alex could stop him, Josh replied, "Can I be your date?"

Alex sighed and rolled his eyes, but Annabel was more sincere.

"Sorry, but I've already promised my dad. Maybe next time?"

"It's a date."

Alex shook his head. Josh sprang back to his senses.

"Alex, what kind of technical difficulties?"

"Pardon?"

"Your phone, douche bag. What happened to your phone?"

"Oh yeah that," Alex smiled sheepishly. "Well, it kinda smashed into a few different pieces."

"Can those pieces be put back together?"

"Not without a soldering gun."

"See? Personally, I think that's evidence enough to suggest you really like Marina. What say you, Annie?"

"Sorry, Alex, I'm with Josh on this one."

"Fantastic! Now could we all possibly talk about this later? I think I hear Dad's car."

Alex put on a cheesy smile that distracted Josh enough that he did not notice that Alex could hear a car a street away.

"Fine, but this isn't over," Annabel reminded her brother. "You can have my old phone if you want. See if you can retrieve your sim card from the wreckage."

"Groovy. Where's your old phone?"

"In one of the drawers in my office. You're good at finding things, I have faith in you."

"Thanks."

The front door opened and the sound of by Bastian's voice put a smile on everyone's faces.

"Mom!"

The boy came running into the kitchen and leapt into his mother's arms.

"There's my boy! How was it at Grandpa's?"

"So cool! We watched *Star Wars* and ate ice cream. Mork here?"

Annabel looked at her brother, who cringed slightly.

"Sorry, kiddo, I had to take him back to the sanctuary yesterday."

"Aawww! Can I go watch TV?"

"Sure thing, sweetheart."

Bastian let go of his mother and ran out past his grandfather standing at the kitchen door.

"Hello, kids. That includes you, Josh."

Kyle smiled, and looked his daughter up and down.

"You're looking lovely, my dear."

"You too, Dad. We're a little early, would you like some coffee?"

"This is why you're the smart one. Thank you, dear."

Kyle sat down next to Alex and nodded at the two boys.

"So, how are things? How did your radio interview go?"

"Well, really well, I think."

"Really? Because I heard you swore at the DJ and walked out."

"Yes, but everything leading up to that was good."

"You're right, though," Kyle laughed, "the standard of music these days is ridiculous."

Annabel chimed in: "Don't encourage him, Dad! He really doesn't need any help."

"But it's true. I mean, I'm not saying that I'm a particular fan of all the music you boys have put out over the years, but at least it's you who's making it. Your voice, guitar, drums, bass. This electronic pop is garbage."

"Thank you, Mr Harris, it's nice to know there are still a few sane people left in the world."

"Son, I'm almost sixty years old. I was alive when pop music was The Beatles, The Rolling Stones and Bob Dylan and they'd sit at number one for months on end until someone actually released something better."

"Well, you'll get no argument from us, Dad."

Just then Bastian walked back into the kitchen with a confused look on his face and something in his hand. He placed on the table the chunk of phone Alex had spat onto the floor.

"Grandpa, what's this?"

Alex cringed; Josh recognised it as a piece of phone and tried very hard not to laugh.

"Really, Alex?" Kyle turned the remnant over in his hand. "Again? Let me guess, you've broken up with Marina?"

Kyle's tone was angry and direct.

"Have I done something wrong?" Bastian pulled himself close to his mother and whispered into her ear.

Annabel stroked his head and whispered back, "No, no, sweet-heart, you've done nothing wrong. Your uncle Alex has done something wrong. You've done everything right. Now go back to the lounge and finish watching TV."

"Don't you lecture me too." Alex's tone was less than amused. "I've had it in the neck from these two already."

"So because you've already been yelled at, that makes it okay for you to throw away another relationship. What did this one do? Buy the wrong breakfast cereal?"

"She signed a deal with *People* magazine to go public about our relationship."

"So what, you're a goddamn rock star, Alex! That comes with the territory. Marina is a great girl and perfect for you."

Alex stood up fast knocking his chair over behind him,

"I'm not having this fight again! You all think Marina is so perfect for me, then why didn't she at least ask me about it? Or know me well enough to simply not do it at all, huh?"

Annabel put a cup of coffee down in front of her father. "Sit down, Alex. You're making excuses and you know it. If anything, you need to call and apologise for yelling at her the way you did."

Alex took a deep breath, picked up his chair and sat down again, but said nothing. Josh and Kyle looked at each other, then back to Annabel.

"How bad was it?"

Annabel pointed at the piece of phone and rolled her eyes. Alex took another deep breath.

"Yeah, all right, I'll call her tomorrow; chances are she won't be accepting calls from me for the rest of the day anyway."

Josh reached across and patted Alex on the shoulder. "Why do you get so angry about this stuff anyway, man? I mean, the rest of us live the same lives, but we've learned to deal, know what I mean?"

Alex looked up at Josh and then at his dad. "I don't know. I just really hate my private life being made public. There's the public version of me that the world sees and knows and there's private me and I just get tetchy when the two mix."

"Yeah man, I know how you feel. I think that's why Danny goes on his little pilgrimages."

"Where's he now anyway?"

"Peru."

Everyone at the table shook their heads.

"Strange boy, that one."

"You said it, Dad."

"Didn't he once buy an entire housing development and turn it into a forest?"

"Yip, he did. Said it was to offset the band's carbon footprint after all the flying we'd done while on tour."

Annabel looked up at the clock

"Oh, time, Dad – we've got to go."

"All right then."

Kyle downed what was left of his coffee and Josh looked at his watch,

"Actually, dude, I should probably get going too. I'm gonna go over to Brandon's and see how things are going. Let me know when you're back online phone-wise so I can keep you posted."

Annabel and Kyle looked curiously at the boys.

"What's the matter with Brandon?"

Alex smiled nervously, "For another time, believe me."

Annabel and Kyle shrugged their shoulders. When it came to Brandon, nothing was ever simple. After a quick stop in the lounge to get hugs from Bastian and tell him that his uncle Alex would be looking after him, everyone left. Annabel was more nervous than usual; she'd never been good at keeping secrets from her father and knew he was holding off asking her what was wrong. When he eventually did she palmed it off as the usual jitters about a work social.

Alex quickly made his way through to Annabel's office to find her old phone, then into the lounge to find his sim card and join his nephew in watching cartoons. A few hours, pizzas and a bedtime story later Alex felt alone in the house. But he wasn't, of course, and it didn't take him long to appear at the door to Charmaine's bedroom with a bottle of wine and two glasses.

Chapter 32

Alex woke up to a hangover and ring tone he didn't recognise. A quick survey of his surroundings reminded him that he was still at his sister's place, and the ringing phone was for him.

"Hello?" Alex groaned into the phone.

"Morning, sunshine!" came the less-than-pleased sound of his sister's voice. "And where did you rush off to last night?"

"What?"

"When I got home, you were gone. Sure, Bastian was in bed, but you can't just leave a six-year-old alone in the house, Alex – you know better than that!"

"Charmaine was there. Where are you? What time is it?"

"It's seven, and Charmaine being there doesn't make it okay that you left. You're still going to have to make it up to me."

"Sure, can we talk about this at a more respectable time, like tomorrow?"

"No, but I'll call you later; I just wanted to wake you up early as part of your punishment."

It occurred to Alex that Annabel had no idea that he'd slept with her nanny, something he'd been made to swear he'd never do. He turned to face Charmaine who by some miracle was still asleep. He looked around the room to see more bottles of wine than he remembered drinking and far more condom wrappers than he remembered opening. He fought the urge to count them so he could brag about it later. Quietly he slipped out of bed and scanned the place for his clothes. Just as he slipped one leg into his jeans, Charmaine's alarm sprang to life, filling the room with a high-pitched beep, over and over and over again. He dropped his pants and clamped his hands over his ears. Charmaine jumped up with a start and slapped her alarm clock to make it stop screaming. Then she noticed Alex, who was standing with his jeans at his ankles, his hands over his ears looking like an idiot. She erupted into a feeble hungover laugh. Alex opened one eye to see a giggling girl, buck naked, looking back at him and instantly felt slightly better. He gave her his signature smile. But the mood quickly dissipated by a knock at the door.

"Morning, Char! You want some tea?" Annabel's voice.

Charmaine's eyes widened. Alex made wild hand movements to indicate she shouldn't mention that he's there.

"Ye-yes please, thanks."

Alex creeped silently onto the bed and whispered into her ear, "I really don't mean to be offensive or anything, but I think it's a really bad idea if you tell my sister about this."

Charmaine breathed a sigh of relief and whispered back, "Oh thank God ... As cool as it is that we did this, I'm not sure how good it would be for my job to sleep with my boss's brother."

Alex kissed her on the cheek. "Fantastic. Okay, you get ready like normal and I'll hide for a few minutes, then sneak out the window and arrive at the front door. Just make sure she doesn't see that my car is still here."

"Wouldn't she have seen it when she got home?"

Alex thought for a moment.

"No, I parked on the street and Dad would have driven up the driveway to drop her off. We're still in the clear for now. It's always possibly, though, she's just torturing me for sleeping with you."

Charmaine took a few deep breaths to fight off her hangover, then quickly jumped to life, diving in and out of the shower and into clean clothes, a quick spritz with deodorant and she was ready to start her day. Alex tilted his head to the side and looked in astonishment.

"Wow," he mouthed.

She blushed, then left to meet up with Annabel in the kitchen.

Alex pulled his clothes and then slipped out a window. He quickly checked the calls received on his phone to work out how long it had been since his sister had called and tried to work out how long it would take for him to 'get up and get back to the house'. The first thing he had done when the band decided to take a break from making music was to buy himself an apartment, one that was ideally situated between his father and sister's place. He waited a few more minutes, then snuck off to his car. For the sake of the show he got in and drove it up the driveway as if he'd just arrived. He climbed out, made his way up to the front door and let himself in.

"If you're making, I'd love a cup of coffee darlin'."

Annabel looked up in shock at the sight of her tired, hungover brother in the doorway.

"I didn't mean for you to actually get up and come over when I called."

"It's okay, you were right, I shouldn't have relied on Charmaine to look out for Bastian, although I did clear it with her before I left."

Annabel turned to Charmaine who was packing Bastian's school lunch.

"It's true; he did come and talk to me before he left, but only after he had put Bastian to bed *and* read him a story."

"Forgiven then," Annabel smiled and turned back to her newspaper. "But if you're making coffee, I'd love a cup. No, actually, not forgiven, you still have to call Marina today."

Alex scoffed and made his way over to the kettle.

"If you think Marina is awake at this hour ... Actually, what is the time?"

Annabel looked at her watch. "Oh shit, school time. Alex, we can get coffee on the way if you want to come for the drive, finally see where Bastian goes to school."

"Yeah, cool, but I've parked you in so we can take my car."

"Only if you promise to drive extra carefully."

"Of course, I only drive like a loon when I'm alone in the car."

"Okay, I'm going to go get Bastian and then we can go. Don't think you're off the hook totally, I still want to talk to you."

Alex gave her the thumbs up and smirked, "Oh goodie."

***

Alex waited in the car while Annabel walked Bastian in. He knew what to expect when she returned: a lecture about life choices and commitment; he'd gotten them often enough before in the past when he broke up with girls his family liked. As much as he agreed with what people had said, he still couldn't find the place inside himself where he felt safe enough to let someone in deep enough to get to know the real him. The idea of someone discovering his secret and it getting out frightened him more than he'd ever been willing to admit. Still unable to shake the guilt surrounding his mother's death all those years ago, he wished she were still around, how much that would have helped Annabel and Bastian. He felt his hackles begin to rise, and quickly opened his door and stepped out of the vehicle, forcing himself to think about something else and to control his breathing. To his relief Annabel was already heading back towards the car. He walked around to the passenger side and opened the door for her before climbing back in and slowly pulling away. The car was silent for a few minutes until Annabel realised that Alex was heading for her office.

"Alex, where we going?"

"Uhmmm, I'm taking you to work?"

"But I'm booked out all day today in meetings with clients."

"Awesome," he said. "Then let's go grab some breakfast."

He fought the urge to do a U-turn in the middle of the street, but turned at the next circle and headed straight towards the harbour. It wasn't long before they were at an isolated table sipping coffee and taking in the sea views. Eventually Annabel broke the silence.

"So what are you going to do with yourself?"

Alex smiled uncomfortably. "Well, I'm rich and famous, what more do you want from me?"

"I want you to be happy … " She paused. "And going from girl to girl isn't healthy."

"I know you and Dad don't really understand it, but it works for me."

"What about long term? What about a family one day?"

Alex's discomfort quickly turned to exasperation.

"Come on, Annabel, we both know that's not an option."

"But you don't know what'll happen,"

"I know there is unknown DNA in my semen that could potentially turn into a litter of hairy babies that eat their way out of whoever is carrying them at the first full moon."

"Disgusting!" Annabel looked slightly sick at the thought. "You don't have to be so graphic."

"No? Well, apparently I did ... We've had this conversation before and you bring it up at every opportunity." Alex's heart rate began to climb and he could feel his cheeks heat up as he got a little louder and a little angrier. "It's like breaking up with a girl apparently doesn't cause me enough grief. No, you've got to remind me of all my shortcomings, too. I'd love a family, you hear me? I'd love to have kids and a normal life. That's not an option, so just let me ..."

"Just let you deal with it your own way. Sure, you've said that a hundred times before – and don't yell at me like I'm stupid, Alex. You've been dealing with it the same way since you were sixteen, how's that working for you, huh? Maybe it's time to start dealing with it a different way."

Alex shut his eyes and took a long, controlled breath. "Well, what do you suggest?"

"Call Marina, for a start. You don't have to get back together, but you do have to apologise. I don't think you realise how terrifying you sound when you lose it like that. Now, I don't know what you should do, but I've watched you do the same thing for years now and it doesn't look like it makes you happy, not really happy anyway. One girl after the next. I mean, how many women have you slept with?"

"That's not really a number you want to know."

"I just want you to be happy and what you're doing doesn't appear to be working. Don't fight me, just help me understand what's happening in your head and maybe I can help. I mean, isn't that the reason the band is taking a break in the first place?"

Alex thought for a moment about making a comment about breakfast really being a client meeting to try to get the band back together and make her company more money, but managed to restrain himself. Rather than retaliate, he decided he needed to inject some humour into the conversation.

"Well, I read on the IMDB that Natalie Portman occasionally takes in stray dogs, and I've always had a crush on her so maybe I can spend a few nights out in the rough as Mork, then go find her and she'll take me in."

Alex forced a smile in the hope the mood would lift.

"Isn't Natalie Portman, like, five-foot-nothing? Somehow I think if a mangy wolf that was just slightly shorter than her while on all fours came bounding towards her, I'm not sure pity and the urge to rescue would be her first instinct. Screaming in terror and running for her life strike me as a more likely outcome."

"Please, what do you know? There's nothing cuter than a giant wet wolf in need of some TLC – it'll be fine."

"Okay, well, you give it a try and let me know how it works out for you."

They both broke into laughter.

"So, what are we going to do today?" Alex smiled at his sister with a glint in his eye.

"Aren't you hungover?"

"Hangovers don't last that long."

"I hate you, but I do have another *actual* meeting later this afternoon. But if you want to pick up Bastian from school and hang out with him, you're more than welcome."

Alex's smile began to fade as his nose sent caution signals to his brain.

"That meeting's not with a client, is it? You're trying to hide something from me. Annie, what's going on?"

She scratched the back of her head and he could detect the faint smell of anxiety.

"Don't be so paranoi—"

"Stop that. You know it doesn't work on me."

She dropped her hand and looked him dead in the eyes.

"In that case, you should know when not to ask questions. If I could tell you I would."

"But you can't? Gotta say, that doesn't fill me with joy."

"Yeah, well, that's how it is, I'm afraid ..."

"Yes. You're afraid, and that why I'm asking. You're beginning to worry me ..."

The table fell silent for a minute until an idea dawned on him.

"I've got it. You have a giant pet wolf, who loves you and wants to look after you, who isn't a person and therefore isn't a liability when it comes to overheard information."

"What?" Annabel frowned.

"You want to tell me what's going on, but can't. I want to know what's going on because I'm worried about you. Mork can go with you to this meeting as your protection or guide dog or whatever. I get to find out what's going on, you get someone to talk to and neither of us breaks any laws." Alex smiled triumphantly.

Annabel thought for a moment. "You know, that's actually not a bad idea. I'd feel much better having Mork around; Dad can look after Bastian."

"What about Charmaine? Isn't that her job?"

"I'd just rather Bastian was with family – you'll understand why later."

"Okay, before I was just offering to come with you to find out what was going on, but now I'm really happy I'm coming with, just to protect you. What have you gotten yourself involved in?"

Annabel bit down on her thumbnail and smiled. "Yeah, well, yeah, you'll know soon enough, and having my dog with me will be fine, even if he is the most intimidating animal in the world."

"Hey, like I said, Mork is a sweet, kind, and loving creature. Just think of this as helping me hone my cute skills for seducing Natalie Portman later."

Annabel laughed quietly at Alex. "Aren't you famous enough to just meet her at some party?"

"Probably, but my way seems more fun and you said you wanted me to be happy."

"How is it that you can take genuine concern and translate it into permission for stalking?"

"Hey, stalking is an ugly word; I'm sure there is a much nicer, less creepy way to put it – I just can't think of one right now."

"You're a very strange human, you know that, right?"

"Mostly human – and, yes, you tell me often."

He smiled at his sister, still anxious about what trouble she'd gotten herself involved in, but happy that they had moved beyond the lecture. Annabel, however, was thinking up excuses on how to get away with having Mork accompany her to her meeting. She also took the opportunity to call her father and make arrangements for him to pick Bastian up from school, then called Charmaine to tell her she could once again have the night off. Charmaine instantly called Alex to find out if he was free but he'd put his phone on silent, just in case. Kyle was suspicious but knew better than to ask too many questions.

So that Charmaine wouldn't get to see Alex arrive and Mork leave, Alex and Annabel went back to his place until it was time for the meeting. This also gave Alex a chance to shower and pick up some fresh clothes for later. He went directly from the shower to his bedroom to transform into Mork. It was just over a week away from full moon so the transformation was fairly easy.

Annabel, not accustomed to having a day off, had no idea what to do with herself. She tried watching TV for a while but quickly found herself flicking through channels, watching nothing in particular. From there she moved to the computer to check her e-mails and browse social media, but realised she might get busted by someone at work and ended up simply following news feeds.

Meanwhile, Mork took the opportunity to catch up on the sleep he had been cheated out of the night before. Annabel eventually made her way back to the TV and settled into a romantic comedy.

She didn't want to admit that nerves were getting the better of her, so found the distraction comforting. She was relieved that Mork would be with her at the meeting, justifying it to herself because she wouldn't be breaking any silence agreements. She wouldn't be the one telling him what he needed to know, would she? She also wouldn't be hiding Mork from them; he'd be right out in the open. Mork woke up a few minutes before the movie ended and nudged her with his nose to get her attention, then motioned towards a wall clock.

"All right, let's go."

Mork narrowed his eyes as he looked her up and down. From her point of view, she was holding herself together fairly well; but from his vantage point, she'd filled his apartment with the scent of fear so he could smell little else. Neither as Mork nor Alex, had he ever seen his sister this scared, not even when pregnant when she was so fearful that he could almost see it coming off her in waves. At least then there was also excitement and understanding. Now she was simply terrified.

They made their way down to the car and headed off towards the docks. Halfway to the venue, Annabel turned to Mork sitting proudly on the passenger seat.

"I need to tell you something ... This meeting, it's obviously not a client – it's the police. I've been working with them to try to un-cover a money-laundering operation here on the island, a big one. Remember, when I started, I said I was auditing bigger clients? Well, I found something. Something pretty interesting, and now they think I might be in danger. I don't know all the details yet, but hopefully that's what I'm going to find out now. But that's why I've been so on edge." She breathed a sigh of relief; she'd wanted to tell him since she was initially contacted by the police.

Mork tilted his head to the side, inquisitively. He was interested to see where they were going and when they pulled into the parking area of an old, burned-out dockside pub he couldn't help feeling uneasy, and the hair on his neck rise. Annabel recognised the other car in the lot and for a moment thought she might be late. A glance at her watch told her she was early, however, so she parked alongside the empty vehicle.

"All right, we can do this. These are the good guys – this is going to be fine."

She opened her door and stepped out; the cool sea air refreshed and calmed her slightly. She peered into the dilapidated building and saw the man she was supposed to meet and, despite herself, smiled and waved. Slightly confused, he waved back, and then Mork jumped out of the car. The man's eyes grew wide and he ran a mental check on the firearms concealed on his body.

"Ms Harris, I presume?"

"Yes."

"And ... pet?"

"Yes."

"I'm Frank Oslo, chief of police. And what is that?"

"Wolf, mostly."

"I've seen smaller horses."

"Funny you should say that ... I've seen it outrun and take down a horse, when he was still a pup."

"Lovely, but look, Ms Harris, I'm on your side – you don't need to threaten me."

"Sorry, I'm not threatening you – I'm just a little nervous about all of this."

"Understandable. Shall we sit down and I can explain what it is exactly you've stumbled upon?"

Frank pointed to one of the old pub booths that were still mostly intact.

"I think ... I think I'd like that."

Frank and Annabel sat across from each other while Mork crouched on the floor.

Frank looked down at Mork. "He's very well trained," he said.

"Yip, he's my little protector."

"Little isn't a word I'd use, but to each their own, suppose. Now down to business ... How much do you know about the situation you're in?"

"Almost nothing, I think. I know that while reviewing one of my company's client accounts I started to see irregularities that sent warning bells off in my mind, so I took it to the investigation department who's supposed to deal with it. They reviewed it and then asked me to do an investigation into the client and their attached company account. I discovered that the personal accounts had a lot of untraceable income and the company had a growth that was unnaturally consistent. At college we're taught that if all the t's are crossed and all the i's are dotted someone's usually trying to hide something. So we called the police, who eventually put us in touch with a detective in organised crime, who then gave me a list of known and suspected dummy companies and asked if I'd looked again and a little deeper and see if there were any connections to any of the companies on the list. I did – and there were. So I called the detective again. He then explained that he'd take it to the right people, and for my own safety I should forget it ever happened. That was some time ago, then two days ago I got a call telling me I needed to meet you here now. I was told what kind of car to expect and the address and time and not to tell anyone. All in all, I've had a nerve-wracking two days."

"And did you tell anyone about it?"

"No."

"Is there anyone else who knew what you'd found?"

"Only the detective knew the exact details."

"No one else?"

"The investigation department would have known I'd looked into it in the first place and that it went to the police but, no, once I started looking in detail I reported only to the police."

Frank took a moment to consider everything.

"Well, you were right, we took what you gave us and added it to what we already had and it gave us a clearer arrow to who was sitting at the top of the racket, it's an investigation that has been going on long before you found out what you did. Normally, once you'd done your part, we'd leave you out of it as a silent witness.

The problem is that it appears as though someone leaked that you were the person responsible and there have been threats against your life."

"You've got to be joking! Tell me you're joking? That kind of thing doesn't happen in real life, does it?"

"You'd be surprised, Ms Harris. Now, we've had a car monitor you the last couple days to see if anything suspicious happen but so far nothing out of the ordinary. Which, if you're wondering, is why we made you wait two days. What I want to do now, though, is come home with you. We're going to bug your house and put you under twenty-four-hour watch until we know more; hopefully we can catch this person before anything happens. At which point we may have to put you into witness protection until the trial. Are you willing to do that?"

"Do I have a choice?"

"Technically, yes."

Annabel looked down at Mork, her eyes were wide and desperate. Mork licked her hand and took a deep breath. She realised what Mork was trying to say and in turn took a long slow deep breath herself.

"Yes, okay ... So what do we do now?"

"We're safe for now, but we really should get this ball rolling. The quicker we can get your son and get safety precautions in place, the better for everyone."

The blood drained from Annabel's face and she was fighting the nausea.

"All right, let's go. Bastian, my son, is at my father's so you can follow me there."

"Fantastic."

Frank got up from his seat and smiled nervously at Mork before offering his hand to Annabel to help her up.

"Would you like me to drive, and I'll get one of the other officers to follow in your car?"

"There are other police here?"

Frank pointed at the surrounding rooftops. As Annabel turned to look she was greeted by a waving police officer, rifle tucked under his arm.

"I think I'd like to not have to drive right now, if that's okay?"

"That's fine. Give me your keys and we can go."

She dug them out of her pocket and handed them to Frank who put them on the table and made a strange hand signal towards one of the closer rooftops. Quickly the officer on the roof lowered his firearm and disappeared from sight, making his way out the building.

"We can go; he'll follow us in your car."

"Okay."

Annabel had slipped into mild shock at the idea that someone might be trying to kill her and followed Frank without question to his car and climbed in. He cautiously opened the back door for Mork, before climbing in himself. Frank had a vague idea where he was going because he'd had encounters with Kyle Harris in the past, during criminal cases that they'd both worked on. Annabel's daydreaming was suddenly shattered when she heard her father's address come through the police radio in connection with a break-in.

"That's Dad's address – oh my God!" Her eyes filled with panic. "We've got to hurry, my son's there with him!"

Mork was on his feet and gnashing his teeth in the back seat.

"Call out directions." Without hesitating, Frank put his foot firmly to the accelerator and flipped a switch on his dashboard to activate his siren. He weaved through traffic like a mad man, following Annabel's every instruction on the quickest way to her father's house. They arrived in record time and before the car could come to a full stop, Mork leapt through the window and galloped as fast as he could into the house. His nostrils filled with the smell of blood and a frantic panic began to set in. He followed the scent up stairs to his old bathroom where he found his father beaten and handcuffed to the toilet. Kyle blinked at Mork, trying desperately not to pass out.

"Black muscle car ... two doors. Has Bastian. Go. Go now, if you hurry you can catch them."

Mork spun around and sprinted out of the house onto the front lawn. Sniffing at the air, he immediately picked up the faint scent of his nephew and took off at full speed in the direction he hoped it was coming from.

By the time Annabel found her father he had lost consciousness.

Chapter 33

Mork spotted a black vehicle at a traffic light not far from the house. From there he managed to get close enough to pick up a much stronger scent – a strange mix of tobacco, fish and his Bastian. He knew there was no way he was going to be able to keep up so he decided to conserve his energy and slowed to a gentle trot. Instinct had taken over. Any connection with his own humanity all but faded as his mind focused on one goal: the hunt. He followed the scent for hours, through construction yards and back alleys, any possible route that wasn't a main road or highly populated, anywhere they might have to stop next to another car long enough for someone to look in.

Meanwhile, Annabel was a wreck; she wasn't sure if she should stay with the police to find out what was happening with her son or whether she should go to the hospital with her father. Frank found her in the kitchen, pacing back and forth, muttering to herself about what to do. Being the experienced police officer he was, he had seen it all before.

"What am I supposed to do? How am I supposed to handle this?"

Frank could see the desperation in her eyes and knew he needed to offer the poor woman some stability. "What you do is stay with me," he assured her. "Once I've sorted out who does what here, I'll take you to the hospital to check on your father. If anyone hears anything about your kid, they'll call me and I'll tell you. Sound good?"

For Annabel, it felt like she could finally come up for air.

"Sounds good. Thank you, Mr Oslo."

Frank smiled and put his arm around her. "Please call me Frank. Now I'm going to go yell at people to make them search harder and faster for your little boy, then we can head off to the hospital. I know this is a hard time, but don't worry, we'll find him, I promise."

He quickly went back outside to debrief the detectives on the situation and outline to them who the suspects for the kidnapping were, while Annabel sat in silence at her father's kitchen table and let the tears come. It then occurred to her that for someone to know to come to her father's place, they must have gone to her house first. Desperately, she fumbled for the phone out of her pocket and called Charmaine. With each unanswered ring Annabel's panic grew. Eventually, she heard, "Hey! Hey, what's up?"

"Char! Char, are you all right? Is everything okay?"

She didn't even try to hide the panic in her voice.

"I'm fine," answered Charmaine, but Annabel's tone sent her into a mild panic. "Why? What's the matter?"

"Where are you?"

"I'm with some friends in a pub downtown? Is everything alright? You need me to come home?"

"No! No, stay where you are. There's been ... uhmmm, fuck it! Bastian's been kidnapped."

"*What?* What do you mean *kidnapped*?"

"I don't know if they went to my place first but they broke into my father's and took him. Took Bastian. I'm with the police now – and they're doing whatever it is they do. Look, stay where you are, I'm just glad that at least you're okay."

"Oh my God! Are you sure you don't want me to come to you? Maybe I can help?"

"No, I think it's safest if you stay there – and maybe go home with a friend tonight. I'm about to go to the hospital with the police."

"Hospital?"

Tears were flowing freely down both women's cheeks.

"They roughed up my dad pretty badly, but look, I'm going to go. I'll let you know as soon as I hear anything."

"Oh my God, Annabel, I'm so sorry. If there is anything I can do?"

"I'll give you a call, promise. Thanks so much, Charmaine."

***

By the time Mork found the car parked outside a warehouse on the docks the sun was well and truly down. He sniffed around it until he picked up his nephew's scent, and a strange calm seemed to come over him as he drew closer the warehouse; his heart reverberated in his chest, his muscles tense, but his mind seemed still as if he knew exactly what he was doing. Operating on instinct he stalked around the building, listening for how many different voices he could pick up inside and scanning the place for a way to sneak in undetected. There was only one way in, which meant there was only one way out – which suited him just fine. Slowly and silently he padded around to the door, which was slightly ajar, allowing him to look in. The two men didn't seem to notice the wolf on the other side of the door. He scanned what he could see of the room and finally his eyes settled on Bastian, the boy handcuffed to an old anchor, bruises on his face, blood dripping from his nose, and tears staining his cheeks. He appeared to be unconscious. The world slowed down for Mork and it felt like a lifetime passed as he stood watching his six-year-old nephew. Suddenly the stillness in his mind exploded and everything every horror story had ever said about werewolves came to life. He burst through the door, appearing to come from nowhere, a massive beast with burning green eyes and gnashing teeth. Both men wailed in terror as Mork launched at them. Savagely he ripped and tore at one of them with his teeth and claws. As soon as he felt the man go limp, he moved swiftly on to the next, who had managed to pull his firearm but got no further before Mork sank his teeth into his throat and shook him like a puppy with a soft toy, thrashing him from side to side until he let go and sent the man sliding across the floor.

Within seconds, it was over and Mork stood panting in a pool of blood. Slowly sanity sank back in and an idea formed in his mind. He nosed around in one of the men's pockets until he found a cell phone. Carefully he dialled his sister's number with his nose, a skill he had carefully nurtured over the years. Mork waited until he heard the desperate voice of his sister.

"Hello? Hello, who is this? Anyone there? Hello! Where's my son?"

Mork barked at the phone a few times, and then waited.

"Mork? Mork, is that you?"

In the background he could hear Frank.

"The wolf? The wolf is calling you? Jesus!"

Annabel turned to face him, desperate to come up with some plausible excuse but failed. "Can we trace the call?" is all she could manage.

"Give the phone to me."

She handed it over and Frank pulled a small device from his pocket and plugged it into her phone. Then he handed it back to her, pulled out his own phone and called the police station.

"Mork, we're tracing the call, we're on our way, just stay there."

Frank tapped Annabel on the shoulder.

"We've got it! Let's go."

"You hear that? We're on our way – just hold tight."

But Mork was already out the door, weaving his way down the docks towards what looked like a cargo carrier. The saner he felt the more scared he was at how good it had felt allowing instinct take over and hunting down and killing his nephew's kidnappers. His plan was to try to stow away on the ship and hoped it was headed somewhere far enough away to not be instantly recognised. He slowed to a trot when he caught sight of a man at the foot of the gangway. When the man eventually noticed him he almost toppled into the water with fright. Mork stopped dead and wagged his tail, a gesture of friendliness he hoped would calm the man. Slowly Mork padded closer to him in the least threatening way he could, and it dawned on the man that, despite Mork's intimidating size, he seemed both friendly and tame. As Mork drew closer he plucked up the courage and walked towards him with his hand out. Mork sniffed the outstretched hand, and then licked it to show friendship. The man smiled and scratched behind his ear. Behind them the boat sounded its final horn for departure. The man said something in a language Mork didn't recognise and turned to make his way up the gangway. Mork hesitated for just a moment before silently following him aboard. Once on board he ducked in behind the large metal containers so that he wouldn't be spotted from the shore and decided he'd wait until the ship had set off before revealing himself to anyone.

***

By the time Annabel, Frank and half a dozen police officers arrived at the warehouse, the ship was nearing the horizon. Frank held Annabel back while other police stepped into the warehouse to scope out the place. Within seconds, an officer ran back out and threw up over the edge of the pier. The blood drained from Annabel's face as the worst-case scenario began playing in graphic detail in her mind. Frank took a deep breath, presumed the worst and made his way into the warehouse to see for himself. To him it looked as though the two men had exploded; their blood sprayed on the floor, walls and ceiling. They themselves had been torn to shreds, body parts scattered across the floor. Never in his life had he seen anything like it. It took him a few moments to realise that boy was even in there. Immediately he ran over to check whether he was still alive. He put two fingers to the boy's neck to check for a pulse. The touch of Frank's hands caused Bastian to stir slightly and Frank quickly put his hand over Bastian's eyes.

"It's all right, son," he whispered to the boy. "I'm a police officer, and you're going to be just fine. But I need you to keep your eyes tightly shut, okay? Don't open them until I say so, all right?"

Bastian managed a defeated groan before slipping back into unconsciousness. Frank looked up at the other officer, who had managed to keep hold of his stomach.

"Quickly uncuff this kid so we can get him out of here. He doesn't need any more nightmares from today."

The other officer did as he was told and as soon as Bastian was free Frank lifted him and carried him outside to Annabel who was now on her knees weeping. She looked up when she saw Frank step out into the darkness of the night. She could make out the limp form of her son in his arms.

"Oh my God! Is he ... How is he?"

"Fine, fine – he's just fine."

Frank gently handed Bastian to Annabel, who dropped back to her knees, folding the child into her arms and sobbed into his neck. A great weight seemed to slide off her. She was relieved to have him back, but it was only when a paramedic arrived and asked whether he could examine the boy that she realised that Mork was nowhere to be seen. She strained to hear what the police officers were saying, their description of the situation in the warehouse, and knew immediately what must have happened.

Bastian was slowly beginning to emerge into consciousness but, still in shock, remained unaware of what was going on around him. She did, however, manage to determine from him that he had been unconscious from about the time his kidnappers got him into their car until Frank found him. And the only indication to what had happened to Mork was a few bloody pawprints that lead down the dock and then suddenly disappeared.

Chapter 34

And in other news, it's been three weeks since anyone's seen or heard from singer- songwriter Alex Harris. A representative for the band Waterdogs says they're concerned but not worried.

'He's a grown man and can look after himself – it would just be nice if he'd let us know where he is.'

Apparently no one suspects any kind of foul play, but doctors' reports and reports from other band members suggest that rumours of Harris having suffered a nervous breakdown and has checked himself into a treatment facility are not that far fetched. According to those close to Harris, he was prone to disappearances for up to three and four days while on tour and was notorious for being extremely secretive about his private life. Others say his disappearance may be linked to a story about a secret relationship with model film star Marina Allan leaked to People magazine.

Well, that's all we've got time for here on the news desk. What do you think, Barbra? You spoke to him just days before his disappearance – did he seem the type to go crazy and disappear?"

"Well, honestly, I'm not sure. He told me he was single, and stormed off before we could really get into anything detailed about his private life. So, yeah, maybe ..."

Epilogue

I spent two weeks on that ship before it docked again in Bergen on the west coast of Norway – turns out that's where Syn gets most of its milk. It was the longest I'd spent as Mork in one go and I'd started to forget what it was like being human. But I still had glimmers, and I remembered Danny telling me about a wolf sanctuary in Norway he'd read about and always wanted to visit. Set up by two women in the Børgefjell, a small mountain region in the middle of the country, and far away from any kind of civilisation. The idea was that people volunteered there for a few months, mostly students doing environmental or veterinary students or the like. They'd work for a small amount of money, by Norwegian standards. There was a small bar-cum-coffee shop, and accommodation was somewhere between a bed-and-breakfast and a backpackers hostel; Then there was the sanctuary and the mountain – and that was it, for miles.

I didn't actually know where it was, but that's where I was heading. I didn't know if anyone was chasing me, but I was running. I wasn't really sure what I was going to do, but I knew I needed to do something, I knew I had to get a handle on my situation. I'd been brushing it aside for too long and a wolf sanctuary seemed as good a place as any to learn about being a wolf.

MOSTLY HUMAN²

D.I. JOLLY

Printed in Great Britain
by Amazon

84738840R00292